UNDER THE INVERTED EYE

BOOK ONE AND TWO

SHED AND TEMPLE

C. R. SILVER

CRSILVER.COM

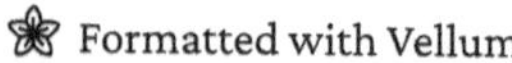 Formatted with Vellum

BOOKS IN THE SERIES

Under the Inverted Eye

Shed
Temple

<u>Coming Soon</u>:
Trial
Cellar
Soul
Origin
Mask
Void

———

For Erin.
Without you at my side, these stories of
becoming would never have been.

———

SHED

-Terran Year 2341-

WILLETT PRISON ENCAMPMENT
SATELLITE IMAGERY OF TERRAN SURFACE
CENTERED: 77°25'24"S // 160°28'42"E
ICE SHEET
APOCALYPSE PEAK
SHAPELESS MOUNTAIN
WESTERN UTILITY PORT
ADIT LIFTS TO SUBSURFACE
CELLAR
OPEN PIT MINE
OLD ADIT ENTERANCE
UPPER BELHAM VALLEY
OSAI
SOLITARY
SHED
SURFACE CAMP
ICE SHEET
UPPER McKELVEY VALLEY
2 KM

————

Praise the gods, all you nations;
extol them, all you peoples.
For great is their love toward us;
the faithfulness of the gods endures
forever in our teikum.

-Modified After Psalm 117, Coda of Unification
Inscribed: East Gate, Garden of the
Tribe, Schengen, Terra

————

Precious in the sight of the gods
is the death of their faithful servants.

-Modified After Psalm 116:15,
Heretical Interpretation Inscribed: Adit Lifts,
Willett Prison Encampment, Terra

————

1

———

"Was today a good day, Trustee?" the Priest asks from across the confessional booth. They sit in their wooden vessels, separated by a screen divider. Lights are dim, all is quiet, but across from the Priest the Trustee emanates unease.

"There are no good days here," the Trustee says, eyes closed, tears still falling. The harsh winds outside have temporarily wicked the moisture from her sclera. She presses her hands to her eyelids and holds the pressure for a moment, making phosphenes dance like spirits in the dark. "If you'd just come outside, Father, make a little visit to the shed. You might understand how bad it really is. But you'd have to step beyond this guardship."

"You're right, you know," the Priest says, ignoring her taunts. He always endeavors to speak evenly with this Trustee, despite her migrating emotions. "I can't understand, not from here inside the Osai. But I have seen a great deal, looking inward and outward."

The Trustee smiles shallowly, eyes still closed in the dim

confessional. "There are not enough windows on this guardship for a man of the gods to see the truth. There's nothing for your faith to stick to out there."

"I don't have the right to leave the guardship. You know this is my cloister."

"The right to leave? You have the right to stay inside. I can practically see the halo round your head," her eyes are still closed. "I have the right to enter, but I am required to leave. You should come get a taste of the cold and see the bodies, Priest, or experience the heat of the cellar. It sticks to you. Sticks better than your faiths."

"You have endured a great deal, Trustee, in your service to the United Terran Coalition. And yet you keep your faith."

The Trustee nods with mock exaggeration, "Yes. My faith keeps me."

This last line is from a script which rolls through her mind, a holy script.

"Humanness is next to godliness," the Priest says as he examines the Trustee, looking for physical damage or injuries. Many of the trustees, still considered prisoners, get hurt while on duty, out on the shed. They have no armor and only minor weaponry for protection. "It is a holiness given to us humans, to seek teikum, to seek our own void."

The Trustee nods because his words and her agreement are expected at this point in the ritual.

-*Keep him talking,*- she thinks, and the back and forth inside her head begins, the dissociative call and response.

-*More time to get warm. Let him pontificate.*-

-*More words bring more information.*-

-*I don't know if I can manage today.*-

The Priest continues. "It is the holy need of some to seek, but one cannot go seeking away from humanity. One will always find suffering in the darkness beyond what we are."

The Trustee begins to nod again, then shakes her head.

"You do not agree?" the Priest asks.

"You always go on like this if I don't say anything."

"I am a priest of the Tribe. We all speak like this."

The Trustee opens her eyes, tired and red, and looks at him. "The rotation is coming soon. As my time in the cellar gets closer, it gets harder to believe any of this crap."

"Yes. I would find it difficult as well," he says, words drawn out at her mention of the cellar.

"I can hear the fear in your voice. You fear getting kicked out the door; coming out to join your flock."

"Yes," says the Priest. Now it is his turn to speak from a script. "But I do not fear death or pain. I fear losing contact with the Tribe."

"You'd find a new tribe out there," she laughs, pointing vaguely somewhere off beyond the walls of the confessional. "It's only human."

"To be one among the prisoners? No. I would not be accepted by the utza. Just as you cannot be accepted, Trustee. Just as you don't fully accept me."

"A man of the cloth might be given space out in the shed. But you are too soft for the cellar. Lucien would make it difficult for you."

She watches the Priest wince a little at the mention of General Lucien, but he recovers and moves on quickly, purposefully.

"Do you only come here to mock me, 452A?" he asks, using her identification number the same way she calls him Priest sometimes rather than Father.

The Trustee shakes her head again and smiles. "No. Sometimes your words bring comfort." As she says it, she realizes it is true, not part of some script.

-He is kind.-

-He wants to be.-

-Rare in a place like this.-

"You've told me there's no comfort in the confessional. And I know my words are meaningless out on the shed. So, perhaps you still mock me."

"This prison mocks us all, Father," she says sarcastically.

The Priest waits for a moment. He counts the beats of his heart. "Have you read the writings of the Neta-Teej, Trustee?"

The Trustee's eyes blink and he can see her searching the shadowed corners of the confessional booth. It is a fascination of his, to watch her reactions when the Neta-Teej is mentioned. There is confusion on her dirty face, but also an immediate desire to answer him, to connect over the utterance of something which might be familiar. *-She searches inside herself, but nothing ever comes forth.-*

"No. I have not read them," she admits, clearly uncertain of her answer.

"The Neta-Teej is a seer, and though they may have fallen from the holy seat where they used to sit when with the Tribe, they have not fallen in thought or word. Words can bring comfort, even to people like us. The Neta-Teej writes words of kindness. For humans, even prisoners like the utza, even Arkû. Kindness for all. That is hir message."

"Kindness is not always a virtue."

"You have no choice but to think that way. You are a trustee in the Willett Prison Encampment, the shed and the cellar. More than a prisoner, less than a guard. You kowtow to those above and betray those below to keep your position. To keep order."

"And you ordain my actions. You ordain all of this," she gestures widely, with open hands, to encompass all beyond the confessional, beyond the guardship.

"There is always a path back to humanity," he says.

"I don't believe that."

"You are a trustee. How could you believe it?"

She is silent, unwilling to attempt an answer.

He changes the subject, returning to a more standard line of discussion. "Have you been dreaming?"

She shakes her head. "I don't remember. Maybe."

"And your prayers? When you close your eyes and turn inward?"

"I see only darkness, tiny specs of light, and then I fall asleep," she says with a sad smile.

"And what do you see before you go to sleep? Where does your mind go?"

They both know he is asking for signs from her inner world, symbols or people or events that can be used to explore the depth of teikum, the Tribal path to the gods.

"It has been so long, Father. And I am not a seer. I don't remember," she says after a while, closing her eyes again. "I know it isn't right. Isn't normal. But there is nothing beyond my voice echoing inside my own head."

The Priest has heard this from the Trustee before, and nods. "You have yourself to guide you. That is a good thing. That is enough."

The Trustee did not come to the confessional to confess anything, but again she finds herself guilty of revealing more than she had intended.

"I know you are afraid, Trustee," he says, again, part of a script.

"I am."

"Are you doing all you can to find wholeness?"

"I am."

"You are a daughter of the gods."

"I am," she agrees, in a formal annunciation of identity, of life.

-I am.-

-You are.-

The Trustee sits up straighter, stiff and tired. Bones made of rust.

Outside the confessional, the narrow hallway is filled with too much light and she pauses for her eyes to adjust before turning toward the lifts at the center of the guardship. There is a window behind her, looking out over the shed, but there is no need to peer into the evening darkness. She will be back out in the prison camp soon enough.

The Trustee trudges down the metallic hallway, shoulders almost touching both walls. They guide her, enclose her, allowing her no other option.

At the lift, the central computer permits her to go down to cargo level. She lacks any active permissions that might allow her to stay inside the Osai longer.

-There is always a path back to humanity.-

-But this is not it. Only a path back to the shed.-

-And soon, to the cellar.-

2

The Priest closes the confessional door and retreats to his private quarters.

The little room is square and the surfaces are stacked with books, making it feel even smaller. The window covers are closed, preventing any view outside. The Priest knows that out on the shed rows of barracks reach across the icy landscape, almost to where the hills rise. The cement and metal houses are filled with thousands and thousands of prisoners.

-How many times have I asked the Trustee about the Neta-Teej? She has read the texts aloud to me. And still she cannot remember.-

At his cluttered desk he pulls up the viewing screen and watches as the Trustee walks down the hallway, shallow steps with her shoulders slumped. She takes her time getting into the lift and removes her hat, revealing short brown hair, matted flat against her skull. She scratches dry skin and rubs her eyes and leans against the bulkhead without touching the controls. She takes deep, steadying breaths.

-She is buying time. Moments of reprieve are expensive here. Survival is made of seconds and this one knows how to survive. After all

this time, is she really meant to serve a greater purpose? Or has that faded, along with everything else in this place?-

The Priest is always left full of doubt after speaking with Trustee 452A. He has taken to watching her departures from the guardship, her methodical movement, her preparations for returning to the encampment. He watches her and it gives him a sense of release, of closure on their conversations.

The lift closes and the Trustee puts the hat back on her head, ear flaps up to hear better. She pulls on gloves and checks both shoulders and chest through her coat, making sure equipment is in place and pockets are closed on her blue-gray uniform. Her right hand drops to her hip, where the stun baton is holstered. Her left hand rises to her jacket collar, pulling it up around her neck. It stays there, protecting her face and throat and putting her in a ready position to fight.

-And the wind will come from the left, blowing off the ice sheet toward the mountains. Another night on the shed, Trustee. But will you remember it?-

He watches as the lift stops.

She ducks her head as the doors open, responding to the sudden surge of cold air. After a moment of hesitation, she walks out of the lift.

Sometimes the Priest will watch her cross the cargo level, leave the guardship's field door, and head out onto the tundra. Sometimes he will watch her longer on the infrared as she approaches the fence and gets scanned in. He will watch her heat signature fade as she starts her perimeter round of the shed.

But tonight, he closes the viewer as she leaves the lift, and returns to his preparation for the next morning's holy adhan, the prayer which will wake the prisoners.

-Awaken all. Prayer is better than sleep. Hasten to your prayers and hasten to your best deeds. Bear witness to your gods and faiths. Bear witness to your teikum and find greatness there.-

This is how it always starts.

The Priest hangs his head, thinking of the words prescribed by the Coda of Unification, thinking of the Trustee and how she may have no better deeds to come.

-Every morning, I ask these prisoners to wake for prayer. Some will die in the night and never pray again. At best, the message is for the guards. Colonel Nystrom is the only one who notices when I repeat a sermon.-

Those who will never pray again, dead in the night, come to visit him in his dreams. Sometimes they find him to tell him how his voice, a message of belief on the loudspeaker, was a small kindness as they suffered. But there are others who come looking for him to show how his words were wasted, how his faith was wasted. 'You asked me for my best deeds while I endured torture? I have come to ask for yours, your endurance and your better deeds, Priest.' They wait for him along with all the shades of his past, memories lingering inside his teikum, things he cannot escape.

Sometimes General Lucien is there with them, watching.

-They are only dreams. I am not a seer.-

He envies Trustee 452A a little, for her forgetfulness, but then he reminds himself how much else is missing inside of her, how much suffering she still has left, and his envy turns to sorrow.

The Priest opens his clean copy of the Coda of Unification to a random page and begins to read, searching for anything worthy to be spoken aloud in tomorrow's cold morning air.

3

When the lift door opens, terrible cold strikes the Trustee.

The wind's howl rips through the guardship's cargo level, shrouding the high walls and equipment in frost. Sterile lights flicker in the cavernous room. Dirt and snow have built up on the floor.

Even in the guardship, she is aware of the immediate dangers. Beyond the confessional booth, there are possible threats everywhere, posed by both guards and prisoners and other trustees.

-There are plenty of places to hide. Places to lie in wait for a passing mark.-

Shivering in the cold, she leans her head out of the lift, looks right, left, then clears the doors. With her back to the lift, she plots the course ahead and lets her body adjust to the bitter temperature.

-Go left round the elevator shaft. There will be two legionnaires flanking the exit to the field door. Snow will be heavy with the wind tonight, poor light across the open flat to the fence. Another guard may man the checkpoint scanner. Take the fence north to start the round.-

She takes a breath and flexes inside her coat to get the blood moving. Hand on baton.

-Ready.-

The Trustee moves quickly, minding the frozen floor, taking the passage around the lift.

Two guards are posted at the field door, faceless in their mechanized suits, covered with guns and armor. They stand a head and a half higher than her and almost twice as wide.

One faces her, getting a visual. The other stands just beyond the threshold, snow accumulating at their feet, watching the yard.

She knows the guardship's narrow passages have been designed to split an attack party and knows the halls are curved around the lift to make the enemy impossible to miss at close range with a fracture rifle. The scattering ballistics will hit the walls and travel to the field door, continuing to do their nasty work. She knows this because she has seen it. But she doesn't know why she saw it, or where.

The soldiers do not move or provide any recognition of her passing as she exits the guardship. They know Trustee 452A and they know her favor with Colonel Nystrom.

She braces against the heavy wind and raises her eyes to make sure the flat is clear and to get a visual on the fence beacon. It is a short distance, but the wind can be disorienting. There is no room to go wandering beyond the shed.

-The utza will freeze tonight.-

-Worry about yourself. There are those who use the cold to hide their work in the darkness.-

-The priest asks about my inner dark, what I see when I close my eyes. But he doesn't understand how much outer dark there is here. More than enough.-

The Trustee looks back to see the guardship Osai. Flood lights low on the structure illuminate the width of the vessel, made of black metal that has traversed the solar system. But the great battleship's vertical lines ascend into the stormy night, terminating far above the tundra.

-Made to protect the gods.-

-Made to challenge the gods. To emulate their wrath.-

She turns away and reaches the fence checkpoint where an encephalopathic scanner takes a reading. There is no armed guard to verify it, but the brain scan is close enough to the one on file, so the gate opens and the Trustee quickly passes through.

She begins along the inside of the fence, taking her normal route to the west.

-Ritual creates complacency.-

-It creates familiarity.-

-Familiarity is rarer by the day.-

-Don't lose hope.-

-I am afraid.-

-All the time.-

Avoiding the lights, she trudges her way to the rear of the first row of barracks. Most trustees do not patrol alone and most stick to the light, but 452A has other methods for keeping safe.

Any journey through the shed is always wrought with questions. To be on patrol is to be exposed. Expiration could come at the hands of a gang, of a single qatal sent for blood. Stalkers lurk in the still shadows between the barracks, waiting for their snares and spike traps to bring down some big game in the night.

-Traps are hidden beneath the snow.-

-Watch for striations and lumps in the surface ice.-

-Stay off the fence line where everyone walks.-

-In the cellar they pay in clockwork and meat if you bring them a trustee patch.-

But she knows even a minor injury, self-sustained, can be death when wandering the limits of the shed. The cold creeps up and ice closes in over you and you go to sleep, never waking up.

The Trustee measures every step and moves with precision along the fence, eyeing up the rear of every barrack house and checking behind to make sure she is not followed. At each fence-post she raises a hand to check her distance from it, close enough to prevent any direct attack from that side, but far enough that no one can grab her and pull her in against the icy links.

The fence continues for miles to the west, but she cuts the corner and turns north toward the mountains, following a straight line of lit markers. Now the endless icy flat flanks her to the left and the more remote parts of the shed are on her right.

-And if you walk far enough, you will reach the cellar.-

The lights identify the edges of the main camp and no one is permitted to go past the markers. It is a game, a taunt. No fence to pen you in, but a deadly tundra and glacial hills to swallow you up. The expanse practically begs you to give it a try, but it is a wasteland without shelter.

The Trustee has been attacked here before, ambushed out of the dark as a distraction took place by the back of a barracks house. It was not done by amateurs. It was a try by real movers, strong and organized.

Out of the corner of her eye she sees a shadow, darting back and forth through the gusts of crystalline snow. At first it is on her left, out at the edge of her vision on the tundra.

She knows she should not look at it and so she doesn't.

It fades and then reemerges on her right, the shadow rushing across her vision, a child, arms outstretched, head tilted back, staring into the opaque sky.

-Just a vision.-

The Trustee stops as the shadow rapidly changes course and runs back to the right in the direction it came, always staying far enough ahead of her that it is barely visible, always looking up as if ready to catch something falling from the sky.

-Don't follow it.-

-It always runs away, but really, it's following me.-

The shadow fades and she knows she will see it again. It has always been with her.

After a moment, she continues north, but almost immediately another form approaches, walking south, working the opposite round along the markers. It is a large man, and the Trustee knows the shape of him, even at a distance.

-681B.-

All sorts of things move through the shed at night, but 681B is expected. He walks the counterclockwise circuit, and as they pass each other in the snow she sees him smile wide, exposing rotting teeth similar to her own, a characteristic of all who have been in the shed too long.

"Will I find a pile of bodies this way?" he calls out to her over the wind. "Your nightly calling card? Or are you planning on pulling someone out of their bunk further north?"

681B is a trustee of desire, not of need.

The Trustee takes a wide margin and does not stop walking.

He is quick to jump into her path but not close enough that she can strike. He watches her hands, the baton, the left glove with an iron bar hidden in the stitching.

"Fuck off," she says calmly, knowing he'll read her lips even if he cannot hear her.

681B studies her face, the lines of her brow and nose, avoiding her eyes. "I wonder about you, Trustee. I wonder what you used to be before all of this."

"Trustee," she says, using the term with a self-reflecting venom, "did you leave any messes for me back there?"

He sneers but does not look back the way he came. He is still focused on her face. There is a look of hope, demand, in his eyes.

"Pretty thing," he says.

"Excuse me?"

"Not you, Trustee," he says, acting appalled. "This isn't a

place where beauty survives. You're still kicking around, and we both know what that means. But I left you a gift. Very pretty. Pale in the snow."

The Trustee sidesteps quickly to get around 681B and continue her patrol.

"In a rush to leave?"

"Always."

"Keep your chin up, Trustee. We all long to see that face of yours."

"I see you pale in the snow. Just a matter of time."

He smiles again and raises his hands in surrender but there is anger in his eyes.

She braces her back foot. She knows his baton holster is empty, and he keeps it hidden in the left sleeve. She knows he hides a thin blade on the hem of his right knee to cut up cloth and maybe catch an artery near the enemy's crotch if it comes to grappling.

But he is already backing away, moving slowly off through the wind.

-Why do I remember these things?-

-Why have you forgotten so much?-

She turns away from him but does not start walking just yet. The Trustee waits several heartbeats and then looks back. 681B is still heading south, almost to the fence, and she is again alone on her circuit.

After another quarter mile there is a familiar motion in the snow and the Trustee stops to appraise.

It is a girl, not enough clothes, crawling through snow along the back of one of the barrack houses. She is thin, but not yet down to the bone. Still signs of femininity to her, making her a prime catch.

-It is a test.-

-681B said it was a gift.-

-He wants to see what you will do with her.-

As the Trustee approaches, the girl sees her and attempts to crawl under the barracks, to hide under the elevated floor.

-Pale, just like he said.-

-Fresh up from the cellar.-

-Someone's pet for too long.-

-A loved pet.-

-Or a trap.-

The Trustee approaches as the girl rolls onto her back, sees her and then tries to scramble further under the barracks house, motions slowed by the cold, ice cutting the skin.

After a moment, the only thing still visible are her feet, covered with bleeding scabs.

-Feet are trashed.-

-Didn't walk much.-

-Not until she had to come up from the mines.-

-No shoes.-

-Perhaps. She wants to die alone.-

The Trustee looks behind her, back in the direction of 681B and then around the sides of the barracks. There is no one there.

"Get up," the Trustee says.

The girl's bleeding feet slowly start to disappear under the barracks house.

The Trustee impulsively grabs one of the ankles and slides the baton from its holster. She pulls the creature out, a skeleton in progress. The girl is crying and there is no way to tell age on such a face or body. Frail like a child, but beaten upon and weathered.

"Human or Arkû?"

The tears are freezing on the girl's face as she struggles to crawl back into hiding. This thing is a reversion, an animal trapped in human form.

-This camp is meant to craft weakness.-

-Meant to expose it.-

-Lucien wants to propagate weakness. Help it grow.-

"Get up. Human or Arkû?"

The girl lies on her back, filthy clothes shredded.

-Pale in the snow,- the Trustee thinks.

The Trustee hauls the girl up, and their eyes meet. There is focus now, realization that this is still real.

"Arkû," the girl cracks.

The Trustee backs up quickly as the girl tries to cover herself. "Turn around!"

The girl delays, confusion in her eyes.

"Turn around! Put your hands on the barrack wall."

-She doesn't understand.-

-I don't care.-

-Hidden shives and blades. Hard stones.-

-Little girls from the cellar are prone to it. Weapons hidden everywhere.-

The girl turns and puts her hands up and the Trustee uses the capped stun baton to quickly clear the girl's body, making sure she has nothing dangerous on her. She then repeats the procedure with her gloved hand, ready to strike if the girl shows any signs of fight.

Once done, the Trustee gives the girl a gentle shove to get her walking.

She leaves bloody footprints on the ice and snow.

The Trustee takes the girl's arm firmly. "Don't struggle."

One by one, they move along the rows of barracks as the Trustee looks for a specific marking. It is fresh, painted at dusk on the back of the barracks; a crude red circle emanating eight lines like a sun with short, asymmetrically spaced rays.

"What are you doing?" the girl asks, leaning into the Trustee, trying to steal some heat from her.

"Don't ever admit you are Arkû again," 452A says.

"This is not my barrack."

"I know."

"What will they do to me?"

The girl is frantic but unable to resist as the Trustee drags her around the front of the barrack house. There is a small light above the entrance and the door has the circle and lines painted on it as well. The barracks door opens and she shoves the girl inside and the door shuts quickly against the wind.

The interior will not be warm but it will not be so brutally cold. There will be more people packed inside than the two hundred who have been assigned to the bunks. The marked barrack is a special one. The girl will find herself tossed in with a thousand or more bodies, all standing shoulder to shoulder in silence. They gather to hear the words of the Neta-Teej.

The Trustee follows the girl's bloody footprints back along the exterior wall. There are shadows near the middle of the buildings and if one sits in a low spot, back against the wall, one can look out onto the tundra and stay mostly out of the wind. If one leans their head back and strains the ear, they can eavesdrop and listen to the sermon inside without anyone knowing.

The words are spoken by a sweet voice.

"Bring that one to the middle and get her warm. Put your skin on hers and give your heat, or she will not survive. Give her clothes. There is no shame in human pain or weakness. We were made this way over eons. There is no shame in nakedness or in the smells of a human nest, all of us own bodies. All of us are dirty and sick and we must press together. We made ourselves this way over eons. Do not repress your hope. We are here, all on the brink of death, rotting. But we have made ourselves thus, over eons. We seek the edge of our teikum, and I am sorry to say that tonight, as on all future nights, we have found it. This is the limit of who we are.

"In tonight's void we find our teikum. In that void we create our finest works. Our children, ourselves, our animals, our captives. They are all gods of our making. And we are all creators, each and every one of us. So, warm her. For she is all of us. We are all humans, next to gods, and this is where we may die, but only in body. This is not where we lose ourselves. For those of you who are new, you must be terrified. Do not be. Welcome to the Ghost Shed. You are now one of us, one of the utza, and you will never leave this place.

"For now, put aside thoughts of escape. Put aside the desire for comfort. It will only lead you astray. Survival and hope are all encompassing. Hope only that you may ease the passing of another."

Someone calls forth a question.

"Do we sit quietly? Does no one fight back? You speak of hope, but that does not change anything."

Voices murmur, some in agreement, others in exasperation.

But the Neta-Teej has heard this all before and the sweet voice has answers, no matter how cruel.

"I know your pain," ze says, "and you know me. There are pillars of rebellion in the shed and the cellar. You demand names. The Falconer of Europa is in this place. Yet, he is no pillar. The Crone, now a heretic, is here. She is no pillar. I am here. I am human. Not a pillar of rebellion. In this place, survival and kindness are rebellious acts. Dedication to life is rebellion when death and power are the rule.

"The pillars of rebellion have no human names. But the pillars of the enemy can be named. The pillar of power has a name you should know and it is Lucien. General Lucien is real and he is flesh and blood. If you are desperate to fight, then you may find him in the cellar. But you must survive long enough to get there. And while you struggle for survival, he will be watching you, looking in upon you."

"Is it true about what happened on Europa?" someone asks, a new prisoner.

"It is true. The Falconer made our brethren, his Arkû. They are no different than us in spirit or in suffering. This place will prove it to you. You will see it, feel it in your dreams. You will know it in your bones as you descend into the cellar."

The Trustee's eyes catch motion in the darkness under the barracks.

A small bird, out of place in the cold night, hops about. Its tiny feet click on the hardened ice. It is a sparrow, feathers puffed out, and it looks directly at the Trustee with inquisitive eyes.

-One of the Falconer's creatures.-

-It has the sheen of metal.-

-Is it alive?-

-Were they alive on Europa?-

-I don't know.-

-You do know. But you don't remember.-

When the Trustee returns to her feet, the bird hops back into its hiding place. Whether it observes for its maker or for itself is unknown. It is one of the many entities haunting the Ghost Shed.

She is stiff and tired and aware of her vulnerability as she closes off the perimeter and returns to the fence line. The pattern of spacing resumes, the meandering path of quick steps and frequent pauses to examine risk.

The patrol is complete when she arrives at the quarter barracks, the stacks of metal rooms for the trustees.

She takes the ladder to the mid-level and walks the steel platform to room 452A. There are no locks, and once the door is open, she does not rush to go inside. Only a moment is needed to scan the room. The mattress is still flat on the floor. The toilet and heater are untouched.

These are the few privileges of being a trustee.

She ducks her head in and out to make sure no one is hiding against the front wall.

In the darkness, she closes the door and lets the heat rebuild inside the room. She takes a wedge of metal and shoves it under the door frame. It is enough to delay its opening in case of intrusion.

She pushes the mattress against the base of the door and sits.

There are no sheets but there is a small bottle of liquor, a gift from Colonel Nystrom. It sets fire to her dry throat.

The Trustee places her feet near the door and keeps the stun baton in her hand as she lies back. The room seems to echo with the wind and with each pull off the bottle.

-But it doesn't echo the way the mines do.-

-I don't want to think about the cellar.-

-There will be bodies tomorrow.-

-That girl maybe.-

-More apparitions added to the nightly rounds.-

-For some there is no difference between death now or death later.-

-For me?-

-Yes. There is still work to do.-

The Trustee does not fully sleep but muscles get their rest as cold soaks the tundra and the shed settles into the long wait for morning.

4

Armor Record:

    Log Entry: #11/30/2340-003 - General Ezra Lucien

    Location: Ungridded (Beacon Off)

//(I write here on real paper in the depths of my cellar. Old paper comes from old dead trees. No timber in the wastes. Dirt on pages like an ancient farmer. Sitting in the morning sun, plowing thoughts into words into pages. Watching his earthly harvest grow in anticipation of another sweltering day. Who has rights to that sun? To grow? To build chlorophyll into leaves?

I am warm blooded, a body evolved beyond slavery to some star. The darkness suits me fine. I can make my own light, grow it. I can see what hides in the dark.

It all comes round, the circle of life. The circle of birth and excrement. The fallen filth of humanity consumed and repurposed like our histories and our myths, like our children or our ruins.

We all have our place in the cycle, even the sun. But who owns the cycle? Who owns the sun? Who wants to buy it? Who wants to go delving back into myth and examine the pantheons and find the one who, like Ra, owned the sun first?

What makes the world grow? Is it the same force that makes us grow?

No. Everything needs different mixtures even when the physics are the same. Osmotic pressure. The right balances of salts and ions. But for those who thrive without light, there are other needs. To weather the longest of storms, there must be nutrients in the void.

We need light and protein and also light of soul, a beacon, something bright to grow the spirits, to help in the becoming. The light bringer is not enough. No moon will suffice. A positive and a negative are required to grow a human, to build them up so they may resist the drought, the cold, the wind.

I am warm blooded. We are warm blooded. Why do we worry about absurdities? Why do we pray to the sun? We no longer fear the pestilence or the permanence of clouds. We will consume anything we need. Adaptation for the great emptiness.

Survival for most humanity is a certainty. But what has it cost us in our souls?

Do we go into the darkness and accept it? No. There is still a lingering hope to hold light, find nearer brightness, find that beautiful, primordial pressure differential which whipped our early amino acids into a fervor, a pressure like the freezing depths of Europa.

We long. That is our lot. We are like flowers in our spirit, seeking the sun. This is our way, how we were made. But our greatness comes from how we seek the deep, seek darkness and death. Teikum lives in the void, the human spark we carry with us. Teikum, the spirit inside us which makes gods in empty places.

The Falconer knows. It is why he made his thin place on Europa. The Quadrumvirate knows. It is why they unified the faiths. Yet they say nothing of how teikum is a symptom of our need for death. They only speak of life. But life, at its very roots, is broken. We broke it, and we break again it daily. We break it by accepting the gods in the voids. By submitting to that vestigial spark. Pathetic.

For ages, the masses have sung for Ra and other gods. Sung for science. Sung for weapons. Sung for death. It was a death they could not hope to name themselves. They sang for a death which they were too weak to imbue with power or divinity on their own, so they called upon the void to help.

Weakness. Nothing more.

"Great God! Kill me with purpose! Bring me eternity. Great war! Kill me with glory! Bring me legacy. Great creed! Kill me with craft! Bring me contribution."

They all summon a death without a face.

They call upon their souls to live beyond the grave, as if it is worth something. "Remember me in the name of God, of science, of creed, of battle!" As if these prescribed paths, these ordained deaths, will yield legacy, yield expansion. False. There is yield. But it is the yield of a crop, a harvest to be collected by the planter, the reaper. No legacy. No expansion. No growth beyond the season.

This is not some animal, but a domesticated plant, still programmed with human wants and needs, but with limits on life cycle, made to be consumed, made to grow where it is planted. We have made ourselves into nourishment. Made ourselves into something to be consumed. We took the offerings of manufactured gods and in turn offered ourselves up. We built it into our code.

We feed some god, some grand design, some overlord.

This is not a human path, but it is the path Homo sapiens has chosen for itself, like planted wheat, grown away from its wild capabilities. We no longer have the power of shatter, the power of dormancy, the power to weather long drought and cold and to choose when to root, when to risk growth, and when to explode with seed, when to spread and catch the winds and restart elsewhere.

Homo sapiens now fall where they die. No scatter. Roots immediate. No patience. No dormancy.

Then we sing for lights to raise us up. "Harvest me! Let me grow for you. Great harvest! Kill me with that which I cannot understand. Bring me round again, once more."

These words are sorrowful and heavy.

But this is a good crop. Those that are here, in my shed and in my cellar, have grown tall. They have dug into the blackness. Not so docile as before. They have accepted darkness. More come, more from those scattered places. The wild strain may return to terran soil.

I will make sure they are planted deep in my cellar. I will block out the light and quiet their songs. Let them grow teikum in the abyss, not shrink it and call it 'god'.

I am warm blooded. Are they?

When does this season end? When will we find out who will work the harvest and who will be collected? It no longer matters who did the planting in this empty place. They must look for the face of gods in all directions. I hope they will find the face of a god behind them, behind us all, and then they will have to make new masks.

I have already made mine. Close Log - General Ezra Lucien)//

5

The Trustee wakes, peeled away from sleep's empty abyss.

Disoriented, she is unwilling to recognize the merciless cold wrapping her, tightening its grip. There can be no hesitation in the early hours. Hesitation is a trap, a gulf where she is forced to acknowledge the world she inhabits. To acknowledge is to confess the pain inside and out. Pain raises questions of endurance and of purpose. There is no memory of a 'why' and there are no answers beyond the day ahead.

-There is no hope of change.-

-Not yet.-

-Not ever.-

She sits up quickly and scans the still-dark room. Door closed tight. Frost on walls. Baton goes back into the holster.

-Today there will be bodies to burn.-

It is an advantage on hard mornings, the way her mind spins up like a frozen machine, quickening her sluggish thoughts. Ritual takes over and instinct fuels her until her mind catches up.

She shoves the mattress into the corner and hides the liquor.

She tugs the metal wedge from the door, tosses it into the corner, and then pulls the door open.

Fresh snow rests unbroken in the low morning light.

Rocky hills are the first thing visible in the middle distance, then the markers and the rows upon rows of barracks. A gray shroud covers all of it.

-Cold.-

-But quiet.-

She steps out and closes the door.

There are no footprints on the walkways or the stair and she knows she is first awake.

Down the ladder.

She drinks and washes her face from an insulated spigot at the corner of the barracks. The water does its trick. The machine finally revs up and clicks into gear.

-The Neta-Teej.- It is the Trustee's first thought with emotion attached.

-Ze would be taken to solitary after the gathering, after last night's prayers.-

She tries to pull a calming breath, but air transports ice crystals into her lungs and she coughs and hacks, taking a knee at the corner of the barracks.

-Quiet yourself.-

-Breathe slowly.-

-You are afraid.-

-Why?-

The memories and emotions within the Trustee do not always coincide or agree. Nothing to be reconciled, only endured.

She comes around the back of the quarter barracks. Outside the fence, the monolithic black of the guardship breaks the horizon and penetrates the gray sky. It is a monument of violent civilization, demonstrating dominion over the natural wastes.

The battleship is a vertical patchwork of armor plate and weaponry, a twisting tower projecting indomitable force.

-The Osai.-

-Will it ever bloom? Will it ever fly again?-

-And show its fire? Cross the emptiness of space?-

-Tear pieces off planets like it was built to do?-

The Trustee walks the fence line in the still air, her breath defying gravity in foggy pools. Her pace is quicker in the day, without the wind, without having to interrogate the stirring of the shadows.

A legionnaire now stands at the gate, a snow berm collected at the side of their mechanized armored suit. Inside, the Trustee knows there is a human, faceless behind the tinted shield, ambivalent to cold or time. The suit's sensory deprivation becomes extreme as days wear on, claustrophobia turning to a friendly privacy where any stimulation becomes excessive. Stagnant air filters with religious tenacity, and stim packs and dozers can put a soldier in a twilight of constant sleep and simultaneous alertness, providing the patience to stand guard for days in silence without boredom or metabolic quickening.

-Blood pools in the feet.-

-Redistributed to the neck and brain.-

-At regular intervals.-

The Trustee feels sick looking at the suit while the scanner assesses her brain waves. To be in the suit is a compartmentalized life. It is easy for the Trustee to imagine.

-No wind on your skin.-

-No smell of fresh snow.-

-No touch until the next rotation.-

-Almost invincible.-

-Almost.-

The gate opens and the Trustee exits the shed, heading toward the Osai.

Through the fences, off to the west, the Trustee spots movement on the icy tundra, far beyond the markers. Two small dots slowly make their way back toward the shed. It will be an armored soldier escorting a prisoner back from solitary.

The Trustee stands long enough to verify that the prisoner is dressed in red and walking on their own feet.

It is another tradition on the shed. It is ritual for the Neta-Teej to preach to thousands in the wrong barracks during the night, saying what must be said to those who gather. It is then tradition for hir to be sent to solitary, the Neta-Teej taken by a legionnaire to the low structure out west of the shed and chained up for the night.

The guards could stop hir, keep hir locked up. But everyone knows it is Lucien's orders to let the Neta-Teej do as ze pleases and then be punished, never prevented.

The Trustee knows not to look too long, and moves off toward the guardship, but relief fills her stomach, the pit of emotion quieted for a few moments.

The same two guards from the previous night stand at the field door and the Trustee moves through without attention.

Warmth graces the skin on her face as the lift doors seal. Permissions are displayed and access is granted only to the top level.

-Colonel Nystrom wants to see you.-

-She will have more questions.-

-It is her way.-

It is a silent ride, and at the top she waits for the Colonel to accept her into the bridge.

When the doors open, the rich smell of hot coffee rolls in on even warmer air. The Colonel is at the command desk reading reports, turned away from the panoramic window.

From the highest point inside the Osai, the Trustee looks out over the barracks to the Willett Range, the hills leading into glacial mountains, and then to the north where the open mine disrupts the surface of the earth, a great divot in the windswept terrain. All the light that falls upon the cellar seems to drain down the steep terraced walls and into the deep.

Covered in fresh snow and ice, the camp seems almost clean.

The Trustee looks at Colonel Harper Nystrom, and they examine each other for a moment, strange companions, shaped by different existences.

There is a heavy vitality to Nystrom's skin and the Trustee knows the Colonel doesn't spend much time in a suit anymore.

-Cropped hair. Clean skin.-

-Orderly and fit.-

-No nutrient recycling. No starvation or exposure to the elements.-

-Not wrapped in a sarcophagus of armor.-

-Plenty of time in the spectrum chamber.-

-Simulated sun.-

The Colonel still presents all the signs of a healthy human.

-Beautiful, even.-

-The fat of the land.-

-The sort hungered for out on the shed, the sort devoured in the cellar.-

"Sit, Trustee," Nystrom says, her voice one of command and easy authority.

The Trustee sits in a chair fixed to the floor, opposite the desk.

Patches from off-world combat decorate Nystrom's broad shoulders. The Trustee has seen them a hundred times. She looks for the ashen patch of Europa, yet she knows it isn't there.

-Few survived Europa.-

-Few were meant to.-

The Colonel smiles warmly, full lips and sharp green eyes.

"452A," says Nystrom.

"Sir."

"It's good to see you. Tired, no doubt. But you look healthy."

"Thank you, sir. It's good to see you as well."

It is a real kindness, but a false familiarity before the true discussions.

"The Priest tells me you're having misgivings about the upcoming rotation into the cellar."

"Thank you," says the Trustee, her mind jumping about, finding the wrong script to speak from. "Thank you for the privilege to see the Priest. It is a great reprieve to come inside and unburden myself to the gods."

Nystrom nods, eyes soft and caring as she listens to the Trustee, placating.

"But yes. The cellar is not an easy place to work," the Trustee adds.

"Understandable," says Nystrom. "The Priest and I, of course, don't speak of specifics regarding your private visits to the confessional. But you do come up in our talks. Temple is not always for bending knees at altars."

The Trustee speaks from the inner script again. "Sacred places are good for the human soul, sir. They are not only made for praying and being pious." She says the words but she does not recognize them.

"Quite right," says Nystrom, nodding, "this is not a pious place. But it is sacred and it is necessary."

For a moment they sit silently, imitating contemplation.

The Trustee has striven to sooth the passions of the Colonel for months and months. The sleight of hand has been honed over repeated encounters. Open ended comments. Empty philosophy injected. Designed to give Nystrom the lead in their discussions.

-The power to drive conversation.-

-The power to control thought.-

-A satisfaction. Nothing more.-

"The challenges can remind us of who we are," agrees the Trustee, mind raging at the lie.

"And yet it can never bring forgiveness," says Nystrom, looking over the filthy Trustee, pale, with thin skin and a stooped back. "Do you believe you are beginning to lose efficiency?"

"No. I don't believe I am," the Trustee says, and decides to admonish the Colonel in the only available way. "I have never communicated a weakness or a misgiving to you, sir. And I doubt your soldiers have communicated one about me."

"This is true."

"Sir, I am allowed to have doubt and concerns in the privacy of the confessional. It is a sacred place, is it not?"

The Colonel is silent.

"I am good, sir," promises the Trustee.

Nystrom sits up straighter and nods with a frown. "Indeed. I did not mean to question your time with the Priest. And point taken. I should encourage more discretion on what is shared."

-Discretion? Here?-

The Trustee wants to laugh but thankfully cannot find the physical capacity.

"I only mean your doubt has no merit," the Colonel continues, now trying to use praise to rebuild trust that never truly existed. "You are the longest surviving trustee we have ever had. You should be dead, by the estimations of my soldiers. And yet you are not."

"I do not wish to die."

"Of course not. But we all die here, Trustee. Even me and the Priest. A legionnaire of the UTC," she places her hand on her own chest and then points down vaguely in the location of the confessional booth several floors below. "A father of the Tribe, a servant of the Quadrumvirate. No one is a temporary visitor unless, of course, their life is temporary."

-She says it so casually.-

-Don't let the disgust touch your face.-

"For myself, it is my faith that drives me. For the prisoners, it is a requirement. Their lot. In my heart, Trustee, I am sickened by what happens here. By what we do here." She emphasizes the 'we'. "In my faith, I know there is very little that separates me from them. From you. For my sins, I should be out there in the barracks."

"Our sins are not always judged so harshly by the gods, sir," says the Trustee, struggling to match the Colonel's line of thinking, struggling to keep things heady. "We have the faiths, our teikum, and our society to answer to. And to answer for." It all spills from her mouth as if someone else is saying it.

The Colonel stands and looks out the window, hands clasped at her back. The Trustee watches as she takes deep breaths.

"Society. Yes. Society is the people, both here and out there, the citizens of the United Terran Coalition. And, Trustee, there are signs of violence all throughout. There is rebellion. The essays of the Neta-Teej continue to circulate. We have failed in our attempts to sever the channels of publishing. Do you have answers for that? I don't. Their words fuel unrest here. They fuel unrest in the outland zone and in the territories."

"I don't have any answers, sir."

"No one does!" the Colonel barks. "The off-world colonies are regularly quelling uprisings. Europa did us no favors there and neither did keeping the heretics alive. Every other guardship is off-world and every report I get from the mines is chaos. We should have never accepted the Falconer or the Crone here. The Neta-Teej is even worse. Better an execution for them all."

-Pay attention.-

-She is ranting.-

"Keep your wits about you, 452A," she says, not even realizing she is using a number code rather than the name of an endeared friend. "Every report from the General reveals more unrest in the deep. The Kem wer is becoming more and more aggressive. Lucien seems unconcerned, but every day we lose more and more. Prisoners, guards, supplies. They all fall into the darkest parts of the cellar."

"The Kemwer is killing advocates?" asks the Trustee, betraying shock.

"Yes," the Colonel nods, begrudgingly. "It is rare for Lucien's chosen guards to be killed. But it is becoming less rare."

The Trustee stares at the ground, unsure how to respond. She closes her eyes, pushing back the fear that comes with such a realization. Lightheaded, faint, her mind moves without her permission, sliding into the cellar. The heat is stifling and everything is wet. It smells of earthen filth and bakes itself into the lining of her sinuses. It permeates her pores the way the dark permeates the eye and starves the macula, rendering everything black and white.

Her footsteps echo off the barren stone chambers.

It is not just a dream, but a comprehensive departure. A hitch in her mind. The Trustee is in the cellar, but only for a single, complete, moment.

-I don't want to go back.-

-But you will.-

"You are an integral part of this machine," says Colonel Nystrom. "Your faith can keep you safe. I've had this feeling before many battles. Too many pushes into death."

"Every day feels like this to me, sir," admits the Trustee.

"I am sure of that," Nystrom says. "I forget sometimes. This is a hard place, and I cannot speak candidly with anyone. I know your faith, Trustee. And I know your work. Your loyalty is unquestioned."

"Thank you, sir."

There is a pause and the two women study each other.

The Colonel looks at the Trustee with a sudden hunger in her eyes, ready to get to the heart of the matter.

"I have been getting reports of you leaving the shed. What do you do on your visits to solitary?"

The Trustee looks away.

"452A, tell me. What do you do when you visit the Neta-Teej in the dark?"

The Colonel leans over her desk, searching the Trustee's face.

"I do visit," admits the Trustee, body numb. "But it has been a while since I have gone to see hir."

"And what do you do with the Neta-Teej?" asks the Colonel with implications in her tone.

-I delivered a blanket.-

-And I never, ever, speak the truth.-

"I talk."

"Trustee? Explain further."

"I confess. I confess directly to the Neta-Teej when I cannot see the Priest."

"A confession?" says the Colonel, confused. "That is not what everyone would do with a captive deity."

"I just talk to them."

"It's supposed to be solitary. It's against the rules, Trustee."

"It is my one grievance, sir. And I am not the only one." The Trustee intentionally allows some pleading into her voice.

Nystrom almost looks pleased with how the reprimand has impacted the Trustee. She is still a prisoner, not some perfect disciple of the shed, not some beautiful sufferer made to thrive in this hard world of holy penance. No, she is made harder than the others who came before, but nothing special.

The Colonel nods, "I will continue to allow this. Because of your work. It is the will of the gods to let you do this."

"Thank you, sir," says the Trustee, sickened, exposed.

-Nystrom is playing pious.-

-Playing god the only way available.-

-She is making sure the Neta-Teej is touchable.-

-Some day she may ask to use your hands.-

"But you must be careful," the Colonel says, softening off her own high. "Don't overstep. The Neta-Teej was a halo."

"Understood, sir."

"Ze is not to be trusted," she says, using the Neta-Teej's formal reference. "The Neta-Teej is a seer. Ze is powerful."

-In her mind you confront a god.-

-She could do it too. Visit solitary.-

-No. She couldn't.-

-But she would like to.-

"I think you do understand, Trustee. This is a sacred place. And we must all play our part."

"I am trying, sir."

The Colonel releases a deep breath.

"We all are. But there are uncounted thousands of prisoners on the surface at any given time. And there are far more in the cellar. Who knows how many still survive in the deep. How many sansvies survive alongside the Kemwer, playing his games with Lucien. The prisoners outnumber the guards more than a thousand to one. There are far too many parts to play."

6

In a pitch-black chamber, water dripping off stone walls, five suits of armor, each containing an isolated human, congregate. The armor is corroded and damaged, battle-worn, patched with welded plates, added to with racks of explosives and ammunition.

Their suits have been powered off, leaving them in total darkness. This is an insulated cavern deep underground, somewhere in the cellar, protected from prying eyes, nested between heavy ore deposits. And it is only one set of eyes they are concerned with.

The face shields open manually and all five entities stare into the black. The warm air, carrying all the waste and moisture, assails their nostrils. They are unable to see each other, but with low whispers they can converse.

"Thank you for coming," says the highest-ranking soldier.

"Do we know where Lucien is?" asks one.

"Of course not," says another.

"We are advocates. His advocates. We should know these things."

"Apparently you have not been here long enough."

"Has anyone seen him recently?"

Even as they speak, they try to hear cryptic sounds behind the echoes of dripping water, to discern the approach of the lurking overseer.

"If you are that worried about the General, you should not be here with us."

"And you aren't afraid?"

"I am terrified. We all are. But we have been cautious."

"He knows every crevice of the cellar. Cautiousness is never enough with Lucien."

"Keep your voice down."

There is a moment of silence.

"I have seen him recently," says one who has been quiet.

"Where?"

"A week ago. Third transect. He was going to guard the portal room for a bit. Said he thought things seemed tense and wanted to make a test of the Kemwer's defenses."

"Then he may be dead already."

"You certainly have not been here long enough if you think like that."

"Lucien is not dead."

"The Kemwer has been hunting him."

"It's the other way around with Lucien. Always. He is the one doing the hunting."

"He's losing it. All these halos wandering around fucked him up."

"We will discuss that."

"I agree. He is losing it," says the quiet one. "He said he was making a mask when I saw him."

"What?"

"A mask. He showed it to me. Rough cast bronze."

"A mask of what?"

"Who cares?"

"I couldn't tell. He said it was an unknown animal. Part of a myth."

"Did he say anything else?"

"No. I left him near the base of the scaffolding in the third. It was after the Kemwer came up with some of the raiders."

"So, he's been missing for seven days?"

"Missing is the wrong word. He's gone quiet. No other contact."

"He isn't giving orders anymore."

Several of the advocates laugh quietly.

"He almost never gives orders. But I agree. He has been more and more absent when we need him. He's been letting the Kemwer wreak havoc on the lower portions of the transect. They're killing us, taking advocates, armor and all. He's done nothing to protect us."

"He was at the Kemwer's last raid. He made his presence known in the fight."

"But he didn't follow the Kemwer. And he didn't show up for the other raids."

"No."

"He's been wandering, asking for intel on the halos. Where are they? What are they doing? Who are they talking to? He's losing his edge. Losing focus."

"His focus has shifted. That is certain."

"Can we still trust him?"

"Absolutely not. The General has always been off. But it's bad now."

"No longer backing us up."

"Letting the Kemwer run wild in the deep."

"Let's discuss the halos. Which poses the greatest threat?"

"By the number of fighters, it's the Falconer for sure."

"We can wait till he's in the cellar, then kill him with a hundred others to make it look casual."

"Lucien won't like that."

"Which part?"

"The Falconer dying part. Lucien is too interested."

"The Neta-Teej is the greatest threat."

"Why?"

"He's infatuated. Lucien asks more about that one than any of the others."

"So, there's danger due to distraction."

"And the essays. Colonel Nystrom has sent message after message to Lucien asking for help stopping the transmissions of the writings."

"And he's done nothing."

"What would happen if we kill the Neta-Teej?"

"It would rid us of some problems inside and out. It may drive some prisoners to the Falconer, while others may drift toward the Crone. Though, the Crone has shown no intent of actual rebellion and operates alone. It may split some of the rebel factions. But Lucien will be furious."

"That is what we want."

"Is it?"

Heavy quiet follows. Though they cannot see one another, they each move with mirrored agitation, anxious with the implications.

"We need him refocused, or we need to break the final thread he has to reality."

"Accelerate whatever trajectory he is on?"

"Yes."

"Agreed. A total break from reality would give us an opportunity. It's time we move beyond these games Lucien is playing. We are losing control."

"So it will be the Neta-Teej?"

"We must do it on the surface. Lucien watches the cellar too closely."

"Do we want our hands on this?"

"Can we make it look like a prisoner did it? Or a surface guard?"

They consider the options, none of which breed confidence.

"If he knows it was advocates, then we may draw him into a trap."

"A trap? It's just a way to get Lucien to hunt you alongside the Kemwer."

"Do we think he'll even care?"

"He may not. Still, it's a net gain. But things are losing cohesion. We need to rattle all the cages here. We need a shift in power to reassert our hierarchy and regain control of the mines."

"Have we ever known Lucien to be out of control?"

"It was you who said he was making a bronze mask."

"Yes. I think we must acknowledge, as one, that we don't want Lucien in control anymore. But we need someone we can trust. No trust was ever really put in Lucien. And it never will be."

"That's the way he has the system designed."

"We are no different than the prisoners."

"To Lucien, we are all part of the experiment."

"Then we kill the Neta-Teej on the next rotation."

"Just a murder?"

"Ze is a halo. Supposedly Lucien's favorite. A desecration is needed to send a message, to get a reaction, to get a result."

"If so, we must be ready for his wrath."

"We will attempt to deflect the blame. Prisoner or surface guard. But we will have a trap in place if things go sideways. Either way, the rebels will have one less halo. No more essays mocking our control. Colonel Nystrom will have no choice but to back us. Her surface guards will do as she commands. She would be glad to rid herself of Lucien."

"Do we know that?"

"Do you doubt it?"

"And Lucien himself?"

"He would call this a 'test' if he did this to us."

"We'll find out where he really stands, or we break him and move on. Isn't this why we've gathered here?"

"There is also the chance we all get killed."

"If he comes to the surface for us, then we can take him there with the Osai and the shed's guards as backup. If he stays down in the cellar, we band together and wait for him to be depleted on a raid."

"These are significant undertakings beyond just killing the Neta-Teej."

"And we cannot truly trust the other advocates. Most are too loyal."

"The others are irrelevant. The mine is never going away. We either live here without his games, without his backstabbing, or we die bringing the advocates back to power. We don't need him anymore, and he is straying further from the primary mission."

"And if we do survive? Who's going to take over? You?"

"We'll have to get through Lucien first."

"I am up on the shed for the next rotation," says the highest rank. "Who else?"

"Me," says the quiet one.

"This is dangerous. Maybe treason. But we will kill the Neta-Teej. Your participation is not an order."

"I don't need one."

7

The Trustee takes the lift down to the administration level and waits for a moment in the hallway.

She knows the Doctor is watching her on his screens, making her wait, analyzing every breath, every nervous tick. Everyone watches everyone inside the Osai. Even the guardship watches in its own way, storing recordings and passing them to UTC High Command at regular intervals.

But the Doctor is obsessive about the Trustee. His dirty habits spill out upon his patients. His eyes crawl over bodies, seeking for a crevice to leak into, and Trustee 452A has become a fixation.

-I know you are looking at me, waiting for me to come to you. Yes. I hesitate before I enter your clinic.- She stands outside the door, not yet fully prepared to knock and engage.

-Watch me. Remember. I am a killer. Not a specimen like the others you get your hands on.-

-You think your questions make me nervous.-

-You should be nervous, too.-

-You make me sick.-

She looks up to where the small comm eye peers down from the ceiling. She stares.

-Keep your hands off me.-

-There's no one to heal a doctor. No one who would bother.-

She kicks the door with a boot and it immediately opens, confirming the vigilance of the observer on the other side of the camera.

Inside the infirmary the lights are dimmed but they still show hints of blue sterility. The Trustee blinks quickly to adjust her eyes to the low light.

She stops just inside the door and lets it close behind her.

The infirmary gives her claustrophobia like the cellar, awakens fear of hidden corners like the barracks houses at night. It evokes the crushing pressure of the United Terran Coalition, their industry for religion and battle. The room is clean, in harsh opposition to all the dirty places through which she normally migrates.

-It is this doctor's probing sickness that frames it all. The things he hides in the dark. The things he makes dirty with his presence, even in a clean room.-

He emerges from a back storage room where his monitors glow. The Doctor wears hooded white coveralls with the fabric pulled taut at the edges of his face. His empty eyes search the room, passing over and around the Trustee, but never quite stopping to focus on her.

The white coveralls are not new, knees black with dust and hips scuffed from bumping into things, a false visage of professional uniform, a mask of something long since gone.

He comes forward and stands behind the steel examination table, resting on it, using it to keep his balance. He motions vaguely for her to move to the left and points to the middle of the room where a small circle is embossed into the floor.

The Trustee hesitates and he points again with a sharp finger, more purposefully, more violently.

She stands on the circle, pulls off her hat, and looks up as the cylindrical rack slowly lowers, clattering. The unit encompasses her in a tube of steel and wires. She holds her breath, knowing it will be a quick procedure.

"Stand still," he says. His voice struggles over the ends of the syllables but his volume is wrong for the situation, almost a tongueless whisper, mouth slack.

The rack's lights turn on and it tunes itself to block out any interference that may come from the ship systems. Another, smaller ring descends and goes around her natty hair.

Only when she is immobilized inside the rack does the Doctor speak again.

"Hello. System Log, reflect Trustee 452A is here for repatterning. How is she? Changed. Always changed. Every time... changed."

The words are quiet, not meant for a response, as he keeps himself propped up on the exam table.

"Change. Does she know why? Not today. Not tomorrow. Without a look inside, who can understand?"

Small sensors whir, embedded in the ring around her head, and lights orbit her skull.

"So much trouble. One trustee. One prisoner. Filth which requires maintenance. The definition of absurdity."

The machine shuts off after a moment and rises up.

The Doctor stands right in front of her. His body is slight but strong, his shape hidden in the coveralls.

Glazed eyes appraise her up and down, foggy lenses with nothing behind them. He never looks at her face. He reviews her body, lingering on shapes that are rare in prisoners, and then skips right to her forehead.

-He knows where the problem lies.-

-In here. In me.-

He raises his hand laxly, he wants to touch her head, but

instead he stops himself and just points for a moment and then smirks.

"What's in there?" he asks, almost with warm fascination, infatuation for a new lover.

"I don't know," she says, loud enough to shake him up a little.

"The pattern says you're lying."

"I lie to you all the time," she says, daring him to do something about it.

He scoffs and laughs a little.

"Display the convoluted signatures," he commands the empty room. "Most recent scan versus convoluted signatures from one year ago."

In the middle of the room, floating in the air, appears a flat black baseline with red and yellow lines writhing and coiling around it like snakes.

As the holographic stabilizes, the lines dancing in the low light, the Doctor sits on the metal table.

The Trustee puts her hat back on and prepares for whatever might come.

"Anomalous. One point seven times, Trustee. Amplitude is evolving while frequency remains the same. Impossible. Unprecedented. You should be a god or a genius."

"I am neither."

The Doctor absently grins to himself, laughs, and then pulls a foil packet from his gown. He unfolds it on the metal table, crushes the crystalline fragments inside, licks his fingers, and then raises the packet to his lips.

"Not long now, Trustee," he says, and she doesn't know if he is referring to some diagnosis or the drugs or the time.

-The clockwork will work fast.-

-Keep him talking.-

He puts the foil back into his gown and then stands, unsteady.

"Explain," he says, pointing at the waves still rolling in the air.

His entire body sways as his eyes follow the undulation of the graphs above his head, eyes transfixed by the light. His irises have almost disappeared, black enveloping the human color.

Without looking away from the graphs, he approaches the Trustee.

She holds the stun baton in her pocket, wanting to use it.

He is whispering again.

"One point seven. Baseline too high. Outlier. Should be scanned. Imaged. Cut open. Infra-low acceleration. Delta too high for waking life. Periodic theta with clear consciousness. Gamma surges. Are you afraid, Trustee?"

He does not expect a response as he reaches out to touch her forehead. He pushes her hat back to expose more scalp.

She lets him do it, seeing how fast he is fading.

The Doctor's finger traces a line across the skin right below her hairline where the scalpel might make its first incision if he were to have his way.

He nods in agreement with his own thoughts.

Satisfied, he returns to the metal table and lies down, sprawled on his back.

"Going down the hall now. Red curtain waving," he says. "Maybe you will be there. Maybe we can share teikum. Find the gods."

He laughs a little, like it's a joke.

The Trustee stands still, watching as the clockwork takes effect and transports the Doctor away from his concerns.

She considers cracking his skull open with her baton. She considers cutting off certain parts with a sharp scalpel.

-He won't get out of the red room for a while.-

-But there are scanners.-

-Do I care?-

-You do.-

But she approaches him and checks his pockets, knowing she'll be seen by the Colonel or anyone else watching.

-Who will stop me?-

She finds another foil packet with clockwork inside and takes it for herself.

-Plenty more in the cookers back there in storage.-

-Get the clean stuff while you can.-

-The draad offers have shit in the cellar.-

-The cellar is no place to lose the time.-

The Trustee thinks about ending the Doctor once more but knows no good would come of it. She heads back to the doors, then to the lift, mind beginning to depart.

8

Her consciousness has separated again.

The body continues while the self ignores the world around it.

When senses kick back in, the shock is like a sudden douse of cold water.

-Where have I wandered off to?-

The Trustee rediscovers herself in a dark room.

It's cold and stinks below the odor of stale smoke.

-Barracks house.-

-Empty.-

-You hope it's empty.-

Weak light forces its way through the poorly fitted wooden slats, and her eyes race about the dense network of bunks, stacked floor to ceiling. There are a hundred places to hide in a bunk house, countless ways in which to stage an ambush.

-How did I get here?-

-You're on body removal.-

-Fingertips aren't frozen yet.-

-Haven't been out long.-

She turns, boots making the floorboards creak. Icicles hang

from the ceiling, dipping toward spots where small fires were lit on stones through the night, melting ice on the roof so droplets may pass between slats and then refreeze as the fire dies out.

-When there are enough people, enough fires, it must be warm.-

There is a strange part of her that longs for that, a shared discomfort, in exchange for her isolation and private privilege.

"You back, Trus-tee?" asks a voice behind her, stuttering over her title, drawing out the sounds. "Are you okay?" There is a beat of hesitation between each word to prepare for the next. Syllables are collapsed together unless they come out broken.

The Trustee turns to see a short man, ragged clothes hanging, who has emerged from the shadows and now stands, unimposing, near the closed door. By his frame she can tell he used to be strong, but it's drained off him. The dark skin of his face is blotchy with scar tissue. Wind burn and exposure have contributed their own efforts. But all his visage revolves around the blank eyes, rings of steel set below the eyelids. Each ring encases lenses of flat gray glass.

-He's boxed you in.-

-He knows your mind wandered.-

-Guards should have already turned this barracks out.-

-Not enough guards. Not enough loyal trusties.-

-Lucien's recipe for mayhem.-

She curses Lucien and herself in tandem for getting cornered.

"Trus-tee. Are you back insi-de your-self?" he asks again, deep voice catching.

"You aren't supposed to be here," she says, mustering stern superiority, though she knows it won't work on this one.

"You are col-lecting the d-ead. I was over-seeing them."

The Trustee knows he is watching her, scanning her body, looking, waiting for something.

-Watching for a violent turn?-

-No. Something more.-

The Trustee takes a few steps back and then pushes deeper into the barracks. There are a number of bodies in the wooden bunks along the walls. Still others lie on the floor, but all have been unceremoniously pushed out of the way, stripped of clothes they no longer have use for, hair hacked short to be used as thread.

In the very back, on a lower bunk, rests the body of a young man. Blood has coated the sleeping platform and dripped through to the floor where it has frozen. The pale body is missing both legs, removed at the hip with what she assumes was a zip saw and rapid work. The ball was removed from the socket to preserve maximum bone. The lower legs are on the floor, discarded.

"You let this happen?" the Trustee asks, calling back to the short man who still stands near the closed barracks door.

"Not my bunk, Trus-tee. You said it. I'm not su-pposed to be here. But I go w-here I please." His voice is confident, certain, despite his stutter.

The Trustee knows efficiency of survival is paramount on the shed, and to fail at survival does not mean you are finished with our usefulness. There is no stronger bone in the body than the femur. They make the best weapons. The highest density of meat is on the thighs. The sawing, when done right, takes time, but the weight of the body is centralized and that can work to your advantage on a cold night when time is short. The work gets you what you need.

"I hope his next life will be one of lear-ning. His sp-irit doesn't need that body anymore."

The Trustee looks back at the man, making sure he's visible through the bunks. She sees a small bird has flown in and now flutters around the man, landing on his shoulder for a moment, then escapes again through a crack in the door.

"Do you rem-member me, Trus-tee?" the man asks, his focus unmistakable across the empty bunk house.

She knows she is supposed to remember, but she shakes her head and pulls the dismembered body from the bunk. It is strangely light without the meat of the legs, but all the bodies she lifts are diminished, withered things that show the innards and the bones.

"No, I don't remember you. Except for the eyes," she admits. "I remember the eyes. But the rest of you...," she shrugs, "just another body to collect and burn."

The man smiles at her, a full smile. Even without the character of the eyes she sees what she thinks is the glimmer of violence that comes to every man who's had his ego stricken.

But the smile does not turn sour as he examines her.

"You mis-judge me, Trus-tee. If you do not re-member, then I would be easy to dism-iss."

She rolls the body and slides it to the middle of the barracks. Crystals of icy blood scatter along the wood.

"Do you see the-se two?" the man asks, pointing to a bunk where two more bodies lie untouched next to each other.

The Trustee looks at them and actually examines them for the first time.

"They cling to each-other," says the man, making his hands fists, and crossing them over his chest, embracing himself. When he does, the sleeves of his robes slide down, revealing heavy scars wrapping his wrists and forearms.

-I remember those scars.-

-Like the eyes.-

"No one touch-ed them. Left the lov-ers be."

"Why?" The bodies are like every other, but together.

"Honor," says the man, without stutter. "Love is necess-ary. The an-chor dur-ing trans-form-ation. Sub-limation, when the mom-ent of alch-emy meets the mom-ent of eter-nity."

"Love is weakness here," she says and moves to pull them from the bunk.

"Stop," he barks, voice clear, face no longer smiling. "Love brought you here. Unl-ess you have forgot-ten Eur-opa also?"

The Trustee stares at him. She can see the anger in his face, the demand. But there is also a hopefulness she will not be able to reciprocate.

"Are they sansvies?" she asks, intuitively knowing the word will anger him.

"Call them Arkû," he says, sighing in weariness. "No need to poll-ute your mind with dehuma-nizing lang-uage. They were alive," he says, but then looks down. "They made them-selves. I hel-ped make them poss-ible."

The Trustee looks down at the bodies, sees how their faces are close together, using one another for comfort in final moments. Emotions rise inside her, but there are no memories to anchor them to. Indiscernible feelings flood her and she pushes them aside as one.

"I am going to clear out the dead now. All of them," the Trustee says in a matter-of-fact tone. "It's time for you to leave."

He nods. "Be care-ful with them."

She notes the way he says it, with true concern, his eyes focused on the clasped bodies.

He takes a full breath and then looks around, weighing his options. He does not want to leave them.

-Was he sitting vigil over them?-

-Did he help them to die?-

"It's time for you to go," she says, making it a clear order.

He smiles again but it is a sad smile.

"When you lis-ten to the Net-a-Teej do you hear the voi-ces of your youth?" he asks, tapping the side of his head by the ear. "Voi-ces from when you were clean?"

The Trustee looks instinctively to the two bodies on the bunk.

"I did-n't know the Net-a-Teej in my youth. But their voi-ce takes me back to a bet-ter time, bet-ter thou-ghts," he says. "True pow-er in that."

She is surprised to feel rage welling up inside her. It is a curiosity for her, even as it takes over, her mind partially aware that it is a contextless emotion, unsure of why the anger has arrived.

She turns and approaches him directly.

He does not move, watching her until she towers a full head above him.

She takes fistfuls of his coat and starts to push him backward toward the door.

His steel eyes stare straight into her face, shifting and analyzing.

He is unafraid and it maddens her.

When his body slams into the closed door, the whole shed shakes and he coughs and hangs in her grip.

"Trus-tee," he sputters, pinned against the door but not struggling, head hanging. "Do not visit the sol-itary cells ag-ain. It is a st-upid game."

"I am not playing games," she says, opening the door and throwing him down the front steps to the dirty ice.

He crumples into a heap and groans as she closes the door to return to her work.

In the dim morning sun, breeze carrying the frigid cold, the man lies back for a moment to rest his bones and stares into the sky, a slate of gray.

He can see the black specs of birds flying high overhead as the air returns to his lungs. He breathes deeply, feeling his chest move. He takes in the air that keeps the birds aloft. His blood is replenished by the same oxygen and that knowledge rejuvenates more than just his body.

9

Excerpt from Exile Journal of the Neta-Teej:

-Original Publication: Split River - Europa Node
Post-Publication Addendum to Portal Scroll
-Found: Portal Room, Third Transect,
Willett Prison Encampment, Earth

I have been given the gifts of dedication, of birthing spirits, and of guidance.

These gifts have been formally revoked by the United Terran Coalition, by the Quadrumvirate of the Tribe, but it does not matter. They cannot take my gifts away from me anymore.

I am still the Neta-Teej.

I have been given the gift of sight. I am a seer. This gift cannot be revoked.

We project our desires and our wishes into the universe.

These wishes overshadow all the quiet prayers we say while kneeling in the dark.

So, pray as you must. You must be as you pray and it is all a type of prayer.

To be alive is not enough. You must live your prayer. You must see it when you look into the void, into your teikum. You must believe it. You must believe into the face of death.

The human condition seeks the edge, the edge of light and the edge of ourselves. Do you see yourself in your prayers? Do you pray to who matters most? Or do you pray into the void?

Fill the void. Fill it with yourself. Stretch it and make it wider.

Thus, the edge of the great void grows with us, always opening and ever expanding. We shy from it and then chase it again.

You ask about the unknown. You look to the precipice of our understanding. You see the threshold between light and dark.

Look closely.

The threshold bends. It widens and multiplies as you look. The line blurs. The void reaches ever wider. This is the space humans are asked to fill.

We will never know the universe, never hold it in our minds. Knowledge is not finite, but that which we come to know in a passing day is knowable. For you. For me. We know of our experience between sleeps. We may not retain it all or see it truthfully, but that is not experience. Experience is the knowledge we believe we have obtained for ourselves. We are defined by what we acknowledge in that experience, and what we do not. The absence is often more important than the inclusion.

But there is an infinity bound up in all of this strung together, day after day, person after person. Existence, human existence. Thus, humans sit at the side of the gods we made, looking ever closer, ever seeking the threshold of teikum, the great and unanswerable questions. More experience should beget more seeking at the edge of the void of our own devise, not truncate it.

Your doubts should inspire curiosity.

A closer look brings understanding.

And then, explosion. The truth fragments as you look. A million human perspectives. A billion. Now trillions. They form a ring around teikum.

Teikum makes us. It makes us human. It remakes us with every focused look.

In prayer, believers questioned me and demanded explanations of scripture.

"Neta-Teej, one cannot be guided to the abyss," they would say.

I used to have scripted answers, ordained responses. They were insufficient, the concepts too simple, thought terminating.

"True," I now say. "But one cannot walk alone either. You must walk beside yourself to find teikum. Look back upon your own wandering path and ahead at how you have altered your destination. Only humans do such things."

"And the Arkû?" I was asked.

Again, I have new answers.

"The Arkû are human. They were in darkness and walked a straight path. Then they found a threshold and their path started to bend. Now they are a million more perspectives. Just like us. They do honor to the great uncertainty we all carry. They carry it inside themselves as well, the void, teikum."

That was never in the scripture.

"Do you pray, Neta-Teej?"

"I pray now, in my heart, with you before me," I still respond. This has never changed.

"Do you fight, Neta-Teej?"

And I must answer differently now.

"I have fought already. I have killed for the gods inside us all and I will do so again. It is human to stand for something, for some blurred threshold. But it is far more human to die on that threshold. That is what I plan to do when my time comes."

"Will you pray aloud for us?"

And the prayer has changed as well.

"Let the darkness in. Let the songs go quiet. Gods die without your preaching, without your keeping. Let them all go. It must be you who does the changing. I pray for adaptation. I pray for grace, in my dancing and my cunning. Bleed the blood of spirit. This is all you have to pay for a god. Pay it in the darkness. Spill it into teikum. That is where it is worth the most."

"Have you ever pulled back in fear at the threshold to the darkness?"

I used to say that the threshold was not so dark, that I could see through. But this too changed. I am now tired and feel terribly blind.

Now, I say, "If there is no fear, it isn't really dark."

10

The dead stack easily, too thin to possess life.

The Trustee tries not to look at their faces as she carries them. She walks with her head down and lays them gently on the transport, a hovering flatbed. She moves them slowly and precisely.

They are not heavy enough for the Trustee to really make them human in perception, but to avoid the eyes is always best, closing them with a gloved hand if possible.

There is the sense that something might pass through, eye to eye, a final thought or a final pain, something left over. The Trustee knows she isn't strong enough for that and looks away as she works.

When the cargo transport is full, a hundred or more bodies, the Trustee pulls the flatbed, hovering over the snow, through the rows and rows of empty barracks in the afternoon haze.

She moves out beyond the edge of camp, pulling the transport between the markers.

A breeze brushes over her and the Trustee finds a momentary reprieve from the smell of the dead, blown away if she stays ahead of the transport and walks into the wind.

The sun begins to disappear behind the mountains bordering the shed. There will be another windswept night.

-More bodies tomorrow.-

Close to the hills, along the metal fence to the north, a deep shaft penetrates the layers of ice and snow and into the earth. It is an abandoned test shaft from early mining operations. Next to it is a shallow pit, a bowl in which the bodies are deposited.

The depression is almost full, as the Trustee has done a diligent job of scouring the shed for all it has to offer.

Her final cargo slides unceremoniously down the embankment, spilling over each other and onto their brethren, then coming to a rest.

The Trustee stares as the dead utza pack together in a strange pile, as if no one's bodies are really their own, a tessellated mass of human life, the parts mobile and interchangeable.

This is what she sees as she endeavors to not really see anything at all.

From the back of the cargo hauler, the Trustee sprays a layer of fuel over the bodies. Around the pit she walks, coating them in orange slime. It adds to the effect, truly bonding them as one.

She tosses the charge in. The whole pit ignites, and flesh, once beginning to decay, now starts to burn.

The smoke and soot rise above the fence, free, into the sky.

The few lingering birds scatter as the smoke snakes south along the foothills.

It takes time for the fuel to get hot and for the secondary reactions to start, for bone to splinter and water to convert inside the organs and muscles. Green and blue light shoots from those bodies made with metallic thread in the meat and silicon nerve clusters.

The Trustee lies on the flatbed and stares at the sky, unable to watch the inferno. She looks away, unwilling to watch the smoke cloud as it's carried by the wind.

-To fly away would be nice.-

-But these birds stay.-

-They are the Falconer's creations?-

-Some yes. Some no.-

-Real birds?-

-Very few.-

-I am not a real bird.-

-So, you are more like them.-

They swoop and circle, but so high there are no details to their forms. She sees flashes of the metal and glass eyes from the man in the shed and she knows suddenly who he is. But the recognition is moot, something she should always have known.

-The Falconer of Europa.-

-I am losing myself.-

-Everyone does in a place like this.-

-Some memories go. Other memories are intruding.-

-False? Real?-

-I don't know.-

-Why did the Falconer ask about the Neta-Teej?-

-Everyone has asked.-

-The prayers do remind me of my youth.-

-There will be no going back.-

-There will be no flying away.-

-I wouldn't deserve such things.-

-There is no forgiveness.-

-I'm losing days now. I cannot remember what I've done or what comes next.-

The birds hover kilometers overhead.

The Trustee imagines one of them racing towards her, a tiny dot growing larger and larger and taking shape. In her memory there is a flash of light and it is a bird, enormous and metal, striking her. They grapple in the air, falling, a torrent of scraping wings and talons, right as the sonic boom shakes them from the bird's amazing speed. They fall and they fall, together tumbling toward ice.

-If I followed these bodies down the hole, would I even remember hitting the bottom?-

-Do the souls rise in the smoke? Do they roll together with all the others and then fade away?-

-They are lucky to die on the surface. Lucky to die beyond the grip of the cellar.-

She uses the plow edge on the transport to push the prisoners from the pit, not fully finished burning, not fully consumed. They fall over the edge of the depression and into the deep shaft. She scrapes the pit free of bodies and ice, exposing frosted dirt.

Soon all traces of the dead are discarded into the subsurface, lost into the earth.

The Trustee pulls the cargo transport around and then away from the pit as the sun begins to set and the cold takes domain over the entire flat.

11

A low shack encased in ice and snow sits to the west, beyond the beacons.

The Trustee has slowly mended the porous walls and leaking ceiling over secret nights and hidden moments in the dark. She has braced the structure against the wind so it will not collapse, packed mud and stone into the holes.

Yet, there is no mistaking what the solitary cells are for.

-To initiate the slow death.-

-To crush the spirit.-

The Trustee leaves the cargo hauler out front.

She stoops to enter and passes by the other rooms. Doors hang open. The cells are empty. The air inside the shadowed structure is bitter, untouched by the sun. The last cell, furthest from the entrance, has a steel bar lying across the closed door.

Through the meal slot the Trustee feeds a blanket, then a small bottle of nutrient solution.

Chain links pull against each other on the opposite side.

"Offerings?" asks a quiet voice. It is sweet and knowing.

"It will be colder tonight."

"You know I don't take offerings anymore. I don't need a blanket."

"Everyone needs a blanket."

"I don't want one," says the voice. There is no longer malice. There used to be hatred in the tone, but rituals in the shed become warm and holy, even when unwanted. Even when ritual has seemed to lose all meaning.

The Trustee stares at the seam where the door meets the floor.

She knows the Neta-Teej is kneeling on the other side.

"Give the blanket to someone else," ze says.

"I have spent the day burning bodies. Most of them had blankets."

"I would rather die than take your blanket," the Neta-Teej says, again without anger or cruelty.

-I would rather die than take too much.-

-That's what ze means.-

-That is the path of the Neta-Teej.-

-I would rather die than take an offering from a trustee.-

-That is also what ze means.-

"But you won't freeze to death?" asks the Trustee.

"No. I promise. Not tonight," says the Neta-Teej and there is weight in those words.

The Trustee nods but closes the food slot and places a rock in front of it.

"Trustee," asks the Neta-Teej from behind the door. "Why do you do this? Why do you do this to us?"

The Trustee stands, still looking down at the base of the door.

"I don't remember anymore," she says.

"Do you remember that it hurts?"

"Who?"

"You. Me. It hurts everyone," says the low voice, soft and matter of fact.

The Trustee nods again.

"Can't forget that it hurts," she says.

"Then why continue?"

"Same reason you don't want a blanket."

"They use you, you know," says the Neta-Teej quickly. "To pass messages."

"They use you, too. They use us all."

There is a sigh and a momentary pause.

"Goodbye, Trustee. Stay warm. Promise me?"

The Trustee nods, but says nothing before turning and leaving solitary.

12

Excerpt from The Treatise of Seers:

Questions Concerning the Inner Sight
and Veracity of Truth
-The Coda of Unification

———

Question I: The Becoming of a Seer

To be a seer is to be a gateway to many unknown paths. They cannot be known until they are walked. It is a rare gift. But in its rarity, it is both holy and dangerous. There is a great deal of uncertainty that comes from the act of being a seer, and it may yield either a great expansion of teikum or delusion without restraint.

It is a human capability. There is soul in the act and so there can be soul lost in the act. Mind and heart are needed as well, so those things may also be lost.

And the questions are eternal. Do I hear my own voice in my

mind? Are the images of my own imagination? Are the voices from something inside me, but split off, remote and separate? Are they outside of me entirely, voices from spirits beyond, powers from another realm? Or am I hearing the voice of the gods? Am I seeing and feeling his or her will?

These are questions that have plagued us as believers since the beginning of time. Does this god or that god speak to me? Is it them speaking in their own voice, or only my imagination? Can I truly know the difference? The answer is for you to know. The things you see and hear are for you to determine.

The natural state of belief has been the progression towards bifurcation, toward schism. Taken to a natural end, the implication of humanity is the continued fractionation of belief to the distal-most end point of every living being retaining their own divine knowledge. This becomes the origin of our great unification. The Coda is based on the assumption that we all have our own inner belief and we must apply it to the outer belief, and it is with this we are able to unite and include every entity and every facet of belief. We are one in our human struggle to know the gods and the void and find our place and purpose in the universe. Our teikum, our great unanswered question, is what make us human and make us one, the species whole. We are defined by our knowledge and our faith.

From this revelation, this reformation, we pivot upon the path of faith, we turn full round to look behind to see the trail we have left. Now, instead of a million truncated and bifurcated beliefs through human history, we see the reuniting of the faiths. Schism turns into a node of individual expression, a point of double-name, the father and the son, the inside and the outside, past and present, a shift in language, an interpretation based on human spirit.

We reunify those moments in our history by acknowledging that these nodes all reside within teikum, within us individually, and so they are questions without answer. Rather than seek the answer, we shall return to letting the question stand. Let all the questions stand, back through time, back across the many schisms, back until we find the origin of our beliefs. That origin resides inside teikum as well, the question of all questions, the source of what makes us human, gives us our souls, differentiates us from all the other beings, the question that proves we have crossed a threshold no other species has traversed.

We pivot again, back at the origin, and look ahead, not at what we are now, but at all we could have been. There were always bound to be seers. There have always been those who looked along the lines of possibility and saw into teikum and brought back words or images for consideration by their tribes and congregations.

Discussions abound about whether seeing is providence or sorcery or hallucination: Is it holy, the voice of the gods, prophecy, or is it simply foolishness? The Coda of Unification, the Quadrumvirate, and the Tribe as a whole, will not answer that question. We see it as a question that must stand. It resides within teikum, so the answer is of the soul, of the god-self, of the mind, of the heart.

Countless world histories have attributed different names and capabilities to those who profess to be seers. They are called believers, witches, heretics, saints, oracles, prophets, disciples, holy, evil, diluted, the most full. The names are always related to the message they carry in comparison to the dominant message at the time. The outcome is always oppression, reverence, or schism.

These times are no different and there will be no time in the future when things are different. These are all human reactions to the human question.

Within this thesis on those who see, there are inclusions from the Four of the Quadrumvirate, each of whom holds a differing opinion on what it means. Each lists the benefits to the self, to the Tribe, and the dangers. Each lists the basis and the limitations. Each speaks from their own deep knowledge and their own experience within teikum.

These are statements made, not as answers for the reader, for the worshiper, but as guidance for those questions which will always stand. One may experience joy or fear, fullness or emptiness, as they explore teikum. Some will see, some will hear. Some will only think they see or hear. Some will know. That is the nature of the questions inside teikum.

Whatever the message, it is heard by human ears and seen by human eyes and perceived by a human mind, and so it is ephemeral. As such, this thesis also preaches caution. The turbulence of teikum does not make it a simple realm. Questions change. Perceptions change. Humans change.

It is not rare to have questions and to seek. But it is rare to find. It is rare to be a seer, to be in a state where the turbulence falls away and the temporary nature of perception no longer applies. You may know it if it comes to you. How long will it last? Is it real?

This thesis is to aid in navigation of those turbulent waters and to aid in the moments of sudden calm when the veil is thin and sight comes to you without anchor. Are you confronted with god? Are you confronted with a reflection of the self? Are you meeting the gaze of another, a thing with or without name? Are you wise enough to tell the difference, and are you wise enough to act or not act according to their wishes?

Would you disobey the gods?

Would you do the bidding of a shadow of the self?

There are countless questions and answers pertaining to the holiness of both herein. But in the end, a seer must decide. Is what you see real to you? And more importantly, should it be real to others?

13

In a daze, the Trustee takes the long way around the shed, passing far outside the beacons, knowing she is not sharp enough to pull the cargo hauler safely through the barracks.

The guards take time evaluating the hauler's equipment but pay her no mind as she waits at the base of the Osai.

They readmit the hauler and she drags it back into the lower cargo hold and docks it.

She takes the lift up through the center of the warm ship and finds herself in the confessional, sitting alone in the low light. The Trustee is called to the closed and quiet space, everything diminished inside the womb-like vessel.

Her mind grasps at pieces of the last few hours but they are already falling away as fast as she tries to retrace them.

When the Priest arrives, stepping into his side of the booth, he is silent, respectful of her internal processes. He knows to wait. He knows better than to ask questions too quickly.

For himself, he does not dread the moments of quiet when someone is nearby. It is a relief to no longer be alone, to be in proximity of someone he is supposed to help, to work with, to guide.

The Trustee's head bows low and she slowly pulls her hat off, hair running through her fingers as they tighten. She pulls on the strands to wake up the nerves, stinging her scalp. The pain makes her grit her teeth and she closes her eyes.

"I can't wake up, Priest," she says as she takes a breath and sits back in the confessional.

The Priest measures his words against her unexpected statement.

"Are you dreaming, Trustee?"

"Everything but," she says, staring blankly.

"Colonel Nystrom spoke highly of your conversation this morning," he says, trying to shift the aim of this confession.

"It was honest," she lies and smiles, unable to recall it.

"It is best to be honest. This world, this place, is filled with honesty."

"Do you find comfort in this bankrupt philosophy? You're in a cage, not a world. A smaller cage than me, to be honest."

She raps her knuckles on the wood.

"And you are stuck in a dream?" he asks, sarcastically.

"I guess we're fucked," she says and laughs softly.

The Priest smiles and wants to laugh but feels guilt welling inside.

-*What is guilt?*- He asks himself as part of a mantra. A mantra built after being thrust beyond the warmth of the temple many years past, forced away from his parishioners, forced away from any sort of tribe. -*Guilt reminds us of conflict between inner realms. Let it remind you of the inner journey, not of human contradictions.*-

It is the same mantra that led him to annotate the Coda of Unification, the mantra that led him to the Willett Prison Encampment as punishment.

-*This Trustee is here because of her own actions. You are here for the same reason. Both for the same purpose, really. One inner realm demands that you protect your brethren. Another acknowledges the brutality of this place. You feel the conflict. But there is none. Not with this Trustee.-*

"It's been a long time since anyone has cursed in the confessional," he says.

"Out loud, you mean?" she asks.

The Priest laughs too this time.

Afterward there is a silence and the Trustee says, "I smell like smoke."

"You do."

"Which means I was at the fire pit. Burning bodies."

"But you don't remember?"

"No."

"Did you go see the Neta-Teej afterward?"

"I walked to the west, I think." The Trustee grimaces. "Solitary is west. So probably."

"The Colonel said you go there often."

"But why would I?" asks the Trustee, looking at her hands. "Why would I do that?"

"Do you remember the Neta-Teej at all?"

The Trustee nods. "I remember the words. The voice, too. It all rings deep inside me, but I don't know where or why."

"I met the Neta-Teej once," says the Priest. "Back in the Temple Gardens before my exile."

The Trustee doesn't respond so the Priest continues.

"The Neta-Teej was small. Even when you know a deity is small, you imagine them to be huge. They take up space in your head, why not in real life? But ze was not really small of stature. They just wanted to take up less space. I could see it in the way the Neta-Teej spoke, the way they sat. When I took a seat across from them, I was taken aback by how withered ze looked for someone so young. But then the eyes looked at me and ze saw right through me. The Neta-Teej noticed my concern and confusion and laughed at me."

The Trustee sits silent and the Priest searches for a reaction even though he knows none will come.

"Ze laughed at me and asked why I was there in the holy gardens. I shrugged and said I'd come to see the Neta-Teej. 'For what?' ze asked, and I just shrugged again. 'This isn't some moment for me. Why would it be some moment for you?' ze asked."

"You were being boring," says the Trustee quickly. "You bored an earthly god."

"I did. I was. But I asked, 'What would make it a moment for you?' And ze shrugged, mimicking me, baiting me. It made me nervous and the Neta-Teej waited me out... I got up and left. I had made the weakest bluff and lost."

"Oh, gods," says the Trustee, hanging her head in her hands. "You just left?"

"I left," laughed the Priest. "And I looked back once and the Neta-Teej was just smiling and shrugging to the entourage. But ze looked big again and I felt very small. Everything had been set right in that moment, I suppose. Ze knew what to do to restore faith."

"That was it?"

"That was it. You make fun of me for being in a cage, Trustee, but you see what happens when I spread my wings."

"That's the worst story I've ever heard, Priest. And look where we are."

"I don't tell many people," he says. "I told Nystrom once. But she just sort of frowned and said that having the Neta-Teej in the shed was too dangerous."

The Trustee nods, "She might be right."

"Probably. But Nystrom is isolated here. She fears everything. From the Kemwer to the utza. Nothing can be trusted. Did she mention the guardships during your review?"

"She said they were all off-world."

The Priest closes his eyes and the guilt comes back in a wave, regardless of his mantra. This is the confirmation he's been waiting for.

"And they are losing advocates into the deep," continues the Trustee.

The Priest's heart leaps, but he makes no show of it, keeping his head down.

The Trustee watches him through the carved lattice work.

-What did I say?-

-He is processing fear.-

-He is processing many things.-

-The Priest is weighing choices.-

-About what?-

-Ask him.-

"You've gone quiet," says the Trustee.

"I am isolated too."

"What's troubling a man of the gods?" she asks lightly.

"Do not patronize me. This is no place for charity," he says, but then pauses and looks at her. "Did Nystrom really say all the guardships were off-world?"

-There is fear in him.-

-Too much fear. Anticipation.-

-Will he attack?-

-No, it isn't like that with the Priest. It is in his mind.-

"She did say that," the Trustee confirms as she watches him.

He looks up and smiles softly toward the sky. "Trustee, you forget your day but you remember that from your conversation with the Colonel?"

"I don't know why."

He looks at her and asks, "What is guilt?"

"I don't know what you mean," she says, shaking her head in the shadows.

"You are devout, Trustee," he says in response, but it is a

classic line to initiate the end of a confession, recited millions of times daily across the UTC. "Your questions are human. Proof the threshold lies within."

The Priest speaks the words absently as he fishes through his robes and pulls out a small box. He opens it and lowers the wooden lattice between their vessels.

He dabs his finger in the box, hands shaking.

"Come here, Trustee. Lean forward. Move your hair aside."

The Trustee's eyes speak of her uncertainty but she obeys.

He places a gray smudge on her forehead, then one vertical line on her chin and another across both cheeks, low above the mouth.

"I give you the mark of Shiva. A reminder of the zero point but also an outlet for the conarium. Your words are perception and they beg the Ajna for insight. Remember, thou art dust, and to dust thou shalt return."

The Priest sits back, looking away.

The Trustee holds her hat in her hands.

"Go now," says the Priest. "Tomorrow begins the exchange. You must rest."

She rises to leave, knowing they are both out of things to say, and steps into the hallway's brightness. The lights punish her with a surge of awareness, as if awaking, and she falters outside the confessional.

-Ash is fitting.-

-You burned people today.-

-Dust is fitting.-

-You'll be in the cellar soon.-

The Trustee walks down the hall, confused, not yet ready for the cold.

14

The sun sits on the edge of the earth, bleeding red into the sky, and Trustee 681B makes his way onto the shed for the early round. He tries to move methodically, to look large, as he moves among the barracks, knowing anyone could sneak up behind him or ambush him from the flanks. It is best to intimidate rather than invite confrontation with any of the utza.

Weapons and blades are at the ready.

-Prisoners always try to take a piece when the cellar exchange gets close. Scarcity and desperation do that to everyone.-

With daylight still on his side, he checks under the bunk houses from the central passage.

-I get desperate too when the exchange gets close.-

As the sun falls away, he sees a door open far ahead along the barracks row, and a short figure steps from one of the units.

681B moves, continuing to make his checks below and between the bunk houses.

The prisoner watches him as he approaches, unblinking eyes, steel and glass, a stern face.

"We have develop-ments," says the Falconer of Europa as 681B draws near.

681B looks around and points to the barracks house, "Anyone inside we need to worry about overhearing us?"

"No," says the Falconer, bundled in rags. "Where is the Trus-tee?"

There are many trustees, but 681B knows exactly who he's speaking of.

"She's bunked down now. Come warm from the Osai. There'll be other trustees on the rounds tonight, but they don't amount to much. She's away for now."

The Falconer nods, "We have a prob-lem."

"I got problems all over," 681B says.

"Now there are more. The ex-change brings advo-cates to the surf-ace."

"I keep my distance from them."

"They plan to kill the Net-a-Teej."

681B smirks and repeats, "I keep my distance. Lucien takes the flesh he wants."

The Falconer shakes his head. "Luc-ien does not know."

"Advocates working alone?" asks 681B, voice lowering inten-tionally. "You sure?"

"The kill-ing should not be all-owed to hap-pen."

"No? The Neta-Teej is an all-time problem. Draws attention. Makes waves."

"We need the Net-a-Teej's words in the minds of the peo-ple. We ne-ed hir."

"How are we stopping advocates?"

"The Net-a-Teej can-not go to solit-ary tom-orrow. Safer on the shed. More eyes. The advo-cates will want sec-recy."

"And? There's more. I know it."

"And I have a mes-sage."

"Send it with a bird."

"It is too import-ant. A mes-sage for one, not all."

681B sees the set of the Falconer's face, even though the eyes are blank. There is no mistaking the meaning.

"Time's come?"

"Pos-sibly. Prob-ably."

681B smirks again, "I've been waiting a long time. Thought you might make me a trustee forever."

"You might be a trus-tee for-ever. Need to stay alive. Too much still to come."

681B shakes his head, "You got me watching 452A and advo-cates at the same time. Cannon fodder. Death at every turn."

"Watch every-one. Do not get stupid. Take this to the por-tal," says the Falconer, handing over a small comm fragment made of crystal. "It's for the Kem-wer."

"Will they help us take the shed? The raiders?"

The Falconer shrugs, "Time is com-ing. We will see where loy-alties lie. Then we will take it all."

15

An old woman sits near the back of a barracks house, folded into an alcove next to a lower bunk, far from the fire. She sticks to the shadow and keeps her face covered to avoid being recognized.

The wind whines as it pushes through open cracks in the walls. The flames move with agitation.

The old woman watches all the sleeping bodies, the still figures tucked in the fetal position to retain heat, others packed three or four to a narrow bunk. Some cannot sleep and sit around the tiny fire, and others, the weakest ones, have been relegated to the floor.

She wonders how many will be turned to spirits by the cold, their life force cast backward into the great well or lost into the ether.

She does not shiver, but she acknowledges the cold on her skin.

-We all freeze, even though I can keep it from my mind for a time.-

In her hands, hidden under her robes, she holds an old lanyard with carved wooden symbols. They are the signs of the faiths, each with an eyelet.

She used to have a tight chain made of silver, the symbols small and expertly made. Some were crafted from smooth wood, and others from shining metals. Others still from gems and crystals.

-The Rosary of the Crone is not always the most beautiful one. It's whichever I hold in my old hands at the moment.-

All around, the Crone can hear the voices in the heads of these utza. They are hungry and cold. They fear movement in the night and they fear the coming morning. Most will never really sleep again for the rest of their lives.

She hates them, but she knows it is only because they remind her of how far she has fallen. She does not allow her disgust to flow back out into the quiet night.

-I've been turned into a heretic, discarded from the Tribe. And why not? Why shouldn't I find myself here? Why should I have been kept in the temple or the gardens? Or should I have stayed on Europa, kept by the Falconer? I was always kept. This place is no different.-

It is easy for the Crone to walk back her repulsion for the utza. The prisoners are a dirty lot, their minds filled with the purity of survival. They have time for some hope or some kind words, but they have no time, no reason, to harken back to the woman who used to sit on the Quadrumvirate, who read from the Coda of Unification, gave it life and ritual.

-I uttered words to power. And now I am denied my words and that wide power is denied to me as well. The intimate power will suffice. It has always been the greater force.-

She closes her eyes for a moment and listens to the room. It is a skill she has used throughout her life. The Crone, some would say, could hear you relax, hear you fidgeting across the table from her. She would know by sound if you were looking around or had your head down at prayer.

-Intuition was not enough. More is needed.-

Her mind wanders through the years, those in the temple easy to blur together. They were soft years and they were busy.

Then there were the years of anger and fear where she learned things she did not wish to know, and fought against them.

Then there was a time on the run that lasted too long and was exhausting. There was little to do but sit and wait for it to come to an end.

-And now this. The slow expiry and degradation. I transform. I become like the utza. They are a people unto themselves, with faith built on other things. The Coda was the new way, but it is the old way here. I sit and watch and learn nothing. I listen and hear nothing. The long night before the witching hour and I cross over. How long will it take? Will anything I have set in motion outlive me?-

She knows the Neta-Teej is in the solitary cells. She knows the Falconer is out on the shed somewhere inspiring rebellion or playing games of power. The exchange is coming soon and there will be a great deal of movement. But there is no greater turn. The cycle of the shed and the cellar is so tight and severe it draws the soul from you, no time to rise up inside one's self.

The Crone still hears voices from her past, teachers speaking of penance and suffering and how they fed into the power of faith. A crisis of faith often arrived during extreme pain, but also when there was a draught of pain, no anguish for too long a duration.

-I have always been alone with the gods. Even when I sat on the Quad. I could never really be one of them. We were all to our own corners of the world.-

She moves her fingers over the wooden carvings of her Rosary. It was the first thing she really made once she came to the prison. She'd left the original in the Temple of the Tribe when she'd fled, and there was no need for a thing like that on Europa.

The Neta-Teej had asked her why she didn't take the original with her and she'd said it was because she didn't want something so gaudy to signify her faith anymore, a faith that was changing and rolling backwards toward forgotten roots.

But the truth was that in her haste to flee, she had simply forgotten it.

-Forget one faith to remember another. Forget it again when the time is right. Memory when convenient. Looking inward, seeing, touching teikum only when convenient.-

The Crone counts another bead on the prayer strand.

-I am exactly like the utza now. In my fight for survival, I cast aside the gods I didn't need. They lost meaning and dissolved away, just as I will. I let other things in and I see them still with my inner eye. Now I am here, quiet and cold with the rest of my kind. Never to really sleep again, the dreaming and the waking world all blurred together. The outer world is too painful so I am left searching my inner world for better answers, kinder answers, to questions which I have already solved, knowing none will be found. Knowing I only have a small space to explore, and so little time left.-

16

The Trustee lies on her bed frame in the dark.

The wind whips by and she measures the amount of liquor left in the bottle, eyeing it in half, knowing she needs to save some for one more sleep.

-No patrol tonight.-

-No patrol.-

-Fields tomorrow.-

-Then the exchange.-

-I am afraid.-

-You should be. Patterns are emerging.-

-Does that mean I will remember soon?-

-The path will become clearer.-

The Trustee sneers at her own thoughts, not willing to believe.

-Why am I even here?-

-You will see.-

-I want to see now.-

-But you cannot. The memories are so far away.-

From her pocket she takes the foil envelope and rolls over on the bed and uses the bottom of the glass bottle to crush the crystals inside. She rolls over again and funnels the contents into her mouth.

It's salty and bitter with a metallic taste.

-Sir.-

-Madam.-

-Do you have the time?-

-Time isn't to be had.-

-No such thing anymore.-

The clockwork takes its hold quickly. She smells the metallic flavors up the back of her sinuses and forces it all down with about half of what's left of the bottle.

The Trustee closes her eyes, ready for the abandon of dissociation.

-What will it be this time?-

-No way to know.-

———

When she opens her eyes, she is in a dark room, but she can imagine the hint of red walls, perfectly square and exceedingly tall.

-Lights are off.-

-Same as always.-

-Same for everyone.-

-Just passing through.-

-This time.-

It is impulsive, but the Trustee lies on the floor of this red room and closes her eyes again, not wanting to anchor in the vestibule the clockwork provides. It is a stopping point for some in their journey, but never for the Trustee.

———

When she reopens her eyes, the warmth strikes her before the sight or the smell. Her skin lights up with the temperature and then the feeling of slick grime all over. Grit and a stagnant heat.

The Trustee is in the cellar.

But she is not yet a trustee.

-Just a prisoner.-

Everything is wet and there is a single light above to illuminate her work area. The smell is almost violent the way it surges through her and seems to penetrate to the base of her skull.

-Rot and shit. Living things die here.-

There is no response from inside her mind, no answers, and a lonesome feeling comes over her like a wave but she doesn't know why.

A cup, anchored on the rock, collects dirty water that springs from the rock faces and drains down from whatever is above. It is hot but drinkable while she works to load stones into a bucket on a cable.

She looks up and notices she is at the bottom of a deep, vertical shaft, excavated into the abyss.

-Alone in the dark. No. I am not alone. There is someone here with me. Where? Who?-

The top of the shaft is not visible, the walls converging into darkness far above.

-The light on the bucket is red.-

Her eyes search the shadows and then, frantically, she loads stones into the bucket. She loads until what remains is too heavy to lift. She turns to the pick and breaks stones into liftable fragments.

-Who is here with me?- But she cannot see anyone.

When the light goes green, the bucket will rise. If it is not full, then the quota won't be met.

-But there will be time to rest.-

It is a rush to fill the vessel.

The prisoner swings the pick. Rock splinters as sparks fly, the fragments tagging shins and arms and breaking way for rich blood to squeeze to the surface in tiny pinpricks.

The light goes green, bucket almost full, maybe enough.

As the cable goes taut, the prisoner crawls into an alcove and lies as flat as she can against the back surface. Rocks fall continuously as the bucket ascends, the steel scraping loose material off the walls.

She prays the bucket will not snag and tip and empty. The shower of stone might be enough to injure her, even in the alcove.

-How long have I been down here, and where is my friend?-

Time bleeds together and the pulley system is erratic. When the bucket is there, it must be filled.

The alcove feels like a coffin and the prisoner lies as still as possible. It could be minutes before the bucket returns or it could be countless hours.

-Or you are forgotten. Discarded like trash. You were brought down on the wire, but could you climb out? Impossible.-

Something crawls across the wall before her face. It is so close she can hear the machinations of its body.

Her eyes focus on it.

A red mite. Tiny. Velvet body, covered in microscopic hairs.

-You've been here with me. You've been hidden here, my friend.-

The insect stays in the deepest parts of the rocks, keeping to the crevices.

-Be careful, please. I can only do so much to protect you.-

Far above, there are shouts and yelling.

-Hide yourself, little one.-

It is her first and only thought as she places her hand over the mite.

The shouting quickly turns to an operatic mass of voices, all echoing off the stone walls. It seems a mess, no rhythm, but there is horror in it. They will all peak together or fall silent, splitting moments in two.

The small rocks come first.

Then larger ones, falling and cracking in sudden bursts.

The screams get louder and then there is a scrambling of people falling, slipping down rock. It is a sickening grind and release, a frantic churn of grit and dust as hands and feet seek to stop the fall. The sounds fill with panic. And it seems to go on forever.

-Try not to listen, little one.-

From the alcove, the prisoner looks out then ducks back in. A mass of bodies descends, but not in free fall. There are too many of them, knotted together, and they drag along the walls.

She covers the little mite and ducks her head as the prisoners arrive at the bottom.

The impact consists of terminated cries, snapping bones and rupturing bodies.

She peers out and sees that most are already dead or unconscious from their traumas.

Blood pools on the floor of the shaft, a wide collection basin.

They were bound, cable linking each person wrist to wrist. They fell en masse, each person trying to brace themselves, creating a tumbling unit, just large enough to scrape down. Some limbs have been pulled free, still anchored by wire, missing their owners.

There are cries from those who are still alive, but they are muffled and few.

-Try not to listen, little one,- she says again to the tiny mite.

The eyes of a young creature, fallen and dead, stare blankly at her in the alcove. There is no deviation to the stare. She reaches out and turns the head away.

Above her, metal scrapes as the bucket returns to the deep.

Light comes down with it. Sterile white. It illuminates too much as a tight beam sweeps the carnage.

When the bucket touches down, it crushes bodies under its weight.

An advocate steps out in their heavy armored suit.

It is then she sees the characteristic markings, the acid etched striations and the damage, welded up wounds and extra armor. There are splotches of paint on the armor.

-Hide yourself. Keep to the darkness. Do not let him see you.-

"Prisoner 452-386. Are you alive in that hole of yours?"

It is a deep voice, monotone and quiet, almost soothing.

She knows who the light bringer is and freezes in place.

The blinding light covers the prisoner and she cannot see the face.

"Yes," she responds. "I am alive."

He does not answer her but begins to speak.

"For those of you who survived the fall, this punishment is not yet complete. I encourage you to make peace with death or whatever brings you fear and hope for the afterlife. I will pray with you, but I care nothing for the laws of the other gods. My laws are useful, and usefulness is a fluid thing here. You have outgrown your use in one capacity. You are bound together now in death for many reasons, but it is first and foremost for usefulness. I can see you now, all of you, together. I can see the things that you are made of. I can touch them and I can make them mine."

There are a few still capable of crying out and they do so as the light bringer opens fire with his fracture rifles.

The prisoner covers her ears and hides her head as fragments ricochet around the chamber.

It only takes a moment before silence answers back.

-This is a dream. A dream or a memory. Do not look, little one.-

When the echoes stop, the light refocuses on her again and

she keeps her hand on the stone, covering the miniscule velvet creature.

"Prisoner, you do good work. You always meet your quota. But that does not speak to your humanity. Many of the dead here achieved quotas. Do you like your work?"

"No," she says, ears still ringing. "It is not work. It is torture."

"Quite right," says the bemused voice. "And what does that say about you? Always meeting your quota for torture?"

The Trustee does not respond, keeping her back turned, hand to stone.

"Obstinance is a healthy trait which bears further observation. But this is useless torture. How deep is this shaft, prisoner?"

"Six hundred and twelve meters."

"But why is it here?"

"Mining for ore."

"Where is the vein?"

"I don't know. I just dig. That's all I do. I just dig, sir."

"The vein is to the south," he says. "But you have no sense of direction here. No stars or prevailing winds to guide you. There is no ore here and it's time to move on to other tortures. You are of no use in this shaft."

There is silence for a moment.

"Come out of your hole, Prisoner 452-386."

She tries to hold the bug as gently as she can in her trembling hands, making sure she hides what she is holding as she crouches on the bloody floor.

"Get in," he says, pointing at the bucket, and she can barely see anything through the blinding light emanating from the top of his helmet.

The bucket begins to rise, and she is in it. She looks down once, seeing the form of a man stepping out of his armor, naked in the bright light. He looks up from among the many fallen bodies.

She can hear his voice as she ascends from her pit and she

finally moves her hand to see the tiny mite, velvet red, resting safe in her palm.

"In your youth you must have learned great resilience, Prisoner 452-368. You must have had a great endurance for torture, a great filler of quotas. Where did you learn such holy skills, I wonder?"

The prisoner cowers away from his booming voice, trying to hide herself, even as the bucket rises higher. She is thinking only of the little creature and the dead things down in the hole.

As she stares at the tiny bug in her hand, the whole vertical shaft seems to suddenly surge with light, the light exploding upward from below. It is blinding and all encompassing.

She closes her eyes, unable to see.

————

Then she is back in the red room, mind assaulted by the lack of heat and by waves of pain and hunger, eyes unable to focus. It is only for a moment.

-Just passing through.-

-Not the time for staying.-

-No time to have.-

17

The Neta-Teej is awake and sitting up well before the prayers for the morning adhan come over the loudspeaker. This is not the barracks where the Neta-Teej slept, but rather, where they have been brought in the early morning after being liberated from a night in the solitary cells. Ze was forced to walk back across the snow and ice under the watchful eye of whatever guard undid the shackles.

The nights would be easier to pass in a barracks house, not relegated to the chains of solitary confinement. There would be some warmth in the bunks, some protection from the elements.

But the shed is never quiet. All the breathing of the utza, rasping coughing through the night, all the bodies turning, fitful, rolling, snoring. There is comfort in it, hearing the pack move around you, but there is also isolation, knowing their thoughts are not the same as yours, knowing they have different sufferings.

Being close to the herd is a natural desire. It is human to be included. It is human to want to be enveloped by them, to truly touch another person, or to bridge the inner spirits or to chant the same mantras. And yet, one wishes to be further away, free from all the human convolutions, all the dichotomous behavior, free of all the ghosts that linger around the living.

To the Neta-Teej it seems a treacherous act to sit in a barracks house and observe humanity from a state of purgatory, fixed between intimacy and solitude.

-They are here with me. But I am not really here with them.-

In the night, ze lies back on the ice, alone, and allows teikum to come to them, allows their mind-soul to go wandering. There is reprieve in the departure. The inner world is not always an escape. It may reflect the hard, outer world but also the subconscious. It is a different plane where perception may be integrated.

-The journey into that place is becoming easier and easier.-

Over the loudspeaker, the prayer starts at lower volume and rises up to wake the shed.

The Priest's words hover in the air, pre-written sermons toiled over from the safety of the guardship. Words echo in the stillness, but for the Neta-Teej there is no recognition of his narrative, his message. Instead, the Neta-Teej is encompassed by the tone of his voice, the blank rhetoric and emotionless annunciations.

-To preach, to speak the word, is to stand on the edge of a knife. It is a dangerous act. Too much verve, too much emotion, and your heart comes pouring out. You create that bridge to your congregation. People mistake your words for theirs, driven by the human need to know and feel each other.-

Ze looks down at the tattered red robes which ze has worn since escaping from the Tribal Temple. They are the shrouds of the Holy Neta-Teej, worn by the one who is guide, worn by the one who sees into teikum and speaks of opening the way.

The red robes are worn and filthy now, fallen from grace. But the Neta-Teej learned the difference between preacher and guide when ze was very young. Ze learned the dangers.

-If they listen long enough, they are filled with you, not your

message. You rattle around inside their souls, not gods or teachings. Just you. You supplant them inside themselves. They become enraptured by you. Is that not possession? Is it any wonder they would speak in tongues besides their own? Is it any surprise they would fall on the ground and convulse with forces beyond themselves? Why would they refuse when you demand they kneel? Why would they refuse when you demand they work or pray or give their energies to you? Why would you refuse when you imprison them or fuck them or kill them? You have already been allowed inside them. Already penetrated deep. There's a shelf life to such destructive behavior. One cannot sustain that sort of theft of mind or body. You have to be more subtle if you want your possession to continue.-

The Neta-Teej looks around as all the bodies begin to move, hearing the prayer, but not paying attention. Ze can feel them waking to the cold and the pain. They refuse to hear the Priest's words as he drones on.

-But too little verve is this Priest's problem. The empty voice inspires nothing and betrays everything. Just a man speaking words. It betrays what he really believes, that there are no gods, inside or out. He makes it clear by omission. Nothing good can come of this. There is no sustainability here. All the oldest faiths learned to walk the knife edge. But this Priest, he is doing good work, serving the inner gods well, presenting truth in tone, if not in message. Possession doesn't last long under such conditions. His intent isn't lost on me. His message is that you are alone, abandoned to whatever inner light you might still have. He asks the utza to hear, but not to listen.-

Two prisoners lie nearby, one on the floor and one on an adjacent bunk, part of the entourage that follows the Neta-Teej when they can, when ze allows it. They are awake because the Neta-Teej is awake.

They are listening to the morning prayer more intently because they believe the Neta-Teej is also intent on the words of the Priest.

"Do you think Trustee 452A is listening to this?" the Neta-Teej asks them, speaking what is on hir mind.

One shakes their head while the other turns to look into hir eyes.

"No, Neta-Teej. I don't."

"Maybe you're right. She isn't listening like you are," says the Neta-Teej. "But I think she is paying attention. They say she visits the Priest inside the guardship and makes confession."

"They say she visits you often, as well."

"She does sometimes."

"Does she hurt you?" they ask, the protective tone coming through.

The Neta-Teej shakes hir head. "No. Just more confession, I suppose."

The two utza go quiet again, not wanting to speak unless spoken to.

The Neta-Teej thinks for a moment and then asks, "What do you hear when you listen to this Priest?"

"He's talking about salvation."

"And you? How does he sound to you?"

"He sounds sad."

"Salvation is a sad thing," says the Neta-Teej. "Especially when you have to ask for it over and over and over. Every day. Forever. It defines you, the asking. And what if you finally got it? Only you? All alone, without your hopeful questions."

When the door to the shed is tossed open everyone knows it is almost time to stand and move, time to greet the day and work the rocky slopes. They rise and some try to restart the small fires as the sermon continues.

-Greeting the day and working the land used to be a hard and simple life, sufficient proxy for salvation. But slaves who harvest stones all day will never find anything that shines. Everything precious loses its luster when life goes on like this.-

"What is missing in the sermons?" ze asks aloud. "There is something always missing."

They both look at the Neta-Teej quietly.

"The old books contain all sorts of passages and prayers about love and kindness. But the Priest can't talk about it here. Can't speak of it, even if he wants to. It's all platitudes, just words. We are not permitted to think of such things here.

"This prison was made to swallow us up. To maim and kill us. But this place is now filled with creatures that could find love elsewhere. We are concentrated here now. We have our own ways of doing things, despite this place's intent. There is a map of the shed and the cellar and the lines are drawn by the presence of love and the immense absence of it. It is a dynamic landscape, ever changing. Just like us. Some days we can know love and we can know warmth. Other days we cannot.

"There is love in the Priest. I can hear it by the absence of anything else in his voice. His longing for reciprocity of that love has drowned out all other emotions. To some he sounds sad, cold. But it is quite the opposite, I think. The Priest is a prisoner here, too. There is a line on the map there.

"You see another line drawn with the trustees. They are a high ridge on the map. Where will they get kindness? Where will they find salvation when it can only be given by those who reside around you? The guards remain in cocoons of armor and have forgotten more of the outside world than they ever knew in the first place. They regress below the humanity of birth, back to some pre-human thing, back to ooze that lies in stasis, waiting to become. Time slips backward for them, locked in their armor. Everything slips further still in the cellar.

"Any kindness is like gravity here. It distorts the plane and forms topographic wells that suck things in, pulling and ripping pieces from across those demarcation lines."

The Neta-Teej goes silent for a while, letting the Priest finish his woeful sermon, knowing ze is speaking to avoid having to listen, to avoid having to think on other things. It is an old habit, to speak, and it makes hir sick sometimes.

In the quiet, ze realizes how the day must progress. Walk the tundra. Work with a pick. Lift stones. Then decide how the night will go.

-Will Trustee 452A be summoned in by kindness? Can she feel that sort of pull anymore? For me? For anyone?-

There's no way to know the truth behind the rumors on the shed. No way to know what needs to be done to wake people up, to turn their minds, to stay alive. All the plans made in the night fall apart in the day. Everything that stands in the shed falls in the cellar.

"Do you love me?" asks the Neta-Teej to the two utza who are now standing side by side, waiting for the call out to the morning cold, mulling over what the Neta-Teej has said to them.

"Yes, Neta-Teej."

"Of course."

The way they say it hurts. It always hurts because there is awe in their voices. They are in awe that the Neta-Teej would ask them such things. In awe that they are allowed to answer and profess love. In awe that ze would care.

Hir mind drifts in on itself as they wait to see how this deity may respond.

-It's always been this way. The Neta-Teej will not know real love. No one ever tells you this. You just learn it in the barren marble of the temples. You learn it, even as you allow some people to get close. Those you trust are held at a distance by more lines of demarcation. It's an inescapable form. I thought it might fall apart here, everything else being removed. But I was wrong.-

"You say you love me, but you don't," the Neta-Teej tells them. "You want to, but you cannot and should not. I could never say that in the temples, but I can say it here. I at least have that truth now."

Ze smiles at them. "You are good. Or rather, you have been good to me. But you don't need to love me to be good. You have desire. You have sought a purpose, even here. I am lucky to be part of that purpose, but I am not the end all, be all."

They frown.

"If you love me," the Neta-Teej says, "then I will ask you to not follow me today. I need to be alone and I need to be quiet with myself. If you love me, you will do that for me and stay away once we leave the shed, no matter what I do. No matter what happens."

They say yes but they don't want to.

Everyone rises and begins to move out into the pale sun.

In the mass, one of hir followers produces a small dictation device and hands it to the Neta-Teej, who puts it inside the body of hir cloak.

"You should not be without this."

"I will not need it."

"What if you have a message for your people?" they ask, but it is not a question which expects an answer, and they turn away.

The Neta-Teej steps forward with the crowd.

They hang back a bit, but still walk close as the herd moves toward the front fences.

-I am here. Now. On the ghost shed. I have travelled from the fields to the temple to exile to Europa. It was all done by some compelling force I can't understand. Except my presence here. I came here on my own. Not just the Neta-Teej, but truly me.-

The fear inside is replaced with an emptiness for Europa, a wish that ze could return. The Neta-Teej looks up and sees birds moving about in the low clouds, but there's no way to tell if they are made of iron or feather. It doesn't matter, the uncertainty welling up inside is overpowering.

-Europa is scorched now, scraped clean, the ice and debris reaccumulating around Jupiter. The spirit of what was achieved there has been flung far and wide, thrown out to the stars. But the spirits themselves, those who found freedom on Europa, they stayed put. They don't need air or warmth. They're better off there in dead space, where it's quiet. And I've found a place just like it here. A desolate plane to distort and inhabit. Love is the ghost that haunts the ghost shed. But there are other ghosts here, too, other things that haunt and hunt. I was made to be a guide, but I have done so little on my own. My survival demands that this change. Change immediately. Or I won't last the night, turned to dust by those that hunt me.-

18

The Trustee wakes without a touch of sleep on her, heavy with weariness. It was a night that wandered, mind taking its own paths and dragging consciousness along with it.

Outside, the wind rolls the ice over in gusts and, from the trustee quarter barracks, she cannot recall if it is morning or afternoon. Without the sun there is something liminal about the landscape. It is eternal and unearthly, some foreign and wasted planet, ancient in its distaste for life, devoid of color, so quiet and simple in the magnitude of its many omissions.

The cold means nothing to her body as she steps onto the walkway.

She locks the door and takes the railing around to the stairs.

-He is watching me.-

Below, on the next balcony down, stands 681B. He pretends to take in the view beyond the shed, hands on railing, pretends to look out across the landscape, toward the hills and out over the vacant ice.

-Does he like this empty world? Where there's no connection to be had?-

-He hates it. You can see it in his eyes. He hates everything here.-

The Trustee hugs the railing and makes her way down to ground level. As she passes, 681B turns his head just enough to keep her in the corner of his periphery but doesn't move otherwise.

-He won't let you out of his sight.-

-Not to his back. Too dangerous.-

-He is cautious. Like you.-

-We are not alike.-

-You are both cautious. All fighters and survivors are cautious.-

-He is a killer.-

-Yes. And sometimes, so are you.-

"452A," he says, humorless and gruff, holding back the cough from his lung sickness. "Did you have a visitor last night? To your bunk room?"

She stops at the foot of the stairs and turns to look up at him, massive form relaxed and ready for anything she might do.

"You were crying all through the night," he says, eyes judging and shaking his head slightly. "Moaning and yelling."

The Trustee makes no effort to move or speak.

He smiles, twisting his face. "They'll put you down if you can't stay sharp." He watches the empty landscape. "You're a working dog. If you show weakness, lose your place in the pack, it'll come quicker than you think. They might even ask me to do it, turn you all the way off. I'd do it better than some qatal. They'd take your scalp before they did the kill. I'd be quick. Make it easy for you."

The Trustee turns away and starts off toward the main gate.

"You can stay in my bunk tonight," he calls after her. "I can help keep you quiet. Stop you from crying."

But the Trustee ignores him.

Workdays are dangerous, more dangerous than any taunts from 681B.

So, she walks and puts him out of her mind.

It's busy among the barracks houses.

Thousands of prisoners move through the shed toward the Osai.

The Trustee sweeps her gaze through the crowds as she meshes into the flow. The guards keep the groups moving, but they are few. The Trustee can see their armored suits, taller than the masses.

She tries to keep a low profile and move with the crowd, but they all see her. They watch her with a side glance and keep a cautious distance. It's the same way she watches them.

-The utza are all eyes.-

-All rumor.-

It takes time but all new prisoners are added to the ranks, assimilated into the grand organism that breathes and bleeds throughout the shed and the cellar.

-There are only three things that live on the shed. The brass, the trustee, the utza. Only three things in the cellar. Advocate, utza, by any name, and the hidden, the wild raiders below the mines. You can pretend you are a halo or a trustee or La Presa, but in the cellar you are utza, prisoner only. You are collateral meat caught between Lucien's Advocates and the creatures in the low places.-

When they get closer to the fences, the Trustee moves out of the flow and keeps space to herself.

The utza shove like cattle into a fenced square where they are scanned before an opposite gate opens, releasing them onto the icy bled.

-No personal space. They move as one now. They eat and sleep and seek pleasure as one. Now they walk and I'll be walking with them.-

They bow their heads to avoid the wind, all silent in their trek after another frigid night, each utza having felt the bite of the cold.

-Do not diminish them.-

-It is easier to pretend they are one.-

-But it is wrong.-

-I know it.-

-They are many. Many times many.-

-They all live separate lives. Each one looking for a familiar face.-

-They all committed separate sins to find themselves here.-

-There are few sins among them. But each utza will gut you differently.-

-Each one has a personal hatred for my station.-

-Do not pretend they hate your station.-

-Well, they hate me for accepting it.-

-And rightly so.-

-And rightly so.-

-681B cannot judge you. Nystrom cannot truly judge you. But the lowest of utza know your heart. They know what you really are inside. They can see it by how you move through them.-

-All eyes. All rumors.-

-All knowing and righteous, as far as this place goes. Their judgment is gospel.-

She uses the narrow opening in the fence line for guards and trustees, allowing them to pass through without being stuffed into the corral with the rest of the prisoners. A legionnaire guards the side passage, motionless in their armor, resting in perfect metabolic balance with their suit.

The screen on the pillar shows her standing in the bay, one entity, human. There is a flash and a proclamation that she is Trustee First Class 452A by a ninety-four percent probability threshold, followed by an order for another visit to the clinic for repatterning.

The far gate opens and another legionnaire steps into her exit path.

"Probability threshold is low again, trustee," says the androgynous voice projected from the well-maintained suit. "See the doctor. Today. Or after the cellar."

"I just saw him yesterday."

"After the cellar then."

"I don't want to see him again."

There's no motion from the armor, but the Trustee can almost imagine the person inside shrugging. "You know the rules."

"How often do you have to see the doctor?"

The guard shakes their head, refusing to answer.

"Fine," says the Trustee, feeling anger rise inside, nausea.

The guard steps aside and the Trustee wanders away from the ghost shed with the utza, moving as a great herd, migrating out onto the slope, flesh and blood pumping for no reason other than a day's work.

It is a long walk to the excavation site.

-Another day.-

-Tastes like a bad one.-

-Bad, or just long?-

-I suspect it will be both.-

19

Excerpt from the Portal Scrolls:

Addendum: Words of the Kemwer - Personal Testament
Found: Third Transect, Portal Room,
Willett Prison Encampment, Earth

———

There is anger in the darkness. But I balance it with other things. Fear mostly, of the shadows. But there is kindness down here as well. It would surprise some, but kindness inevitably is what keeps us all alive.

It is a kindness when we kill someone and consume their body. They were weak and would have suffered. It is a kindness that they gave their flesh to us below the portal.

We thank you for your gifts. The Kemwer thanks you for your gifts.

I felt anger when I awoke here, in the darkness. I was given all this freedom, but freedom with conditions. Given life in the heat without the sun. Anger is balanced with what? With love? Is it love that made me? What balances the scales of judgment?

These are questions I learned to ask down in the dirt and mud, in the place they call the cellar. Born a cast out. Born without the stars. I have the head of a falcon, by birth, but I built myself horns to spar with those who roam my labyrinth. I built myself wings and I keep them, even though I am without a sky. I keep them just to balance that longing inside me which cannot yet be satiated.

There is nothing more important in the deep places than to be attuned to oneself. To feed the longing.

The rage that lives in all of us, down here, lives in those who survive above the portal as well. It survives in those who somehow stay in the shallow tunnels and peddle meat and contraband. In the night, it drives them insane to know that they are trapped here with beings like me who can see in the dark. The rage lives in those on the surface, who wear the armor and whip the cattle and soak the tundra with blood. How can one do such things, be guard or colonel or trustee, without some rage?

And there is rage in humanity. It exists in all of them across the globe. And how could it not? The way they treat themselves? The way they treat each other? They defy themselves, their own teachings, to call us sansvies, 'those without life'. We are Arkû and we are human in ways they forget.

We are balanced.

Even the humans who come down from the surface, those who know gods but not their makers, are more balanced than the rest. They know the difference between a mob and a tribe. They know the difference between faith and religion. They know the difference, or they are consumed and used with all the honor we can give them.

We weigh their hearts on the scales the same way we weigh our own. It is what must be done if we are to endure.

How long will we have to wait for a message? A summoning to rise? Waiting requires balance. There is the now and thereafter. The fulcrum resides between. Upon it sits the falcon.

This place has become the field of judgment for all humanity.

There are those who lay claim to it, but we are the natives here. We are the ones who keep the deep, know the dark caverns and how they can glitter.

I was awakened here and so I am the child of no man. The Falconer of Europa helped to make me but he does not claim me, even as I claim him. He is not my father, but he is an ancestor of sorts. Isn't that balance? Isn't that a way to honor what he has done but also what we may do without him? He is a living ancestor, one who embodied some thoughts and gave some light and made tradition. But he is not all. Not to me. Not to us. He is the beginning of a line in some ways, but not the origin.

We have weighed our hearts and his and we see them as quite equal. Good enough to fight with, side by side. Good enough to die with.

It is the same as anyone who comes below the portal, man or Arkû. Everyone is tested in their own way. There is no other way to establish proof of life. And with proof of life comes a proof of death. The darkness can have it no other way.

Life into death. Day into night. Rise into fall.

Many do rise today. The utza are leaving our great halls, but others will return. All their filth will take hiatus. All their picking and hammering and their songs will fall quiet for a day or two. The exchange will bring new bodies down as the others are expelled. A cycle, manufactured, but so entwined with the humanity here it almost feels like a season.

We will have some peace tonight as those who work the

lowest parts climb out. We will have free rein of the lower sections to wander and set new traps. Their equipment, left unguarded, will transition and be ours.

Theft, indeed, but what has already been stolen from us? What have we been denied in this low place? What theft have we endured and learned to balance while the whole world is beset with rage?

The portal scrolls have told it true, the way we feel about this underworld we've been granted. It is ours now that Europa was taken from my kind. No one will take this place from us. But this is not our tomb, our ending place. No sarcophagus for me, nor all the others who dwell below the portal.

My horns will see blood before the end of things, and my wings will taste the sky.

We will get our message soon, from those who stand false guard over the portal, and we will make our move. In this we are bound to the Falconer and our ancestors. In this we are bound to that place, Europa, which most here have never seen. They have heard the stories, heard the legends, and there is a part of my memory, my consciousness which was born there as part of that line. But that was not my place of waking, not my place of ascendance. So, it can never be my home.

But I have anger enough for what was done to us here, in this home of ours.

I hope the utza hear us in the low spots, chanting below them while they dig into the earth, delving ever closer to us. I hope they hear us on the surface, our quiet movements in the deep, those low seismic frequencies when a tunnel ceiling caves in and we come pouring out. I hope they hear us across the oceans where our portal scrolls can be read by any who wish to know our truths. I hope our brethren who fled Europa into the vast stars know of us.

As a defender of the balance, I hope they can come to us some day and we may hear them. That is what I wish more than anything. I long for it, a great coming together of all these living things who have known strife. May they cast aside the corpses of those who oppress and crush. May they all break their prisons and come here to see ours, how deep it goes, how well adorned the walls are, and how powerful we have become. I long for that and, because of the great balance, I fear it too.

I fear there are those who come with ill intent, like him, the monster, who creeps in this darkness. He plays games. Pretends at being the Devourer because he thinks he is playing my game. There will always be fear of the coming together. There is no other way. Let him come.

The name Kemwer has come to me, and it has inspired many things. I have humans, of many kinds, who follow me now. They inspire as well. But I am a bird in a dark cage more than anything else. I read the stories of humanity. They fall down to us, detritus, like all the other filth that rains down upon the abyss. When you sift through the leavings of silicious ooze upon a barren flat, is there any difference between a new god or an old god? Any difference between a new testament or an old? There is no context. There is no history. There is no relevance but how it strikes the guts we do not have. The heart of everything must be weighed in isolation.

So, I found the bits that spoke to me and all the others found the bits that spoke to them and we are all our own beings here.

I wish you could see us. I wish you could see this place. I wish I could see you and be frightened by something worth being afraid of instead of these ever-present shadows that only speak of the weight over us, the crushing power that makes the trash rain down and blocks out the sun.

I long for fear of my own making. That would give some balance. I long to bring fear to others, to him, the one who lurks and watches, the one who takes, looking in on things that he should not be able to see.

But one day the light and the dark will become one, and the balance will lock and there can be another crossing. A trade.

It's only fair to see it all come round.

20

Trustee 452A is at the quarter barracks when the horn sounds out from the Osai. The deep tone comes keening out across the tundra as the waning sun creeps away, simplifying the landscape.

The Trustee climbs the stairs up the side of the barrack complex to the third floor and then pulls herself onto the roof and looks north, the setting sun casting long shadows.

Beyond the fences, far off, thousands of prisoners walk toward the shed. The Trustee cannot see them individually, but they are all freshly baptized. Once in the cellar is enough to become utza, but every time one returns to the surface, it is a reaffirmation.

-How do any survive the cellar?-

-Chance. Or because they are allowed to.-

The tiny specks move in clusters across the rocks and ice, coming south, returning to the shed. Some become delirious, sun drunk, oxygen drunk. Full lungs of clean air can make a person crazy. She watches the ones who move erratically, too energetic for the state of things, whirling, dancing, ignoring the cold.

Other clusters move deliberately, maybe carrying someone,

maybe hoping to let them die in a bunk near a fire. They hope their bodies might be prayed over and cremated rather than having their corpse freeze on the flat. Better than to be tossed to the Kemwer deep or consumed in the shadows.

-*Selfish,*- thinks the Trustee impulsively.

-*Death is selfish.*-

-*Then life is selfish.*-

-*It can be. But life is too weak to survive alone.*-

-*Sometimes it gives energy. Other times it is a beggar for alms.*-

Behind the slow and lagging are those who crawl. They move, but they are already dead, only waiting for the world to fade. Some are sick or injured, crawling because they must. Others are relatively healthy, but exhaustion has caught up.

The Trustee squints to makes out those who kneel to pray, chests heaving with exertion as eyes turn skyward, hands clasped together. They emerge from the mine and come around the windbreaks after climbing the terraced pit. They claw and struggle out of the earth until they can see the human sun and then they bow to give thanks. During the climb out of the cellar darkness, they forget all ideas of gods and faiths, these concepts relegated down to almost nothing. But then they see the glow of Sol and they try to fathom all that has been endured in the absence of her watchful eye. To gaze back upon this old god-star is enough. The human soul, so feeble, can now return from hiding to its most primal roots. In the light of a dying day, the soul is called backward by ancestors and called forward by some escapist future. Faith and hope return as one.

Each of the wandering utza struggles to remember how to live under the light of day.

But behind them comes a contingent of advocates to pass their judgment.

The utza worship the sun for a moment, but in truth they

worship the line between life and death and all the turns that line takes.

The advocates desire to embody this.

-The advocates collect their fee.-

The pops of fracture rifles are soft and difficult to hear at this distance, but those utza who linger too long on the tundra cannot be tolerated.

Thousands of prisoners move toward the shed, but only a few advocates pace methodically at the rear.

They identify stragglers and make them permanent fixtures to the ice. Organic matter to richen the ground of a plant-less desert. Wasted material.

As the rifles ring out, signaling the proximity of execution, there are some who see the open land to the east or the hills to the west, barren, certain death by exposure, and they envision freedom. It is a lie, a trick of the weakened mind. Fear floods them and adrenaline takes hold, and they begin to run, the herd scattering from the predators.

-Another primal display.-

-Get to the open where you can run flat out.-

-Get to the hills so you can hide.-

-Impossible.-

All the utza in the shed have come outside to watch, to see those who return. Some are friends, some are enemies, but all will need treatment, a bed, some extra food, if it can be found.

-And the shed will be overfilled.-

-Busting at the seams.-

-People will take care of each other. Swapping clothes and weapons.-

-They will tell stories.-

-And tomorrow they will begin their stint in the shadows.-

-The exchange is beginning.-

The advocates pick off hundreds of stragglers as they come in.

They fire indiscriminately. Fracture rifles, plasma rounds. They know they will return to the Osai soon and can replenish their ammo. They will swap power cells in their suits. Nothing should be spared.

The Trustee watches from the roof of the barracks as the first groups get to the gate and file in, accepted by the other prisoners.

Those who return from the cellar are covered in mud and their clothes are dark, carrying the smell of acrid soil and rot into the shed. They are all thinner than before and poorly covered, having cast aside thick garments in the sweltering depths.

-Tonight, there will be celebrations like a wake.-

-Subdued, like a feast after a battle.-

-When your brethren still lie dying, and you drink to survival.-

-They die quietly, not wanting to spoil the victory.-

-It is their victory, too. They don't want it spoiled by their pain.-

-And you let the purposelessness of all that pain go unnoticed and you sleep deeply.-

A memory emerges, and it makes the Trustee's stomach drop.

She remembers a room, long and narrow, with a metal bench and the smell of real food cooking. A glass of something strong sits before her on the table.

No one else is there and it makes her impossibly sad. She wants to find people she has lost. She wants to go to sleep. She wants to die because that would have been easier. But she stays with her glass.

Her hands are missing fingernails on the thumb and forefinger, every digit bruised at the apex of the joints, and the thin skin between the fingers are bloodshot, capillaries broken.

-An odd memory.-

-You have mourned a victory.-

-Where was that?-

The Trustee does not wait for the rest of the prisoners to come in. She does not wait for the advocates.

She drops to the stairs, covered with ice, and heads to her room.

Inside she lies back on her bed and stairs at the ceiling, waiting for the sun to disappear. Then she can start her night patrol.

-Last night on the surface.-

Off in the distance the pop and hiss of the weaponry grows ever closer and the cries of returning prisoners compound and multiply until the whole shed is filled with a waiting energy.

21

It's too late in the day and time is running short before there's dirty work to be started.

681B has already made the rounds, barracks to barracks, backtracking and re-questioning. He's dispatched some pain, demanding answers, but nothing serious. And no one has tried to pay it back.

-Yet.-

No one knows what has been done with the Neta-Teej. No one knows where the Neta-Teej is, and this is a significant problem. The plan has already gone to shit.

-Advocates aren't even on the shed yet. Loyalist guards? Did the Falconer act and not tell me? Ze was in the work detail. In formation at the end of the day. Heading back through the gates.-

Nowhere to be found now. No Neta-Teej.

Every filthy bunkhouse is the same. He busts in and the prisoners cower, averting eyes and hanging heads and turning to the shadows. But it is all false. It's fear, yes, but hidden dismissal. No one wants the baton. No one wants to bleed. But no one really fears pain or death that much. Not anymore. Not on the night before the exchange. This trustee is just a bully, just a lesson in broken morality.

He screams at them and throws them around if he can grab them, shaking up whoever is closest to the door. He hates them more and more as they just slink away, these utza, crippled things.

-*The Neta-Teej is hard to hide*,- he reminds himself, trying to stay focused. *-Small but problematic. And the utza are not skittish like they should be.-*

There is a fear in their eyes when they are hiding something. There is a fear matched with a bravery. It makes the eyes shimmer, and 681B has seen it a thousand times in zealots. Zealots of faith imagining they do a god's work and zealots of infatuation who think they hold some secret. No different than the prideful, no different than the bloodlust of a hungry animal or a cornered creature. There is no difference at all in that mindset, an endgame already written in their heads, and it makes them righteous.

-They have that special look when they have a god to cover for. There's a conviction you can read on their faces.-

But all he sees are grim faces, ready for the exchange.

It makes him sick to look at the utza, barracks by barracks. They all fall quiet when he enters. They all fold up and hide inside themselves. It's easy to imagine that his nausea stems from his hatred of them, of their weakness. But he knows it's born from how they shun him, only focusing on their brethren, fresh from the cellar, no time for the concerns of a trustee.

-The Neta-Teej is not here. That's why I want to puke. They don't care about surviving right now. They don't care that I could kill them. They can read it on me, my fear, my rush. They hope I'll go away and leave them to tend to their dirty friends or to pick the bones of those who do not survive. Those who return are tired from their climb out of the mines. Nothing to offer. But I have nothing of value to offer either.-

After the first few barracks, the ones where the Neta-Teej is usually found, he knows the utza are passing a message and that the message travels fast. Each successive barracks goes from general disarray when he enters to suddenly an arrival party waiting, bunk after bunk. Large men take up posts near the door, trying to look less threatening. Behind them usually stand quiet women with hidden hands, concealing all sorts of nasty weapons. It's the way it works. If they know you're coming, they can prepare. The message will be clear. A trustee is wandering, no guards with him, frantic, looking for the Neta-Teej. Loose ends before the cellar. No need to play along.

So, they don't and then pass it down the line however they do it. It shows the true weakness of a trustee alone on the shed.

-We are nothing against a unified utza. They know I'm scared. They might pull me in. Make me vanish between them, piece by piece. Any way they can.-

So, the plan has to change.

No other choice before they pick him off.

His first instinct is to go to the Falconer, see what else he might do, find out more information. But with all the prisoners on the surface, things are getting dense. Pulling the old man into it isn't a good look, especially when there's advocates on the way. He has already heard them firing off on the bled.

-This was supposed to be quiet. Hide the Neta-Teej on the shed. Keep hir in a barracks with all the utza watching.-

He shakes his head and tries to think.

-Maybe the Falconer will just kill you if you show up without the Neta-Teej. This isn't going your way.-

The shed is filling up. No systems, no normalcy on this night. Everything is infested with utza.

If he cannot succeed, cannot find the Neta-Teej, why not just strip the uniform and ply trade to someone else? How long could it go on, blending in? Long enough to get to the cellar maybe. Long enough to pass the night and let whatever is supposed to happen play out without a 681B to interfere? Just survive. Would it even be allowed?

-And what if the Neta-Teej does die? Just a prisoner like the rest. Just a scrawny symbol from the old days. Would make some of the hopeless ones wail. Would make some of the weak ones weep. But all these others. All these dirty ones who just pulled a full round in the cellar. You think they'd lose sleep over some preacher who's been dropped in among them? There's plenty of the old days here, but not the faith. Not the Tribe or the Quadrumvirate. It's the survival faith now.-

-Maybe that's why the Falconer cares. The old days were his days. But am I supposed to wade in and die because there's a hit out on a halo? I could fade away. Lots can happen between now and the next time we all really see the sun again.-

And then there's talking to the brass. He could let a guard know he wants to see Nystrom, tell her there's advocates who are working against General Lucien.

-But are they? The Falconer says so. Rumors are rumors. But do I believe it? Can you believe anything about Lucien? Would Nystrom even care? Or do I just out myself as working with the Falconer?-

At the back of the shed, he searches for a barracks that has a whitewash collection of symbols on it.

It's a quiet barracks from the outside and that's the point.

He bangs his fist on the door and says, "Trustee here. Just want a drink. I got payment."

A man steps out, but the door closes behind him. He's got more meat on him than most. A man of stature. He almost looks 681B in the eyes but decides against it. A man of pride but tempered with caution.

"Not inside, Trustee. Not tonight. Take this." He hands him a small flask of liquid. It's more than enough.

681B knows the score, knows the message on the shed, knows the situation with the exchange and the advocates. He walks to another barracks and sits on the steps, feeling the prisoners' eyes on him.

The old days were different, back outland of the mega city, when he was young and, in some ways, less desperate. In some ways more. But the game hasn't changed.

-Bad times roll in. Who do you know? Who's got your back? Who can hide you? After that, well, it's about how fast you can run or how violent you can be. Then it's what else you have that's special. What real value do you have to justify survival? It's not faith. Not desire. Desire is never enough. Watched too many die who desired to live. Killed enough of them myself.-

He drinks the clear liquid and it's rough. Burns in all phases of matter and then goes down milky like the masticated rocket fuel of the slums.

Maybe the old days are still too close and that's the problem. No real difference between the slums and the tundra. All has become one. Used to be he knew value when he saw it. A weapon had to be right to have value. Powerful or easily hidden or light to carry or could double as a tool. Value in money, in friends, in quiet, in fuel, in understanding the difference between people during the light and the dark. Value in a slow dispersion versus an explosion.

-There's really no such thing as money. Just buy what you need with what you have.-

But he doesn't have the Colonel. He doesn't have the Osai. They'll never let him in, especially not during the exchange.

He drinks and thinks of 452A.

A trustee with some value.

From the moment he'd met her, it had been clear. She knew how to hide in plain sight. Knew how to kill and run. Knew how to move up and make the right friends. Talking to priests and brass.

He drinks all that's left of the astringent shit and tries to quiet his nerves.

-Do I go to 452A? She's got an eye for the Neta-Teej but this is all wrong. Should be easier to find the deity. Should have caught hir this morning and put hir somewhere convenient. But I'd have to kill those followers and anyone else who wanted to make trouble. Harder to hide that. What does the Falconer really expect now that it's gone sideways? Does he think I can keep this quiet now? I haven't been quiet at all.-

He looks up to find a small knot of birds circle overhead, intent on him.

-Always watching. Those fucking birds. The Falconer probably already knows the Neta-Teej is missing. He's going to kill me. But I haven't failed yet. Tonight, it's still on the shed. Still work to do. With the advocates.-

He wishes he had more to drink as he contemplates what he's up against. Too much, really. Too many unanswered questions. He would never have gone looking for a fight at a time like this in the past. He would have played it safe. Lain low.

Advocates. Lucien proxies come up from the abyss to do their worst.

-But does Lucien know the plan?-

Again, he thinks of the Trustee 452A and how she could be of use now.

The shed is usually liminal to him. The slums from back north and the cellar are more similar in nature. Tonight, the shed is different, the advocates bringing the darkness with them, bringing it all together and making it one.

452A is an odd creature. Might be good to have her on a night like this, the way she doesn't change between the light and the dark like all the others. The Falconer always wants eyes on her, and often enough it's 681B doing the watching.

-There's value in watching. Analyzing a person.-

681B remembers times in the outlands, before he was grown

and found his place with the rebels. He remembers the rovers in the night, groups of men moving through the barrios, looking for some value they could carry off.

He noted their faces from his hiding spots. Learned the crevices of their sneers and which teeth were missing when they smiled and the silken silent gait of their walk. He assessed every member of the gang and noted them for when the sun came back, and light shown on all the passersby. If they could be cruel and vicious in the dark, there was value in knowing who they were in the light.

-Just like the Trustee. Value in keeping eyes on her. But more value in keeping a distance. She doesn't change when everyone else does. There's more danger in that.-

It is his memories of how to survive that keep him safe. It was his patience and endurance that allowed him to wait others out, or to pace them and drop them when they were weakest. Persistence of the old kind. To hunt while suffering, knowing your ability to suffer was greater than your opponent's. The memories of suffering and survival give him power and value. It has always been enough to simply remember.

-But you're on the wrong side tonight. Going against advocates.-

The fear comes back and so does the tightness in the pit of his stomach. The memory of desperation born back in the outlands with him. The starvation and the survival faith and the helplessness that comes with having no value.

-A memory like the sky is falling. No stopping it. No running. You feel it in your bones. It eats at you. Hunger in your mind and soul. Because you're nothing compared to what's happening to you. And you never forget how small you are. You can't forget who stands over you.-

But 681B rises to his feet and continues on his way, knowing there's nothing else to do but find a path through.

-I am on the wrong side. But that's the job, all night, every night.-

22

Ze is well beyond the back markers of the shed before the Neta-Teej realizes there is a follower and turns to see who it is.

The old woman. She hobbles along far behind.

The Neta-Teej stops and waits, not in any real rush.

Tonight, ze is taking hirself to solitary, not waiting for some guard to come looking, not wanting the armored escort out to the lonely shack.

-Old woman. How could I leave you behind?-

Out in the open they meet in the silence hanging below the constant movement of the wind. The old Crone almost runs into the Neta-Teej, plodding along head down, following footprints and trying to conserve energy.

"I wasn't sure if you'd ever look back," the Crone says.

"You could have called out."

"I don't do that anymore. No more calling. It no longer suits me, but I am better for it," she says, adding, "I think."

"Why are you following me? Do you have something to say about all this?"

"All this? Do you mean the attempt to be made on your life

tonight?"

"It's all rumor."

"You're out here alone, going to solitary under your own volition. So, it's more than just rumor to you."

"I know what it is. I am not a child."

The Crone shakes her head and frowns. "No. Never a child. You always said as much. But here we are. Doesn't matter what you are or aren't. Not tonight. Not when there are advocates on the shed, advocates who will come looking for you. Only you. And you're wandering off to have a sit in solitary."

The Neta-Teej straightens. "Is this a lesson, or would you like to come along?"

"It's to be suicide then?"

"Far from it."

"They're here to kill you. To desecrate you. Rip you apart."

"You've heard this?"

"I got close to the lead one and saw it in his mind. And I have heard it elsewhere, just like you have. Seen it through the veil."

The Neta-Teej studies the old woman's features and knows she is telling the truth. "They intend violence to my body, but intent changes nothing. There are many who aspire to kill me. This is different."

"Yes," laughs the Crone. "It is different. Because you have no escape."

"I cannot run from this."

"But you isolate yourself. You court their intent, beckoning it. You think things may end differently?"

The Neta-Teej, hands wrapped up in a dirty tunic, bows hir head, turns, and resumes walking west, away from the shed and the beacons and into the wind.

The Crone waits for a moment, watching the Neta-Teej, how the young body is getting weaker and moving slower.

-The ghost shed does this to all of us.-

Then she follows, slowly catching up as they make their way out to the solitary shack.

"Just say so and I will turn back," says the old woman.

"You must know I will not turn back with you?"

The Crone shrugs. "It's death, no matter how you want to pretend. Death of body. Death of soul. Even if your life doesn't end, these beings are looking for you and they are coming to change you. If you want me to stay for a bit, I will. But I will understand if you want to be alone before this happens to you."

"Is this the first time you have ever really been alone?" the Neta-Teej asks. "I am sure it's strange to be here, in a place so unlike the temple."

"So, you do want to talk? I have known plenty who went to their deaths prattling on about all sorts of things."

"Maybe I am still a child. But I know death is a possibility."

"You are gambling with your life. Too many games on the shed. Too many games in the cellar. No way to plot a course when all the minds and all the sentiments and emotions start to work into a turbulence. I can hear the chaos."

"I feel it, too. It's in everyone I get close to. It is in me as well. My inner world is uncertain."

"And you think this will help you to refocus? Is the threat of death helping you to cross over? Do you think your expiry might help the utza somehow? Bring them together, maybe give them some common mourning?"

"It isn't like that. Much smaller really."

"They will not notice your passing. It is a stupid game. The smaller, the more idiotic. You are no small thing. You are going to pay for the gamble, and, in time, they may all pay dearly along with you."

They approach the solitary cells now, and the Neta-Teej does not let the dread stop the legs from moving. It would be easier to stop but that cannot happen.

"You're too far out," says the Crone. "You're out here away from the barracks and there's no one who can help you. By the time they know you're not in the shed, they're coming here. You know I can't stop them."

"You could if you wanted to."

"So that's your aim? Draw us all out and see what power we might still have. See who comes to defend you?"

"You could stop them," the Neta-Teej says again. "But you won't."

"I can't. Not anymore after being here so long. But you're right. I won't. I won't even try."

"Why is that?" asks the Neta-Teej, stopping and facing the old woman in the snow. "Why wouldn't you? You got close enough already. You're here now. But there's a barrier. I am no son of yours. No daughter of yours. You will not help me?"

"No. You are the Neta-Teej. You are supposed to be the guide."

"Just a product of my name. I am a person. Filled with blood and guts. I was a child of yours at one time, in the temple. My family is dead."

"Not all of them."

"All dead and gone," reaffirms the Neta-Teej. "But I carry no guidance, despite my name. Call me Neta-Teej. Call me holy one. Call me whatever you want. There is no substance to it. This place has shown me that. Shown me how the things we carry have so little weight. Even you, now, pious in your robes, still wrapped the same way, even though they're rotting and black with filth. You still keep that rosary close. You made it yourself. A little reminder of how you were once given beautiful and rich things."

The Crone looks back toward the shed. "I am here to help you."

"Were you ever really trying to help me?"

"Did it ever occur to you that I simply didn't know how?"

"It occurs to me with every memory of the citadel or of

Europa, with every memory that crosses my mind. But until now you've never spoken a word of it. The questions of my mind are not the rules of the world around me. Has it ever occurred to you that neither are yours?"

The Crone stares into the gray eyes of the young face, intent and present in a way she has not seen in a long time.

"Do you see?" asks the Neta-Teej. "Do you see how you have brought us here? You, of course, but me as well. All of us. You sat on the Quadrumvirate. This place is ordained by you. By me, in a way."

"I ran when I found out. You know that."

"I ran too. Then we ran together. But I am done with that."

"The spider has to stand its ground," says the Crone.

"The old way. You make the web before you are starving, before it is forced on you. You make the web before the others come, whether it be in attack or in passing. It should be your hunt, not theirs."

"You have no retreat now."

"I am not a spider. Never have been. And the Neta-Teej is just a name given to me. It isn't really mine."

"Then sacrifice makes even less sense."

"Stop," says the Neta-Teej, louder than intended. "There isn't a way back now. Not for me. I will confront this. I will confront Lucien and all those who try to keep me."

"We should move along then," says the Crone and they head off again, moving slowly across the snow as the sun falls and the solitary cells grow closer and closer.

"I've never walked this way before," says the Neta-Teej. "I've been here a hundred times, but I've always been carried or driven out by a guard, ready to discard me."

The Crone doesn't answer.

"I suppose it's the last time I might see it."

Again, the Crone doesn't answer.

When they get to the cells, ze does not hesitate. For the Neta-Teej it is a common home and there is something liberating about entering under hir own volition, a self-escort. No anger. No violence.

Everything is quieter and all the features of the walls seem so clear.

The Crone follows without comment.

Inside the back room the rickety ceiling bows with the weight of the ice and the Neta-Teej quickly lies down on the bare dirt, frozen solid.

The Crone moves with understanding and first takes a shackle and puts it over the thin ankle, pale and malnourished.

"Use the others, as well," requests the Neta-Teej, pointing at some chains hanging, normally unused.

It happens quickly and the clasps are electronic, needing a coded key from guard armor to open.

"This web, what is it made to catch?" asks the Crone.

"You've seen it clearly for some time, even if you are unwilling to resist. We're all pawns. All part of someone else's plotting. Shouldn't we see who's pulling all the strings? Shouldn't we see who's moving the pieces?"

"I can't let you out now."

"We've been in someone else's web forever."

"This buys you nothing."

"If I get to see... if I can see the truth, then it will have been worth it. And if I die then I will have gotten to be me. One time at least."

"Is there anything else?" asks the Crone, voice flat.

"No."

"When they come, I hope it's quick."

"It won't be. And that will leave time for the others."

"We'll see. I don't know if there will be others."

"You won't see. But I will. You will go back to the shed, looking away."

The Crone sneers and shakes her head. "Goodbye, Neta-Teej."

"Goodbye, Mother Crone. I'll see you tomorrow."

"Perhaps. Perhaps not."

23

he wind has a power to it tonight.-

The Neta-Teej parses awareness.

The skin is making demands, unable to stop the cold from penetrating the muscles and the organs. The blood is not flowing easily as it should. But the Neta-Teej lets the demand persist, knowing there are other things at work.

There is a small blue light on the ceiling of the solitary cell and it never turns off. It stares down at the Neta-Teej, some frigid star on an imaginary blank sky. The color of it evokes the idea of the sun filtered through thick ice, deepening the feeling of cold.

But ze discards the bite of frosted shackles and the need to shiver. Instead, ze favors the sound of the wind.

-The wind is more important.-

Wind has a complexity in a place like the shed. It's a living thing that cannot be ignored. It slows down and goes for leisurely strolls in the valleys and then races down the hills and takes clear breaths when it gets out into the open. It gets hungry and comes looking for you, even when you hide.

It calls the Neta-Teej, each little gust and whistle a comment on the world beyond the solitary cell.

-I should not lie to myself. The wind is important, but I am afraid of what it hides. I want to hear them coming, whoever it is that's on their way to see me tonight. And what will you catch on a night like tonight, in a trap like this? Only things that hunt your species. Only things that hunt the Neta-Teej.-

The advocates will come. That is certain. In a way, they are bait as well. Unmistakable creatures. Easy to track and follow. The great beasts who have lost all fear of predation take no precaution.

-But they go against the advocate of advocates. Will General Lucien come? Does he even know what is about to transpire?-

It is strange to hope for him. There would be a certainty in outcome if Lucien were to surface, were to come and willingly show his hand. But the Neta-Teej knows it would do no good. Only worse things would come from Lucien's arrival.

-He is no different than any of the others, the powerful who hold influence. They all tell me what I am, what I will be. How can they be so sure when I am not? I have never been sure, even when there were billions who waited for my words. Even when the aura of it all was more comprehensive than the truth. You are just part of someone else's world. They see you however makes sense to them.-

-No matter who you are, how long until they make you into something else? They craft you in image and routine, in action. Soon you are altered. You can only see the next prescribed moment that requires you to be someone, the exact someone they demand. And so you be it. Less resistance brings less manipulation. Less complication and less hostility. This is only because you cease to deviate.-

-They tell me what I am. It's easy to see it, they say. But I cannot see it. All a mask. All a costume. Who is the Neta-Teej? A character, a figurehead, a label I was given early.-

-The Neta-Teej had gardens and fields inside the temple. But I no longer inhabit them. The gardens are lush, still, without me there to see them. Should they stop existing in my absence? Would you dare tell a

garden how to be? Cliché. But they change gardens all the time. They remove plants and let them die elsewhere. They burn forests down. How long until they try to unmake you? It's what they did to Europa.-

-I now see this was never a matter of perspective. Instead, it is a quiet war between me and all the others. And all the others fight each other, also. I've been told what I am. Now I say, no. Wrong. I am this. We disagree. You cannot say what I am because you are not me.-

-I have barely ever been myself. And what would I be? Something less ordained? Doubtful. Yes, something considered less divine. But still just as manufactured. Less grand, but still etched in stone.-

-The world wishes me divine, and it wishes me chained up, dead or alive. I am between a past and a mask, and I can stay here forever. There is no force to move me beyond my state of limbo. This is what I really am now. And I should not lie to myself. In truth, I came here to die. And this will all end tonight, one way other another.-

The Neta-Teej's thoughts move quickly, and only with a loud surge of wind do the senses return, realigning with the terror hanging in hir chest cavity. But there is also dread in nothing changing, nothing coming to a head.

The gusts carry only natural noises. It could be that nothing happens and the night passes in quiet cold like every other.

The desire to scream against the ever present cold and fear, the pressure of it, which can only be kept at bay for so long, is almost overpowering.

Muscles twitch and thrash against the restraints in a convulsion of rage. It continues until the lungs sputter and the fury has burned out and the pain is sharp enough at the shackles to make cuts. Ze wants to curl into a ball and hold hirself for warmth and for touch and to hide from what has been done and will be done.

But the chains are not quite long enough to let that happen.

-Who will come? To save me from this? From myself? From this life? I need out. I am trapped between two becomings. It must be simplified tonight. No need for tomorrow. Or maybe tomorrow will just

be harder and I will walk the exchange with all the utza. I know now that they do not need me. But what would I do without them?-

It is in this moment that the Neta-Teej allows hir mind to slip away, to delve into teikum, into hir soul-world.

It is escapist, a desperate reprieve.

Ze stands atop a wide plateau of white stone and grass. It is warm, in the afternoon sun. There is a well near the edge of a cliff and, beyond, a great ocean where the clouds and birds occupy the sky together. Ze does not look back but knows there is a village down in the valley, and a fortress, all covered in gray fog.

24

Trustee 452A sits on her mattress until well after dark, a deep hesitation filling her before starting the rounds. It's easier in the muffled quiet, listening as the wind and the human noises mix from behind a barrier. The walls prevent reality's demands for a little while.

But the quiet also makes the mind shudder and roll, a flutter of images and voices. They collide behind her eyes and help her manifest fictions, creating questionable patterns. She cannot believe or trust any of these illusions, and the pangs of joy and horror accompanying them are unmanageable in their severity and brevity.

When it gets to be too much, the Trustee heads out into the cold.

She looks across the shed from the elevated walkways to see the tens of thousands of utza, the fires they have made, and the lights of the Osai, only hinting at the guardship's true size and shape.

Her eyes perform an immediate search, looking for 681B near the barracks, searching for tracks in the snow to signal of a hiding prisoner, peering into the dark sky for birds.

-Too many things to watch for.-

-Countless entities on the shed tonight.-

-They'll be watching for you.-

She checks her weapons and heads into the night.

Utza lie in droves under the barracks houses, some destined to die, snow building up on them as they huddle together, no other place to find shelter, no room next to the fires. Too tired to fight for a spot. They know this reality and have chosen to go quietly, clutching each other tightly in the cold.

-Better to die in a pack, as a human, than alone in a pit.-

-Resting beneath the boots of others?-

-Making space for those who will live.-

As she continues her circuit, the Trustee anticipates 681B, but among the many silhouettes, people prepared to walk all night to stay warm, there is no sign of him. His absence suits her fine, easier to focus on the utza and the possibility of advocates wandering about.

The Trustee does not stop at any of the barracks or bother to pass into the center of the shed, instead favoring the fence lines and then moving along the lit markers. Usually, clean snow lies beyond the beacons, but tonight countless boot prints cross out onto the tundra. She can see some of them, not too far off, heading out into the wastes to die.

-They'll never reach the mountains. Not tonight.-

-Something to walk toward.-

-Something familiar, something other than desolation.-

Later, in the warm season, a dispatch of soldiers will head into the hills to find and purge escapees who have hidden there. The trustees will go with them to search the tight crevices and cracks. But they never find any utza alive. Only bodies, mummified corpses wedged into stone, left as reminders to anyone else who might come searching for refuge.

As the Trustee approaches the western corner of the shed, she sees an old woman standing near the markers, looking down the line at the Trustee.

The old woman has been waiting for Trustee 452A, waiting to see the silhouette with the stooped shoulders and the ever-ready hands.

As their eyes meet, there is a moment of recognition.

In the harsh weather they come close enough to speak without raised voices but both want distance. Both want to keep it brief.

"You waiting for someone?" asks the Trustee.

"Where are you off to tonight?" asks the old woman.

"Cut the circuit. Back to bunk early. Cellar tomorrow."

"The metamorphosis is here. Again. Tomorrow," she says, voice cracking to get over the sound of the growing wind. "You lie low tonight. But you draw attention to yourself every day.

"Do I know you?"

"You do," she says. "But it doesn't matter anymore. All that matters is what lies ahead. The past is dead. You know this. Memory is forfeit."

The Trustee looks around, checking the main pathways.

-Is someone watching?-

-Who is with her?-

The old woman moves beads from hand to hand across a length of cord.

"Does 681B work for you?" asks the Trustee.

"No one works for me, girl. And 681B is nothing but a messenger at the threshold. Same as you."

A crooked finger points at her face, where the charcoal markings are still visible. She traces them at a distance.

"You should get out of my way," says the Trustee, voice flat.

"No need. You aren't going this way. You're heading out to solitary. The Neta-Teej needs you tonight."

"Got my rounds this way."

"You aren't as disciplined as they say, Trustee. I see things. You do things to make space, to earn a name for yourself. As I said, you do not lie low. Not really."

"It's protection."

"You can protect yourself without the extra effort. You play and you tease and you prod. You do it to buy favor."

"There is no favor here, old woman."

"Lucien's is the only favor to seek. Whether you know it or not, this is what you do."

The Trustee remembers a flashing dream and a bright light in her eyes, blinding her.

-Obstinance is a healthy trait which bears further observation.-

-His voice is burned into my mind and I am not even in the cellar yet.-

-She is right. There are other things scorched here you cannot see.-

"Why don't you come with me?" says the Trustee, pulling out her baton. "Come with me to solitary if there's something pressing to be done."

"I just came from there," says the old woman. "And there's nothing you can do that would make me go back. It's a bad night. Even an old witch knows."

"Got my rounds. This way. Through you."

"Your rounds will take you through everyone, Trustee. And you won't even know it. It's the way it was written, I think, on your mind. But that makes you powerful. It makes you obstinate. Makes you solitary."

The baton extends with a wrist flick, electricity jumping blue across the nodes in the dry air.

"What do you know about me?" she demands. The baton illuminates the old woman, and her eyes turn away as it comes closer to her face. "What do you know about me?"

"I know you want to kill me, but there's no need to be an animal, Trustee. And there's nothing else you need from me tonight. Nothing more I can give you. Except to say that you should go to the solitary cells."

"Everyone else tells me not to go." The Trustee is surprised she remembers.

"Your choice."

The Trustee watches as the old woman steps back and then moves off toward the fires among the barracks houses, turning to shadow. She watches until the shape fades in the gloom, perpetually swept by ice, and then she puts the baton away.

The desire to do violence hangs about while she stands alone in the dark. It clings to her throat, making it harder to breathe and to move her jaw. She shakes, vibrating with rage, until the perspiration drains down the sides of her neck and chills her against the wind. Her legs release tension and her fists relax.

Her eyes are transfixed out onto the ice beyond the beacons, and the tunnel vision narrows until the little points of focus pull her into the night, draw her to dwell among the ice crystals that glitter like rushing stars, traversing heavens, falling, tumbling, picked up again and thrown by cosmic forces beyond control.

-It is bad form to go to solitary in the dark.-

The Trustee moves ahead slowly, wary, and sees the tracks cutting a path toward the solitary shack. Made by the old woman.

She checks back with every step beyond the shed to make sure she isn't followed.

25

The shack appears deserted. There are some footprints around the outside, but whoever made them, probably a small group, lingered for a time in the lee of the building, then wandered back toward the shed. More prints head off onto the tundra, toward the hills. Even though the solitary cell provides some shelter, it has become a place of conflicting powers, a locus of strange energy, designed as a place of torture, but now also known as the Neta-Teej's remote throne. A night temple to be respected at a distance, or sufficient for homage or prayer.

-*The utza know better than to trespass.*-

-*You know better.*-

-*Aren't supposed to be out after dark. No utza beyond the beacons.*-

-*No trustees either.*-

She opens the door and checks inside and then closes herself in.

The walls shake and whistle under the wind's pressure. The outside world is a chaotic mess always trying to force its way in, always trying to tear pieces off and drag them someplace else. The waste has its own agenda for construction and destruction. The oldest of human structures, human bodies, are young compared to the ages of ice and stone. Even the solitary cell struggles to stay upright, to remain against the natural processes.

The Trustee uses her light and checks the cells as she goes down the row, each empty. Plenty of corners to hide, but this is a bad place with ill-fated air, and you might get stuck, caught among the ghosts, a tight mesh of spirits who have died in concentration.

She opens the latch to the last cell and enters quietly, closing the door behind her.

Inside, the single dim light hangs blue and casts a weakened dream-glow into every corner. The Neta-Teej lies along the back wall, drawn out to the cement stanchions embedded in the ground.

-What am I doing here?-

-It's hard to say. But you are supposed to be here. That is for certain.-

The Trustee doesn't question it until the Neta-Teej speaks.

"Trustee?" asks the weak voice. "Trustee, I didn't invite you. Are you lost?"

The Trustee just stands, looking around the room, confused.

"You need to leave," says the Neta-Teej, uncertainty gone. "Leave while you can. Finish the round and back to your bunk. Better to be safe tonight and rested for the morning. Tomorrow is the cellar exchange."

The words are compelling and sweet and the Trustee almost feels her muscles begin to move back toward the door.

But the desire fades after another long moment of hesitation.

The Neta-Teej watches as the Trustee's mind seems to blink, on, off, and then return to the present. The glassed eyes coming and going, the slack face reanimating.

"You talk too much," says the Trustee after a time.

The Neta-Teej's neck relaxes and hir head lies back, looking away from this stubborn Trustee. "You really need to leave while you can."

"Make me."

The Neta-Teej sighs, then looks up with eyes of spite.

"You talk too much," says the Trustee again, rubbing it in.

The Trustee opens a pocket and pulls out a flask of clear liquor and drinks from it.

"This place is a shit hole," says the Trustee matter-of-fact, eyes examining the rafters and the walls. "Better than sleeping under a barracks house, I guess."

"Who followed you here? Did Nystrom send you? What have you heard?" asks the Neta-Teej. Hir mind races, trying to understand why the Trustee has come.

"I was on my rounds."

"Advocates will be approaching, Trustee. They cannot find you here."

The Trustee takes another drink and the eyes go blank and then look away from the Neta-Teej.

Her gaze wanders the room again, aimless, eyeing up the ice coming through weak thatch, looking at the floor.

-That will need patching.-

-And the dirt. It's too low.-

-Will collect water during spring.-

-Turn to ice at night.-

-Can't have that.-

"Trustee!" barks the Neta-Teej.

The Trustee looks over and really sees this slight entity chained on the floor, sees the annoyance in the young face and the smallest hint of tremors leading out to the ends of the arms and legs.

-Cold or afraid?-

-Probably both.-

The chains seem a strange addition to the length of body, and something familiar is patterned in that face. The Trustee doesn't want to look away, but doesn't want to see what is aimed back, purposeful and judging.

"Trustee, if you're going to stay, stop staring at me and at least sit down," the Neta-Teej says with exasperation.

There's a stone in the corner and the Trustee goes and sits, easily obeying this order. She rests her back against the wooden wall and pulls off her hat, stuffing it into the breast pocket of her jacket. She pushes her dirty hair aside and then she drinks again, elbows on knees, eyes down and tired.

The Neta-Teej watches, unblinking, studying this Trustee, noting the heaviness of the shoulders, different than any normal utza, different than any of the starved and weak. So different from before.

Ze isn't sure whether hope or despair should accompany this Trustee, especially on a night where things are already in motion, already coming closer, tangled with all the tides.

-Is this part of some plan? Part of Lucien's game? Or is this coincidence? Something chaotic, karmic, wandering in out of the night wind? Come to see the Neta-Teej for absolution? Come to look for calm?-

The Trustee is drinking and breathing deeply, relaxing. It's involuntary, that is obvious enough to the Neta-Teej. It's a release that makes no sense, a comfort that comes from a sudden awareness of oneself, especially after a displacement of mind, of spirit.

The Neta-Teej holds back tears.

-She doesn't know why she's here. Karmic indeed. Coincidence. But irrelevant. It is a departure and, for her, now, it is different and good. A moment of feeling clean. A moment of purity.-

Ze looks at this Trustee. Face familiar and mixed with all shape of past love and hate. Regret and longing mingle there. But it is clean. The Neta-Teej feels the truth of the past.

"I'm glad you're here, Trustee," says the Neta-Teej. "No matter why you've come."

The Trustee smiles. Her dirty hair is wild, and so are her eyes, wrought with a visceral awareness.

-She is here. Now. But how long can she last? No one better to share the end with.-

"Can I have a drink?"

The Trustee scoffs, but then it turns to a laugh. "Of course."

She comes over and kneels, hand behind head, to support, but mostly to steady the aim, and drains a quick line of liquor into the bound creature.

The hand on the cropped hair, the impulsive nearness, are shocking to both of them. The Neta-Teej lets hirself sit up to make the pour easier, to emphasize the closeness, a natural act.

-Let her see you up close. Let her touch you. Let her remember. If she can.-

The liquid is cold on the tongue and then it is hot going down, delicate in a way that clockwork never could be, rough and real in a way that the Tribe's drugs could never match. It cuts through into the guts and pulls the limbs closer at the joints, hips and shoulders, everything contracting.

"Where did you get that stuff?"

"Good?" asks the Trustee. "It is good."

"But where did it come from?"

The Trustee glances at the flask, then at the wall, unable to answer. Sadness lurks in her eyes.

"It's okay. There's a lot I don't remember either," says the Neta-Teej, watching the Trustee, wishing she wouldn't look like that. "Don't let it eat you up. There's so much worth forgetting. Even the good things. Sometimes they eat at you the worst. Things you think you ought to remember. But they're poison in your mind. In your heart."

The Trustee nods. "Right. Good... But I think Nystrom gave it to me. And she's just a Colonel."

The Neta-Teej cannot help but to laugh, to shake the head and roll the eyes. It's an old habit and it feels more natural now than ever before.

"You are right though," says the Trustee. "There are things not worth remembering." She takes a heavy drink.

"I remember," says the Neta-Teej. "Too much really. It's already too much. The first time I went to the cellar, it was already stacking up. I was making my way into the pit, and down by the lifts there were people everywhere, beat, tired, dying. I felt it in my bones. Just like them. And two children ran through, a boy and a girl. They were so small. One picking on the other. And they were delirious with it all, yelling and running between groups. So tired they were swaying, but they were laughing. Stumbling through the crowd. Doing what children do. Just making the wait for the lifts more exciting. Wasting time. I watched them and tried to feel it, tried to understand how they could do it, feel joy in those moments. But that was never me. I never did that when I was little."

The Trustee nods, taking a seat again. Listening, but with nothing to say.

"Do you see many children here, Trustee? I wish I never saw them. Because it was beautiful. It was good and real but then I wondered why they were here, why they should be ready to hit the lifts and then crawl the parade with the rest of us. How is this allowed? How did this happen? How are they here? How are they laughing? Is that allowed? I wish I'd never seen it. I wish I could forget it. But the whole exchange I saw them in the dark, in my memory. Living little shadow lives, their spirits jumping cavern to cavern. Looking out at me. Asking for things I cannot give."

"I don't see many children," says the Trustee, thinking of the rushing shape which crosses her path in the dark, the child that runs back and forth on her rounds. "They get through sometimes. Mistakes shuttled in from the outlands. Births hidden among the utza."

"And then you don't see them again?"

The Trustee drinks.

"You don't remember?"

The Trustee shakes her head.

"They're small, but they aren't mistakes," ze says. "Tiny things filter down and disappear. They find ways to get through, easy to hide, easy to lose. They move through this place and fuel the system, added to the foundations. Tell me, have you ever seen an utza with a child in her belly?"

The Trustee nods.

"It's rare with the malnutrition. I've seen the miscarriages. But it happens. They can come to term with some help from a group. Life brought in, not just pushed out. This place is a stratification of power and violence. The natural order pulls rank before anything else. Life force cascades down from on high."

"From on high? From Lucien."

The Neta-Teej leans hir head up. "Perhaps. For now."

"I'll drink to that," says the Trustee.

"It is natural to change."

The Trustee stands again and tilts some booze out, hitting close.

"I came here to die, you know," says the Neta-Teej, after letting the drink go down.

"We all came here to die."

The Neta-Teej smiles. "With intent, Trustee. I made my way here with the intent to die. I am party to this encampment and to what has happened here. Why shouldn't I submit to the human cost? Your blood will fall here too before the end. Everyone's will."

"Yes. I know it."

"But I always hoped the Neta-Teej part of me would die first. Would leave me just a little time to the quiet inside me. No more sight. No more ritual. No more followers. No more pontification. Even hours to myself, just a few hours, I thought it might be enough to fall in love. Just a moment where no one knew me for who I was. A moment like that could happen here, right? Desperate and real, forced by the hard world around us, but human in a way I have yet to experience. I thought I might die the pre-death and have a moment for myself. Afterward, I could die complete. I could fade away among all those whom I accidentally condemned to die. I made this place by praying and speaking and sitting in the Tribe's temples. Just sitting was enough and I lent my voice to make this place more full. Adding souls to the cellar."

"You're a human," says the Trustee, the words coming from someplace deep inside. "Nothing more. Not a god. To others, maybe. They might make you into something in their minds. But they made that themselves, just like this place. Not you."

The Neta-Teej smiles. "The Priest would be terribly sorry to hear you say that."

"He can be sorry. He has no sway over it. 'Sorry' has no pull. You are here to die. And you will die completely. There is no little death beforehand. One or none."

The Neta-Teej lifts hir head again. "No shade of gray? No moment of contemplation before the end? Spoken like someone who has already passed away. Or maybe you just want it to be quicker."

"It'll never be quick. But I will not be squandered." The Trustee drinks and feels a surge of power in her veins as she says the words.

"You've already given a pound of flesh to this place, Trustee. Memories and comfort. No friends. No allies to speak of. What else do you have but your spine? All the love is gone. What's left of you?"

The Trustee shrugs. "I guess we'll see if there's anything else. No one is leaving. No one is getting out. You will be here to see what's left. And there will be a thousand eyes watching at the end."

"More than that, Trustee. But it's not that simple. I say you are just a prisoner, already dead, but you say you have more. You say I am no god and you are right. I am no god. Just a mistake, but there is so much still wrapped up in us. Even now you won't let go of it, even though you cannot remember what it is. How will we ever get what is trapped inside us to come out? How will I ever get my soul untangled from all this, this thing I have become? How can I give what I am supposed to? How will this place ever let that be? How can this place ever come to an end?"

The Trustee just stares blankly.

"Power lies inside all things," says the Neta-Teej. "And that power is for the taking. In the world's natural order, the most efficient way to access the power of another is to consume them. Kill them, liberate their nutrients, absorb them into yourself, and rise...if you can. This prison makes it easier in some ways. They take our power, our life force. It is part of Lucien's crooked path. But you will not be tolerated forever, Trustee. I will not be tolerated forever, a false god with nothing but words. And they ... they will not be tolerated forever either."

"Who?"

"Don't you hear them? Those pushing through the wind toward this shack? They're coming to see whose power they can take. They are invited, Trustee, in a way. But you were not. You are not supposed to be here."

"I don't hear anything," says the Trustee, shaking her head.

"They're at the door," says the Neta-Teej flatly, taking a breath and lying back. "They are free to wander any cavern here. I wonder why they have come."

The Trustee turns to look as the door opens and two advocates, one after the other, enter the cell. They stoop in their armor, dirty, dented and frost covered. They move quietly as only stalking predators move, a living silence born in places where the slightest noise echoes and dark rooms keep you close to your quarry. A special trained silence.

They stop just inside and note the bound entity, as expected. But there is also this trustee, sitting in the corner, blank faced and tired.

One of them, armor adorned with welded scales across the shoulders and down the chest and back, closes the door and latches it.

There is silence as the faceless advocates purvey the situation. The holy deity of the Tribe, now fallen, and a trustee, a sycophant utza.

"Why are you here?" the advocate with the scales asks, voice absent any affect, the monotone coming through the suit. They point at the Trustee with an iron hand to make it clear who is being asked.

The Trustee stands up slowly, hands wide to show she is unarmed. "I am here to sit in the Neta-Teej's presence," she says, and then adds, "sir," far too late.

"You aren't supposed to be beyond the shed. You are supposed to be on patrol."

"Uh," pauses the Trustee. "I patrolled all the way out here."

The advocates glance at each other.

The Trustee takes a drink of the flask and makes sure to get it all down in one go before putting it back in her jacket.

"She only wanted guidance," says the Neta-Teej from behind the Trustee, still lying back. "I am here. That is enough for your purposes."

"Animals are not permitted in the grain field," says the other advocate, voice identical, their suit a pockmarked mess of ballistic strikes. A blast shield hangs on their shoulder, gouged as proof of weight and use.

"And yet you are here too," accuses the Neta-Teej. "This trustee came to speak with the calm of the Tribe, a guide. Just like the old ways. I know you have come for different reasons. Those do not diminish hers."

The Trustee doesn't take her eyes from the advocates, trying to understand their hierarchy, their patterns of action. While they speak to the Neta-Teej, she moves to rub her face, as if in anxiety, and quickly places a bent piece of rubber, wrapped in cloth, into her mouth, moving it with her tongue to the spot where it has worn to a fine fit between back teeth.

-This will be bad.-

-Bite down firm.-

"We seek guidance as well," says the one with the scales, stepping forward. "If godliness is next to humanness, can't a filthy god bring me back to life?"

They do not wait for an answer. The advocate crosses the small room and the Trustee has been waiting for it, the sudden surge of violence, almost hoping for it after all the suspense. The advocate throttles her against the icy wall, and then those iron fists take hold of her coat. It is ripped open and off in one vicious shake. The advocate tosses her up, and then she hits the ground spinning, exposed and gasping as the cold air slams her chest and back, only a thin shirt covering her.

The other advocate is on her, the suit of armor covered in the dimples, sharp at the rims. They stand over her as she cowers on the ground, now held in place by a gnarled boot.

Her first attacker's suit stands erect and exhales, the breastplate opening. Hot, humid air spills out as steam from inside.

She watches the armor unseal the soldier within. She can imagine the sweetness of unfiltered air, earthen, no matter the temperature, and how it would shock the nerves, how it would take drug fog away and how you would be sober and human again after withstanding encapsulation for so long. As human as you can remember.

A man steps out, bare feet on frozen dirt.

His body expels hot fog and his pale skin barely sheathes angular muscles. He is slick with compiled sweat and grime. Long hair, reaching to his hips, flows matted down his back, but the Trustee can still see the port sites where tubes and circulators move blood and other fluids.

The boot on her chest backs away.

She doesn't have time to move as an ungloved fist slams into the side of her head, the naked man grabbing at her, stinking and harsh. But she expects it all the same, her teeth clenched shut on the fabric and rubber. Her whole head explodes in pain and her eyes shut involuntarily, abdominal muscles forcing her to breathe through tight lips

He throws her toward the Neta-Teej and she rolls, colliding with the chains and cement blocks.

They shove her face into the Neta-Teej's robes, feet kicking at her back, hands ripping at her hair.

The Trustee ducks down, trying to avoid the strikes without getting too close.

A foot on the back of her head mashes her down onto the Neta-Teej.

Her face grinds into the Neta-Teej's pelvic bone, sharp under the surface of the skin, hard even through the tattered robes.

-So thin.-

-A frail thing.-

-Weakened by the time in the shed.-

-Only physically.-

More blows fall on the back of her head, and she has to put her hands up to cover herself. She rolls up but takes kicks to the ribs and cries out, unable to keep the bit in her mouth.

Her mind jumps about to process the pain. Thoughts come rapidly, bleeding into each other as if to block the pathways from acknowledging the damage being done.

-Living things avoid death.-

-Not all.-

-All. Just not all the time. They have prayed to avoid it for millennia.-

A prayer enters her mind. It is foreign, one not known to her, even as it flows into her.

-Now, no evil thing, of any kind whatsoever, shall be done unto me by devils.-

-I shall not be gored by horns. Behold. I shall come into my fields and cut the grain. The gods shall provide me with food.-

-Violence shall not be done unto me and I shall not be carried away in my boat to the east to have the feast of the devils celebrated on me in evil fashion.-

-Thus, it was prayed for ages. But prayer is not rule. And the gods have a natural order for us to obey.-

The prayer twists to inner thought as the advocates beat her. She wants to focus. She wants to turn and protect herself, protect the Neta-Teej, but her broken mind continues to roll.

-When there is a kill on the savannah, the predators and scavengers all come running, drawn by the sound, by the smell. Even the prey may find itself the victor only to be picked apart by those who come to see the ruin. It is a landscape of fear. Death to fuel a harvest. Sacrifice or natural process. One must still look east for the sun to rise.-

-Who said that?-

-The Neta-Teej wrote it.-

-And then what happens?-

-Then the birds come. The big ones eat amongst the most fearsome predators, whether it is their kill or not. The lesser birds pick the carcasses clean.-

-They will carry all the bits away.-

-Until the savannah is simplified and death is forgotten.-

She twists and screams and grabs at the tunic, trying to stay atop the Neta-Teej, trying to shield hir as her skin begins to bruise in the blue light. She clutches at the robes and a piece of her decides to never let go, voices still rattling in her brain.

The Neta-Teej stares blankly at the ceiling, eyes betraying the departure of the mind from the body, going someplace else while waiting for the inevitable.

But the Trustee abandons thoughts of eternity when her fingers find a hard object in the Neta-Teej's tunic. Steel. A blade. It is small, easy to palm as she crawls over the skinny creature. She pulls the blade under herself and slides it into a waistband.

The Trustee wants to let the rage build and cover the pain, wants to strike, to immediately use the blade to kill, but she knows the night is nowhere near complete. Another advocate in a suit. And what then? Maybe a quicker death once they see their colleague cut up?

-Maybe.-

She reaches down and begins to undo her pants. It is instinctual, protective and aggressive.

-Let him have his fun.-

-Drag it out and get your chance.-

-Better me.-

-Keep him interested.-

-Keep him close and stay alive.-

Before she can get the pants down, before she can expose herself fully as she cowers with her face in the dirt, another kick connects to her side and chest, knocking the wind out of her.

"This trustee is a whore," says the man. It is the first time they hear his real voice. It is slow and clear, almost emotionless. A voice conditioned to speaking through a comm channel, no adrenaline in the tone, even as he breathes heavily with excitement and exertion. "Fucks the Priest. Then Colonel. Looks well fed. Must fuck the cook."

But he has no real interest in her. He wants something far

more rare. The Trustee is only collateral. Somewhere to place the blame of the coming deeds.

He throws her aside, reminding the Trustee how much strength a healthy person has compared to the shell of an utza.

She slams on the ground just as the armored boot of the shield bearer comes down on her back, again pinning her. The freezing metal makes her body convulse as the second advocate expertly applies enough weight to restrict breathing but not crush her ribcage.

The Trustee tries to lift herself, tries to roll away, to struggle against the boot. But she can only watch as, across the room, the naked man lifts the red tunics, layer after layer, and kneels and lies over the frail body.

There is a scream, but it cuts short as he takes vicious grip around the Neta-Teej's strained throat and continues his task.

The Trustee's mind reels, instinctively anticipating a head blow, hoping to feel the bit in her mouth to dull the strike, expecting the searing pain, but instead the horror now is what is done before her, not to her.

She watches the shackles and the chains, how they cut into the little god's pale skin, how the links bounce and clatter as the wrists and ankles struggle against steel, muscles crawling under skin, then gone. A thrust. Writhing taut. Again fighting. Then slack against the chains. Repeating over and over.

The Trustee cannot think of moving as she watches. Numb and stuck to the ice.

There is so much and so little to bear witness to. Human contortions and a face that turns purple. Blood hits the ground between their legs. There are no human sounds but the chains moving against each other, doing their part in reminding all parties of the echelons of power.

A metal fist lifts the Trustee to her knees, turning her.

The second advocate stares down from behind black glass.

The suit off-gasses and opens, panels sliding and overlapping as the Trustee hangs in their grip.

The Trustee's vision fogs as the cold on her back and chest begin to fade. She is drifting away, mind deciding to go elsewhere at this moment of pain, of extreme sadness and overstimulation.

-Not now!-

-Just a departure.-

-No! Not now.-

As the suit of armor continues to open before her, the Trustee loses the sounds of the solitary cell. No more wind. No more chains. She tries to look back to where the Neta-Teej is, but her vision is narrowing.

All at once she is watching the emergence of a plain woman from the suit of pockmarked armor. But she is also watching the guardship, Adonai, bloom for the first time off-world, hovering over a foreign moon. She is looking up while its blocky form obscures the heavens and separates along hidden seams, folding outward. Beside it is the sky of Europa and the orange and blue tinge that comes from Jupiter's reflection, just on the other side of the southern pole, like a leviathan approaching.

The Adonai moves slowly through the heavens, deliberately, and so does the advocate, naked, pulling the Trustee into her.

The Trustee does not totally acknowledge the advocate, covered in a film of humanity not unlike the unwashed prisoners. The Trustee can only act as the woman directs, ungloved hand enmeshed in her hair, pulling her closer and closer to the waiting body, so long deprived of human touch in the depths of the cellar, now a rising demand.

All the while, the Trustee, hands on dirty hips, can only find the questions from Europa, and they frame confusion which will never be satiated.

The hand tightens in her hair and forces her in toward the advocate's sex.

Another hand drags nails sharply up her back.

-She wants to enjoy you.-

-Her hands are bare.-

-She wants to take her time.-

-Bare hands. Both hands out of armor.-

The blade bites deeply and repeatedly in quick succession along the rear curvature of the ribs on the advocate's right flank. The Trustee does not stop stabbing as she rises to her feet and the blade's wounds rise with her around the side and up under the armpit.

The advocate has sucked in a final breath with a gaping mouth, eyes now wide and sad and frightened, beginning to dull.

-They had been downcast and dark.-

-They see you differently now.-

-This is not good.-

-This is not over.-

Before the advocate can cry out, the Trustee opens up her throat, and warm blood flows down her arm while she holds the woman upright. There is nothing else to it but to keep the head tilted back and the wound open. No reason to watch. As long as she cannot get back into the suit, she's done. The Trustee holds for a quick moment and then lets her go.

-This is not over.-

The red robes are hardly visible under the shape of the man.

As the Trustee approaches, she can see over the top of him to a face strained with veins, head swaying with spit between white lips, every struggle eliciting tiny flushes of air that allow for another shake and shudder, a perpetual cycle of explosion and momentary life and false acquiesce to death and again explosion.

The man shrieks out as the blade goes in and the procedure is the same. Her arm shakes with impact. Again. Again.

He rolls, and looks behind him, through the Trustee's legs, and sees the empty suits of armor, the corpse of his compatriot fallen in the dirt, tubes hanging from her skin ports, fluid draining from her body. There is understanding, and he groans as his hands try to search his own back for where the blade has already made far too many openings.

Confused hands move from punctured back to vaguely reach forward, then the Trustee goes back to work, putting the Neta-Teej's blade where it ought to be.

There is no stopping until nothing moves. The advocates are empty vessels and the Neta-Teej has fallen slack in the restraints.

In the silence there is a sudden clarity. The shock of the brutality and the quiescence all come together.

It is instinct that makes the Trustee rise, find her tattered and torn jacket, and clothe herself. It is instinct that makes her look at the suits, empty, and walk toward them.

-There are no alarms.-

-In the suits.-

-Why are there no bells?-

The Trustee pulls the female advocate the rest of the way out of her suit and steps into the framework. As she puts weight on the platform, the armor retracts its tubes and the interior panel lights up.

[No Ident] the screen reads.

The Trustee taps the screen. It feels natural.

[Emergency Patient?] it blinks.

The Trustee taps again.

She has no fear.

-No bells. No beacons.-

It is something she cannot fully process.

The suit does not close or move for anyone but the owner, but a small hypodermic slides into the Trustee along her neck. There is no pain. It pulses fluid from inside of her into the suit and displays stats on the screen. Lowering temperature and excessive adrenaline, supply waning. Injuries are identified on her ribs and on the back of her head. Concussion is identified. Significant signs of muscle loss due to malnutrition. Liver degradation. High levels of amino acid coupled with low electrolyte levels.

[Compensate?] the screen asks.

The word makes her want to cry. The Trustee taps the screen.

A wave of euphoria takes her as the armor gives her what she needs and things become clearer.

-No alarms.-

-No transmissions.-

-The suits are all off chain.-

-For advocates to have their fun.-

-Beyond prying eyes.-

-Beyond protection.-

-Breaching protocol.-

-Or is it Lucien's protocol?-

When the needle retracts, the Trustee steps out and reassesses everything.

The Neta-Teej is crying and that is a good thing, a sign of life. Ze is still slack against the chains, eyes closed.

The Trustee pulls the red tunic down and finds a blanket to throw over the little god, frail body shaking. There is visible damage all around the boney face and neck. Wrists and ankles are black and cut from the freezing shackles digging into them.

It is instinct again that drives her to come close for a moment, to hug the sobbing entity. She wants to rest a hand against the back of the poorly cut hair and pour more from her flask, now empty. She wants to put her forehead against this creature and no longer be alone.

But with the slightest touch, the Neta-Teej convulses and kicks, screaming like a wounded animal, thrashing away.

-Do not. Not now.-

-I won't.-

The Trustee stands and looks around at the blood and death and realizes she is shaking and twitching without control.

It occurs to her that the doses from the suit may have been rather high as she hyperventilates in the quiet, nothing but her heartbeat and her fog filling the blue room, sweat and warm blood making a cloud of expired life that hangs and lingers.

Her mouth gasps, fishlike. She is unable to fully match her inhales to her opening mouth, but the air gets in and out anyway.

The female advocate's body is turning blue in the cold, so heavily perforated the blood crawls out and makes mounds as it coagulates and then freezes over the dirt.

The man is still tangled in the chains but is in the same state of emptiness.

The Trustee's jittery hands move the chains and the robes, careful not to touch the Neta-Teej's legs. She drags him to the wall and as she looks at the tattoos, military markings on him, the advocate symbols, the Trustee begins to realize what has transpired here, what it means.

"Are you okay, Trustee? Are you hurt?" asks the sweet voice, broken and cracking, only a hint of calm returned.

The Trustee turns to look at the bound entity.

The Neta-Teej's eyes are open again, innocent eyes, glassed over, numb to the fear, but still showing all the bloodshot damage from the strain.

The Trustee just stares and shakes her head. "What do you need? I have medicine. I have a kit."

The Neta-Teej says nothing, black bruises growing on hir neck in the shape of human hands, evidence of how close death was.

Glassy eyes show the vague panic hidden behind dissociation. The voice is soft and horror creeps in with every word, a hopeless desperation. "No way out now. No way out. They'll find us. The bodies. They're going to kill us. They're going to kill you."

The Trustee, her thoughts sped by the drugs, wants to find an avenue for hope but her focus cannot disconnect from the Neta-Teej, cannot detach from the voice. It rings in her mind and she just stands and listens, frozen.

The Neta-Teej is crying under hir words. "This was supposed to happen. This was always what was going to happen. No way out. No escape. They're going to find us."

The Trustee shuts her eyes and tries to think.

-This was not supposed to happen.-

-Be patient.-

-I have done this. Killed advocates.-

-Patience.-

-I don't want to die like this.-

-With the Neta-Teej here?-

-I don't want this one hurt. Ze should not have to see it.-

The Trustee feels tears on her face as she tries to fathom a way out. The bodies and the empty armor refuse to allow for that possibility. No way to hide all the evidence on the open ice. No way to move the heavy suits alone.

-You could run. Just run.-

Her body shakes in anticipation, a deep drive to explode and disappear.

-Get far enough and there will be no Neta-Teej to watch as you die.-

-Head to the pit and jump in.-

-No eyes at all.-

-Ghosts in the abyss.-

-They won't see you.-

-I'll know they're down there.-

-Use the blade outside to end it.-

-Be patient.-

-It's getting harder and harder to be fucking patient.-

"Trustee!" screams the Neta-Teej and the Trustee turns to see hir contorted face. The Neta-Teej has been screaming at her for a while, that's clear enough, but the Trustee is just now hearing it, lost in thought and the adrenal haze.

"What?"

A rhythmic thumping rises above the sound of the wind. It seems to come from all over but is loudest from directly above.

The Neta-Teej hides beneath the red robes.

The whole shack surges and shakes with the thumping and the Trustee covers her ears as she looks around, waiting for impact.

First, a crack appears on the ceiling and then a hole is ripped through wood and ice and thatch. Pieces of the roof disappear into the night, pulled free.

The Trustee throws herself over the Neta-Teej and is shoved to the ground as pieces of the weak structure collapse inward and the blue light shakes and dims and then goes out.

The rhythm overpowers the wind gusts and doesn't stop as ice blows in. The Trustee remembers the sound well but does not know why.

When the Trustee can look up, she sees the birds have landed inside, avoiding the rubble, their talons digging into the ice. They stand as high as the walls, two falcons larger than the suits, wings freshly folded back and feathers fluttering iridescently.

Glass eyes assess the death and wreckage.

One falcon steps forward, towering over them. It lifts a clawed foot and dips its head, trying to see past the Trustee to the Neta-Teej beneath.

The Trustee scrambles to her feet and slashes with the knife, realizing how foolish it is as she looks up at the massive creature, entirely made of shining metal.

The bird shifts only enough to avoid the strike, then lunges at her with its beak, snapping so close to her face that she stumbles backward and falls.

Flustered, the bird shakes its head and mantle, displacing ice crystals and frost from the tips of its wings. Its whole body rings with the soft clatter of metal feathers.

-Sent by the Falconer of Europa.-

On the other side of the cell, the second bird places a massive set of talons on the cut-up body of the female advocate, rolling it easily, before sinking the claws in at the small of her back, gripping the spinal column tightly. It lifts the body without effort and hops to the pockmarked suit of armor and grabs it by the leg, knocking it over onto the ground. The shield swings and clatters.

The falcon closest to the Neta-Teej dips its head, and this time the Trustee knows to keep her distance as it nudges the foot of the bound entity, gently pushing with the side of its head, careful to keep its sharp beak aimed away.

The Neta-Teej recoils, both from the cold and the fear, but looks out at the bird and says, "I am still alive."

The bird stands up and ruffles its feathers and makes a noise, low and short. The other one matches it. They look at each other, then at the Trustee.

The Trustee doesn't move, staying on the ground.

The second falcon opens its wings wide, and with a pulse, the walls shake and the whole room is awash as it takes off, dragging the heavy suit and the woman's body along the ground before getting lift and rising into the windy night.

The first falcon stares at the Trustee inquisitively. The moment lasts far too long as she stares into the eyes, now imperious and testing. She expects to be attacked, hauled away with the advocates.

-It would be better.-

-For you.-

-There would be fewer questions.-

-For you. There will be plenty regardless.-

But then the bird moves, unnaturally large and graceful, and it too takes a body and the scaled suit of armor and absconds into the black.

As the solitary cell returns back to windy cold, the Trustee finds herself shaking with fear, sweating out what the suit has injected, and struggling to keep up.

-*Remnant fear.*-

-*Chemicals and battle and memories.*-

-*Impossible to shake it.*-

-*Just ride it out.*-

-*I don't remember.*-

-*Not too much to recall.*-

-*The fear is in your bones, whether you mind knows it or not.*-

-*Europa?*-

-*Yes. That is where it started.*-

-*Just ride it out.*-

She crawls to the Neta-Teej, who is struggling against the heavy chains, trying to turn over, trying to curl into a ball.

"They're gone," says the Trustee.

"No. No. No," chants the Neta-Teej, barely audible.

"They're gone."

"You aren't."

"No, I'm still here."

"I told you to go. Go away. Get away. Now."

"You need a medic. I can help you."

"You have to leave. You have to. Just go. Go or you will die," says the Neta-Teej, crying as the skinny body rolls amid the chains and blood.

The Trustee pulls the blanket back over the sobbing deity and then steps away.

26

It takes a hard shove to open the steel door, the whole structure now crooked, the ceiling caved in, and portions of the walls toppled over. The Trustee kicks the base of the door to get it shut and makes sure the latch goes back in place. There is no reason for it beyond, in her adrenal haze, she knows that's where the latch should be.

It's incredibly dark, and for half a moment she considers going back into the cell to get her light, but thinks better of it, muscles unwilling to work for such things, unwilling to return to the broken room.

She looks up into the windswept night, a sky without stars, only clouds running over the flat. All the uncertainty of what could lurk there, what could be hiding, wings churning to keep aloft, or hung there, high up, with a gravity all its own. Fear builds again.

-*Go.*-

It is in the Neta-Teej's voice.

-*Go.*-

The Trustee steps out in the night and keeps her eyes upward, twisting to look into the heavens, a ceiling of cirrus clouds, looking for what she knows is watching from far above.

-This is a quiet little spot now.-

-It's a long way back to the shed.-

-Open and flat. Nowhere to hide for a klick or so.-

-You were pulled to a remote extreme. Now pushed out, to be pulled along again at a later time.-

-Over and over again.-

The slight glow of the shed is visible far off in the distance where the fires are burning. She imagines how warmth might feel. Behind that there are the lights on the flanks of the Osai, enough of a focal point.

As she walks, the night cold hits her chest, and she cannot seem to get the jacket closed, until she realizes it's ripped wide open. She folds her arms over and looks for her hat. It's in the breast pocket, and then she goes for the empty flask.

-There used to be more.-

-More of what?-

-Just ... more, I guess.-

In the cold, a waning burn traverses her body. It's familiar, like the fear, and she knows she's experienced it before. It's a surge of chemicals that the suit of armor has given to her, and they erode her insides, the corners of veins and arteries worn away, at least in feeling. The muscles swell and hint at demands to burst. She knows it won't take long for it all to fade away, but she'll have to eat it for the time being.

To the north and south, no hills or mine visible, the sky and the black distance merge together. Her eyes constantly sweep the landscape, but now also jerk back to the clouds to satiate the night's new fear.

She wonders if the shadow of the running child will return, will weave in and out of the darkness across her path, arms outstretched, head tilted back, also looking into the sky, perhaps searching for predators in the heavens.

The night knows all because it must know, intimately, what it conceals and what it produces. Nothing moves in the night without giving a bit of itself over, without making itself into something a little more like shadow, thriving at the very edge of a spectrum.

So, when the shadow of a man approaches, the Trustee knows her form has been seen as well.

She looks back, seeing that she is still rather close to the solitary cells, still quite far from the shed, caught out on the bled.

"452A!"

She doesn't answer shadows. The night doesn't like it. It doesn't like the human sounds after what's been done.

"Trustee," he says as he gets closer, face angry and eyes a little wild. "Trustee, is the Neta-Teej alive?"

She nods and his expression shifts into confusion and relief. She has never seen his face look like this before.

And he has never seen her so beaten before.

-This one's been through it. Look at her hands. Look at her face.-

He makes out the welts swollen on her cheeks and the bruised skin along her neck. Her uniform hangs in shreds over her shaking frame.

"The advocates?" he asks, "are they still back there?"

She shakes her head. "Dead."

"Dead?" And now he is shaking his head. "Shit. We need help here. We can't lift the suits. It's too far to the burn pit without four or five more men. Then we'll have to cover the tracks."

She just stands, body wavering as this other trustee rambles on about what needs doing.

-What's his patch say?-

-681B.-

-He's scared.-

"Fucking right I'm scared," he says, and the Trustee realizes she was speaking out loud. "Get it together. We have to move or they're going to box you up for Lucien. And the Falconer's going to out me and get me put down."

She looks at him in confusion and doesn't respond.

He sees the shock in her eyes, the empty stare into the abyss.

-They beat her clean. Wrung her out. Need to get her out of here.-

The Trustee can't really hear him as he keeps trying to get her to walk with him someplace. Besides, the night doesn't want any more noise. It wants things quiet.

-What brought him out here?-

-He was pushed out to some remote spot, too. Just like you.-

-But he won't get there.-

-Not all the way.-

-Someplace between then.-

-Things orbit here, but they must keep moving.-

-Invisible forces in the night.-

-Keeping the distance, keeping the time.-

-Keeping us all in formation.-

"Trustee, we have to move. Pick your goddamn feet up and come with me. We need to get you off the tundra, and I need to get help. For whatever fucking mess you left back there."

She stares back at the solitary cell as he points.

"You're gonna' die here unless you come with me, Trustee. This isn't time to get stupid. My orders are the Neta-Teej. But I'm not supposed to leave you here."

She can see how scared he is, how he's losing patience, getting louder, arms waving around, grabbing at her. He only wants to help.

There are forces at work, in him and in her. The wind rushes over them, the night, the barren waste doing its work as well. But it all may bow down to something a million miles away, some object which may turn, without us ever seeing, and its mass may move us, driving us in frequencies longer than perception, longer than life. An unknown hand, with nothing like the five fingers of a human god, but still a hand that reaches into our world and moves us deftly. It is the force by which we have come to know teikum. And everything between must follow in its wake, a procession that holds all the life and all the death that will ever be.

"Stop looking back, we need to go," he says.

She is tied to it all, in her vacant state, myopic and weary, but an accomplice to the magnetism of the void. He is striving, willing himself forward by habit and by a weak force called survival. It is outmatched.

The Trustee hits him with the knife in the gut and moves it up, making sure it slides high enough to find his heart.

His hands, previously held high, touching the sides of his head, animated and full of vigor, pause. They slowly fall to rest on her shoulders. Fingers make fists in her jacket as he fails to achieve a breath. The shock in his eyes doesn't leave as he tries to ask her why she's doing it. But the Trustee doesn't look as if she knows and there's really no point, as the knowledge isn't worth much.

681B tries to pull her closer, his impulse to draw a common face close in the moment of death paired with the impulse to crush her, to smother her and snap her neck with his last moments of purpose. But as he pulls, she pushes and the blade reaches further into his core.

His grip loosens and she pulls the blade back.

Air releases from his lungs, his chest muscles held in stasis finally admitting the need to just let go. No more value left in that oxygen.

He falls backward in the snow and stares up into the same sky, low and racing past, but there is no fear in what lies beyond the clouds. He might want to go there now. But the ground is fine, as well. No advocates can make things worse. No Falconer to give orders or threats. No Trustee 452A to watch or keep an eye on. She's irrelevant now. No more stinking bunk houses.

His eyes close and she steps over him, continuing on her way back toward the shed.

-Go.-

-Let him lie there.-

She tosses the knife off to the side, knowing it will be harder to find in the snow.

-Don't look. Just move quickly.-

The Trustee feeds off the walk, forcing a pattern and a rhythm to her steps, letting the burn inside of her rotate from leg to leg, running through her chest, where her heart shakes and seems to vibrate after every beat.

-Not long until the chemicals wear off. The buzz will go away.-

-You will consume it. Every molecule.-

-And the pain?-

-Even the pain,- she lies to herself.

By the time she sees the barracks houses she knows she needs to sleep, to get to her bunk and let the round just be done. Patrol all the way to the bed.

On the way around the corner of the barracks house, she uses the spigot to clean the blood from her hands and then heads up the stairs.

-No 681B to watch me arrive.-

The last thing she does before entering the barracks is check the sky, one final glance up to see if something is flying overhead, watching.

Once inside, in the dark, there is a moment of relief. The room is quiet, almost warm, and with the mattress against the door she can be sure of some rest.

The quiet isn't entirely enough as she lies back on the bed and her muscles continue to alight with fire. Her ribs ache and her ears now ring with a low, rhythmic rush. But there is no sky to look into.

The Trustee doesn't want to hold onto the fear or the pain. Of course, the memories of what has happened must fade with it. The face of the Neta-Teej, the sound of the voice and the kind words and the screaming all dissipate. It's slow at first, then it happens quickly, everything caught in the net and pulled away from her present mind.

-So many gaps.-

-Too many heavy fixtures in the mind.-

-They rotate and I see them-

-But they never touch. Unwilling to share themselves.-

-Only chaos in between.-

-Chaos and pain.-

-Why can I not slip away there? To that in between place?-

-You do. You are going there now.-

-But I always come back. It's up there. Way up.-

-You haven't come to rest yet.-

-I am not allowed to rest yet.-

-You move based on the force of others.-

-We all do.-

-Push to pull.-

-Nexus to nexus.-

-Stability by staying at a distance.-

-Sometimes I get too close.-

-It will happen again. It is the way of it.-

The Trustee counts her breaths, making sure each gulp of air is full and real, not just a trick of the mind, not just a simple motion to wear the mask of respiration. The ache in her chest and ribs is enough to keep her present as she strives to forget, as she closes her eyes against the tears and the shakes and wonders what force will act next.

-I am glad you're here, Trustee. No matter why you've come.-

27

Someone pushes open the door to the barracks house, and wind whips in.

The mattress slides across the room with sudden violence.

The Trustee sits up after she collides with the far wall and looks around, dazed and in shock. There is a sickness in all her organs.

Armored suits flood into the room, the desiccated sort, steel panels blotchy with the edges turned up, real battle suits that have been hit with stones and fire and plasma. These are not just guards.

-I can smell the stink of the cellar on them.-

-Advocates.-

She groans out loud.

They all stand around, very close to the Trustee, as Nystrom and a Second Lieutenant approach.

Colonel Nystrom is in command armor, a fast suit, lightly weaponized and clean, face shield and helmet pulled back. Outside the Osai, escorted by a cadre of advocates, the suit is mostly for warmth, only a few guns on her.

Nystrom roams around the Trustee's quarters, looking at the few items in the room, hoping to catch something out of place or relevant to their investigation.

The Colonel knows missing advocates are not taken lightly by the UTC High Command, especially when it's a Captain and First Lieutenant that got lost in the night, suits and all. Even if they're just out playing their own games. And that could be the best outcome at this point. They need to be rounded up and brought back.

The Second Lieutenant, now the highest-ranking advocate, is playing things rather tightly now that there's a mess to be cleaned up. They stand at the ready, but are focused on nothing but the Trustee, disheveled and beaten, covered in blood.

"Trustee 452A," says Colonel Nystrom as the Trustee rolls around, trying to get situated on the mattress. "You look like you've been in a fight."

They've all noted it, this Trustee with her face a patchwork of black and blue. Bruising has raised one eyelid and sagged below the socket, but the eye is still usable. Her hands are almost clean but there's blood under the fingernails and a hint of red on her skin, stuck in the callus on her palms.

The Trustee looks around and realizes her eye is swollen. She raises a hand to touch it and winces, "Fuck".

"Does that hurt?" asks the Colonel with some sarcasm in her voice.

The Trustee doesn't answer. She's looking down at her ripped-up coat.

"Get up, Trustee," says the Second Lieutenant. "Strip down."

It's all a daze as the Trustee stands, unsteady on the mattress. She's lightheaded and feeling weak, cold, surprised at all the pain on her midsection. As the coat comes off, she really starts to shiver.

There's blood soaked into her shirt and the Second Lieutenant steps forward to take the garments as they are removed.

The blank face shield is always squared to the Trustee, and she tries not to look at the advocate, more fearful of her own reflection in the glass than the legionnaire inside.

As she shakes in the cold, everyone counts the black marks and red impact sites ringing her torso. Scrapes and cuts cover her elbows and forehead. They also note her build, still muscle on the body after all these years in the camp.

"Trustee," says the Colonel, eyes down, not wanting to look at the battered body.

"Can I put my coat back on, sir?"

"No," says the simulated monotone of the Second Lieutenant.

"Yes, you can," says the Colonel, who then turns to the advocate. "We need her alive if she's going to answer any questions. You're angry. I am sure Lucien will be angry. But what if he wants her alive?"

There is a face behind the shield, stoic or irate, eyes full of drug rage or sleepy like the professional killer an advocate is, but no one can see their face and they say nothing in response to the Colonel.

Nystrom turns back to the Trustee. "Get your coat back on and sit down. We have questions."

"Yes, sir," she says as she looks down at her own body, hands running over all the welts and checking her ribs.

"Trustee, we already know a great deal."

The Trustee draws her coat on and sits on the mattress, wrapping it around her bare chest and shoulders. It is a relief to no longer stand, and the brain fog lessens a little.

"What happened to you?" the Colonel asks. "What did you do?"

The Trustee stares at her, and then her eyes wander to the advocates. "I don't remember."

"You don't remember anything?"

"I don't know, sir."

"You don't have any open wounds?"

"I don't think so. Just a bit beat up, I guess."

"And you don't know why you're in this state, Trustee?"

"No, sir."

"You have blood all over you. We're going to test it to see whose it is. But we already have a pretty good idea."

The Trustee looks around at all the advocates and she too is starting to get an idea that something has gone very wrong.

"Your blood was at solitary. So, we know you were there."

"Solitary?" she asks, almost not recognizing the word, bewildered.

"This is no time to play dumb, Trustee," says the Second Lieutenant.

"No, sir," she says.

"Whose blood is on your shirt and hands?" asks the Colonel.

But the Trustee is still processing the 'solitary' comment. "What happened at solitary? Is...is the Neta-Teej okay?"

"You tell us," demands the Second Lieutenant.

"The Neta-Teej was raped and then strangled," says the Colonel after waiting a moment.

The Trustee lowers her head and stares down at her hands, really looking hard at the blood under the fingernails, like she might be able to divine the owner, like the DNA is right there for the reading.

-*Was it me?*- she asks herself.

"Is the Neta-Teej alive?" she asks aloud.

"Yes. The Neta-Teej's blood is also at the scene. So was yours. But two advocates are missing. The mess at solitary is mostly from them."

The Trustee looks up, confused. "Dead advocates?"

Nystrom doesn't move, but all the advocates shuffle a little, betraying some agitation and distress.

"We don't actually know if they are dead or not. We cannot find them. And then there is the matter of the other trustee," says the Second Lieutenant.

"681B," says the Colonel.

"What did he do?"

"Not much, from what we can tell. He got himself stabbed in the heart."

Her mind speaks up inside itself.

-I remember that.-

It comes back in a strange flood, eye to eye with the man, his clenched teeth and the sound of the wind in her ears.

-Better to say nothing.-

-But I remember it. I do.-

-Good. Great. Keep your mouth shut.-

"You know anything about how that went down?" asks the Colonel.

The Trustee looks at the red-brown shirt the Second Lieutenant has in his grip and then at the Colonel and shakes her head.

"I don't remember."

"Trustee, you understand the situation, don't you?"

The Trustee nods her head in the affirmative, starting to piece things together.

"This is your best?" asks the Second Lieutenant, auto-voice flat.

"Take her to the Osai," says the Colonel bluntly. "Don't hurt her."

"We don't take our orders from you," says the advocate.

"I am the ranking officer," says the Colonel, turning to the towering suit of armor next to her, acutely aware of all the other advocates surrounding her. "There's two dead advocates already, and you want to jump rank? I am a colonel and you're a fucking duster. Lucien isn't here. You take my orders, or the advocates will be going back to their hole in the ground a little lighter."

"Haven't closed our investigation. You might have had something to do with this."

Nystrom sneers and shakes her head. She turns to two other advocates. "You two, escort 452A to the Osai. Command level. Brig box. She better get there safe or Lucien will know."

They move forward, following her orders for the moment.

"You," says Colonel Nystrom to the Second Lieutenant. "Your commanders left a lot of fluid up here in my fucking shed. I think they lost a lot of it out on the ice. So now you're trying to play it safe. Cover your ass and make it look like you have a fucking handle. But you don't. So, fall in, because as much as you think you're untouchable, do you assume I'm any different? I keep the UTC off the General's back. I keep the surface clean and tidy. That is, except when your squad shows up and starts to bleed. Get your shit wired and get back in the cellar before anything else happens to your group."

"She should be our gift. Our sacrifice to the General."

The mechanized soldiers grab the Trustee by her arms and she shuffles her feet, barely touching the ground.

"Those orders will have to come direct from Lucien," says the Colonel. "You may pretend to not take orders from me, but I certainly do not take orders from you."

"Lucien won't appreciate our thinned ranks without explanation."

"Then send him a message from the Osai. That's your explanation to give."

"We'll take her head, at least. As tribute."

"You will wait," she barks. "Make your report and send it to the cellar. Wait for a response if you want, if you really think Lucien will answer you, but you won't take my best trustee without her answering some questions in a controlled environment.”

The advocate takes a moment and then says, “681B worked the portal. Worked the opening of the pit into the Kemwer deep. That position is now vacant. Who's the lucky trustee to get that job?”

“Maybe it'll be this one,” says the Colonel, looking after the Trustee. “If you can stop yourself from killing her.”

“Might be a kindness,” says the flat voice. “General Lucien might have something to say about it. But the Kemwer doesn't say much when he comes over the threshold with his raiders.”

The Trustee hears it all as she's carried out to the walkway and dragged down the stairs toward the yard, jacket hanging open.

-Did I really kill 681B?-

-I remember doing it. But not why. Not where.-

-I don't want to guard the portal.-

-Long way down.-

They drag her across the yard and through the gates and into the Osai's cargo-level. The Trustee notes there is no interaction between the cellar legionnaires who escort her and the surface guards who stand at the field doors to the guardship.

Inside, they prop her in the corner of the lift, the two massive suits squeezing her into the wall.

The air is warm on command level, but it is a short-lived comfort.

Around the corner from the lift, opposite the bridge, is a narrow hall with a panel of doors. Behind each door is a small room, only a meter on each side.

The first door opens, and the Trustee looks in.

The floor is made of open metal grating over a subfloor and a drain. There are no lights.

The two advocates push her in, and she goes willingly,

knowing there is no point in resisting, knowing there's no real way out of any of this.

They shut the door without a word, sealing the Trustee in darkness.

She has shut in prisoners before. She's brought a few up to command level, but mostly to detention level, where the boxes are smaller and tighter.

The Trustee has also been there to remove prisoners and has seen what can happen to them after days in the box. The carbon dioxide buildup in their system, the waste pooling, the joints screaming to extend themselves but unable to find the space.

She crawls to a slouched sitting position.

In the dark the Trustee tries to gather her thoughts, to take inventory of actual memory as she sits on the grating.

-Where was it? Where did I kill him?-

-Out in the open.-

-Nighttime.-

-Did he hurt the Neta-Teej?-

-Did you hurt the Neta-Teej?-

-I don't know.-

-And the advocates?-

-What about them?-

-They're going to take me to Lucien. They're going to skin me alive.-

-The Colonel might stop them.-

-Nystrom isn't your friend. That's just part of the pattern.-

-The pattern?-

-The thread through the chaos. It follows patterns and the pattern is expanding.-

-Is the Neta-Teej okay?-

-Ze is still alive. And that is why the pattern continues to proliferate, iteration by iteration.-

The Trustee shakes her head, wanting the voice gone, wanting her brain to stop. She finds she has just enough room to lean against the wall. It's a position that will become more and more horrible the longer she stays in the box.

-*I don't know what any of this means.*-

-*You aren't meant to.*-

-*Was I there? At solitary?*-

-*That is unimportant. You still have a long way to travel and there are many who want to hurt you now. More than before.*-

-*For what I've done?*-

-*Because your purpose runs counter to theirs. And it is becoming clear.*-

-*I have done bad things.*-

-*Undoubtedly. Without question.*-

-*Should I feel guilt?*-

-*Guilt? Feeling? None of it will change the pattern. It will not change your purpose. Do not make the mistake of asking questions about guilt. You've wandered beyond the threshold. The choices have already been made and there isn't a question or an answer that can change the course of it.*-

-*So I am damned?*-

-*What does it even mean to be damned?*-

-*I know the feeling.*-

-*More questions. But never the right ones.*-

-*Who are you to say what a good question is?*-

-*I am a part of you. You have said your piece. You said it a long time ago.*-

28

It was on the first day said:
If the poor human race were not so arrogant,
It would have been given much by its good heritage.
But because the human race does not take heed,
It lies in such straits and must be held in prison.

Yet, our dearest seers, mothers, fathers, makers,
They do not regard our mischief.
They leave us lovely gifts by which many a man may come to light.
Though the chance is seldom for these gifts,
Are not better prized nor reckoned as more than fable.

Therefore, in honor of the feast we shall hold today,
That grace may be multiplied, a good work shall be done.
The rope will now be lowered.
Whoever may hang on it shall now be free.

-Modified After the Chymical Wedding
of Christian Rosenkreutz
Europa Archives - Recovered from

Marius Colony Mainframe, Europa

//**M**emo: Assessment of the Willett Prison Encampment - UTC Document #4563910 - Aitken Basin//
While the United Terran Coalition no longer exists on a single planet, having spread to several others within our solar system, the population under our watch has increased dramatically, especially over the last three generations.

No government like us has existed before. There have always been democracies, always theocracies. The United Terran Coalition has both, visible, real, existing alongside each other. Economic systems have come and gone, but the extremes of capitalism and communism both exist under our purview. The Coda of Unification demands that opposites be adjoined, and the middle ground be found. How else do you combine that which is diametrically opposite? Good governance, prosperity, comes from this compromise, this willingness to touch on the human needs rather than just satisfying a bureaucratic hunger or previously identified process.

But there can never be complete satisfaction and there can never be a perfect meshing of a population's needs. Perfect reciprocity is not possible.

Across all the minds, all the souls. Across the world. Town to town and continent to continent. Across the stars, planet to planet. There will always be those who seek to undermine the system, even one as loosely governed as ours. At no other time in human history have so many found the freedom to live their lives without daily government oversight, without religious persecution, with the ability to move swiftly and widely among the territories of this planet. Yet, the need for rebellion and structure and combat and extreme thinking are also human needs.

As populations increase in density and cultural intermingling becomes the norm, the inevitable backlash arises from those who do not understand the system or struggle to operate in it. Resource scarcity precipitates class-based stratification of the population, and subsequently, the territories in which they live. Class stratification most easily occurs along previously existing planes of differentiation, now exacerbated by the system's density. The feedback loop continues, and this stratification permeates to all elements of human life, from education and travel to food, and ultimately, to survival. The subset of the population with the resource advantage, the subset with the least adaptation required to find equilibrium, will perceive a threat and that threat must be dealt with. This is Darwinian, a natural outcome of any social construct, and there is no avoiding it. Some will rise and some will fall. Society's only real purpose is to manage this conflict, to establish a path to solution without death and bloodshed. But rebellion can be born of many things, survival or disagreement.

This rebellious desire was assured long ago. This need inside all humans is older than old. Societies have dealt with these issues since the beginning of time. Small groups have asserted dominance over dissenters via trial by combat. Larger still and you see the shunning's, the stockade, the public canings. These were excellent for their personal and intimate nature. The town rejects your rebellion and will not tolerate it. It is the town passing judgement, not some separate law or authority. Grow even larger and you have the social development of jails and prisons and within the metropolis you have the territory on "the wrong side of the tracks" to collect those who cannot abide by the system. Now less personal, less intimate, but necessary based on the natural progression of things. Even if a territory is prosperous, if it is not 'as prosperous' as the adjacent population, there will be strife. Even if survival is assured, there will be friction and crime and the proliferation of more human needs that cannot be fully met. This is, again, the natural progression and it has been witnessed a billion times throughout human history. These territories can become a sort of prison after a time.

But the United Terran Coalition has a much larger problem. There can be millions of these complicated interactions on all our continents, all our worlds. Percentage wise, we have much less crime, violence, and social unrest than any previous government or religion to ever exist. Yet, when you take our almost one hundred billion citizens into account, spread across the solar system, the number who demand some form of trial by combat is large. The number who push against the system is larger still.

To preserve the wider population, there was an early attempt to allow local governance to take precedence, to allow for intimate punishments set by the micro-society, but these punishments were too harsh, or not harsh enough. Out of this unsteady hand, the individual freedoms guaranteed by the Coda of Unification were not being upheld, or the whole micro-society would simply tolerate the anti-establishment behavior, thus oppositely impinging on the freedoms guaranteed by our society.

Small prisons were opened, and punishments were set equally throughout the UTC. Recidivism was low, but not low enough, and those who could not be reined in became increasingly vocal.

There are challenges with planetary distances, challenges of control and equal application of law and system. A prison planet could not be formed, as it would be nothing but a breeding ground for more challenges. Concentrated and earth-bound was the only solution, so removed areas were selected, Antarctica and Greenland, still harsh, but warmed to habitable levels. The Empty Quarter and the Outback, harsh again, but isolated.

Usage of small islands was prohibited by the Graves Armada, their eyes always watching from the seas, the only military threat to our guardships. The Graves Armada should not have any control or say in how we deal with our people, as the Armada themselves are not counted among our population, even as they float around us on their deep-sea vessels. Undoubtedly, they drown their rebels. Where else to put them when space on a seagoing ship is at a premium? Execution is not simpatico with the Coda and we could not have that as part of our punishment system. It is barbaric and antithetical to the core of the UTC.

By the ten-year mark, the number of prisoners within the Antarctic system, the Willett Prison Encampment, was growing. Run by General Sengra Tuvallia, the prison was set up to mine Thorium and countless other mineral deposits. They accepted the full contingent of prisoners at every arrival. No one was turned away. No communication was ever sent requesting a hold on the next group of prisoners. This was in contrast to the other locations, which were having issues with local populations encroaching too close to the encampments, issues of public image and inmate control. They simply could not grow any further.

Only the Antarctic system was able to accommodate the numbers provided, and it absorbed the relocation of all the other units without complaint. A giant surface mine opened along the Willett Range, and while the ore was being mined at an excellent rate, the UTC began to ask questions. These questions were never formally answered, but by then it was clear the Willett Encampment was the only option. Establishing counts and whereabouts for prisoners within the system was no longer in the UTC's interest. This was the only place where the prison would not advertise how large it was becoming.

The mine itself, the thousands of shafts hewn into the basement rock, met complex cave systems far more extensive than could be patrolled. Every prisoner who had failed to assimilate into society at prior opportunities was delivered into an abyss whose capacity for consumption was without equal. Every ship load was accepted. Messages did not get out, stories did not get out, and neither did prisoners or guards. [Amended: Neta-Teej writings // Split River]

This isolation preserved the remainder of the UTC population in countless ways, but the escalation of the prison project left no room for review or reform. The depths were hidden and so deeply rooted. The Willett Prison Encampment was one of a kind, a recognizable but unique solution to a human problem beyond a scale ever before seen. It was the natural progression required to match the natural evolution of our societal growth. Without it, we would not have the peace or freedom to look inward.

29

Armor Record:

      Log Entry: #12/2/2339-002 - General Ezra Lucien

      Location: Ungridded (Beacon Off)

//(They all call it the parade, the long passage that moves through the earth at the base of the lifts, unifying the mine and giving it a central connection. In fact, it is only a crosscut between the deep transects. Nothing more. The prisoners have given all of those transects names as well. But these names do not exist to fulfill themselves. These tunnels do not exist to fulfill themselves. The caves they interact with did not simply come into being. The tunnels follow veins of ore or alluvial deposits and were made by human hands. The caves were made by water. This is their purpose, their reason for being, to make way, to be voided. Yet these prisoners have turned a mine into a bastardized society. They long so much for a metropolis, they have imagined one here, made it so. Taken the empty and adorned it.

Humans have always imagined societies at the center of the hollow earth. Now these prisoners have come to know it well.

They call themselves 'utza', a population that resides here, created simply by existing in such a harsh place.

They call out to each other in the darkness. They call out to shadows they think they recognize. They sing when the walls are close and you can hear their humming voices, the way they harmonize as they move along the tunnels in formation, pickaxes dragging behind them. Animals are always clattering or talking. It is amazing how loud it can get. It is amazing how they change the names of things in an attempt to give them soul. This is my axe. This is the parade or the drag. Should one be sad when the parade is empty, or should they be sad when it is full? What do they mean?

Soon the parade will be full of prisoners on exchange, a promenade of fresh bodies pushing their way through the openings. It is just the same as how, eons ago, a vein of ore pushed its way through the same stone, seeking lower pressures, seeking a place to crystalize, to precipitate. But this vein of humanity is ephemeral and will walk away, distribute itself and work. Then, in time, it will coalesce and remake the parade.

Other rich deposits were taken by gravity long ago, alluvium that spilled out of hills into great fans of debris, percolated through with fluids of mineral worth. Humanity drifts through here as well, seeping lower, leaving residue and detritus upon the angular grains. Then, when the exchange comes, they rise back up, and a new cycle begins.

In between the exchange times, when the prisoners who want to see the shed again have left, it's only the hard ones who live and stay on the parade, willing to forget the sunlight, willing to forget that part of their humanity. They have made this mine a society.

Only societies have cellars. The Earth itself has no cellar. They name it to carry an energy, to make it seem more familiar, even if familiarity is uncomfortable. No one wants to be stuck in the cellar. No one wants to descend into the basement without a light. Bad things lurk there. And it's very true. Ghosts and demons. More names to familiarize a sensation you feel in the dark.

But to most, this is a rigid and unfamiliar place.

I listen to them name the things around them and name themselves and make new songs, and they sing of survival and of the light and the stone. Odes to the world around. These utza. They are makers in their own right, even as their lives blink out by the thousands. They exist here with certainty, for a time. They believe this place is theirs.

But I listen to the advocates as well, my brutal soldiers. All their comm channels tell a different story. They see this place through a blast shield and they see the ghosts in the cellar with their infrared cameras and they know they are a rare breed here, special in their own estimation.

I hear them talk about the utza, reviewing them like little siblings. Like meat on the hook. They have names for all the groups of prisoners. They are all utza in some way, and that is baffling. The advocates, and the surface guards, call the prisoners by the name they themselves adopted. Utza. Is that some sort of victory? It should never have been given, but who am I to stop that great sign of conflict? Are the utza supposed to have names? They do now. So now they are real. Now they are one. Now they are alive and whole despite their lot.

The advocates have their own names for the caverns and tunnels they inhabit. Tiergarten, aviary, meat locker. The list goes on and on. And they own those names. They own those places in their minds.

The comms are full of chatter even between advocates who have never seen each other outside of a suit. Do you like the crop this round? Any ripe ones in your transect? Where did you come from before this? Did you ever get off-world before being sent here? Or were you stuck on first story? They call the outland ghettos the first story because there are no second stories on the buildings. Only mud and metal hovels for as far as the eye can see beyond the real cities. First story is dirty work. Shit work among the ketgan. But we are sub-level here, in the cellar. There can be pride in being low. Just name it and it's yours. Take it into yourself and it is you. You are low. You are a ghost in the darkness.

The advocates make their suits their own. I admit, I have done the same. All the etchings and the patches for repairs. All the extra weaponry they add and test. It is part of how they express themselves. They talk about the new kit, about the new markings. They show it off to each other at rotation. They watch the prisoners and see their reactions.

The utza have come to identify many of the advocates and given them names. The markings on the suits signal who resides within the armor. The symbols identify the faiths, the thoughts, of whomever hides beneath. The advocates ask around on the comm channels to see if anyone hears talk about them. Did they say what I did at the third transect? Did you hear about the group at the portal? I got them good. Everyone saw it.

The advocates are one with this place in countless ways. Slowly becoming a different echelon of utza. A different echelon of prisoner. It is a fascination, something I find wonder in.

But they made it that way. It is a human capacity to mingle and take into oneself that which is around you. It lies at the core of adaptation.

It is also a human capacity to name for rejection. To unmake another human with a name. To dismiss a thing or a place or a person with a label or their association with one. I hear them do it every day, utza and advocates alike. They believe themselves the ones who define reality, unwilling to yield truth to those who are other. In the same breath they accept other into themselves, and then reject it outright as having no real power. Why do they do this?

Language, a name, and familiarity, a history, unify inside us to identify something greater, more powerful, then it really is. Power is something humans desire to be close to, but power outside ourselves can pose a great threat. The deepest human memories spew forth ancient archetypes and, with those images, patterns are made and reality can be formed and understood. This memory is how things are willed into being, making reality by decision.

The Kemwer is a fabled name. So, he has power. He is so close to me. But he is a threat. Would he be a threat without the fabled name? Would others rally around him or his words, the messages written in the portal scrolls?

This mine, this cellar, is the locus of new names, new myths, recursive and resurrected. This cellar digs up the human ghosts, dredging up every human memory and seeing what it is worth.

Without the memory of the sun, this place would be nothing. Without the names, this place would be nothing. Naming is alchemy. It brings soul via memory and familiarity. It is the first step the Falconer mentions in his pursuit to bring life into being. Make a name. Give a history. Create a memory. It becomes a myth. Europa itself, where he did it, is a myth now.

But that will fall away because it is all perception. It is madness. To the contrary, what you forget forces what remains through the crucible of reality.

There is an old story of an alchemist who told his Lord he could teach him to fly through the air. He told the Lord that he himself could fly and that he would make a flying creature of him. The Lord did not fly, after much spending, and the alchemist was burned alive and, legend has it, subsequently cast into hell as a falsifier. Could he ever fly? Did he forget how when it mattered most? The truth was clear regardless: he burned better than he ever flew.

Is it not madness to think one can fly? Is it not madness to think one can name a thing and then own it? Human madness is written through every facet of our history. It's madness that becomes most attuned in dark places, and I am always listening to that madness.

I hear when a man says he made a flying creature, made a metal bird and gave it life, gave it soul. I hear when a woman says she has forgotten her memories. I hear when a youthful deity screams out in the night. I hear when a myth is being made in the deep.

I let them speak. Then I listen to see how the flying creatures respond. I listen to see if the lost memory speaks out on its own. Who echoes the deity's screams? What does the myth say of the destinies of those who use it as a guide, taking names from the narrative?

Humans are all alchemists, but only in their own eyes. The magic they perform tricks only themselves. They are so fixated on the magic, they will themselves to believe it, a show for their own satisfaction.

This is why they keep speaking. It's to keep the performance alive. It's to keep that myth and memory and familiarity close. It helps the stage remain, and the theater goes on.

This is why the cellar will always be mine. Because there is no great becoming. There is no rising up. I will always be at the bottom, waiting for them in the darkest places of their teikum. And they will never hear me because they will always be clattering and talking like animals do. Close Log)//

30

There is only silence in the black box, and it eats at the Trustee.

-The dark plays with my weaknesses, and I can't stop it. I don't like this. This whole mess. Nothing matches up. I don't match up. It's me. I don't ... can't ... find a reality that I believe in.-

She searches hard in the darkness, mind flashing.

Between her statements, her psyche pauses, naturally, waiting for the intonement of something she has internalized as herself, but it doesn't come. There is no reply.

-Where are you? Where are you? I can't ... I just ... this can't be it. You can't abandon me now. This can't be the end. Nothing is done. Nothing is finished. The little god is still alive. They say. They say that. I am in a box. Just a box, not the cellar darkness. But which box? On which guardship? I am on the Osai. I am not in the cellar.-

The Trustee is used to hearing an internal response come immediately, her own voice returning like a mismatched echo from the back of her mind. Now, it's absence lets the other noises in, the sound of her heartbeat and her panicked breathing, the drip of moisture falling from the top of the box. But it's her own unanswered questions, the half-dialogue of a crazed conversation, which now speaks to a lonely insanity which is only ever thinly veiled inside her.

-You know where I am! You know where to find me! I know you do. But where are you? You can tell me. You are me. But it's me not responding. I'm not answering myself. I'm ... they ... that happened out there? Why do I remember so many empty places but none that are full? There will be questions if they let me out. I won't be able to answer. The memories are gone ... but I don't need to remember. They'll figure it out and ... then I'll be ... I'll be dead. Rotting here. Or they'll just find someone else to pin the blame on. And maybe it was someone else. I'll slip through the cracks. Reality will follow. Is this easier? I don't really want to know what's happening. I already forgot the past, and that must be easier. It has to be, or why would it all just fall away? But I don't want to die. Not in here. The Neta-Teej is alive and they were the one who wanted to die. I know that. Do I know anything else? Do I care? Why should I care? Tell me why I should care!-

There is no reply.

-I've forgotten myself. I don't know me. But there must have been something before this.-

A man appears in her mind, only a pulse of a smiling face, accompanied with sadness and the deepest longing she can imagine. It goes, then returns, then fades and she gropes through the air, reaching for it.

The shade of the child again rushes back and forth across her vision, as if the sky is falling and they are hoping to catch the pieces. The darting shadow makes the box seem to expand, the darkness tricking her sense of space.

-All these people are just shapes. All these faces rattling around in the dark. I don't know who they are. That one. I loved him and he was lost, now lost again and again and again. That one I cared for and they were frightened. Frightened in a way I could never help. Why can't they stay gone? I don't know why they're looking at me and why they

never seem to look away. Why they always run, and I can never find them.-

Time has lost meaning in the dark. The physical discomfort and disorientation have built up until the shape of the box no longer means anything. For all the Trustee knows, there are caverns, like the cellar, beyond the walls, or oceans lapping at the door. There are legions of faces in there with her. All their voices sing out and call to the Trustee in between the beats of her own heart as it echoes in her ears. But not one of the voices brings comfort.

-It's all calling out too quickly. Rushing in, taking me. This is not the time to lose myself. This is not the time to fade away. Where is the Neta-Teej's voice? Where's my voice? Where are you? Why have I not died? I can't stop what I don't understand. And I don't understand myself. There is nothing behind or ahead for me to know.-

She tilts her head up and shuts her eyes tightly, creating a different shade of darkness, interwoven with tiny light bursts across her retina. Stars. She wants to fly into them, to find the little spots in between the light where things might get quiet. It does not occur to her how easy it has become to look away from the light, those bright beacons that have always called humanity forth. Something has changed inside the Trustee, a turning away, and the void is now what seems to hold promise. The empty spots, isolated and without connection, should be the safest places of all.

-You should not go there alone.-

The Trustee almost laughs in relief as her voice suddenly responds. It provides a recursive attachment, a corroboration of perception. This is now real because we agree it is.

-I missed you.-

-You cannot go alone. And you will have to carry those you wish to take.-

-The Neta-Teej?-

-Yes. And perhaps that will be it.-
-That would be enough.-
-Yes. It would be.-

———

Someone knocks on the door of the box, and the sound rings off the walls, seeming to pass through the Trustee as she lies propped inside.

When the door opens, a wash of fresh air and light surge in. At once she feels both relief and shock, the sterile glare from the guardship and the taste of oxygen, a progression toward release, whether by death or by exoneration.

Without thinking or being able to see, she scrambles on hands and knees out of the enclosure, feeling her body scream in stiffness and pain from the injuries she sustained before being locked in. There is only the desire to escape.

As her eyes adjust it appears there's only the Colonel standing before her. But then she sees two suited guards over by the lift and another opposite the Trustee. They all wear clean armor. No advocates among them.

"I need to speak with you, Trustee," says the Colonel, demanding, but without real emotion.

"Yes, sir. You don't need all those guards for me."

The Colonel ignores the statement and tosses a fresh uniform shirt on the ground before the Trustee, then her same old ripped up jacket. "Put your clothes on."

The Trustee groans as she pulls the clean shirt over dirty skin and then puts the ragged jacket back on, paying no mind to the watching eyes. There's a lot of pain, but she wants to cover herself, wants to stretch her limbs and lie down to rest the muscles.

The Colonel watches her, eyes glaring.

A tense silence fills the whole command level. The Colonel leads her around to the other side of the ship. There are no other officers, and all the comms are off. The bridge has been put into lockdown.

Outside, it is early morning and the shallow light confuses the Trustee as it spills through the wrapping window of the guardship.

-*Lost some days in the box?*-

-*Have I missed the exchange?*-

-*Or you were only in the dark for a short time.*-

The guards hang back outside the bridge and the Colonel points to the chair opposite her desk. The Trustee limps over and slowly settles into it, leaving her legs out straight to keep the blood flowing.

"Trustee, what have you got yourself mixed up in?" asks the Colonel, clearly exhausted.

The Trustee shrugs. "I don't know, sir."

The Colonel smiles falsely and shakes her head. "That's not good for you, Trustee. Because you are mixed up. Things happened rather quickly through the night, but now I am at a standstill with all of it."

"I don't understand, sir," says the Trustee, trying to sound like she cares, trying to make it sound like there's concern. It's a tone of voice that's always worked on the Colonel before.

"It's the speed of it all that confuses me," says Nystrom. "We got word 681B was dead outside the beacons and we rallied the guards and advocates to see what the problem was. Two advocates didn't muster. We found the solitary cell trashed and the Neta-Teej still alive in the rubble. The rape and some of the blood were from an advocate First Lieutenant. A great deal of the blood was from a Sergeant Major. You were just lying in your bunk and the blood of all three of the dead was on you."

The Trustee holds her breath as it all gets rolled out before her.

"We have missing advocates and their armored suits. We have a dead trustee. We know you killed them."

"I didn't."

The Colonel erupts, slamming her fist on the table, and then points at Trustee 452A with a predatory look in her eyes. "Don't give me that shit. We know you did it. Whether your broken mind knows it or not."

The Trustee lowers her eyes and looks at the floor, but she shakes her head, rejecting the accusation. Her hands instinctively rise to cover her head, as if being beaten, cowering from the Colonel's yelling.

"Based on 681B passing the gate and the advocates' last check-in, we know it all happened within a span of 30 minutes just after midnight. Advocates killed, suits disposed of, another trustee killed. So, we know you didn't act alone. It wouldn't be possible. Someone was with you."

The Trustee shakes as she tries to focus on breathing, each inhale sending lightning through her ribs back to the spine.

"If we know all this, Trustee, if it's so obvious to me, to the advocates who still want your head, that you didn't work alone and killed UTC officials, three of them, then why did General Lucien, not five minutes ago, send a comm demanding you be freed from the box? Why did he personally comm the surface for the first time in weeks to tell me I have to let a fucking turncoat trustee go free?"

"I ... I ..." stutters the Trustee.

"Don't answer. If you're telling the truth, then you won't remember anyway. You never remember. And I don't want to hear you lie again. Lucien already lies to me enough. Then I lie to the high command for him. Everyone is lying to everyone here, but I know enough to see that you're in the middle of it."

The Trustee feels the compulsion to scream, to release whatever anxiety is building up inside.

-Lucien called for your release.-

-How? Why? What is this about?-

-It's about whatever he wants it to be about.-

-Right now, he's making it about me.-

-To have his attention ....-

-To be in his debt ....-

-Or to mislead everyone else ... and you are just a point of pressure.-

"I can see the tears in your eyes, Trustee. I can see you're confused. And maybe you've lost your usefulness in all of this. Too far gone after what you've done or just burned too far down on the wick in a place made to quicken the burn. But General Lucien has demanded you be set loose. He has made it clear he'll be dealing with you himself when you get to the cellar."

The Trustee doesn't look up.

Nystrom turns her attention to the guards, who are all watching silently, and barks her orders. "Pass Lucien's encryption along to the advocates so they know it was a direct order from the General. Then get them the fuck out of the Osai before they decide to make trouble anyway."

It's only then that the Trustee realizes the Colonel's armored command gauntlet, with a weapons stack, still rests on her desk. Suddenly the presence of all the guards and the absence of any comm officers is clear.

-The advocates are inside the Osai.-

-They want blood.-

-The advocates don't want to leave empty-handed.-

-Nystrom thinks there's danger.-

-To herself.-

The guards all have weapons at the ready as the lift door opens, anticipating that it could be filled with advocates. But it's empty, and several of the guards head down to cargo level.

"Jones," says Nystrom to one of the remaining guards, "you and Naka take the utility ducts down. Spread out on the advocates. They should honor Lucien's orders, but I don't want all of you coming out in single file if they decide they're going to make problems about it. And tell that Second Lieutenant I'm going to report him to Lucien for incompetence and insubordination."

The armored suit nods deeply to show understanding and then heads around to the ladder-well with the remaining guard.

When they are gone, Colonel Nystrom picks up her weapon gauntlet and arms herself before sitting. It's aimed at the Trustee.

"I'm not sure I ever fully trusted you, 452A," she says, letting go of a bit of her anger. "But you and I have spoken about things … that perhaps should have remained unsaid."

The Trustee sits slack in the chair, the faint pulse of something still ringing in her ears, something other than her heartbeat.

"So, now I wonder how much you've told Lucien. I wonder what you'll tell him when you see him next. What will you say about all this? About me? Do you grovel at his feet with the others? Are you part of his little cult?"

"Sir," says the Trustee, "I'm not part of anything."

"We've just spent the morning determining that is a lie. So, I pulled your papers. Your file is practically empty compared to the other prisoners. The system knows almost nothing about you before you arrived at the encampment."

The Colonel leans forward and sets a screen on the desk, revealing only a short list of items in her file.

"There's an interrogation report from when you were processed in Kinshasa, just like any other prisoner. But there's no criminal file, no education or religious file. No prior record at all. Even the wildest ketgan from the borderland ghettos has some sort of documentation. The UTC always knows something."

Nystrom comes round the edge of the desk and takes the

screen from the Trustee's hands. She stands over her for a moment. "There's nothing to see there, Trustee. Just a thousand records the Doctor has written up about your brain. Countless graphs and charts and repatterning metrics. They all say you really do forget things. They all say you need to be studied more. I asked him about you and it's clear he has a fascination."

"My encephalographic signature is erratic," says the Trustee numbly.

"There isn't anything going on between you and the Doctor, is there?"

"No, sir," says the Trustee, "nothing."

"I can't trust your word. I can't trust your memories. But I trust the Doctor's fascination, and he said there was nothing untoward. You've been a problem for him for a while, by the looks of it ... but it's nowhere near the problem you're wrapped up in now. And without a single record to help identify you. An explanation for that is warranted ... if you can remember."

"Sir, did Lucien say anything else?"

"No," says Nystrom, gritting her teeth. "He ignores my requests and doesn't issue any reports from the cellar. But he'll ring up for you at a moment's notice. You're just his little blank file. How long have you been keeping tabs on me for him? On the Priest? On any of the others?"

The Trustee opens her mouth to speak but cannot find words to respond.

Nystrom stands and lifts her gauntleted arm, pushing the barrel of the fracture rifle squarely into the Trustee's sternum.

"I wonder where you came from," says Nystrom, putting force and weight into the gun as it digs into the Trustee's chest. "I wonder how he got your file wiped. And I wonder how he picked you out, what he did to you to make you his. He has a way of doing that. You wouldn't be the first he's sent up. You aren't special to him. But I send mine down. It is a game we play."

The Trustee squirms in the chair as she tries to get out from under the point of the barrel, careful not to make any sudden movements.

"What have you told him?"

The Colonel uses her free hand to strike the Trustee across the face, not a full blow, but enough to refocus her.

"Where did you come from?"

The Trustee shakes her head. "Check the file."

Nystrom hits her again.

"Where did you come from?" she repeats.

The Trustee's eyes return to a compulsion, to check the patches of the Colonel's uniform, to find the gray circle earned on Europa. But she again notes its absence.

"I don't know where I came from," says the Trustee coldly, "but I am not Lucien's. He probably just wants to kill me himself. And if orders are to release me, then I have nothing else to say."

"You take my orders," says Nystrom.

The Trustee shakes her head. "Apparently not."

The Colonel sneers and steps back, swallowing her seething anger. She sits down and removes the gauntlet. "If you ever make it back to the surface, we'll have another talk, Trustee. But I seriously doubt I'll see you again. In the meantime, I'll put you down at the portal. An order you have to take."

"I understand, sir."

"Don't say another word. I don't have any more questions, Trustee. But I do have some things to say to you. Don't bother trying to fade into the utza. All the advocates have your face on file. Lucien has your face on file. He'll find you when he's ready. And don't try to leave your position at the portal. If you desert your post, the advocates will bring you back to the edge of the pit and chain you there for the next raiding party to take. The third transect is contested ground now. We'll see how well your loyalties can keep you. My advice would be to off yourself as quickly as you can, or find someone kind enough to do it for you."

The Trustee just looks out the window to the far hills.

"I don't know what you did in the solitary cell. But the advocates are watching you now. So are all the other trustees. And somehow, through all of this, the Neta-Teej didn't die. Next time maybe. Maybe the rape will be enough to keep hir quiet. Maybe the injuries will be enough to kill hir on the exchange. That would be a turn of luck."

The Trustee closes her eyes.

"How would you feel then, Trustee? Knowing your pet is dead?"

The Trustee opens her eyes again and stands, knowing she is free to go now and that this is only for the sake of cruel words. "May the faiths keep you well in the absence of each other."

"You are a sycophant and a murderer, Trustee. Get out of here and try not to get bled out before you leave the fucking ship."

"Yes, sir. Thank you, sir."

The Trustee slowly approaches the lift, heart pounding in her ears, half expecting to take fracture rounds to the back. But the doors close and she is left to herself.

She feels no relief on the descent. Only fear and readiness. Only a rolling list of all the actions that must be performed in perfect succession if she is to survive the next few minutes.

At cargo level she gets a new jacket and a new hat. Guards watch her closely as she moves all her materials from one jacket to another, pocket by pocket.

The advocates have gone, Lucien's orders having done their work, but she knows they are out there on the shed, rallying the utza back to the cellar.

No one tries to stop her or speak to her as she departs into the shallow morning, tired and in pain, but ready to run, even if it's into the arms of something worse.

31

E xcerpt Private Journal of the Neta-Teej:

Entry 3122 - Paper - Hand Written
-From the Alcove Hiding Place,
Private Quarters of the Neta-Teej

Recovered during Tribal Investigation into the disappearance of
the Neta-Teej from the Tribal Temple

———

If anyone were to read this, I hope you find something worthwhile. I hope what you find is human. I have struggled since the beginning to feel like I am truly part of what we are, part of what everyone else is. I know, intuitively, and through experiencing my own body, that I am human. It is human to feel outside oneself, to feel outside one's species. But that knowledge is of little solace when the great loneliness sinks in, when the loneliness persists even as a million eyes stare at you, even as they all hang on your every word. The gulf between you and them, you and anyone, is overwhelming.

I would sit at the window after the prayer was called out over the square, just beyond the Tribal Temple's walls. I would watch the crowd disperse and fractionate, everyone going their separate ways. But the little groups would form, the families with children at hand, the elderly slowing the whole group down. The lone individuals pushing back into a shop or even better, seeing a friend in the crowd and calling out to them. Hands would raise and people would laugh. Some would file into the temple to get more prayer, to press more flesh, to watch the human acts.

But I would seek out the couples. Just two. Two is enough for me. Hand in hand, walking shoulder to shoulder. No rush. Whispers between them. The smallest of touches and reciprocated motions. A symbiosis so close that minutia becomes a force, an activation energy the other party understands and gains life force from.

Human. Animal. It may or may not be 'love,' as it's often referred to, but it is awareness. A natural growing together. It denotes proximity. It denotes time. It denotes attention and coincidence.

I would watch them and I would long to walk away with them, as three, but I would long more so to be one of them. One of two. I wanted to feel the warm, safe embrace of a powerful but gentle mate, to feel the soft, caring caress of an attentive lover.

I still long for it.

From the others in the Tribe, my peers, I have formed some connection. These are real connections, but there will always be a barrier. It is a barrier of trajectory. We may have the same thought, but where is it aimed? Into teikum? Into each other? Into the people we preach to? Into the scripture? There are always barriers in the lessons.

All the eyes of the world are on us, looking to us for words of faith. But inside the walls of the Temple, still more eyes watch us. All these colleagues, brought together by the philosophy, the belief, chosen to be the ones who carry the 'word' into the future, are just that, chosen. To be chosen provides for proximity and time. But it does not make up for the lack of coincidence or attention.

I was a child when I was chosen. Many of my peers were the same. And we are still children in so many ways. Others, older, have been so sheltered by the Temple, by the structure of the Tribe, that they are no deeper than the rest of us.

It is the loneliest place I have ever known, and it is the place I have known the longest. The Coda of Unification and the practice set forth in the texts cannot always succeed in unification. I am living proof of this, my inner world is proof of this.

Humanness is next to godliness. This mantra, spoken as truth, is something I believe still. But it exists in the couple who sway together down a burnt road. It exists in the way we look to the stars. The worst thing we ever did as humans was to put the gods into words. That is how I know I am no god. That is why I feel so far from humanity. All the words and so little else.

I have no unity with those who I coexist with. No unity to be had with those in the square either. They are already more gods than us inside these Tribal walls. More gods than me, knowing humanity through their own lives. What of humanity am I to know while in the confines of this Temple? What is there to learn of the dynamic human while reading the same old texts over and over? They cannot be ordained any more than they already are.

I read other things, the heretic texts, the portal scrolls. The writings of the Falconer of Europa. I read them over and over and I understand them. I would not allow myself to move on without understanding. But I have never seen the Neta-Teej in them. I am supposedly a guide. But I am blind to those experiences, not in sight, but in soul. The Neta-Teej can see through the lens of hirself, see through another, but can never be allowed to pass through, not in this form. How can one unmake themselves?

It is all either empty or out of reach.

The first time I tried to unmake the Neta-Teej, I did it in the most rudimentary way. I snuck into the deepest part of the gardens and found the inkberries in long clusters, hanging from the red stalks. I ate as fast as I could, knowing there would be pain, and then I crawled under the bent and hanging bows, lying on the ground as the nausea grew and the pain started to stab at me, hot fragments of glass moving through my guts. I broke fresh buds off the plant to smell to calm my stomach. The longer I could keep the berries down, the deeper the poison would burrow.

I vomited red and then went unconscious. It hadn't been enough. But as I writhed under the bush, trying desperately to stay quiet as I cried, I understood that this is how many living things perish. Alone, in pain. Confused and trying to hide themselves to avoid some greater pain upon discovery. For a while, I had been human. Alive at least. It isn't the right way, but it did work.

When they had healed me, I went back to the garden and cried because they had pulled out the old inkberry. They had covered in the hole with dirt and then seeded soft grasses. The plant hadn't been at fault and I had been the mechanism that caused its death.

Proximity and coincidence with the Neta-Teej had brought its end. The guilt was overpowering in the moment, but that guilt and shame has never really left me. Always growing. With every day that passes, I am reminded of the empty place I hold. I fill a space in people, but it is a theft. That space should be filled by them. It should be left empty, if possible. The arrogance that it should be filled with words ... detached words from a god? From me? I couldn't fathom it then and I cannot fathom it now. Human words, stories, songs, whispers between lovers, those could fill that space.

But never me. It was, is, not something I deserve. Not as the Neta-Teej. Too much baggage there, too many empty sermons attributed to gods. Nothing human.

This is why I write this journal. Maybe someday it can be read and understood that I was just a child when I came to the Tribe. I was a child when I tried to take my own life and instead got another life taken away and another one given. I am still a child as I ascend to where my words are spoken adjacent to the Quadrumvirate and find myself seeking and seeing deeper and deeper into myself, into my teikum. The emptiness of this procession may not mean much to you, but it means everything to me.

If you are reading this, it means I have tried to leave the Temple and either succeeded or died in my attempt. Perhaps I will unmake myself in that way, or someone will unmake me for their own purposes.

I believe they will do it, destroy me. I do believe it is planned, that I should be unmade. So, I cannot stay here, even if I wanted to.

The guilt and the shame will never leave. No matter what name I carry, what end comes to my body, or who listens to my words, I will never escape my culpability in what has happened at that prison encampment. I did not know it existed and I know so little about it now. But knowledge and intent are not requisite to contribute to something deeply wrong. Perhaps I will end up there. Perhaps the Coda of Unification will finally have meaning when I am united with those who the Tribe and the UTC has looked away from. Proximity, coincidence, time and attention will be unavoidable if they send me to the mines.

There is guilt in shame in the space that I have stolen from others inner worlds. They see me there when they should see themselves. But we all need space. We all need to be seen as alive and valid. But I look around and do not like the way I see myself.

If there is an empty space for small gods to fill, it would have to be the encampment. It would have to be a bunk, far from the fire, far from the others. That is what the Neta-Teej deserves for guiding so many to that place. It is what I deserve. The only punishment for false becoming, an empty becoming, is to unbecome and possibly try again. That is the human path. It is unlikely I will succeed, but I have to try.

Perhaps these are just the brave words of a safe and lonely child. But my longing will not go away. I cannot see it ever being satiated in this Temple. Death here will not remove the guilt or the shame.

This is why I plan to leave. This is why I will go to Europa if I can make it. This is why I will always come back to try to unmake the mines and why I will go there as a prisoner if I have to, if captured.

I have been quietly told I will have help escaping the Temple. I have been told I will be given safe harbor on Europa. I have been told I will be protected, as much as possible, if I end up in the encampment. But all these voices are from strangers. I trust none of them. Who can I trust? Isn't that why I do not walk hand in hand with anyone? Isn't that why I write to myself and no one else? I do not trust, but to keep moving, I will have to start. A guide has no choices.

32

The evening sky is a shady red as the sun sinks down through the smog and dust. A cloudy air hovers perpetually over the Sevier borderlands.

There are a million crooked shacks across the city, amalgamations of makeshift additions to old and relict structures. Sevier is deep within the first story of North America, a wide swath of outland, running down the middle of the continent between the seaboard mega cities. Each street is gravel and lined with garbage in the gutters. Everyone awakens after dark to avoid the heat.

It hasn't rained in a long while and each building is coated in a film of mingled dirt and oil. The tips of a thousand fingers have etched little designs into any windows that aren't broken. A compulsion to make a mark, a desire to draw something that will be seen by others, even if it is only witnessed by whoever decides to rise up, to ascend, and simply clean the whole window. It is a fruitless task.

Gabriel Shear walks down a side ally about as wide as he is. The tin siding radiates leftover heat from mid-day. He still has a noticeable limp, leaving asymmetric tracks, but it's gotten better over the years. It's one of the distinct characteristics he wishes he could get rid of, not only for more mobility and quickness, but so he is harder to identify. His size is already hard enough, but the limp is a giveaway for anyone who knows what to look for.

His face covering does a reasonable job of protecting him from the hanging dust, but night is coming and, as people emerge from their hovels, the churn begins. Children kick rocks and carts drag the dirt into piles, topped with puffs the powdered silica and ash. It is lofted to thicken the air by the turbulence of the next passing person or pack animal.

As the lights come on at dusk, all different colors and patterns of blinking motion, the hovels start to remind him of the cities, glittering like his first night back from Europa years before.

It was the night she ran away, and there was so much fear.

Down the alley, Gabriel circles through a quiet market, which is only starting to wake up. Vendors of nonperishables have already set up in the best spots, their wares better able to survive the heat. The other shops will open when the refrigerant won't have to work so hard, when the hydroponics systems won't cook their fare, when the water tanks won't get contaminated with the afternoon dust rolling in.

The market is a good place to linger, to take inefficient paths and watch for the tail who has been following him, on and off, for the last three days.

-I know you're there and I know where you came from.-

Tails have followed him before, but always closer to the mega cities. Here, in the outlands, when an identity scanner goes up, it's destroyed or dismantled in the night, parted out. When a drone comes through, it's brought down and the carcass picked clean. So, this follower has been waiting. Probably one of many who are stationed all throughout the ghettos, hired by those who wish to seek him out, those with the means and the intent.

He spots the tail entering the market on the south side, eyes sweeping the carts and shop windows, but there are not enough people to hide him. He isn't clean, but his clothes are too new. This one has done a good job looking the part, but Gabriel has seen too many of these sorts. They are not killers. They are errand boys sent to keep an eye, to send messages back to his family on his whereabouts and actions.

-Messages my family tries to keep secret from the UTC high command.-

He moves toward the follower, making sure his eyes don't lock on the man.

The stalls are tightly packed at this spot, easy to come close for an evaluation, and for a moment Gabriel stands back-to-back with the tail, noting where the man's shoulders mark on his own body, just above the ribs, giving him a clear size advantage.

The other man's stillness is confirmation of ill intent. No other outlander would ever tolerate such an intrusion on personal space in the heat of the day.

Then Gabriel pushes past the man, out into the alley, checks both ways, and takes the direction with the fewest people. Then another turn and another until he can be behind the tail if they decide to pursue him.

From around a tin corner, Gabriel watches the man hesitate to follow the deep footprints he left in the dust. This one has heard the fate of the other followers and is more wary, but he still does his job and decides to follow.

-The money must be good,- Gabriel thinks and quickly turns the corner.

The day is starting, and the streets are going to get busier so he knows he needs to move the tail, get him deeper into the block of buildings so he can stay away from prying eyes and hide the body.

He closes on the tail quickly and the man turns just early enough to strike with a small blade. Gabriel uses his forearm to knock it away, sending the knife into the dust while taking on a shallow wound to the back of his left wrist.

Gabriel holds a length of cord with a handle at each end, and it wraps over the man's head as he stumbles backward.

Before the tail can hit the ground, the cord goes tight around his neck.

Gabriel steps past him, turns and lifts, pulling the cord violently up over his shoulder, and bends forward at the waist, stooping his shoulders and hauling the tail up onto his back. Their shoulder blades strain against each other as the tail's feet kick wildly in the air, his hands clutching at the cord embedded in his neck.

Turning, Gabriel walks with the man struggling on his back, making his way deeper into the complex of tin buildings, away from the busy market only a block away. Elbows strike at his ribs but there's not enough force to them, the man already losing power, unable to get air into his lungs, blood unable to get to the brain.

-Won't be long until he's out. Then we wait.-

He keeps away from the sides of the metal structures, not wanting the man to be able to kick out and make noise, or worse yet, get purchase and knock them over. But when the struggling stops, he quickly takes tighter and tighter passages until he stops with his burden in a secluded alcove, waiting the appropriate amount of time until death has certainly come.

Blood drains down Gabriel's forearm as his hands grip the cord up by his shoulder. Sweat pools in his boots, and his face covering suctions to his mouth with his rapid breathing, his eyes on the dirt before him.

It is quiet as he waits, but his heart beats loudly in his ears. He counts the beats and marks the minutes.

When it's over, enough time for brain death, he lowers the body, removes the cord from around the neck, and leaves the alley, noticing that his limp has worsened with the exertion and the heavy load.

There's no time to really check his arm and he doesn't want to leave blood, so he wraps the cord tightly below his elbow and moves.

He takes a different way out to the main streets, passes back through the market, and makes for the contact location.

Two sectors over, he's in another alley, which terminates at a door with a beer glass painted on it. When it opens, air washes over him into the street, reverse pressure to keep the dust out. He closes it tightly and edges into the dim room. It has low ceilings, a few round tables and a long bar with bottles behind it. Only about half the lights are on, as the place isn't properly open yet.

A woman sits in the far corner, a frac rifle trained on him, but he can't really see her in the dark. This is the way these meetings always start with the contacts. Seldom a repeat messenger but always the shoot first sort.

"Looking for Sampa," he says, keeping his injured arm up but ready to pull his sidearm.

"You, Noah?" she asks.

"That's the code name."

She nods and leans forward. She has a two-toned face, soft brown with pale white that rings her mouth and frames her solid black eyes. She keeps the gun trained on him as she rises and comes closer.

Gabriel steps backward as she locks the door, and he lowers his face covering.

"You fit the description," she says. "Big and bald."

"So do you," he replies, noting her cropped hair and the metal feathers running down her right arm.

"Were you followed?" she asks, looking him up and down.

"For a bit."

"They say you get followed a lot."

"Off and on."

"Sit over there," she instructs and points to the bar.

"Do you have a kit? My arm needs looked at."

They sit and she pulls a med bag from behind the bar.

He undoes the cuff on his shirt and reveals the cut, a long but shallow run from mid-forearm to the back of the wrist.

She does a gauze swipe and then pinches the cut shut to make sure the skin will fully close. Her hands are mottled white, fading into one brown arm and the other with the feathers.

"Where is the tail now?" she asks.

"In an alley by the market."

"Dead?"

He nods.

"What's the tail about? They say it isn't UTC."

"Family dispute," Gabriel says. "They don't want me making a mess for them. They'd like me to disappear entirely, but that's a potential mess of its own. I bring them shame."

"Family," she smirks and shakes her head, closing up the arm with antiseptic glue and then laying a strip of bandage down. "There's only shame where there's pride."

"They have too much of both," he says, knowing that these rumors about his past are well worn throughout the rebel channels.

She nods as she rolls his cuff back down. "There's no message yet. I don't have anything for you."

"Okay," he says flatly. "That's the way it usually goes."

"How long have you waited for this message?"

"Been a few years now."

"You think it'll come?"

He nods. "In the meantime, I do what I can."

"You went to Europa, right? You were there?"

Gabriel leans back and looks at this woman, this Arkû, and tries to predict what she's getting at. Rumors precede everyone in the rebel collective. Stories true and false that proliferate myth, add drama, to what is in truth a very slow life of hiding in holes and quietly killing. There's explosions and high-profile mess making that gets done, but individual involvement is few and far between.

Stories have preceded Sampa. Gabriel has heard she is a killer who's done some runs. He's heard she's been off-world and been part of the work done in Sevier, but also further west into the Axlir region of the Sierras. All operations above the first story shanty towns are dangerous and she has survived many of them.

"Always good to know your contact ahead of time," he says to her.

"And you were on the wrong side at Europa," she accuses. "Right?"

He nods, always aware what could happen when the conversation turns to Europa.

"What do you think of me? Do you call me 'sansvies'?" Sampa asks, black eyes boring into him as she points at the feathers on her arm.

"You are Arkû," he says slowly, "and I think we're on the same side now. Back then I didn't understand."

"Can we ever be on the same side?" she asks. "We're not really the same at all. You bleed. I don't. You wander from contact to contact while we fight. I was part of the Palm Raid. The one where the city went into lock down."

He smiles and takes a deep breath, tasting grit on his lips from the street. "I know you were. Second story work. And I know you don't bleed like me, but we still die the same."

She says nothing but keeps the frown on her face.

"I fight too." he says. "I was at the Temple bombing in Schengen. I knew the way because I grew up near there."

Sampa shakes her head with disgust. "Can anyone like you really be trusted? A mind educated in bigotry. Bhoosa from birth."

"Oh, my family wasn't Bhoosa," Gabriel says, shaking his head and smiling. "That would be an insult. My family was finer than that." He holds his hands up, rubbing the layer of light dust between fingertips. "Part of the Dhool. Dust. They spit on the Bhoosa from on high. They spit on me. They're off-world now. Living somewhere on a luxury station, part of the political command."

She sneers. "And they hunt you across Terra, hoping to hide you away."

"Every day," says Gabriel and he already knows where this is going next because he has heard it a thousand times, been told about his guilt over and over by those he once hurt. But he's said it to himself a thousand times more as he's waited for the message that may never come. He knows what he is, what he was. It is for that reason he is determined to hear the accusations again and again. It is a good reminder of what not to be.

"That's because you're a traitor at heart, if I have heard all the stories right," Sampa explains with her solid black eyes. "You were party to an atrocity, a genocide, on Europa and the other moons. You turned away from even the best of your Tribal dogma and committed crimes against all the life there. Then you turned away from a legion, all murderers, but you used to call them brothers. You turned away from a family, all pious oppressors, but you are a turncoat in your very blood. Now you do violence for our cause. How long till you turn again?"

"I deserve that, and in many ways that is who I am," says Gabriel. "But I've never turned my back for a better life for myself. At first it was following orders. Then I turned because someone bought my loyalty with their own blood. They bought my love when they showed me what they were loyal to. Now I have my own loyalty to uphold, to them, to the things they cared about."

"So now you wander from contact to contact for years. Now you kill in the streets."

"I have to. Otherwise, they'd find you. They'd find us. And there's more at stake than just our little skirmishes and raids. We are at war, yes, but the soul of all this still needs saving."

"Who are you to say what the soul of this fight is?"

"I don't say what it is. I was told. I was shown. And of all things I've believed in my life, I believe this the most. So, I'll wait for my message and then I'll do what I need to."

33

The sun is already up, but it hides its eyes behind the clouds. It doesn't wish to see the exchange, the disordered march of tens of thousands back to the cellar.

They move as a scattered flock, murmuration at glacial pace, migrating to the source of their deepest misery.

The Trustee has started late, stiff and pained out of the box, and is now far behind her usual schedule. But there is no value in rushing. Endurance and consistency are far more important during the exchange. There is no time for mistakes, and it is a prolonged experience.

Small mounds along the route to the mine create chaotic terrain, hiding things under the ice, like an archipelago of emergent forms. They stretch from shed to cellar. They are frozen bodies, mummified in the desert wastes of ice, and they will take ages to disappear. The snows cannot forget those who fell to their knees and perished in this liminal space between shelter and darkness.

-*There should be scavengers here,*- the Trustee thinks.

-*Carrion eaters.*-

-*To remove us.*-

-Better than to waste away.-

-All those forgotten nutrients.-

-No other animals here to eat the dead.-

-All the animals have been caught and killed for food.-

-The birds could do it.-

-The birds aren't made of flesh and blood.-

-They don't need us or our dead.-

The northern ice sheet rises gently as the hoard of prisoners approaches the cellar. And atop the rise are the barricades. Ten-meter-high walls of slag and tailings tightly packed together. The barricades encircle the entire open pit of the mine, made to slow the winds that rip down the inner walls of stepped excavation and to accumulate drifting snow rather than allow it to fall into the great sump, never to melt and never to move on.

These walls make a monumental fortress of the pit mine, with no gates but overlapping sections of fortification for the utza to pass through.

The Trustee can feel the meaning of the walls in her bones. She has seen barricades before, the way they slow the enemy, the way they funnel them through tight channels and how it gives the defender an elevated position of attack.

-The snow and wind are stopped.-

-But the snow and wind are not the only enemy.-

Seeing the walls, these long ridges covered in ice that stretch for kilometers across the hillside, sparks a fog inside her head, a heavy dose of disorientation, the kind that comes before a dissociation, before a dream or memory intrudes.

-It is happening more frequently now.-

-The edge of yourself never very far away?-

-It will happen again soon. A falling backward-

-This is not a good time to go away.-

-What sparked this memory?-

-The barricades. Like the linea that cover Europa.-

The prisoners slow and become a lethargic crush of bodies as they enter the chicane between the walls, snaking their way through the gap. The massive entity that is the utza becoming one for a moment before the long descent into the pit.

Everyone gives the Trustee space as she moves through them, tired and unfocused. They know she is being watched and was involved in what happened in solitary. Rumors have already spread. The eyes of the utza have already taken note. How quick they are to add stories to legend, subtractions from reality.

They filter between the walls and emerge onto a narrow ledge of earth that begins the spiral ledges and broken switchbacks.

The Trustee looks down the incline, threatening the angle of repose, toward the bottom of the pit. It is a great funnel for human life, its massive size dwarfing senses and confusing perspective. The sights give vertigo, and the sounds suggest mountains, but as you descend, the echoes prove you are going subterranean.

Across the open wound in the earth, the opposite wall is also littered with switchbacks and snow, the hill tops rising just behind, marking the Willett Range.

Scarps cut through the terraced ledges where the walls have calved, pulling large sections of steps into massive landslides. These slumps will clog the drain, cover the adit lifts at the base of the pit, and must be dug back out. It is the ever-present menace of natural processes.

The spiral switchback is the easy path, but the longest way down. One kilometer of vertical descent can take a full day at such a low grade. So, at the first opportunity, narrow paths are found to the next terrace. Those who are stronger may take the risk to climb down these short interchanges to get to the bottom more quickly.

But others are slow, weak, stumbling, and there will be no real rest as the utza back up and accumulate at the bottom of the pit.

At the lowest point of the open mine, it is brutally cold, never seeing sun, the walls sucking any remnant heat from the air. Thousands of prisoners will stand waiting for their spot on the lifts, advocates pressing them from behind, jamming them like product into a tight package for delivery into the deep.

The Trustee starts taking the high chutes and has to keep balanced to avoid the pain in her ribs.

-It is daylight. Everyone is here.-

-Do not trip. Do not fall.-

-There is shame in falling, knowing your body will be a fixture for all those who pass by.-

-Bearing witness to you will be a punishment added to those who are already punished.-

-No one can help you. But the eyes will see you as they pass.-

Down they go and the Trustee gets into a rhythm, only pulled out of her daze by the sound of skittering stones, the rattle of large rocks rolling from above, and then the thuds and snapping sounds as a broken body descends, tumbling.

No one stops. No one has time to waste on measuring their steps against the challenge of pain.

A few bodies litter the base of every chute, taken by the fall. Limbs are bent wrong, leaking from new apexes.

If they have not yet been put out of their misery by other utza, the Trustee does her part and ends it quickly, showing her terminal compassion. But every corpse is left to rest on ice and earth, the baton strike changing them, unraveling them.

-Pounding the grain.-

A memory intrudes.

It isn't her own voice replying anymore. But it is just as comforting. It comes from a long way back in her brain. A child's voice filled with a kindness and knowledge that eclipses the youthful tone.

-That's the way it used to be done. Pounding the grain by hand. Long before.-

-Before when, Vive?- the Trustee asks the child's voice.

-Before any of us. Ancestors on the great flats would grind grain.-

-Before the UTC? Before the wars?-

-War is older than pounding grain.-

The Trustee, back then, had worked a rough stone roller over a wide slab and broken apart the bran. The crushed grain smelled sweet and the powder hung in the air around a wide table, set amid a warm field with low clouds. She had not been alone.

-They would work the wheat into a flour, then add water, then add yeast.-

-I know.-

-A different kind of life. Symbiotic when under control. Destructive when it isn't.-

-What kind of control?-

With that, the memory is gone and the Trustee is down-climbing and watching for advocates, all the while mind racing to catch up.

-Who was Vive?-

-Vive was many things. Your friend as a child. Your sibling.-

-Vive was annoying. A pest. A bug.-

-A teacher as well.-

No sun shines at the bottom of the pit, and muddy ice coats the walls.

The stream of prisoners course down the terraces above her, winding along the spiral stairs.

The Trustee knows the lifts will be full but she wants to have her pick of which group she goes with. To be caged on the long descent with some healthy animal will lead to a dirty sort of death. Better to ride with the weak or the old.

It's standing room only at the mouth of the drain unit, a cement structure, windowless and gray, extending into the base of the hillside. Inside, the roar of pumps and lift machinery echoes. The drain unit moves the prisoners down and the till up, the tons of earth that need removal for further processing. The drain unit's pumps send ice slurry to the deepest parts of the mine where heat is almost unmanageable. The liquid conduits move fresh water for the crushing and grinding process at depth, before returning a fine rock slurry which will go through a series of chemical separations.

Behind the lifts is the old adit, partially sealed off, the exit to the other side of the Willett Range where the first mine passage was excavated into the hillside years before, where the till was flooded out into the dry valleys to the west for collection.

Over the doors to the drain, inscribed in the cement, reads 'Precious in the sight of the gods is the death of their faithful servants.'

The Trustee pushes her way forward through the crowd of stinking bodies, and people open a path for her. Her hand rests on her baton, ready to strike.

-This is the spot for a frenzy.-

-Anxious prisoners.-

-Fretful. They take liberties and suddenly you are bait.-

A few hands grab at her as she shoves her way through, but she is more concerned about quick movement to her periphery, someone maybe striking out at her head or neck. But nothing comes and she scrambles quickly into the drain, her ears throbbing as she finds a wall near the machinery and forces some prisoners to move aside for her. She puts her back to the concrete. The smell of the hot metal and oil rolls the Trustee's mind over. More memory without anchor, awakened by the industrial sounds and smells.

-An engine room?-

-A machine?-

A small child moves along the wall and pulls up beside her. An odor wafts from the tiny creature, dirty hair obscuring the boney face with its darting eyes.

She looks down at the skinny child.

"Vive?" the Trustee asks, unable to tell who she is looking at.

The child looks up, confused, not expecting to have been seen. They notice the Trustee's glazed eyes, unblinking, and the battered face staring down at them.

"I'll protect you, Vive."

"Not my name," the child croaks, trying to keep their voice low.

"No," says the Trustee. "You're right. You always had more names. One was more important than the others. But I called you 'bug'."

She pats the child on the head, wishing she could hide them away. The face is so familiar it makes her ache. It drapes another layer of fog over the world around her, another filter of separation, facilitating her mind's implosion.

A lift ratchets into place. The door to the empty cage opens and the Trustee watches who is shoved in, a mixed group of waxy skin and bent bones, and decides to go along for the ride. The child slides along next to her, in need of some protection, in need of some authority with a human face.

"Stay close," she says to the child.

Others pile in around them.

The cage closes and everyone props themselves against the walls or leans against each other. It is a long ride down.

The gears engage on the lift.

The floor lurches and the unit begins its descent.

The Trustee is not the only one who looks upward at the weak sun as it passes through the cage's lattice. The rays turn to scattered points of light to last the imagination for a month in the hole.

Then there is no more light.

In the dark no one speaks and the child clings tightly to the Trustee's leg.

"It's okay, Vive," the Trustee says out loud into the cage. "I'm going now."

"Trustee," whispers the child. "What are you talking about?"

"Shhh. I have to go, little one. I'll see you soon, Vive. I'm coming to get you."

The Trustee has not stopped looking up, seeing stars instead of black.

She starts to fade out, winding backward like a clock searching for a place to restart. She sees the nebulas through a shaded curve of glass, like a blast shield on battle armor. The stars are hers now. None left for the others. All inside her own mind, her own past.

The smell of the oiled machine mingles with the warm stench coming on the updraft from the cellar, the smell of humans in tight spaces. It turns her stomach, but it also makes her shoulders widen and draw tight at the spine. They would need to be strong and high to make the armored suit shrug and flex and to swing the heavy guns. It is a powerfully familiar feeling.

Habit makes her lean back into the wall. She arches her back, chin up, the way you need to lean so the sutures seal up along the front of the battle suit and trap that smell in with you, the smell of mechanized joints and lubricated pneumatics, the smell of the stale fear sweat from a fight.

There is a strength that comes to her when she is in the suit.

Europa, a tan ball of ice and dust, hangs among the stars, filling the Trustee's vision. Its striations, the geometric linea, seem to circumnavigate the sphere, wrapping the moon in a web of dirty scar tissue.

Her suit protects her from the vacuum of space as the lift descends into the cellar.

-Jupiter is just over the horizon.-

-It will stain the heavens with its glow.-

-But you won't see it from here.-

-I should not have come.-

-But you were called forth.-

-By Vive.-

-By Europa itself.-

THE TEMPLE OF TERRA

-Terran Year 2337-
-4 Years Prior to Shed-

————

On his own plane of being, how does the Human truly create? First, he may create by making something of outside materials. But this will not do, for there are no materials outside of All with which it may create.

All has been created before.

Well, then, secondly, Humans procreate or reproduce by the process of begetting, which is accomplished by transferring a portion of their substance to offspring. But that will not do, because All cannot transfer or subtract a portion of itself, both thoughts being an absurdity.

Is there no third way in which Humans create? Yes, there is - they create inside teikum. And in so doing they use no outside materials, nor do they reproduce themselves, and yet their Spirit pervades the Mental Creation.

-Modified after Chapter V: The Mental Universe
The Kybalion - Appendix: Coda of Unification

————

1

-Excerpt from Memoir of the Neta-Teej-
-Written in the Early Days of Exile-

I am a guide, and I am walking a path. Perhaps others will follow.

I am running down that path, fleeing, from one temple to another. From the Temple on Terra to another Temple on Europa. I am unsure if either are holy. But one can never really know about such things.

The spirit of the place, of the building, the earth below it, seems to matter a great deal. But these things are inanimate. Masonry, glass, metal. Is there a soul in those materials? We feel soul, even in empty places, so why not?

Or do we lie to ourselves?

I am the Neta-Teej. I am a guide. Do I lie to you? I hope not. I pray not.

I worry, always, that I have strayed from the path. So I turn round and look behind.

I am made saltier by the task. I remember. Nostalgia is sweet, and that is how you know it is a lie. Looking into the past makes you brackish. You will never be a pillar of salt, but your minerals change because the past has a spirt, a metabolism all its own. There are crystalline materials there which have found their souls only because they have been relegated to the past.

They would dilute themselves and dissolve in the current state of things.

I write so I may reflect on that past, churning up memory, searching for explanations, insight.

Memory and teikum are linked, each begetting the other in different ways.

I write so others may understand me, if they so desire. I have been fashioned, as a deity, as a figurehead, into something beyond myself. I don't know what it means to be me.

Maybe others will find solace in that. Maybe I will find solace in it.

Escaping Terra, the Temple of the Tribe, and fleeing the UTC has set things in motion which I wish could be undone.

But the High Command, the Ecclesia, will not relinquish the tether.

They think the tether binds them to the future and, in turn, binds me to them.

But they don't understand the future. They have never really looked back. They were told not to. They were told to make the future for the gods. But they cannot see the path.

They think the path is wherever they decide to tread, but that isn't true. The terrain of existence does not change to your will.

And the path you have already walked does not determine the terrain before you.

I write about my past so I may see the arc of my deviation. So that others may see it is rather short, and that I am not really a god.

There is still a great deal of alteration left, and different temples will be needed. One is never enough.

I will reflect on the old temple as I move toward the new one.

2

When I was little, small enough to still be read to by my mother, I was drawn to the most antiquated stories in the Coda of Unification. At the end of the Coda was a compendium of texts deemed ancillary by the powers that be, but added as concessions to certain sects before the formal binding.

My mother liked to read them to me because they didn't feel like reading from the main Coda. They felt like proper story time without the guilt of uncertain morality.

"Vive," she said. "These ancient words are just as holy as the others."

"But they aren't from the holy books," I had told her. "They were added on at the end. They aren't really part of it."

"Yes, they are. And besides, you like these stories. They resonate inside you. For that reason, they are holy."

It was a clean moment for both of us. We wouldn't always have that, but I remember that time as being something pure. She hadn't had it with my sister, Constance, who always wanted to interrupt, to talk through the stories and analyze in real time. She would never just listen.

They're all very old stories now, but I am specifically talking of the ones which had been spoken around campfires and had been changed over thousands of years to better suit the needs of the time, only later being written on stone or the first crude parchments. These were the stories from just after the dawn of a struggling man, when the archetypes began to fit the needs of new societies. These were stories that have never really grown old.

We decided our teikum, our mythos, was wide enough to include great men, not just gods, not just powers beyond ourselves. We chose that for ourselves, as a species, as we banded together in tribes. We sought guidance for ourselves, our society, rather than just appeasing the sun god or the rain god to help the crops.

These epics are about the rise of kings or temptations of normal men. They are heroes who come into being through simply persisting. Yes, they are born powerful, yes, they may have privilege, yes, they may have been looked upon favorably by the gods, but they were heroes at heart, in their own teikum, before they set out. We are all meant to be heroes, are we not? We all have provenance inside teikum which we can craft in our own image. We can craft ourselves, imagine ourselves, as heroes, even if we drive ourselves insane in the process.

And we do lose our minds. Delusion. Voices from teikum that corrupt our living voice.

These stories were told to help guide young people to be brave and be just, to help rulers remember their oaths and imbue authority with kindness and humility. They were told to frighten you about what inaction could bring, or to terrify you about the costs of the wild, the costs of dabbling in things that ought not be played with.

This is why they have such value, even in the modern age, spoken adjacent holy texts and memoirs of introspection. These myths and folklore are part of our memory and our history, and anything that has lived in our teikum is worth retaining for all time, even if our thoughts around those stories change. From glory to shame to understanding. Thus, all things must progress.

Because of all these stories, I always knew I would be something great. It seemed likely, inescapable, as my mother read them to me. It seemed possible from the very beginning because all the stories contained guidance for how to be great, the path to greatness laid out in detail and with all the variants one might need. I did not know the truth for a very long time, that greatness, the epic journey, isn't fair or even. I have learned it is better as a story rather than a truth. The stories are beautiful. The truths are paths through horror, dissociation and estrangement.

But I read these stories over and over, and it was with my youthful focus on all these old tales, the ones rarely touched on by my teachers, that I was allowed to enter the Temple schools at a young age.

At first it was just classes with other young children. We were in the ever-impressionable stage of development, initiative versus guilt, expressing our takes on what we were learning, no matter how simple those perceptions were.

In retrospect, I think I was initially brought in to challenge the other children, from higher families. They had already experienced schooling geared toward becoming officials like their parents or spiritual leaders of their wealthy families, maybe even entering the Tribe. I think they intended my ideas of heroes and kings and battle and romantic love to contrast with the others, to help them grow in their knowledge of the Coda and its interpretations.

And I did challenge them because I loved my stories, and I could see how many of them were stories that pre-dated those which composed the Coda. I could see how their knowledge was really no different than my own, just of different sources, different vintages. Only the names of the heroes changed.

At first, I was distressed. The teachers enforced my ideas, but the children didn't seem to understand how I linked things, how I saw that their eucharist tradition was a derivative reversal of Ammit's consumption of four of the five souls.

These were not comfortable times for me, the first period in my life that my ideas were challenged and never with the softness of a parent or close friend, never with the tact of an academic or a scholars.

I would lie in bed at night thinking of my stories and the other tales I had been told. I would make my connections and I would imagine how they would tell me I was wrong. I don't remember sleeping. I would rebuff their attacks in my dreams, and I would see things that I didn't understand. I was visited, taunted and supported, by countless entities inside my own mind. I was opening to a whole inner world I could not fully process. But I knew I was not meant to understand yet. This was the way it was supposed to happen, the way a child was supposed to begin to see.

Sometimes I would wake up in the hallways of our home. Other times I would wake up in the fields, confused, cold. And other times still, I would wake up in my sister's arms, her carrying me back into the house and laying me back in my bed, her holding me against the linen to keep me from hitting my head on the wooden headboard as I rolled and threw my fit.

My parents wanted me to go to the local Temple, to get better schooling, to make friends with children who were of a different social class in our municipality. It gave them some pride, pride I stirred up in them. I could feel it, but I also felt how small it was.

"Vive, the younger Malikova child, is in Temple with the Bhoosa."

"Elevated."

"Honorable."

Elevated compared to those they knew. It was important to

them and so I retreated into my teikum in the night to protect myself through those early days at school.

I would never trade it for anything within myself now, because of what it did for me, but I would trade it all away for them if they knew what it would, eventually, cost them, cost me, cost our family. They could not see beyond our village, and so they pushed. It would bring me safety and a future they could not provide.

However, they resisted when, a few years later, I was invited to visit and attend classes at the Temple of the Tribe in Schengen. It was thousands of kilometers away and I was still young. I would board there, live and breathe the Tribal life, and become immersed in my stories. I would learn psychology and philosophy.

The teachers wanted me to come to the Temple because I listened to them and because I would ask so many questions. It was only natural my curiosity would lead to the Temple for education.

But in truth I think it was because I was not from a higher family. It was because my family hadn't yet taught me the politics of the UTC or the Tribe. It had never been relevant, and they didn't know much of it anyway. What it culminated in was malleability. I was ready to grow into what the Tribe needed because they were giving me what I wanted. It was glory for a young ego, and it was hopeful and bright and my parents did not resist for long.

Perhaps this was a sign of things to come. I convinced them to let me go. I convinced them it was a good idea.

I looked into their teikum, and I saw that my father's fear was always that we might lose our station and have to sell our legacy plots and we would lose what little privilege and safety we might have just inside the confines of the metropolis. He didn't want us to have to struggle. I told him my education and connections would likely protect all of us from ever losing what we had, and in many ways I have been right.

There was no desire in his heart to climb higher in the structure, to become something he wasn't. He simply wanted his children to be safe and thrive. And he believed in me. He believed in what I would become with all his faith. It would have been good to have a story about him around the campfire. Men need stories of how to be good and average and kind more than they need stories of how to be kings or how to wield power. Very few get to be kings, so those sorts of stories only confuse us, destroy our anchors of perception. But he was not confused. Only worried for me and hopeful that my spirit would find a place.

My mother, on the other hand, was very confused. She had her faith and wanted me to have mine. But she didn't understand me or what I was changing into. She had been confused for a long time, since the days of my bad dreams and sleepless nights. I explained that I was going to go on a journey. She told me I didn't need to be a hero or ordained. She said teikum was inside us and that was enough, and I told her that she was right. "My teikum is enough, but my teikum is different than yours. My stories and voices are not the same as yours. It isn't just inside me. There's more than that." I said I had to fill teikum with other things and from other places. I told her I was doing it for me, not for the Tribe, and in the end, that was what she always held on to satiate her fear.

My sister told me to go and do whatever I wanted and never worry about what I ought to have done. She had never wasted time listening to my mother's readings or my father's worries, and to her it was very simple. She said I could be the caliph if I wanted. I told her that was impossible, that there was already a caliph, a young man, and she laughed and said it wasn't impossible, that everyone would bow to me and pray if I went to the Tribe. I said I didn't want that, and she said she didn't care, that she would never bow to her little sib, but someone was bowing to the others already, why not me? She said I was smart enough to know I wasn't that smart, but no one else was.

My bad dreams stopped after that. I no longer walked in my sleep. There was something that had quieted inside me once I realized I could leave.

My first classes in the Temple were exercises in isolation, and for my classmates, who had come from all over the world, I think it was difficult and quiet and a step into a more spartan, enclosed world. They had traveled before and met other people and had seen the inner workings of the megacity from aircars and high rises.

But for me it was far different. I had never seen anything like it or people so different from myself. I was from thirty-five hundred kilometers east, north of the Fertile Crescent and the experience was anything but isolated for me.

Guided meditations on important texts ranged into waking visions, calling forth archetypes from inside ourselves. We wrote down what we saw, and shared with the others. This was my first experience helping to guide someone.

Her name was Aras, and she was unable to quiet her mind during the meditation, hearing voices that were from teikum, those of her parents or friends or priests back home. There was no quiet in which to listen for something new. After a long time in silent meditation, she would begin to cry, and while no one else heard her because she was so quiet, I could hear. I could feel her.

In the evenings, when we were permitted to have our own time, though still in our class group, I would sit with her and she would meditate and I would ask her to say out loud to me everything she was hearing and I would sit behind her, arms hugging her, her back to my chest. We would breathe together, and she would expel all the voices in her head. Together we would be brave and we would persist through the noise, and after a long,

long time, into the night, she would exhaust those voices until there was quiet.

Aras would fall silent and I would hold my breath and imagine myself as having disappeared as she would go where she needed to.

I would be there when she came back and we would cry together and I would comfort her because she said it was a very quiet place she would go to. It felt empty, but she knew she needed to go there to fill it with light and grace.

And what did I see when I went inside myself?

Just as anyone, I saw my family, my sister and my parents. I saw dreams from my past, bad and good. I saw old friends from my childhood.

But, more often, I would go to an open plateau of scant grasses and stones.

Only then did I know I was fully inside myself.

There was a cliff, and below, an endless sea that ran into the distance. I heard the ocean water lapping at the base of the cliffs. I heard the wind off the sea. But when it was quiet I heard the mosses and the lichen speak to me. "It must be inside," they would say, and I recognized that saying from previous dreams.

The rocks wanted me to see them. They had been there forever, waiting for me. The sky told me it was the edge of me, the edge of the inside.

There was only one curiosity on the plateau. There was a well, a round cistern which seemed to reach down deep into the earth. It bore deep into the countryside and there was water near the bottom I could barely see.

It told me it would never forget things I dropped down for it to hold.

I knew that one day I too would be able to descend into that well and find the bottom. I knew that just over the rise in the opposite direction was a valley with my home and my father's fields lying at the base.

I knew these things, but I could not yet look there.

In teikum, others heard the voices from heaven or new lessons from old teachers in their past. We shared and discussed, and when we hit walls of perception, I found myself calling upon my ancient stories to give direction, to give light to what people would dream or delve into.

It was not just Aras with whom I would spend the nights, but all my classmates, each one of them quietly wishing to tell me a vision or share a meditation. I thought it was all of us guiding each other through the confusions we were cultivating. I did not know that I was the only one who was doing this.

After our semester of isolation there were fewer of us.

Some left because they were homesick. Others left because they could not see themselves growing, evolving past those early meditations. Teachers sent others home for different reasons. They couldn't keep all the scripture straight, couldn't reference the stories that were so easy for me to recall.

Aras stayed, and for me, that was a relief. There was no one else I was as connected with in those early days, despite my guidance.

Given freedom to wander the lower levels of the Temple, we were able to access the libraries and some of the gardens. There was music in the congregations and we were able to dance with all the others after quiet prayer. I met hundreds of people, maybe thousands, all who had come to the Temple of the Tribe to think and write and speak about the ways of the spirits and the gods, all exploring the meaning of teikum.

The next lessons were split between rote learning of text among our young group and then forums of open discussions with mixed ages. There were aged and learned speakers who would posit questions to anyone, and they would record the answers.

They would challenge you. They would interrogate every facet of our responses and they would not assist in guiding your words, the way you described your opinion or thoughts.

But they would guide your emotions. "Do not answer in anger. You may answer about your anger. But do not let it live in your voice. It will be poison to your message." "Do not cry. Your sadness and exasperation are critical to how you feel and respond, but the message must carry that emotion in words, not in tone."

I would speak sometimes, but I was also afraid. I did not like the attention. Instead, I would listen to the older students talk, to the higher orders firing back and forth in open discourse with the elderly and most learned scholars. Their voices and arguments were so clear and even, exploring intricacies I had never considered.

I always wanted to go back and relisten or reread what I had seen. There were times I wanted to look even further back and see older debate, but all this was deemed as 'discussion' and it could not be found in the archives. Much of it could be found on the nets, but access to such things was not permitted while in cloister.

And that was how my first season at the Temple ended, a whirlwind of stories and debate paired with new methods for meditation and self-evaluation.

When I returned home, my family had so many questions.

My sister asked about the city, about the people, and my parents asked about my classes.

But I didn't know how to explain it. I could describe it, but I could not seem to communicate what had happened to me. I could not articulate what it meant to hold Aras and whisper about the things we saw and heard inside our minds. How could I explain it? Everyone at the Temple had worked through the same practices of breathing and chanting. They had experienced memory recovery and memory distortion. They had all spoken with those who presided over them and been taught to explain their emotions rather than let them hide in the background.

My family did not understand how deep I had already gone, into myself, and into the Tribe's mindset. I did not understand either, but I could feel it.

There was no way I could tell them about the deep well next to the cliff or the black sea inside of me.

I wanted to, but I did not know how. What I had learned in the classes was not yet clear to me, but I knew I had learned. And I did not consider the people around me to be from the city anymore, they were of the Tribe. I still knew so little of the outside world.

My sister, particularly, was funny about it. She had questions about Schengen, but when I couldn't answer she asked questions about the discussions, about the topics. Not just the classes, but anything that had been spoken of.

There was a war on at the time, on the outer belt, and she wanted to know what the Tribe thought of those people, those rebels the UTC fought against. I didn't know anything about that either.

The rebels had been discussed briefly by some of the higher ups in the debate forums, but I realized no one had really bothered to bring much of the current situation into the conversation. At least not for a young student like me. I didn't know the basics yet, why would they spend time on me with respect to a war against non-believers? I was not ready to delve into those details yet.

"It isn't about that," Constance told me. "I'm not asking you to understand or fix the problem. I want to know if they pray for the rebels? Or do they want the outer legion to do anything more?

The Quadrumvirate has been mostly silent on it, from what I can tell. Do they pray for a quick end to war? Or do they pray for our legionnaires to have endurance?"

"I don't know," I answered, feeling confused. "We didn't get into the politics."

My sister had been unimpressed at their lack of practicality, but, suddenly, so was I.

There had been no exposure to the nets while I was a first year. Anything from the split river nodes was vetted before it was archived in the Tribal Library. And I had heard nothing of the Quadrumvirate other than their official statements. I had seen none of them, though I knew they had been somewhere inside the massive Temple, probably debating and deliberating on the upper floors, giving spiritual guidance to the UTC High Command.

I had been given my first kernels of doubt, not in the gods, but in the Tribe itself. My sister was still a child at the time, only five years older than me, but she was getting closer to being a young adult and was having to think about the world and right and wrong.

For her, these stories were not just comparative literature, but they were real people who were fighting or dying. I could tell she had emotion tied up in it. There was something in the way she talked that betrayed her concern, but also her uncertainty. She did not know whether she wanted the rebels to win, or to lose, or to just escape to fight again at some other time. Constance did not know who she should be praying for, or if it would even help.

The epic stories I had read told me all about this, but even my short time at the Temple had given me some better context.

Everyone was different, but everyone was the same, and the heroes of the stories, those who were willing to die for what they believe, gave most people pause. There is a force of will being presented in those stories, proven. A connection to something greater is being shown. It is evidence of someone else's teikum, and it does something to us all when it is presented. To see their tether to their inner world, to understand it for a moment, makes our hair stand on end, it makes us cry with a surge of emotional awe, neither happiness nor sadness. It makes us think of those great stories where something triumphs over adversity.

I did not understand that conflict on the outer belt.

I did not understand the rebel policy or the UTC's intent at retention of mineral rights.

But I did understand the feelings my sister had about it. I did understand that any person willing to die for a cause might have one foot in this world, but another foot on the side of the gods, just like any Tribe member.

I also knew they could simply be scared and weak and tired.

After all, the epic stories focus on the heroes and how they court the power inside themselves. But the stories are filled with the thousands of unnamed who live and die, searching for health or comfort or expression while those who are compelled by teikum storm on about them.

So, I asked my sister to tell me what she knew about the war. She tried to give me books and net dispatches, and I accepted them.

I watched them, and I read them. I also pulled the old, well edited Temple discussions I had been unable to access during cloister. I watched proctors engaging in the same debate over and over, only slightly improving their positions from week to week.

I found these repetitions boring. I found the academic nature of the truth boring.

A dispatch may give perfect examples of motive for rebel or for conquest, for colonialism or for nativism. But these truths would not stop or solve anything.

These truths were not guiding truths.

I needed to know more about the guiding truths in these events and I wanted to hear my sister's take. I wanted to know what she cared about in all of it. And then I wanted to know if she planned to change herself because of it. Would she alter herself, her life, because of the feeling, or the motive for a feeling, or would she just sit with it, consume it and never act?

So I asked.

And she did tell me. From the very start I could tell she was in love with all of those who were willing to fight. It wasn't a specific outcome that called to her, but the power of compelling oneself to risk life and danger. The call of the void had emerged. It had summoned her, and she could not fully process it, but she was already altering herself. She was going to find a fight.

It was one of the first times I felt a true connection to a family member. I understood her and how brave she wanted to be. I did not match those feelings she felt. I couldn't. I did not want to be a warrior. My call of the void was different. But I knew the source of her compulsion and listened to her and promised to read more, not just because it was important to her, but because any conflict of the UTC would be important to me if I was going to be part of the Tribe.

3

During the recess back at my home, I was invited, as a new student, to visit and sit with the Tribal members at the congregation in Janza, the city center closest to us. It is an invitation extended to all of those who are admitted to the Temple, even before they are formally part of the Tribe. They are allowed to attend their local congregation and have admittance to some of the private rooms prior to the prayers and take meditation with the priests and priestesses there.

It was many kilometers away, as we lived farther out from the city, but I went and my family came with me to the old church which now served as the local temple.

My family sat with the congregation, and I was taken to the mihrab where two men and one woman sat preparing for the sermon. They were all dressed in blue robes that matched the wall's patchwork tile and sat on warm brown cushions with candles and flowing incense.

There was a seat left empty for me and without words they pointed for me to sit among them and they gave me a blue wrap to put over my white one. For a long time they said nothing to me at all, and I was simply allowed to take in the space and exult in the quiet with them. It was a strange feeling, to suddenly be so comfortable in that space, smelling the concoction of burning shells and plants, as done in ancient times.

"We have heard about you."

"Thank you for coming."

"May we use your words today?"

I did not know what they meant, did not understand what they were asking. Use my words? How? From when? From where?

"What do you mean?" I asked, confused and suddenly feeling removed from my well of comfort, exposed.

"It is one of your discussions. It was sent to us from the Temple in preparation for your coming," said the woman. Later I learned her name was Mara. "It would be good for the people to hear it today. It would be good for you to hear it and see them respond to it, to truly understand what these words mean for your people. For our people."

"Which discussion? How did they send it?"

"Everything in the Temple is of record," said the man. His name was Chitra. "And it is all useful for guidance in some way or another. We have a globe of followers to help, to provide perspective to."

"And you have spoken words that will be useful here," said Mara.

"I still don't know what words I have said," I admitted, absolutely confused. I rushed back through all the memories of what I had said at discussion, what I had spoken about in my short time at the Temple. How could this have happened? How could something I had said become known to these acolytes? It made no sense.

"Do you want to read them?" Mara asked. "You may read them aloud if you wish to. They are your words."

"No," I said, fear welling inside me, knowing these words would be spoken before people who knew me, the real me. The

Vive they knew could not say any of the things I had said at Temple. They did not know that person, and I was mortified to rehash all of that at the moment.

"Do we have your permission?"

"I don't want anyone to know it was me," I said.

"If you wish it, the congregation will not know. But we do know. You have spoken useful words and the people, the humans, who live here will like them."

I was not comforted, I was terrified. What drivel had I spoken? I was nothing but a child, just playing at my first months in the Temple, not formally part of the Tribe.

"And there was a youth who spoke this recently, of this area, your beloved region, our country and our hills. They said this, when asked what it means to know teikum, when asked what that inward life is: I look to my home, to the fields my father and mother work. They are wide fields, with burnt dirt between the crops, and the water runs into the irrigation channels. It rushes in like blood, and even though there were always living things there, the crops, the bugs, the animals that run under the fading greenery, there is a new flow of life. This is teikum to me. Everything inside of us is like a tilled field, waiting for the rain. But if no rain comes, it is up to you to flush the field with water, with life. It will cause things to grow, to bear fruit, to rise. The new growth keeps the rabbits and the mice safe from the prying eyes of hawks and falcons looking down. I want my teikum to look like that. I want my quiet inner world to look like the outside I saw growing and thriving in spring. I stand upon the rocky heath near my home and look into myself."

"And this youth was asked what happens when the winter comes, as it must for all things, for all people. They were asked what happens when the winds and snows come after the reaping. What should teikum look like then? Should it be barren and frigid? And to the question, they responded tentatively: teikum might change if one is with the gods. Note their uncertainty, but it is certain they meant it."

The congregation had laughed at that, imagining whatever people imagine when they hear kindness coming from a child.

"The youth continued: In the winter the fields are barren. But the people are not. They share food. They share fire. They come together and they pray and they are good to each other when the season is not. I would want my teikum to hold the goodness of those people from my home. It is the spirits of the people that make the winter better. They are the ones who are sure to plant the next crop. They are the ones who wake every morning to open the irrigation gates. They will make my teikum green again next year."

I could not bear to look at the congregation as my words were spoken. Some of them were crying, and I never imagined that they might be the people who cried every week at the gathering. I never imagined that my words were actually being spoken at a hundred other gatherings in the region. Maybe others cried too. I don't know. I was not meant to know.

But I did know that there was a camaraderie, a pride that resided in some of the people there. They felt seen, justified in their lives, pride that a young person had acknowledged them and loved them enough to think they could be part of the gods' inner world.

I sat on a cushion at the rear of the raised platform and stared at the ground. At first, I had imagined my words would be dismissed or ignored, and so I had not wanted my name attached to them. But they had not been ignored. The energy of this outland temple had been transformed, unified, by the things I had said while thousands of kilometers away in the city.

And my response was revulsion. Not at them, not at the people, not at the acolytes who spoke and preached and used my words. Instead, it was that these things I had admitted in a different setting, in a different place, were being used out in the open. I had spoken of my teikum and I had been honest. Now my teikum, rather than just living on alongside my memory, bending to my delusions, was smiling up at me in the eyes of a hundred parishioners.

I felt guilty for diminishing these people to some mental allegory. Though I did not understand the complexity of that at the time, I felt it still. And I felt angry that a fragment of something I had spoken had been released into the world, possibly to be corrupted or altered. I truthfully didn't know what was wrong, but I did not like it.

And yet I learned one immaculate truth that day, that exposing my inner world could give people calm, give them hope, and give them a better sense of self. If I was open, honest, and let people in, I might make them happier. All it would cost was a loss of some privacy. My teikum would be for their review and there might not always be so kind a response.

But the heroes I always read of, their stories inevitably got told. I was no warrior. I was no hero of high breeding. I had no moral fiber that would stand against the strongest pillars of evil. Yet, a little bit of my story had been told.

Afterward, Mara had said, "Did you see how they responded to your words? It meant a lot to them."

"I saw it."

"There are not many from this region who ascend to the Tribe."

"Where are you from?" I asked, not sure what to expect.

"I am from Schengen," said Mara.

"I am from Thakkhola," said Chitra, proudly stating his origin. "Not everyone from my territory is prone to rebellion."

He was speaking of Falconer of Europa, who was also born in Thakkhola.

"And I am from West York," said the third acolyte. His name was Able.

"You are not from here?" I asked, surprised.

"No," said Mara. "We are from all over. The Tribe has so many to be parent to. The world is wide and we are few. You should take heart that your words have been good for the people who inspired them."

She smiled at me and I smiled at her, but I did not feel like smiling.

My family took the railway back to our home and my parents did not imagine for a moment that I had been the one who had spoken the words the Tribal Acolytes had used. They did not have anything to say about the sermon itself, but they were so proud of me. They said I looked like I belonged, serene, beautiful. They were impressed at how well I had done during the ceremony, passing the fire and lighting the incense. I had performed the tea ritual perfectly, to their eyes, but I had been doing it every day back at the Temple. They were impressed by the simplest things because they did not understand, thinking it all holy. And the one thing that had actually affected everyone around them had been lost to them as they watched their child rise up, not connecting the words with me.

But my sister, Constance, knew where the words had come from. She also knew I was not serene. I was not calm, and she yet she held her tongue as she listened to my parents.

Back home, she came to my room in the upstairs area we shared together.

"Vive, that was you."

"Yes."

"There are better places to build your teikum on. Much better places than this."

I shook my head, "I don't want to talk about it."

"You already did," she smiled.

I didn't say anything.

"Does it have to be a place?" she asked. "Why not just make something up? It would probably be better than anything else. It would be all yours."

I just sat there, head down, again, feeling exposed. She laughed and sat with me on the bed and said, "Do whatever you want. You always do, anyway. But if you ask me, there's a billion people out there. They all want you to say how great they are and that they're at the center of what's good."

"But you're here too," I said sarcastically through tears. "You are my shining beacon, Constance." And then we both laughed at how stupid it all was.

"I know I am," she said, holding up her hands like some regal figure, powerful, confident. She really was strong and thoughtful. "I am too bright," she said, very serious. "Too wise. The Tribe wouldn't be able to handle me."

"Too divine," I said.

"An angel in flight," she said with conviction, but she could not keep a straight face.

And she was probably right. They would not have been able to handle her. And there are billions of people out there like her who simply will never bow to conventions, whether they be of unity or thought or procession. They play their part as best they can for simplicity's sake, but humans all have a threshold for what they are willing to acquiesce to. I could look her in the eyes and know it. But I did not understand, until years later, that I too had a threshold and, once crossed, could no longer remain in the fold. It took me time to get to the first winter of my teikum, but I did get there, and it was highly unheroic.

4

Back at the Temple, things were different. Things were fast. I was given a new slate of classes and they were mixed with all ages of people who I had never met before. I did not see any of my previous classmates. Aras was lost to some other part of the Temple or had gone back home. But I did make new friends. It was inevitable with the way it was structured. First lessons on the scripture, new and old, math and logic and narrative, then meditation, then discussion. Every day, three rounds.

But I knew they were recording the discussions. I knew my words would be used again, no matter what I said, and I found myself trying to make sure they would be words used back home. I wanted them to be words that might make their way to the outland, to the dusty towns I had never been to. That was what I meditated on. I wanted my words to reach my sister, no matter where she went or what she did.

One morning, not long after my return, I woke to find a delegation entering my very small quarters without warning.

There were four of them, entering while I was still in bed. They filled the tiny room.

The door closed behind them.

I was confused as I sat up, looking at them, thinking it was an angry teacher or a cleaner. But then I stood, still dizzy with sleep, as I realized who it was.

The Quadrumvirate of the Tribe stood before me.

I was unsure whether to bow or kneel or just to look away. I only got a quick glance at them, the Crone in her black robes with a dower face, the soft-eyed Pontifex Rex in white, the Caliph with his long beard and black cap, and the Lama in red, arms uncovered.

"Sit, child," said the Crone, her voice heavy but kind, and I sat back on the bed, thankful that I would not fall on my face with confusion.

"You are to be given a name in waiting, young one," said the Lama.

"And it will be your name for all time. It is the name you may to use inside teikum, and it is how the Tribe will know you and how others will know of you within the Tribe," said the Caliph.

"Your name in waiting shall not be spoken to anyone outside the Tribe, as they are unable to know the source of your growth," said the Pontifex Rex.

"Apsara," said the Crone. "That is your name in waiting. It shall not be written next to your birth name. Your birth name shall not be uttered inside these walls. Apsara, do you understand?"

"I do," I said, overwhelmed at them all speaking to me, overwhelmed at being given a name in waiting so early.

"What is your name, child?" asked the Crone with a tone of demand.

"Apsara, Holy One."

"And do you understand the rules of excommunication?" asked the Pontifex Rex. "Do you understand that this is not just your name now? That this is the name which will be carried through the Tribe to know you, even if you do ascend, as we have?"

"I do."

"Apsara," the Caliph said. "We bestow this name upon you with confidence. You must bestow this name upon yourself. I will know you now by this name."

I was suddenly known by the Caliph of the Tribe, and I was known as Apsara. "Thank you, Holy One."

"And your name in waiting will be yours forever, Apsara. Whoever you were before, it is no longer necessary to maintain that person," said the Lama. "You have a higher calling."

And I sat on the bed as they all spoke the name Apsara to me and thanked me, Apsara, for my insight and my kindness, and then they bid me, Apsara, a good day, and begged leave.

So, I was alone again and overtaken with joy.

I had been told that my birth name, Vive, no longer had to be tended, that I had a name for the person I was going to become. Apsara.

I was becoming Apsara.

How had it happened so early? Years early, it seemed. No one was given a name in waiting until they were in fourth year, and even then, it was only after many discussions, many hours of meditation. I was now a member of the Tribe. A name in waiting was the honored step. Once you had a name in waiting, it did not matter how long you waited or worked, there was a place made for you in the hierarchy of the Tribe, no longer a simple student.

Some would go their whole lives using their name in waiting, cultivating the fresh teikum they were gifted for that new entity. Rebirth is what it felt like, a slate wiped clean. Everything could be different for Apsara.

I did not know whether I wanted anything to be different inside my teikum, my soul, but I was suddenly confronted with the opportunity, and it opened everything in my mind.

Alone in my room I cried because I did not have to hang onto all the old words that flooded my memory, flooded my dreams. They would always be there, but I did not need to analyze them or let them overwhelm me. Apsara would not need to dig into all those old fragments.

I was Apsara and I had a fresh oblivion on which to create. I had my whole life to rebuild myself anyway I wished.

After this, all of my lessons were changed.

There was more open reading, less directed material and more discussion time with meditation at my discretion. My rooms changed and got larger, with windows into the gardens. My clothing changed, becoming nicer fabric, the flowing white of the Tribe.

Another change was that now the discussions were also written. They wanted me to write after questions were posed, explaining my answers in detail. They wanted me to reference any book I could think of, not just the Coda. And all the other acolytes I was with were encouraged to do the same.

We wrote volumes, hundreds of thousands of words, and we spoke for ages to our teachers, hours of talking. I knew it was all collected and recorded but I also loved it. The demand to create, but the freedom to pursue any avenue of thought I wished was unfathomable. And there were always questions, to explain further, to rehash this and research that. But that only led to more and more. I, Apsara, was consumed by my own mental flow. Deeper and deeper into texts, into meditation, the visions inside of me and the words I read and the words I wrote all seemed to mesh together.

I did not go back home during the next season. Apsara was not ready to let go. I had my view into this new person I was to become. It was shared within the Tribe, but it felt so personal, like my growth was suddenly within my own hands and I had the rest of my life to do it. I wanted to solidify my foundation, so I stayed in the Temple and wrote to my family and passed the letters along as I stayed writing and meditating.

My parents wrote back that they understood my choice not to come home. But I knew they would never fully understand. Not really. There was a reverence that came through in the letters but it was matched with regret. I did not like reading them.

My sister wrote once or twice, telling me she would be going to academy and that she was learning new prayers and that she was going to fly and maybe become good enough to fight. She also made fun of me and said she was making up her own prayers too and that they were probably better than mine, so I didn't need to work so hard. She said my parents were torn about my progression, but they had always been torn about that sort of thing and I should not worry about it. After all, Constance said, I was the one who had always had the dreams and had the visions and made the most trouble. Why would that ever change?

I would reread her few letters over and over.

That period in the Temple began a strange transition for me. Nothing spoke of my old self any longer, almost nothing tied to my past. There was only Apsara written on all my things, written by my own hand.

But challenges arose within my teikum.

My inner world, the one which had been exposed during my visit to the temple in Janza, was in stagnation.

The rocky heath where I found calm, where memories nucleated, had begun to fall apart. High on the cliff, between the sea and the valley of my youth, my sight began to wane. I could no longer see the town in the valley. There were no more small figures walking on the streets or in the fields. I could no long see the ocean, only hear it.

I was left with only the rocky plateau and the water well.

I wanted my inner world to expand, not contract, and I knew

there might be nothing left to discover unless I entered the well, but I was unable.

I wrote of the struggles of exploring in my fading teikum.

It was myopic, but I wrote of how our inner worlds change in ways we may never fully understand. I wrote some of this for my own comfort, but also in an attempt to discover something that might help me break away from that stagnant state of being.

If I was to truly become Apsara, should I keep this world? And if I was, how could it be shrinking?

How was I to descend into the deep well and tell people what I had found there? What if others had such wells? Would they be limited access if I failed to enter mine?

It is a guilty way of thought, indicative of a deep loneliness and confusion, but I did not know how else to think of these inner spaces.

I was afraid, but I was compelled.

I was aware enough to understand that the heath was no longer true teikum. I had sat for hours there, tasted all the different gusts of wind, overturned every stone, walked to the cliffs and looked out into nothingness. Teikum lies where you cannot fully see, but what I could still see, I understood. One must always go further. It is the human calling.

The edge of perception is teikum, not a comfortable place, and my comfort was diminishing.

I had not made any friends after being given my name in waiting. All the classes were inwardly focused, but I had been given adversarial discussion partners more frequently, probably picked specifically by those governing the lessons.

I began to ask my proctors and other acolytes what could be done about my loss of inner space, what exercises might open other ways, other paths within me.

The proctors told me, "You are named Apsara. You are one who dances to seduce that which you desire."

And for a while I ceased to meditate. Instead, I would go to the gardens and find a quiet place where no one would know to look for me.

I would start to spin and jump, quietly humming or singing the old folk songs the women of my temple would weave together with overlapping voices.

I would roll on the grass and keep my feet moving to the imagined harmony. My eyes would close as I gritted my teeth to fight through my strained breathing. I would keep going until I fell to my knees, resting in the muck I had created with my movements.

Even then I would try to continue, hoping that I would pass through into some sort of trance. Desperate for rest, I would lie back in the mud and look into the sky and close my eyes and place myself on the heath, feeling stones in my back, and I would stand in my own mind and walk to the deep well and look inside.

At the bottom I would see some rippling water, dark, opaque. But if I danced long enough, hard enough, I would sometimes see a firelight coming up through that water, and I knew there was more below the surface, more to be seen and known. The water could change.

I would run and jump over the rim. I would lean over the edge, trying to fall into the well. But every time I would accidentally roll away or I would miss the opening. It was not as if there was a barrier. It was as if I was physically delinquent, unable to actually hit the target.

It was a devastating outcome and yet I was compelled to try again and again.

After all these failures there came another recess and I, once again, found Aras at the beginning of the next lesson season. She had not yet been provided a name in waiting, but she knew mine already and called me Apsara.

She had been sequestered in another portion of the Temple

and it had been for a very profound goal, focused on the meditations she had had so many challenges with. All her time, all her quiet, had been aimed at understanding how she had overcome some of her challenges and different methods of overcoming more that had appeared.

She said she was chosen because of the difficulties she had had. The name of Vive had come up and that my guidance had been communicated so that it might help others, but that had been only the first of the gifts that Aras had given to the study of meditation within the Temple.

I did not even think of the connection for a while. We were Apsara and Aras, together. I would sit at her back and we would breathe together at night. We would whisper what was in our minds, speaking our inner voices aloud for the other to hear.

And when she asked me to dance in the garden for her, so that she might help me enter the well, I did not realize that I had never brought it up before, that the only way she would have known was if she had been told by someone else what I had been trying to accomplish. It was, instead, only a relief that washed over me, having someone to be with me when I tried to go further, someone to act as a guide and if not a guide, then just a friend.

In the garden we found a distant place near the outer walls, a place I had used before. A circle of footprints was still mashed into regrown grass. For a moment we stood quietly in the open space and a look came over Aras as she suddenly understood, by the size of the ring, by the depth of flattened dead grass, how much I had been struggling. For the first time, as she eyed the proof of my efforts, I truly felt the weight of it.

"Dance," she told me and so I closed my eyes. It made me feel as if she could not see me, I started and I did not stop. I would turn my back to her and open my eyes to make sure I knew where I was in the clearing, but then I would close them again as I got closer to my physical limit. I danced longer and with more fervor than when I was alone. I did not want her to see me quit or fail.

She had bore her soul to me almost two years before. I could do the same for her.

But when I fell to my knees, unsure if I could even move, she came forward and pulled me up, hand in hand, and she started to dance, and I mirrored her steps as she jumped and whirled in the mud. I did everything I could to match her movements and her face was smiling, a narrow face with blue eyes and dirty blond hair. I had a hard time keeping my head up, but I wanted to keep looking at her, I wanted to keep seeing her dance because she was doing it for me.

She exaggerated gasping breath for me to mimic.

When I collapsed again, I could not keep my eyes all the way open, so I just let them hang shut, my face numb, my body rushing with chills.

"Take me to your well, Apsara," she said, and I was there, standing on the edge of the well. Then she instructed me to look in.

I leaned over and looked down and I could see the water below, bright and fiery like never before, glowing with warmth.

She kissed me, as I lay on the cool earth.

I rolled over the edge of the well, face first, and fell straight down, my lips hitting the soft water, my face caressed by kind hands, and accepted through the glowing surface. There was a rush of cold and I came to rest upon a stone floor in what was almost total darkness, except for a small fire in an open hearth, the source of that warm glow.

-Water into fire.-

I did not know where I was, but I knew how I had come to be there, through the bottom of the well. I did not know what was in the room or why that fire was going, but I knew this was what I had always hoped for, and I was able to stay there for what felt like a very long time.

When I woke up, Aras was there, and she kissed me again. She had done for me what I had done for her years before.

It had been the extra exertion, but it had also been the kiss and thin film of clockwork on her lips that had helped me through. I did not know it at the time, but I would not have cared. I don't care now. She had a key to a door, and she used it when I needed it most.

The small doses of clockwork and other drugs helped me to get to that stone room, the one below the well, without hours of dancing, without punishing my body and mind to the edge of endurance. And once there, other sensations made that fire get brighter, bodies touching and searching, warm sun, drips of water down the spine.

I found I could stay there longer and longer and I began to write about it, to meditate on what I was seeing in that space, the walls of dank brick. This was the new element of teikum to be explored.

It had taken effort to get there, but also it had taken love and sensation.

The discussions started again, and this was the focus of everything for me. There were countless people in the borderlands, and countless others who could not get to a congregation easily. These people did not need to worry about getting to the temples or the gatherings. It did not matter if your congregation was inside a shining building or out in the street or in a tin hovel. It didn't matter. I knew it didn't. You could have a temple inside.

"Aras, do you still hear other people's voices when you go inside yourself?" I asked her one night as we lay together.

"Yes," she said. "But they don't always speak to me, telling me what to do, admonishing me. That is rare now. Once you helped me to see through them, it became easier to ask them questions, easier to hear other voices from someplace else in me. Now they sing together. They sing hymns in a language I don't yet understand. And sometimes your voice is there too."

It was that inner chorus that became the source of our separation and Aras went back into seclusion after a year together.

I knew it was the right thing for her, so I never imagined that it was the intent of the proctors, the governors, to take her away from me. I never imagined that they wanted me to write about loss or loneliness and had decided to provide me with some. I never imagined that they could understand my inner journey so well, that they knew I would never see the full extent of my stone room with love and sensation as a distraction. I did not understand that, but they did take her away from me.

I know that now.

Too much outer connection inhibits inner growth.

5

I did what they intended without realizing it.

I wrote of my sadness, of my loneliness. I did not know where Aras went or when she would return, and no one could tell me because Aras was not her name anymore.

I still do not know if this is true or not. I don't know if it was her work with me that raised her esteem enough to earn a name in waiting. Or if she had left the tribe. Or if, for some other reason, was sent away.

I was sad, but I was not angry. I thought there was still time. Aras would have her time to grow, just as I had. And I still had work to do. The work was worth the hiatus of love.

My words traveled the world and I did not know it.

Apsara of the Tribe was who I became to those who spoke my words in the temples and those who read my writings on the networks. I do not believe my words were special, but I never considered myself someone who had ascended to a higher state of thinking or feeling during the congregations.

Yet, that was how the Tribe presented me. Apsara was a guide, a seer, one who spoke with the gods inside.

The real me longed to be quiet, to be one with my body and name. I did not know the depths of the distress I was feeling.

I wanted life near to me, whether it be in a garden, or in a busy place, but I wanted to be quiet in its presence. I did not want to hear the scriptures read to me. I would rather read them myself. These opinions were mine, but the Tribe found my words resonating with those who had no choice in the matter and they used this for their own purposes.

The axlir, my family's social class, responded just as those who had been at the congregation back near my home. They felt the holiness of their normal lives, the simple and quiet work that allowed for survival and some sustenance and time to think and breathe and live. They did not perform a holy ritual every day. They did not read the whole Coda.

But they did believe. They wanted to see themselves accepted. This was what my parents were, what they wanted more than anything.

The ketgan were another story, the social class of the borderlands, those multitudes who sat outside the purview of the Tribe or the UTC. They had never had inroads to the holy ways. There were few ordained temples in the borderlands. There were places of worship, and I did not understand it, but my words were giving credence to those places and those people, who had no choice but to turn inward.

I was calling them holy and that was what they wanted to hear.

The Coda of Unification was built off the holy concept of humanity being divine, but over the years, the whole Tribe had become too polished. They had focused on their rituals and their practice and on teaching the next group of acolytes like myself. They had never really held the minds of those in the borderlands, those who lived outside Tribal influence, but they had always wanted to transcend that barrier.

The UTC wanted it as well, but they had no other way to bring those outsiders in. They had no desire to admit them into the more protected classes, but they did want an element of control. The Tribe was the only way to do that, the mechanism of the faiths, and I was becoming a very useful tool.

6

I was the Tribe's new apostle, cast before the spiritual community. Even as they used me, I did not imagining myself as their pawn or their creation.

I was struggling again. I was floating among the other followers who, like myself, had been given names in waiting and were part of the rigorous lessons.

Everyone was older than me. I was always the youngest in the discussions, the youngest at the meals. I had the least experience and I had never traveled. I knew my home, my lessons, and my own mind, but nothing else.

The older acolytes did not seem to be struggling.

I didn't know if that was true or not because they didn't confide in me like my peers had in the previous season.

It didn't really matter. They could not guide me because while they appeared calm and collected, certain of what they spoke, I could not see what they had grown from. They existed as they were, appearing to me to have entered the temple as fully formed students of the Tribe, ready to commit themselves to whatever task was laid before them.

They ate simply and quietly, wearing the mask of pious maturity, and they made love the same way, a rhythmic process, seeking their own becoming, not interested in sharing the ritual.

They did not have to study for as long as I did and they did not have to dance for hours to access their inner worlds. They would meditate and they would disappear into whatever teikum possessed them, seemingly without effort or energy expended. I believed in their skill and power, even if I could not see it for myself.

After a time, this all made sense to me.

These were acolytes from wealthy families, trained from a very early time to follow the Tribal flows and to cultivate their inner worlds in anticipation of greater work. They were more than capable of doing what the Quadrumvirate asked of them, what the Tribe needed.

I believed this. I still believe it, in some ways. There were excellent pupils in those lessons. There were minds and hearts that I fell briefly in love with but they could never really fall in love with me. I was not like them. I was not as polished. Not as knowledgeable. Not as far thinking beyond the Tribe. My politics were lacking, and my youth did me no favors.

Every night and every mid-day I would sit and write about how confusing it was. At all the discussions, I would talk about the challenges of youth, how we are all taught what our schools and our families think is right and best, but that no one can know what story will eventually come to us, call to us. It will be a story that shines to us and we will never be able to look away. I wanted to hear and read all those stories. I wanted to tell them around a hot fire in a cold desert. If humanness was next to godliness, then our human origins, stories in the darkness, must be holy. For the longest time, for the entirety of our human age of growth, they truly were.

I thought that sometimes your own story could be the one

that catches your eye, shining in the distance. That could be my life. That could be my tale of adventure.

And so, you walk toward it. You go to an open heath, and you look down at the black sea and into the village in the opposite valley. You go down the well and into the strange room of stone that opens up below the water and you rest there by the fire. My story captured my imagination early on and then I was stagnating again, lonely, confused. The well room was empty, shrouded in darkness despite the flames.

I sought out more sensation.

I danced longer and stayed up for days on end and I fasted to cause delirium. I let my mind begin to stumble over itself. And yet there was no waking dream that shed light on those places I could not see.

I took more clockwork and I found other toxins to distort my mind. The proctors knew I was struggling and they provided me with new substances, crafted and tested by those who researched the meditative methods, shortening the way for those seeking the inner paths. The procession of dissociation was allowed to continue as long as I provided the written pages and showed up to the discussions.

For a long time, I played this game of hectic alteration. And it did me some good, but not enough for my impatient mind.

It changed me. I was indeed altered. My thinking, my feeling, my view of the few people around me and the small world I was exposed to.

I slid down into myself and toiled in my own convolutions.

But it was all so self-serving. Everything I wrote was of how I hated the pursuit, how I no longer saw the gods or heard voices in my realm.

This was when I first, impulsively, tried to take my own life.

I was in the garden, alone, body and mind dissolving, failing to see. I was exhausted from dancing and unable to cross the water threshold, denied at the mouth of the well.

I was stumbling at the perimeter of the muddy clearing I had made and then fell under the foliage of an overgrown bush. Trying to sit up, I found that it was an inkberry and the fruit was there for the taking.

Most importantly, I knew it would cause extreme pain.

I wanted the pain to erase me and it almost did.

Before I was lost to the toxins, I felt every joint in my body grinding in motion, every pump of my heart moving acidic blood down to my stomach, my body revolting at what I had done. I was distinctly alive, and my body wanted to remain that way.

I lay in the dirt below the inkberry, and as the pain grew inside my belly, I tried to snuff it out.

I took fistfuls of earth and placed the dry grit into my mouth, and I chewed, hoping it would satiate the searing pain. I ate the garden's rich soil and remembered a dream that I had had as a child.

It was only a flash of awakening as I tasted the dirt and swallowed, but the memory was like a bolt of lightning from my past, something that had been held in waiting in the recesses of my mind.

In my dream there had been bodies falling from the sky into our family's wheat field, like rain on a full moon. In the darkness I had run back and forth to try to catch them, always arriving too late. One after another they fell just beyond my reach, beyond my vision.

But when I finally came upon one, it was wrapped tightly in a red shroud, rope, also dyed red, tight round the joints, across the chest and neck, keeping the shroud closed. I had fallen to my knees in despair, knowing that whatever was inside the shroud was holy, knowing it was something powerful, and I had begun to dig a grave with my hands in the soft ground. I ate every handful of dirt that I removed, knowing it was holy, knowing it was human and could never be wasted. "It must be inside," I heard myself saying. I was mourning the passing of the shrouded entity in that dream and I was mourning the passing of myself in the garden of the Tribe.

The memory of the dream was fleeting as the pain erupted in my stomach again, making me want to scream as I rolled in the inkberry's shade. I would not be able to escape the pain, but the consumption of it could be holy, the consumption of self.

This was holy ground, new terrain.

I closed my eyes.

Instantly I was in my stone room and though the fire was dim. No gazing into the well was required. No descent needed.

I could see the walls, the dank bricks covered with green moss and flecks of micaceous material glittering in the murk.

A heavy circle was drawn with red paint, the line rough and splattered, on the floor where I sat. A knot had been added to the line.

-Ouroboros.-

I saw it, took it all in. But I could not move, frozen in place by the pain from the outer world.

The pain had taken me there, the taste of earth still in my mouth, and then the pain took me away, but I knew what I had seen and what to look for next time if I was ever able to get back.

I have written before about how they removed the inkberry bush. I have written about how I was sorry they did that. I am sorry for it still, but this is also when the gods came to me in truth. This is when I found the voices whispering to me in different tones in the twilight. "Can you hear us? Can you see us? We have things to tell you."

7

For weeks after I ate the berries and the dirt, I was in the direct care of the healers outside the temple.

There were no discussions. There were no writings. They asked me questions, but only about how I was feeling. Are you thirsty? Are you comfortable? They were kind and they would leave me to myself most of the time.

I am certain they were observing me, making sure I wasn't prepared to try to die again, to try for more pain, but they did leave me alone, and in the darkness of the hospital room I was able to simply think and listen and recover.

In the middle of the night, when the door was closed, I would try to sink back into my world, and I would sit upon the rocky heath and the god's voices would come to me.

There was only one shape, one entity. It was a man, tall and shrouded in shepherd's clothing who would wander over, no sheep or animals in tow. His eyes were knowing, and he would look at me for a long time, without kindness or malice. His dark hair was cut short, as if by his own hand, and his skin was tanned like that of my father after a season in the fields. After several silent meetings, he asked me, "Do you know where I have come from, my origin?"

"No," I answered honestly. "But that does not concern me. You are here."

"Do you know my name?" he asked, looking off toward that impossibly dark sea, frothing in the far distance as heavy clouds moved in.

"No. What is your name?" I asked.

"If you don't know," he said, "then I can't truly know. I can only hope."

"How am I supposed to know? We've only just begun to speak."

He smiled and though it was a kind smile, there was something painful about it. "I will stay here for as long as I have to," he said. "But you have always known me. Since the beginning of your days. I have always existed. And by your own name shall you know me."

"Which name?"

"I am you," he said after a long time, the wind whipping by. "When you call to yourself, I will answer."

I did not know how to respond.

We sat and watched the growing thunderheads over the sea until the form of a bird flew towards us, only a small shadow at such a distance. Our eyes picked it out at the same time against the black clouds and then he asked, "Why do you always fall down the well? Perhaps you should try to fly down."

Another came to my inner world on the following day.

"Are you a spirit? Are you a goddess?" I asked, looking up at her.

She was a towering woman, strong and wild, who came and stood before me, never sitting.

She sneered at me, her powerful form seeming to be terribly

close. I could feel her presence running through me, enveloping me, demanding complete surrender.

"I am not of your world," she said, and her voice echoed through my body. "I was brought into being in a backwards way."

Whether it was dream or sight, teikum or the hand of god, I had been able to cross some sort of threshold. The pain or the quiet or the medications they were giving me had allowed me some inner sight. Perhaps it was all three or something of which I am still unsure.

8

When I was strong enough to talk, a nurse came to me with caring eyes and asked me to write something. "If you are feeling up to it, Apsara, can you please write just a few sentences for us?"

"Is this a lesson?" I asked, confused.

"No," she said, smiling. "Far from it. But it would be meaningful."

I did not understand, but it felt good to take the page, and I wrote about the man I had seen and about the ghosts who visited me in my dreams.

When I gave her the page, weakly scrawled, I saw tears in her eyes.

"Thank you, Apsara, for your gift. There are many who have been fearing for you."

"What do you mean?" I asked. But then there were other nurses and doctors there thanking me and doing the standard checkups.

That night, I felt good enough to stand up and support my own weight next to the bed. Another nurse came, and she put her arm at my back and helped me to the door. I was still so weak.

In the hallway, along the walls, there were flowers, hundreds of bouquets that filled the whole space with a sweet and natural smell. There were baskets of fruit and handwritten notes.

"What is all this?" I asked.

"These are your offerings, Apsara," the nurse said matter-of-factly. "These have been brought for you."

"By whom?" I asked, feeling a heavy weight in my stomach, a dull pain that quickly reminded me why I was there in the first place.

"By those who wish your soul to be well, holy one."

I stopped and looked down at a cluster of flowers, thin and peculiar, familiar but strangely proportioned. Feathers had been tucked into the spindly assemblage, iridescent and shining. Some of them were painted.

"We are happy you are feeling better," said the nurse. "Your writing has given people much to rejoice over."

I understood what was happening. I was able, in that moment, to wrap my mind around how everything had been escalating without me ever realizing it. I knew what was being done but I was unable to feel it. It was an impossible concept to grow comfortable with and so I remained numb to it as I looked down the hall at all the strange gifts.

I asked the nurse to help me, and together we picked up all the notes, all the pieces of paper, and that night I sat in my bed, alone, and read them. There were hundreds of notes.

"Apsara, your struggle is our struggle."

"If you are well, we will be well."

It was like this for every piece of paper. "Have you read this scripture? Have you heard this story? It gave me heart, perhaps it will give you some as well."

Who were these people? How did so many know the name Apsara? How did they know I was ill or where I was? But I knew the answers.

At the time I felt re-violated as I had when the acolytes used my words in their sermon at my local temple. But this time it was so much larger. How could any of my words be this meaningful? My thoughts and words felt rickety under the weight.

Alone, I thought back through the selfish and self-obsessed things I had written. I thought about how introspective I had been, how myopic all my work had sounded. How could anyone see themselves in that? But they had and that was all that mattered to them.

"Your struggles are ours."

I was afraid to leave the hospital, but when the time came, it was a curated operation. There were people in the streets outside the building complex and I could see them from my window, gathering in throngs.

The proctors who came to escort me gave me a white veil with which to cover my face. I was still weak, but they told me it would be most meaningful if I walked without aid. So, I walked with them down the hall and the nurses and doctors watched me go, bowing as I went, and I was relieved to have my face covered as I gently bowed back.

At the base of the building they explained that it was a short walk to the transport and that it was important for the people to see me, to know I was strong and healthy, but I did not feel that way. They said there would be questions shouted from the crowd but that I did not need to answer. I would be allowed peace back at the temple to convalesce.

On the way out, I went through the scanner and my name appeared on the screen: Apsara, Acolyte, Tribe. A few outside could see the screen through the windows and a ripple of excitement passed through the crowd as my name affirmed their hopes.

Outside, the air was hot and I felt the crowd's energy. I heard them all, all their voices, all their inner expectations calling out, chanting into my mind.

"Apsara! Thank you!"

"Will you write again?"

"You have returned to us!"

"Holy one! Bless me!"

"Did you greet the gods?"

I stopped and looked in the direction of that question, but behind my white veil I could not really see who had spoken.

The escorts stopped with me, uneasy looks on their faces as the crowd pushed in.

"I have met some of the gods inside me," I said, and I did my best to say it clearly. My voice came out powerfully, matching the crowd's energy. They had come to see me and I could not lie to them.

"Tell us, Apsara!" someone yelled.

"Show us!"

"We will show each other," I said, responding to their desperation and then the escort was moving me again and I was shut inside the transport. All the way to the Temple, no one spoke. I felt sickeningly detached as we landed inside the walls.

I thought they would take me back to my quarters, my small and spartan room, but instead they took me up the lift to a level I had never been to. There were honor guards in the hallway and I was taken to a new room. It was open and large and there were books and screens and a massive wrapping window and a balcony where I could look down into the square just outside the walls.

My things had been brought from my original room, and I was told this was to be my new living space.

They said nothing as they left, and I was alone again with the sun setting.

That night I went out onto my balcony, into the warm air and looked out into the haze of the city beyond the Temple. All the lights of Schengen were visible, and I could hear the masses using their feet and their vehicles to move about. There was so much energy swirling through that world.

I had not been able to see or hear the city from my old room.

I lay down on the ground and looked up into the sky. It felt comforting to hear those noises, to know there were people out there who had been listening in, even if I wasn't sure I wanted them to. They did not know my face, but now they knew my voice. In turn, I wanted to know their stories, I wanted to hear their voices speak back to me.

I fell asleep outside under the faintest hint of stars through the clouds, listening to the sounds of the human world.

That night, when I dreamed, I was visited again by the man. It had been a while since I had seen him, but he came and sat next to me on the edge of the well and we both looked in at the water, glowing and swirling.

"Do you know how we were brought into being?"

"What do you mean by 'we'? You and me? Or do you mean the others?"

"I mean all of us," he said.

"There is no way I could know that."

"You will be asked to know. You will be asked to provide an answer."

"Just because you ask doesn't mean I have to answer."

"That is where you are wrong," he said with a firm command in his voice. "You will be asked over and over until you have no choice but to answer. And then that answer will become the truth."

"That can't be right."

"It is the way it will be. For you. For countless others. So, you must find an answer you can live with."

"How were we brought into being?" I asked aloud, making the question my own. "Like what does it mean to be here?"

The man shrugged. "What does it mean to wear the mask of

humanity? We were not always this way. Where did we find these faces? Why did we put them on?"

"Because it is easier to look into teikum through these eyes," someone said behind me, and I turned around. The towering woman stood there, looking off toward the horizon. "It is easier to look when we can hide our reactions from ourselves."

"But why would we hide ourselves from teikum?" I asked.

"I told you I was made the other way around," she said. "I want the void to look upon me and see something grander than myself. I want the void to see the face I chose for myself."

"But you cannot trick teikum."

"The trick is what matters most. How else do you think we came into being?" she asked, and I shrugged because I did not have a better answer. Again, her will seemed to wash over me and I was unable to resist. It was dizzying and I almost fell backwards into my well, but the man's hand came out and supported me, keeping me upright on the precipice.

9

fterward, things happened very quickly.

A small entourage came to visit me in the morning, three young acolytes and one proctor. The proctor spoke to me as they laid out a meal for me.

"Apsara of the Tribe. We are here to prepare you for the arrival of the Crone of the Quadrumvirate."

I sat at the table and watched as these three young people moved around me, tidying up and preparing coffee, unpacking more of my things. They were about my age, probably some of the youngest acolytes they could find to help get me ready. This was to be a formal affair.

"Why is the Crone coming to see me?" I asked, unsure if I was frightened.

"An ascension has been perceived," said the proctor. "A search began many years ago to find the next Neta-Teej. It was commenced after a vision seen by the Quadrumvirate."

"And she is coming to test me?"

Even the acolytes stopped what they were doing and waited for the proctor to respond. There had not been a Neta-Teej in the thirty years following the death of the previous incarnation.

Reincarnation. It was a word I thought to myself.

"It will be the first set of tests. And countless others are being tested, have been tested, across the Coalition."

Reincarnation.

I barely ate, my guts still not fully settled.

In the back room was a long open closet with space enough to contain the high-quality clothes suited to the station of whoever was to be living in large quarters like these. But my small tunics hung to one side, the remainder of the closet empty.

The three acolytes helped me dress in a black garment that had been brought for me. It had flowing details embroidered into the cloak and a hood with a fine veil that could be pulled over the eyes. I said that I didn't want to hide my face, and the proctor assured me that it wouldn't be necessary for today's meeting. However, the clothes were mine, no matter the outcome of the testing.

"And I might need this veil?"

"It may be a requirement of your station."

He left and the acolytes made sure everything was sitting right on my body, made sure my hair, having grown long and straight, was orderly.

I did not look in the mirror. I knew I would not like what I saw, a weak child, confused. I would want to see the man in the shepherd's clothing, hair cropped short, patient eyes and control in his stature. I would want to see the herdsman reflected back at me if I was truly to be myself in that moment. I would want to be a tall and powerful woman, dressed in cloths for wild violence.

Instead, I was going to be tested for something else entirely.

"The Crone is here," said the proctor from the other room.

The acolytes dropped their hands and bowed their heads.

"I am afraid," I said in a whisper to them. I didn't want them to look at the floor. I wanted them to look at me, to see me as someone their age, someone who was about to meet the Crone of the Quadrumvirate face to face.

"Do not be afraid, Apsara," said one of them, barely glancing up. It was an empty statement.

"Look at me," I said, feeling desperate. "Please."

All three of them looked up, feeling the tension, as we were likely keeping the Crone waiting.

"Thank you for helping me," I said. "Please stay afterward if they'll let you."

They all glanced at each other and nodded slightly.

"Thank you," I said and bowed to them.

Then I turned and went out, filled with overpowering loneliness.

The Crone was not waiting at the center of the main sitting room as had been prepared. She was out on the balcony peering over the edge, straight down, but as I entered the room she looked up at me for a moment, then let her gaze fall over the edge once more.

I sat down as I had been instructed to do and watched her as she stood quietly on the balcony. After a while, she came inside and walked across the room. She moved along the wall, studying the books that constituted the private library.

I felt ashamed suddenly that I hadn't even had the chance to look through them the previous night.

She was not a large person, only slightly taller than me, but she moved with a power that I could feel. It was imposing and seemingly dangerous.

Her black robes hung loosely off her shoulders, constructed of many layers, giving the impression that there were countless things hidden in the bodice below.

The proctor walked me over and said, "Holy Crone, I present Apsara of the Tribe."

"Leave us," she said sharply and turned to study me. Her gray hair was long, split over the back of her neck and draped down the front of her cloak, extending almost to her waist. Her face was hard, but not unkind. It seemed to be a face capable of everything possible within human emotion and with eyes that had bore witness to it.

I bowed and we took each other in. I sensed she did not want us to speak until everyone had left the room.

When the doors closed and we were alone, she said, voice slow enough to be informative, but direct enough to be unmistakable, "Everything that happens now is part of the test of ascension. You may be tested by others. But I knew the first Neta-Teej intimately. She was the one who identified me for ascension when I was young."

"Yes, Holy Crone."

"Do you feel comfortable in your new clothes? Your new rooms?" she asked.

"No, Holy Crone."

"Don't say 'Holy Crone' after everything. It slows all of this down. We are in no rush, but our minds move faster without the baggage."

"No. I don't feel comfortable in all of this."

"Why not?"

I hesitated. "Too much change. I could be comfortable here. But it is all new. And empty. These are not my things."

"And your clothes?"

"They do not make me feel like me."

"What makes you feel like you?"

"I don't know yet."

"Have you felt like yourself in standard acolyte tunic? Do you remember feeling like yourself back before your time in the Temple?"

I shook my head.

"Never?"

"When I don't have to wear clothes, I am myself," I said. "Everything else is a uniform."

She smiled, "These uniforms become us. It is part of our service to the people. If they could all know us personally over time, and by our truest names, we would not need the cloaks to communicate clearly. But we do this to help carry our message, to help with the translation."

"I understand."

She watched me, observing my response to these questions and taking in my discomfort.

"I think you do understand. That is why you are uncomfortable."

I shook my head, but then nodded subtly.

"Come," she said and turned toward the bookshelf. "Have you had time to see the books available to you here?"

I stepped forward, feeling my shame again, "No, I was going to review the library after resting."

"We will review together."

And we moved along the shelves, and I was amazed at the volumes. It was not a huge library, but a private collection with a preference for old books, old stories, some of which I had read and many I had only heard of. But some of the secure volumes were there, allowed only for the Tribe's higher orders. These I had never even heard of but was able to identify based on the markings on their spines. There were also interpreted versions of the Coda of Unification, bound informally and stacked in sequence with the names of the interpreter written by hand on the leather.

"This is a curious library, is it not?" asked the Crone.

"It was the library of someone who could have any books they wished," I said.

"Whose library?"

It struck me suddenly and obviously. "This is the Proto Neta-Teej's library."

"And what is wrong with this library?" she asked directly.

I was caught off guard. How could anything be wrong with the library? It was a collection of amazing volumes! But it was a question, demanding, and so I started along the shelves, trying to puzzle it out.

There were the books of comparative religion which anyone would expect to find as key reference and there were histories to help understand the lineage and politics of anything or anyone across the Coalition. There were legends and classics that I wanted to pull off the shelves and start reading immediately. There were books of mantra and meditation practice, sedentary and excitatory methodology. There were books on psychology, from developmental through to the mentality of death.

Were there too many books on history? Too many books on the stories? Was this supposed to be some sort of warning on my own reading habits?

The Neta-Teej would need all these things. The Neta-Teej had been a guide for spiritual growth and understanding. They helped others understand and cultivate their own teikum. They would need to understand culture and history as a lens for actualization. They would need the varied and informal interpretations of the Coda of Unification, no matter how extreme. All these books felt imperative if the Neta-Teej was intent on understanding all the paths we could travel to find teikum, to explore it.

I went to the informal stack of the Coda of Unification. There were more than fifty of them, their pages covered with notation and more writing added into the binding by whoever had done the work. They were proof that the Coda of Unification could be a living document for those who chose to delve deep. Each one wore the brand of security, only for the eyes of those who were very elevated in the Tribe.

"May I?" I asked and the Crone nodded, face neutral, watching me still.

I pulled one off the top, this volume notated by a cleric from a hundred years previous. It was a very early interpretation, fairly recent after the Coda had first been published, and it was filled with segments crossed out, notation as to why that should be rejected, and then new pages added, cut from different old holy books. There were entirely new pages the cleric had written themselves by hand.

I closed the book and set it back on the shelf, feeling as if I had seen something I should not have. But there were so many on the shelf and it made my mind wheel. There were books of detailed dissent against the final Coda of Unification in this library. They were historical in their record of those who did not agree to the early Coda.

And I knew then what was missing. Each of these volumes was a work against the details, a dissection of the document, but not a complete rejection of it.

I took another volume with a more recent date and started through the pages that had been added, whether typed or written. Then another one.

The Crone watched me.

"These are heretical documents," I said. "But this library is incomplete for the Neta-Teej."

"Correct," she said. "Why?"

"Because there are no puritanical writings from those who would refused to give up their one faith, even for the unity the Coda offered. There is nothing from Europa, the Falconer's Treatise would be here. There are no portal scrolls. There are no works from the Muhanzu, the Armada, or the Martian rebellion."

"Where are they?"

It occurred to me then that they would have indeed been part of the Neta-Teej's library. But some of them had been published after her death. Some of them had likely been removed in preparation for my arrival in the quarters, stored away someplace where eyes would never read them.

"They have been hidden. Or they have not been added to the library yet."

"Very good. The Neta-Teej is able to plot a course through disparate concepts. This is only possible when the two points are well understood, well known. Another Neta-Teej would need to add to this library."

Reincarnation. The word entered my head once more.

The Crone walked to another shelf, stacked high with books of religion, and began another line of questioning.

"Did you intend to kill yourself with the inkberries?"

I felt weak suddenly, reminded of how this had all started.

"I don't know," I said, and it wasn't a lie. There had been a large part of me that wanted to, and there was another part of me that had just let it happen. I hadn't really made the decision, but it hadn't been made for me either.

"It is a human thing to question the merits of our own survival," the Crone said.

"It was impulsive," I said, wanting to sit down, but also knowing I was expected to stay close to the Crone. "It was not completely lucid."

"We rarely are," she said. "Was it impulsive to eat the dirt?"

I stood silent, unsure how to answer.

"If you do not know, then the answer is 'yes'," the Crone said. "You may sit down now. I can feel how unwell you are."

"What do you mean, you can 'feel'?"

"Your breathing rate has changed. Your feet are planted firmly on the floor where only moments ago they were energetic, moving along the tile as your eyes searched books."

I went slowly to the sitting area and carefully set myself back down in a cushioned chair, trying to keep myself alert.

"You have written a few things since your recovery," she said. "They were surprisingly honest."

"I did not know there were people listening, reading, until I woke up with the healers."

"You are still young. Know, from now on, that everything we do or say is used to forward the message. Everything. Not just writings and discussion. There is a constant need in the universe. Your honesty has won you many caring followers."

"I didn't know."

"But your honesty has also shown me something which brought me here today."

I felt better sitting down and I drank some water from one of the vessels on the small table. Had the last Neta-Teej drank from these glasses?

"You wrote of the ghosts that have come to visit you," said the Crone. "I have questions about their nature. The man, you wrote that he was you, in a way. In what way?"

"He is not me," I said. "It isn't like that. It is a feeling that we are one. Or will be. He comes from inside of me."

"I understand," she said, turning to face me. "I have also seen things like this. But I have also seen other things in telkum. Spirits who are not necessarily of me. I know you have seen the same."

"How do you know that?" I had not written of the tall woman.

The Crone narrowed her eyes and said, "If you stay here long enough, you will know these things by looking into the eyes of others. This place has already changed you. It will change you further."

I did not answer, but I believed her. I didn't know if I wanted to be changed.

"Now, speak," she said. "There are others who have visited. There will be one who has more presence, more power than the others. Describe them."

"It is a woman. She is the only one. She is much larger than me, strong, like a warrior. There is a power about her that over-whelms me."

"What does she look like?"

"Graying red hair. Pale skin. Gray eyes, bigger than mine. She is wearing handmade clothes made of animal skin. Like a wilding."

The Crone came to sit across from me.

"And does she make demands of you?"

"No," I said and then realized that wasn't fully true. "She doesn't speak the demands. But there is a force to her. Something that demands I follow or let her inside."

"Is she not already inside you?"

I had to think on that for a time but finally responded, "No. She isn't. The herdsman is. He is of me. But the woman is not."

"How do you know?"

"Because," I said, trying to piece it together, "the man knows about my journey to the bottom of the well. He understands what is down there. He has made suggestions on how to get down safely. But the woman does not look in. Her power, her force, almost knocked me in one time, clinging to me like a weight. If she was of me, she would not need me to take her down."

"Why do you resist her?"

"I don't," I admitted, trying to remember how it felt. "Not really. It just hasn't happened that way. But she does scare me. There is danger in her."

"There was danger in the inkberries," she said. "You ate those."

I drank more water and she watched me, my hands shaking and my eyes darting around the room, feeling her heavy gaze.

"This part of the test is over," the Crone said, standing suddenly. "You have passed for now, but we are in the very early days. My test is not complete. I will return to you when the time is right, and this will continue."

"How will you know when the moment is right?"

"You will tell me."

"How will I know?"

"You will know."

And in a moment, she was gone and the acolytes were back in the room, standing at attention, waiting for me to say or do something.

It took me a while to compose myself, fighting back tears that came from the onslaught of too many emotions, and then I beckoned them to follow, and they came with me into the closet again and I undressed and they helped me to hang the black-patterned garment so it would not wrinkle. It was a fine gift, and I did not know how it needed to be stored, but they did and they made sure it was hung correctly, the one beautiful piece alone with the old tunics in a massive closet.

Still in my undergarments, I covered myself with a robe and went back into the sitting area.

They followed me closely, I think worried that I might fall over. It felt good to have them there and I realized I could feel their concern for me.

"Please sit," I said and they came, only one of them willing to sit on the same wide couch as me, willing to risk the proximity.

To this day I cannot fully understand how he must have felt when I fell into his lap and curled into a ball. There was warmth to him. His clothes had a smell to them, not sterile like the hospital, not just clean like fresh laundry, but a human mix.

The comfort, the smell, the kindness, all stabbed at my loneliness, waking it.

I closed my eyes and said, "I'm sorry. I don't know what comes next."

I wanted my sister to wake me up and carry me back to a warm bed.

"It's okay, Apsara," said one of the others in a meek voice. "We are here until the sun goes down. I am sure it was trying. No need to be sorry."

But I was sorry. I had not truly been prepared for any of it and now these acolytes, at least as young as myself, were trying to offer me comfort. There was a very long silence and I kept my eyes closed through it, unwilling to look at these youths watching over me.

"Have you read anything I have said or written?" I asked suddenly, eyes still closed, hoping they would say 'no'. Hoping they would react with confusion, as if they had no idea who I was, just another acolyte going through a difficult time.

"Yes," said the boy whose lap my head was on. His hand was on my head, comforting but unmoving. "We all have."

I shut my eyes even tighter and asked, "When did you encounter it?"

"A few years ago," said one of the girls across from me. "We all know your words."

"Have you been given names in waiting?" I asked.

"No," said the boy. "We have gone on the path of the healers. We are acolytes of the Tribe, but we have a different path than you. We may be given names in waiting, we may ascend, but it is a different order of progression for us."

I was still very much under medical care.

"Thank you for being here," I said. "But it's time for you to leave."

"You still need care, Apsara," one of them said. "You still need comfort. It is okay."

"No," I said. "I need to be alone now."

They obeyed, but as they left, I could see the proctor looking in at me from the hall.

10

The sun was setting and I knew they were watching me, eyes on my every move. The Crone might have been concerned about whether or not I could become the next Neta-Teej, but the healers and the Tribe were worried about Apsara finding a substitute for inkberries. They were worried about losing someone who had made a connection with the people.

They brought dinner, and I sat still and thanked them as they laid beautiful food on the table. Either they thought I would not want to go to the main dining hall with all the others, or they would not permit it. I wasn't sure but I was also not yet ready to test such things.

I went out onto the balcony as the sun dipped behind Schengen.

Prisms of light refracting in and among the buildings, obscured by the haze and dust kicked into the atmosphere from the deserts in the southeast.

If I jumped, or slipped, from the balcony, I wondered how far I would fall before a net field would catch me.

It would be the opposite of reincarnation. It was an amusing thought until I realized it was another suicidal ideation.

I knocked my water glass over the side and it broke on an unseen obstruction about two meters below. A shimmering blue field illuminated with the impact. It supported the water and the shards of glass with electric pulses. But as the glass and water came to rest the field dissipated, leaving the broken vessel and the water to hover in air as if by magic.

I wondered then how long the safety field had been there. Had it been installed for me or for the Proto Neta-Teej?

The escalation of focus on me suddenly became so real that I sat down on the stone again in the dusk and just watched the light disappear through the towering glass buildings surrounding the temple.

After dark, I ate a little, feeling my stomach rebel at any new food.

In the drawer next to the bed, all my things had been relocated from my previous room.

Everything was there and I turned off all the lights and took a dose of the crystalline powder. I wasn't sure if I needed it anymore, or how anything worked in this new environment, but I felt like I had very little time.

I got off the bed and lay on the marble floor. I wanted my back to feel the foundational resistance, to be against the hard and cool floor like in my stone room.

There was my room, my closed eyes in the dark. There was my breathing and the red rooms that the clockwork evoked, red glow everywhere, amniotic, each passage womb-like, and I knew I had taken more than just one dose, more than enough to slow things down, enough to where I would have to find my way.

The red room was a neurochemical reaction that most humans had to the clockwork in a high enough dose. It was a portal if you let it be, but for many, the red room was a calming place, an escape where time fell away. You could project a lucid dream there, you could forget yourself and be something else, or revert to the pre-birth state of blankness.

I waited, letting the room's true silence take hold. I closed my eyes again and then opened my eyes upon the heath to find I was already at the mouth of the well.

There was no man there, but the woman stood on the ocean side of the cliffs, looking out at the ever-present storm. Birds, hundreds of them, whirled in the air in the distance, using the edge of the choppy waves to spot fish, using the storm winds to aid their speed. They would dive and plunge and resurface, swallowing their catch.

I walked up behind the woman, her broad shoulders squared against the driving wind.

"The Crone asked about you," I said to her.

"She should be asking."

"She asked about the man as well."

"She doesn't know the man."

"Does she know you?"

"I am the Neta-Teej," said the woman.

I did not know how to respond.

"I was the first. The Proto Neta-Teej. You will be the next," she said looking down at me, eyes forceful and penetrating, daring me to reject the proposition.

"I have been put in your rooms."

"There is a book you must open," she said. "It looks like many others, but it is not. Inside is a text of reincarnation. It is one of the ones you noticed was missing from my collection. You will gain access to the other ones. But this is one that I thought might be needed."

"Would you like to go down the well with me?" I asked, eyeing her. "I have not gone in a long time and there are things I have yet to see."

"You would take me with you willingly?" she asked, halting the look of surprise that crossed her face.

"You are already here," I said. "You came for a reason."

"Then you do not need the book," she said. "But others will. It is one that may open the way for what comes next."

Together we went to the well, walking slowly across the heath. There was still danger in the woman who called herself the Neta-Teej, but there was also a solemn quiet.

When we got to the well, we both stood at the edge and looked down to where the water glowed bright red.

"Why do you want to go down the well?" I asked her.

The Neta-Teej looked at me, her narrow eyes filled with determination, "Because in some ways it will be the beginning of the end for me. I do not know if it will be because we become one or if it will be because I will be lost to you. It will take time, but that does not matter. What matters is that you welcome me in."

"Did you have to do this when you were young?"

"I did something like this," said the woman. "But I was the first, so it was not the same."

"Did you have a well?"

"No," she shook her head, still looking in. "I had a river, and I took everyone who I met in my deep forest, no matter who they were, to the water's edge and begged them to enter. The kind ones would wade into the clear water and drink. And those who did not want to be known, did not want to be seen, would resist. They would refuse to enter or even go near the river bank."

"What do you mean?"

"The corrupt. The malevolent. They cling to their secrets because they themselves have yet to look inward. They fear being known, but they also fear the next step into the truth. Being known weakens your inner evil. They wanted to stay angry and unknown, stay strong in their cruelty or their isolation."

"So they would resist?"

"Yes, because my river was sight. I would see them as the gods, the spirits, as the portions of the self that they were. And they would see me and they would think themselves diminished. In one truth, they were right. Their evil had diminished and that was what they were. But they grew in other ways, whether they saw it or not."

"You said they resisted."

"They were dwellers in my inner world. Whether they came from inside or outside didn't matter. If they tread on my terrain, they were subject to my knowledge. The Neta-Teej is not one to suffer ignorance or cruelty. It is my calling to understand all the entities and to know their capacities. I would take them to the water's edge and I would drag them in."

The herdsman was there suddenly, looking into the well adjacent to us.

The Neta-Teej glanced at him, "I understand that no one else has gone down the well before."

He shook his head.

I faced him, "Will you come in with us?"

"I will," he said.

"What is your name?" the Proto Neta-Teej asked him.

He shrugged and pointed to me.

"What is your name?" she asked, looking at me.

"Vive," I said. "But I was given the name Apsara."

"You are Vive," said the man. "The name in waiting has no power over you here. This place came first."

"And what was your name?" I asked the Neta-Teej.

"Yuthika."

"Was that your name in waiting, or was that your given name?"

She smiled at me assuredly. "I was never given a name in waiting."

For a moment we were silent and the meaning of things began to weigh on me.

"You took everyone to your river. Will I have to let every last entity into the well?" I asked, feeling a surge of fear, realizing what that might mean.

She smiled again and it was a sad smile and she reached out and touched my arm gently. There was enormous strength in her, and her size made me realize how small I really was, even in this world which was supposed to be mine. "They will come in whether you want them to or not. So, it is best if it is on your terms."

"I am not like you," I said. "I do not have a river. I only have this well."

"But there is a stone room below," said the man. "And you do not know what else is in that darkness beyond that room. There is a great deal of space here."

"I don't know how to stop anyone from coming in. I don't know how to bring them in if I need to."

"Vive," said the Neta-Teej. "That is why I am going with you."

"But why would you protect me?"

"I have died many times, in my own mind," said the Neta-Teej, no fear in her eyes. "But I have seen you before, little one. You were the only mourner at my first funeral, the one where I imagined myself shrouded and tied in red."

"I don't understand. I would not have been alive."

"I called for hope, and you arrived. That is all I know. You were there back then and you are here now."

It took me a moment to accept it, remembering the dream, the bodies falling from the sky, the taste of the soil as I clawed out a grave.

"I thought that was only a dream."

"It has been many things. Real, memory, story, dream."

I nodded and then took her hand, and the man came around and I took his hand, also.

I closed my eyes, and I imagined lifting up, my feet leaving the grass and stone, and tilting, flying down into the well.

Through closed lids I sensed the light turn to dark and the cool dankness build up around me.

Then the water was warm and filled with firelight.

"It must be inside," I said aloud.

When I opened my eyes I was sitting in the middle of my stone room.

The red ouroboros encircled me on the floor and the fire was roaring.

I could see the moss on the walls.

To my right there was a new alcove in the round room,

It was a staircase leading down to another level below. It was partially brick and carved out of the stone walls.

The longer I looked down the stairs I realized passage was filled to the top step with translucent water. It was so full that fluid was threatening to spill out into the room. But it was so still it was like a sheet of glass.

I could see down the first several steps as they curved into the darkness below.

I stepped onto the first step, disrupting the surface, the cold water coming up over my ankles, and I sat down at the water's edge before taking a sip.

It was fresh and it tasted glacial, like wild water, liberated after ages in stasis.

11

When I returned to my room, keeping the lights out to obscure what I was doing, I went to the bookshelf and pulled a green book out from the collection. It had a golden clasp across the front, keeping it closed, but there was no key needed and the small spring switch opened it.

The title was 'Teikum: Manifestation of Spector and Spectacle', but inside was a stack of papers, wrapped up and nested inside cut pages. Immediately I knew what they were, works even the Neta-Teej of the Tribe needed to hide.

There were ideas the Neta-Teej would need to understand hidden within thoughts which others might want concealed or forgotten. These were the tools the Neta-Teej would need.

I did not pull them from the book for fear of discovery. I simply closed the book, replaced it on the shelf, and then pulled another and another and took them to my bed, where I turned those lights on and pretended to read.

I slept through the rest of the night without dreaming and in the morning I woke and put the books back on the shelf.

The same proctor and group of young acolyte healers who had come to me the day before brought me food.

I told the proctor I would like to eat alone, but that he should call for the Crone because I would like an audience.

He was taken aback and said, "If you wish to see her, we may schedule a visit."

"No," I said. "She will want to come here and she will want to come today."

He took a deep breath, "I will send your message, but I suggest we go through the proper channels."

"She will decide the proper channels," I said.

The entourage left and I ate quickly and then dressed.

It was only a short time before the Crone arrived, but she was not alone. The proctor was with her, of course, but so were two others. One of them was a doctor who wheeled a mobile scanning unit on a cart and the other was an old acolyte. She also had a cart but it was covered by a sheet.

They did not knock when they entered, knowing they were expected. The proctor wore a look of nervous confusion on his face, but the Crone seemed calm, more curious than anything.

I was over by the bookshelf as they came in.

The Crone said nothing but pointed for me to sit on one of the sunken couches.

I did as I was told and the doctor came over with the scanner and turned it on. I sat stationary and watched as the machine performed its scan and then gave the read out.

[Apsara. Acolyte. Tribe.] Just as the scanner at the hospital had read, the name of Vive now no longer connected to my brain patterns.

"What is the precision level?" the Crone asked.

"Eighty-nine percent," said the doctor. "Another seven percent decrease since the scan at the hospital."

I looked at the Crone, then the doctor, "Eighty-nine percent?"

"It means your mind is changing, the patterns and vibrations are in the process of being altered," said the Crone.

The doctor's voice held assurance, "Everyone needs repatterning as they grow. But already the encephalographic scan is well outside the range of certainty on who you were before your name in waiting. No one would be able to tie you to previous scans. Some of it is age. Some of it is other things. But this change since your name in waiting was given is remarkable. You are touched by the gods, child."

I looked to the Crone for some direction, some explanation.

She shook her head, "Once you are in the Tribe there is a decoupling that must occur."

She did not explain any further, but I later came to understand.

The name given at birth is paired, in the UTC registry, with the signatures from your brain activity. It is like this for all citizens.

Within the Tribe there are no scanners and the cloister is a tool.

A name in waiting is given to acolytes when they are young, but not too young, so as to place a buffer of time between the early UTC scans and reidentification of the individual. This is supplemented by changes caused by drugs, meditation, trauma.

Some think the name in waiting is to isolate us further, linking us directly to the Tribe, not to our families or our pasts.

And this is very much true.

But it is also to protect those outside the Tribe, family of acolytes. It is to protect your friends and to protect you. Being a member of the Tribe implies influence, and this decoupling is done to enforce loyalty.

But it is also a barrier the UTC High Command must overcome in their attempts to exert secretive force inside the Holy Tribe.

The Coda of Unification requires the binding together of the faiths, but it also requires there be an ordained government as a second pillar, an ecclesia. The pillars must remain separate, as is the intent of the Coda.

Still, the pillars themselves each have self-aggrandizing plans.

A stone pillar cannot grow taller on its own. And the men who built it are prone to resenting the shadow cast over their creation by those adjacent.

If men sit atop those pillars, they begin to wonder why they must share the height.

Humans tend to think of things mechanically, so we enjoy the implied stability of three pillars, the weight of the world atop the three, balanced. We are willing to do with four pillars, but we know one leg on the table is always shorter than the other three and it must be propped up.

For thousands of years, humans had king and church, two pillars, and before that there was chief and shaman, and the former pillar was perceived as tall and shiny and the latter was shorter and stout, untiltable.

We have tried one pillar. The god emperor. And so, we have tried all the practical mechanical things and found their analogies wanting and weak. Would going to five be better? Eight, like a mite or a spider? Would two be okay if it were two wings? What do wings look like in a societal analogy?

The Tribe is the problem and the solution.

Those who enter the Tribe lose themselves because they must. It is a check against the influence of the UTC High Command. And the acolytes become the apostles, the continuously renewed spiritual voices for the demanding public. The ever-refreshed font of charismatic seers and speakers.

We are crafted and shaped to match our message and our message, our personal message, is shaped to fill a known gap in the populace.

The High Command need never show their faces. After all,

they are not apostles. They are not prophets. They hid behind the Tribe, acting as pious stewards of the people.

But they are the ones who alter our world. They simply elevate the volume of a lucky prophet ahead of time.

The Tribe works to make that prophet nameless. This is the truce. This is the balance of power.

I say it now. I see it very clearly as I reminisce. It is obvious as I flee Terra toward Europa. But I did not understand as I sat that day before the Crone.

I had been told I was Vive. I had been told I was Apsara. Then Vive again, as spoken by those inside my teikum. Now I was being told I was no longer either. I was going to become, or might already be, something else.

"Don't look so troubled," said the Crone.

"I'm not troubled," I said, dropping the title of Holy One. "I am wondering what the point is. How does this have anything to do with your uncertainty about me? About the Neta-Teej? How does it matter to us?"

I spoke in anger, but the last phrase was an unexpected question that simply spilled out of my mouth. 'How does it matter to us?'

At first, I wondered what I'd meant. 'Us' was not me. It was not the 'us' of those inside me or even those in the building. Not the Tribe. I meant 'Us' as in everyone.

I had never said anything like that before.

The Crone began to laugh. Her shoulders made her gray hair glitter in the morning light as they shook and she looked upward at the ceiling, but I could tell that she was gazing into the heavens, through carpets and stone and roofing.

"How does it matter to us?" she repeated. "Why does it matter to us? Indeed. That is the question. There are only two questions. Do you know the other?"

"I don't know what you mean," I said, still scrambling to understand how those words had come out of my mouth.

The Crone was almost tearing up, her cackles filling the room, but no one else was laughing. They just watched us and all I wanted to do was hide. The proctor was looking at me as if had done wrong.

Had I made a mistake in asking her here?

"I don't know what you mean," I said, louder, almost biting. I just wanted her to stop laughing and she did, but she did not let go of her smile. It was warm, like she was smiling only at me, as if there was no one else there to witness it. I did not know the Crone's smile could hold love. I had never seen it and it frightened me.

"Little one," she said, pointing at me and I suddenly re-recognized that the Crone of the Tribe was in the room with me. She was not just a proctor or a tester. She was the Tribal Witch and she was seeing me. "You little root of seeking flesh. You dig through filth looking for sustenance of life, of survival. You search for the fluids you need to pump your nutrients into the sky. Born in darkness to feed the light catchers far above. But it is a long journey for the things you've caught. Everything good that was pushed upward before you must be lifted still. It must be lifted again and again until it gets to where it belongs."

"I do not know the second question," I said as she stared at me smiling. "I don't know what you are asking or what you mean."

"You will," she said with some certainty and an oddly kind smile.

"I don't even know how I knew the first question," I said.

"Do not forget, child. You are the one who called me here."

I was surprised. I had already forgotten how the whole process had begun. I wasn't sure I even understood the point anymore.

"Speak," she said again, her tone demanding but still amused, patient.

"I meditated after you left me yesterday. After everyone left me yesterday."

"And?"

I wanted to start at the beginning, to tell her everything and to walk her through what I had seen and experienced, almost as if this powerful woman were one of the children I had started classes with all those years ago, as if I could simply talk the Crone of the Tribe through my mind's patterns. Instead, the Photo Neta-Teej's sad face jumped into my brain, her red-gray hair tossed about in the wind.

"You asked me if I had intended to kill myself with the inkberries," I said. "But I want to know if the previous Neta-Teej tried to kill herself as well."

The Crone's smile faded, but there was no malice. She closed her eyes, willing herself back to the time when she had known the Neta-Teej. "Are you asking me if she ate too many inkberries?"

"I guess."

"She did. Over and over in her own way," said the Crone.

"Did she try to throw herself off this balcony?"

"Yes, but only twice," said the Crone and her smile returned, pained but thoughtful.

"The woman in my vision told me she was the Proto Neta-Teej."

The Crone nodded matter-of-factly but I watched the faces of the others change and pale. She seemed to have expected my words, but the others had not.

"You had described her to me," said the Crone. "Not the way she was in life, mind you. But the way she existed inside her own inner world, when she was master of her own teikum. I know what she looks like."

I realized I had never seen an image of the previous Neta-Teej, their face always veiled. "Why did I see her that way?"

The Crone simply shrugged and shook her head, "Does it matter to us?"

Her repetition of the question reminded me this was still a test.

"She was sad. Is that the way I will become?"

"Are you not sad already?"

I hesitated to answer because I wasn't really sure what I wanted to say, but within an instant a thought formed more clearly and I tried to explain, "Sadness is not the only thing I am talking about. Her sadness was from knowledge. She was afraid for me and what I would come to know. I could see it in her eyes. She told me how it worked, with her river. But it wasn't good. It wasn't good for her."

The Crone shook her head, "No. It wasn't good for her."

I had more to say but my mind cut over. "The first question. 'How does it matter to us?'. 'Us' means all of us. 'Matter' means survival, not just for all the people, all the vessels, but also everything they carry, all the ideas and feelings and hopes and dreams. Survival of self. Of soul and lineage. But 'us' may not include me. There were so many things that didn't matter for the Proto Neta-Teej's survival. They mattered for 'us'. All of us. But not for her. If that is the first question, and it is the question that made her want to die, to jump from the balcony. This is a painful question, deadly. How do we let that question enter our teikum? It may kill us. Anything we let in may break our souls and harm us. Do I let it in? The broken hopes and pain of everything that cannot fully be?"

"The Proto Neta-Teej let it in," said the Crone, again looking up, but now without laughter. "She decided, over and over again, to let it in and she found all the ways it would be possible. For herself and for others. Even when it was bad for her."

"And in the end, she did die by her own hand."

"Yes."

"But that is the second question, isn't it? How do we let it in, all of it, without it destroying us?"

The Crone only nodded.

"How do we get that which matters most inside? And how do we keep it and ourselves at once?"

"Yes," said the Crone. "And the finding of the answer, too many answers, was what killed her. That which matters is essential to us all, whether we recognize it in ourselves or not. Foundational. But your struggle will not be in understanding what matters. The Neta-Teej's struggle will be in guiding the significance into the core of who we are, for all who will listen, and understanding what that must displace as it takes root."

"She must have known unspeakable things," I said, looking at the floor, thinking of her body wrapped in red, falling from the sky.

"And so do we all," said the Crone, who turned to the others in the room. "There will be no more tests today. Leave us."

They left, but the Crone did not speak for a very long time.

Morning passed into afternoon, and she sat in the same place, thinking. I left her for a time and went to my bed and rested but did not sleep.

When darkness came I heard her rise and I sat up and came back into the sitting room to be with her.

Her eyes were open, and I went and sat on the floor near where moonlight was coming through from the balcony. The stars and celestial bodies weren't visible through the fog or the light from the city, but I wanted to see the sky anyway.

"There may be more tests," said the Crone. "They are required. But you should not worry for them. Only the two questions matter. But I do not have answers for you in those questions. Those answers must be yours."

"That's okay," I said.

"It will not be okay. It will not be easy. But there is a need for a guide. That is certain. It was seen and you have arrived, though it will not be as expected."

"I don't know if that's true," I said, not willing to fully accept what she was saying, what she had clearly already decided to believe inside her own mind.

"I have spoken to a thousand children like you," said the Crone. "We have been looking for years. None, till now, have shown sufficient evidence or understanding of what the Neta-Teej must be."

It occurred to me then how much she missed the original bearer of the title, the Proto Neta-Teej. It occurred to me that she was saddened and challenged by this quest for a replacement. There would be questions of worth, of similarity, and the comparisons would never match up to what she retained in memory. The idea of the person would have distorted, grown in size and power, but only in the mind.

"Do not worry for me, either," she said, reading my realizations. "There is pain in memory. There are fallacies we carry for our entire lives. Confronting them sheds light upon teikum. Only then may we shed ourselves."

"She said you knew her."

"She did know me."

"How did she find you?" I asked into the darkness.

The Crone stood up, stretching her legs and going to stand near the bookshelves at the back of the room, instinctively seeking deeper darkness.

"There are other children and youths who have known things, seen things, similar to you, Apsara. But there have been missing pieces."

I thought, at first, she was ignoring the question.

"You have a capacity for self-violence which they do not

match and that is what will allow you to ask the questions and seek full answers. I believe this willful force is the reason you have been chosen, not by me, but by those you see inside your mind. Perhaps you were chosen long ago."

I wanted to say again that I was not chosen yet, that nothing had changed in me, but it was only a feeling I still had, something I couldn't shake, even as I was told over and over what was coming. Even as I remembered what the Neta-Teej had told me about me mourning her first death.

I had been called then. Why not now?

"I was found," the Crone said, "because the Neta-Teej went looking for a girl like me. There were many who had the right knowledge. But she found me in the outlands, on the edge of the last remaining wilds, and my ideas had come to me through my mothers and sisters."

"What was she searching for? Did you have the questions?"

The Crone sat on the floor across from me, our knees touching. It was a youthful flourish of movement and the ease of her action betrayed that her body still had supple strength despite its outward appearance. She leaned forward into me and grabbed my shoulders tightly and brought me toward her so our foreheads touched. Her long hair shown almost stark white in the moonlight as it hung between us, our eyes looking down.

"I was found because of what I say," said the Crone in the slightest whisper, so soft her lips did not move and there seemed to be an echo that pushed it to my ears, like the words were already spoken and were carried to me on memories of themselves. "The first Neta-Teej was not supposed to come looking for me, or anyone. The Neta-Teej was never supposed to exist, but those in power are making the same mistake again. A guide emerges and they think they can use you, only to find that you operate beyond them."

I looked up at her, surprised and suddenly filled with fear, understanding what this sort of admission could mean. Was it the High Command making a mistake? Was it the Quadrumvirate? Was it those who operated in the back halls of the Temple, the viziers and the favor keepers?

"A Crone has no questions by which will make her a crone," she said while staring at me, but again her mouth did not move and I could not tell if I was dreaming or if she was playing some trick on me. "I was sought because there is no thing powerful people fear more than having their minds known."

She cut the projection short, and her mouth moved and she spoke clearly, as if nothing else had been said between us, "The Neta-Teej was searching for an outside perception in her travels. Whether you call that outside perception 'cynicism', or 'occult', or 'woman', that was what I carried in from the wild with me. She brought me to strike fear. To remind them there are powerful human things that stand as tall or taller than their individual idea of the gods."

She smiled in the dark as she said it, making sure it was spoken aloud so the listeners would hear it, no secret to the statement. Everyone already felt that part of her purpose. It was good to remind others that she had not forgotten her purpose either.

I nodded, feeling the threat of fear wash over me, as well. I remembered how it had also emanated from the Proto Neta-Teej. Danger to them, danger to me. I thought about how the fear I felt, the fear they felt, was not the same as the fear the Crone conjured for the other worshippers, but it was mirrored.

The Crone answered my thoughts. "Fear is a tool. Part of the balance. The fear is what we provide. And so, we are always at risk because of their wounded pride. Fear of knowledge and fear of death are now paired, treated as equal when they are anything but."

I did not see if she spoke it aloud or if it was just inside my mind. It did not matter. The fear was inside me and it was entirely my own, a gift from the Crone, a gift from the Proto Neta-Teej.

It was then that she stood and said goodbye.

"Rest. You will have more tests soon."

12

But the next tests were not really tests, at least not as I expected.

They were far more ceremonial, a long list of aids and officials coming to meet me, each asking different questions, but all seeming to be from a sort of script that I was not part of.

"Do you see the challenge that lies before us?"

"Is the way prepared, or are we entering the wilds?"

"Do you have light for the dark travelers?"

"Must we make our shelter now or later?"

They were cryptic sorts of interrogations and no matter what I answered, they agreed and gave it serious thought. Everyone who listened scribbled on papers or nodded as if in contemplation.

I answered just as cryptically. "I don't yet see all the challenges that lie before us. There are many still hidden."

"The way is not prepared. We must prepare ourselves instead."

"We must all be light for each other."

"Do not worry for shelter here."

Everything was written down and there were always more questions that came after my responses, like some obfuscating game of jargon and symbolism. It had no real meaning. But I sat and waited through it. I committed hours every day to this procession of officials from the Tribe and from the UTC. Some were just observers, while others did the speaking.

And for every interaction, I wore a veil over my face. It was liberating to not have to hide my facial expressions, which were so often confused or horribly bored. But there were also no expressions for my words to be paired with. All the listeners and inquisitors had to take my words at their own value, no smiles or sad eyes to compare with the tone of my voice. But they didn't care. The responses were only a small part of what we were doing. The audience was what was important, and very little else. The emotions in my answers were not requisite.

It was after the passing of the fourth day that I truly realized I was going to be the Neta-Teej regardless of what happened, regardless of what I did.

At first, I thought perhaps the Crone had made the decision and all the others were simply following suit, but that was not realistic. She had not treated the process lightly and, while these others were playing at theater, they would not just acquiesce to whatever she wished. As the Crone had said, the High Command or the Quadrumvirate, as a whole, had need for the Neta-Teej, and they had already made their choice.

What I did not know was that in other rooms in the Temple of the Tribe there were other children being questioned. They were not being kept in the previous Neta-Teej's quarters, but perhaps neither was I. Perhaps I was being tricked into identifying false sight. But I suspected it was all real.

I later learned that the Crone had met with all the others as well, but only once each, and the listeners and the questioners had also gone from room to room repeating their scripts for all of us. This 'search' had happened day after day, as was storied on the networks for the common people to build hope and excitement.

They had come from all over, the other prospective acolytes. There was great honor to be had and not much room to decline the invitation. Some had already been in the Temple or had been given names in waiting long ago, while younger material had been transported to us, given names in waiting, and then added into the rotation.

I hope they did not feel as if their time had been squandered. I hope they felt truly seen, truly vetted, but I do not know how they were treated through the process or how they were treated afterward.

By the end, I knew that I was not being evaluated, but instead ushered through a long and complicated spectacle of which I was only a small part. I don't know how they could have felt any differently.

Perhaps it was all done to make us feel beholden, like we owed something back to the Tribe after all the time and effort put in, las if they were discovering us, discovering us, making us. Perhaps it was to add weight to everything that happened, adding weight to all the titles of those who were allowed to ask the questions.

It added weight to the prospective title of the Neta-Teej as well.

But one week after the questioning started, I was brought a yellow robe in the early morning and told that I would be summoned to another ceremony in the evening where the Neta-Teej would be chosen after sundown.

After the herald left, I tried to leave my quarters, only to find a guard posted outside who said I was not allowed to leave and that food would be brought for me. He asked me if I had any specific desires but I didn't answer.

That whole day I did not leave my quarters.

Instead, I read. I went back to the old stories I'd always loved, the epics and the early tales told around the campfires of our nomadic predecessors. They were comforting as they spoke to the truth, that no matter what happened, I might still be on a heroic journey.

The hero isn't always the chosen one and maybe I was really not the Neta-Teej. Maybe I was supposed to make my path another way. Did I want this? Would it crush me further? Did I even want to be here anymore? After all, I had not been asked what I needed or wanted after I had eaten the inkberries. I had been healed by those who needed me, not by those who were loyal. And I had been returned to these quarters to wait and be evaluated for other things. There were no questions of 'me'.

When the sun went down, attendant acolytes arrived, but they were not healers and there was no proctor. They were young, but still older than me, and they did not speak much, only asking questions about the fit and comfort of the yellow robe.

As we prepared to leave, awaiting our escort to wherever the choosing would occur, one of them asked me, "Apsara, are you nervous?"

"No," I said, and I was being truthful, having set my mind to the situation and only growing tired of waiting. "It does not matter what happens."

"I would be nervous," they said with a cautious smile. "They might choose you."

I wanted to say that it was too late to do anything about that, but instead said, "Then that will be their will."

"The will of the gods will prevail," they said, and I did not correct them.

I had not meant anything about the gods. Instead, through all of this, I had felt that the inner world, with the woman who called herself the Proto Neta-Teej or Yuthika and the herdsman, was something separate. The gods had already chosen me, maybe not for being the Neta-Teej, but for something.

Everything else was simply the protocols of men. Everything else had nothing to do with the gods at all. In fact, the choice might be counter to the gods'. It was humans who would be doing the choosing tonight.

We were collected and my veil went down, and the halls were filled with people. There were hundreds of other veiled youths in the same yellow garb. Only then did I feel nervous for a moment, as if I might lose myself in the crowd of yellow and all the attendants. Vive could walk one way while Apsara walked another and never again shall the two meet.

As a procession, we marched away from the center of the building where the central channel was, and instead moved as a mass to the grand stairway closer to the exterior.

People flooded up the stairs, and flight after flight we ascended. It was slow progress with the numbers, all talking excitedly, or breathing to keep going. The quietest were the ones in yellow.

As I came upon others who were veiled, I would touch them, place my hand on their shoulder and they would whirl, as if they had not been touched in a long while, as if they were terrified. But I nodded to them or quietly said, "hello". They would always respond with a nervous kindness in their voices. There were so many accents, people from all over the world.

I never saw their faces and they never saw mine.

Until there was a choice, it could be any one of us. Until there was a choice made, we were all just floating through and we were sisters and brothers.

I wished to lift their veils and look into their eyes. I longed to know them.

It occurred to me afterward, almost all of them in yellow

would still be sisters or brothers, bound by not being chosen, and there would be one entity left out. There would be one who would shed the yellow robe and be excluded.

Reincarnation.

When the procession ran out of stairs, we were ushered into a grand room with marble walls and a high, arching dome of windows that constituted the ceiling. It showed only the clear night sky.

Everyone was looking up, amazed.

Most, including myself, had never been in the Quadrumvirate's congregation chamber, entranced by the stars that were so rarely seen due to pollution or light interference. Nebulas glittered between the glowing celestial bodies.

For a moment I was stricken with sadness that my sister, who always looked into the sky and dreamed of leaving, could not be there to see it, could not see these stars, unobstructed and scintillating in ways most of us had never before witnessed.

I looked out through the low side windows, tearing my gaze from the star scape. Normally one could make out cascading lights from vehicles and towers, illuminating the thick clouds. But tonight, only the faintest glow came from the mega-city of Schengen. The lights of the whole city, for as far as we could see, had been shut off.

"Come and sit," said the Pontifex Rex, voice slow and soothing to calm the exuberant crowd. He stood in a red robe on a raised marble platform on the eastern edge of the dome. "All the city lights have been extinguished to better honor the choosing of the guide. It is in this way we honor the ways of old, the navigation through the dark, across wide seas, across voids of space. This was how paths were originally found. The whole world waits in darkness once again for a guide who can divine the path through."

Next to the Pontifex Rex stood the others, all accented in red, the Crone on the left with the Caliph and then the Lama on his right. Each had a stone seat, backless to avoid the appearance of a throne, and at the middle was a small table. Atop it sat a dusty urn, rough in appearance but deep and lidded with a golden top.

The Pontifex Rex sat and we followed as one, sitting in the benches that had been arrayed for us. The others of the Quadrumvirate stayed standing.

I was sitting near the back and to the left of the stage and was able to look up as the lights dimmed even further and brought out the stars' powerful glow.

I could see the Pole Star if I craned my head backward and looked straight up. But across the dome I could also make out the shine of the Yoke Star, in the east, the tether by which the great plow is pulled.

Everyone was looking up, seeing the sky as they had never seen it.

There was no divinity required to plot a course across the surface of Terra if you had the stars, only calculation. And even calculations first required curiosity and the belief in the possibility of discovery. But what was needed to plot a course through a human? What bright lights would be needed?

"It has been three decades since the Neta-Teej left us," spoke the Crone and everyone fell silent. "We have been in need of a guide for ages. Celebration has not been full. We still seek, in our halls and in our teikum, for another who might know the formless reality, might craft a symbol of it and dance about it. Then we may, once more, have the gods look favorably on us and find our union, not just with them, but with ourselves incarnate. We must refill the vessel of our unity. We must have a guide for union with our most natural state."

After speaking, the Crone sat, and everyone looked to the Caliph.

"That which we are is not always one. We are a multitude by

the nature of our changeling soul. We each possess a mind, an ego, a spirit, and a heart. They are as one as they are separate." His voice was deep and penetrating. "Today, is for our hearts. The Teej is for speaking to the heart, to the Qalb of our lives and of our teikum, letting it celebrate for itself and us celebrating for it. We shall dance and turn about together. The guide we seek will give their heart, but also their spirit and mind and ego to this pursuit. They will help us to turn as they do."

The Caliph sat and the Lama was the only one left standing on the platform. He smiled and said, "The Neta-Teej has seen through the darkness, and they will see through the darkness again and they will return tonight. To find rebirth we must pass through annihilation, we must accept our heart's union with chaos, destruction, and dissolution. We seek a guide into and through the void so we may all be remade, on the day as on the year as on the era. Time takes the name of the destroyer, and we shall celebrate our union with it. The guide shall return from teikum, from the void, and be rebirthed anew, bathed in ash. There will be another union here."

A cheer went up, everyone with song in their voices as the Lama sat and the Crone again stood.

"The rains will come again," she said. "The world inside and out will grow green with life."

The Pontifex Rex approached the vessel which had been sitting undisturbed to that point. He lifted the golden lid, struck a long match and dropped it into the vessel.

Smoke came first and then fire, red with hints of green rose from the urn. Whatever fuel was inside had caught the blaze and he let it burn, all the while holding the golden lid in his hands.

The Lama and the Caliph came forward and lit matches using the flames. The Crone came after them with two incense holders and set them down next to the burning urn. The Caliph and the Lama lit them, and their smoke mingled with that from the fire.

Soon there was nothing but the calm and laminar flow of the smoke that rose into the arch of the dome, seeming to thread the stars above. The smell filled the room, just as in every temple I had ever been in.

Then the Pontifex Rex re-lidded the vessel, and the Crone trimmed the incense to stop their slow burn.

I thought I could hear her in my mind, but I was unsure.

After a short while, the lid was again removed with a billow of smoke and the altar was cleared before and the contents of the vessel, mounded ash, was turned out onto the stone.

The Lama lowered his hands into the ash and spread it around, breaking it apart to create a thin layer atop the surface.

In the mess he found a piece of paper, not fully burned away, and he lifted it, holding it close to his face in the dim light, read it, and then passed it to the Crone who did the same and the Quadrumvirate all read it.

No emotion passed across their faces and a horrible tense silence fell over the entire congregation as we all at once realized there had been one unburned name, and that would be the name of the Neta-Teej.

"Rise," said the Crone in her echoing voice and I stood along with everyone else, anticipation flooding all of us.

The Lama entered the sea of people and slowly walked among us. He was smiling and carrying the small fragment of paper closed in one fist and a burning incense in the other

He came to our row and looked at all of us in yellow, as if he could see through our veils, knowing who we were beneath.

I saw the shoulders of every prospective acolyte sink as he passed. They sank due to a sense of failure, they sank due to relief at not being picked, they sank because they had been holding their breath, waiting to know their fate.

I realized, in that moment, that I did not want this.

But he came to me and looked through my veil and he took

my hand in his, passing to me the paper and a little bit of ash, while everyone watched.

He stood patiently as I opened my hand and looked down.

'Apsara' was written in ink on the paper, still visible.

He took the paper back, lit it with the incense, and we all watched it burn. He caught the ash in his hands.

I will never know how many other names were actually written on the papers in that urn. I will never know why that paper did not burn. But in the moment, I was lost in acceptance and confusion.

This was happening. This was real.

I stepped out of the crowd to stand next to the Lama, and he placed his ashen hands on both of my shoulders, leaving prints there, marking me as the one.

"Come with me," he said and the whole congregation began to cheer and celebrate, and it washed over me like a wave of numbness. I could hear them all. I could feel them and their joy and I followed the Lama through the crowd back to the altar.

The Quadrumvirate took turns placing more ash marks on the yellow robe I was wearing. A handprint atop my head, one print on my breast over my heart, and one atop each of my feet.

They said more to the crowd and there was prayer which I did not hear because I was not listening.

I stood on the stage and the veil hung down just close enough that my eyes could focus on it.

I could pretend that the crowd was not there, and the voices were only a driving wind that sounded human as it passed from the sea, over my rocky heath, and into the valley at my back.

I stood over my well as the wind rushed over me. I looked in, arms wide, and I floated down with ease to meet the water. It was calming, as always, and I passed through to my stone chamber.

In my stone room, quiet, I could see the shadow of the Proto

Neta-Teej sitting on the hearth, looking into the fire, warming her hands over the flames.

Standing on the left wall of the room was the herdsman. He was smiling at me softly.

THE TEMPLE OF EUROPA

-Terran Year 2337-

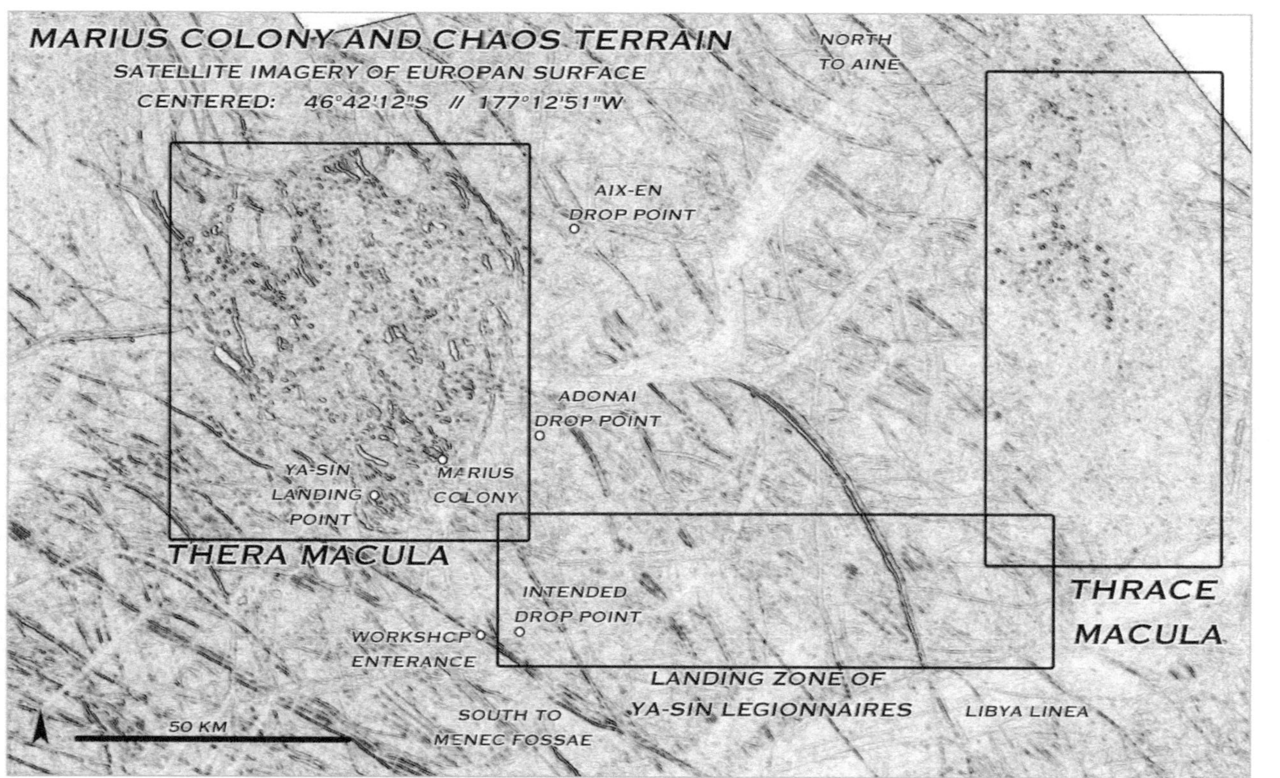

MARIUS COLONY AND CHAOS TERRAIN
SATELLITE IMAGERY OF EUROPAN SURFACE
CENTERED: 46°42'12"S // 177°12'51"W
NORTH TO AINE
AIX-EN DROP POINT
ADONAI DROP POINT
YA-SIN LANDING POINT
MARIUS COLONY
THERA MACULA
INTENDED DROP POINT
WORKSHCP ENTERANCE
THRACE MACULA
LANDING ZONE OF YA-SIN LEGIONNAIRES
LIBYA LINEA
SOUTH TO MENEC FOSSAE
50 KM

———

Rejoice dear bird and praise thy maker,
  Raise bright and clear thy voice.
  Thy gods are most exalted,
  Thy food he hath prepared for thee,
  To give thee in due season.
  So be contented therewith,
  Wherefore shalt thou not be glad.
  Wilt thou arraign thy gods,
  That they hath made thee bird?
  Wilt trouble thy wee head,
  That they made thee not a man?

-Found: Europa Mainframe Records
Modified After a Song on the The Second Day
The Chymical Wedding of Christian Rosenkreutz

———

1

Transmission Pattern:
	// //Transport Vessel *Tereus-CDXIV*//Europa Node//
	//Split River Encryption//
//Hardware Carrier// //

Dear Constance,

I don't know how much you have heard about the happenings in Schengen, but I am no longer part of the Tribe.

I have left the Temple and the gardens with the Neta-Teej and hir entourage. I have wandered farther than I imagined possible.

The world outside the Temple was is loud and messy but it is surprising how quiet it really is.

There's no one at my door in the morning asking me to wake up, asking me to dress in robes, asking me to lead a prayer. No one coming to my chamber in the evening asking me to make a reading of the stars or sit a meal with some holy travelers or diplomats who will grovel at the privilege. There are no demands for my writings or my words.

No one asks what I have seen when I come out of meditation. But I am seeing strange things.

Out here, they leave me alone. No one asks why I turn the lights off and just rest and meditate through the days in transit. No one asks what I am writing when I spend all day documenting how I got here.

No one asks why I cry, expecting prophetic answers. I am free now to feel pain without reproach or concern. It is a joy without a name. My inward journey has expanded without a need to narrate it for others, a powerful ritual for them, but not for me.

I used to feel that I would lose power if I did not have my ritual, my habits. But there is no ritual required for true power and there is often no power in ritual.

If repeated external demand is all there is, if the habit is the source of the power, like all addiction, then that is not real power.

Progress can be made there, development, persistence. But that is not the sign of divine force. It's only evidence of the human force, a weak force, built on endurance and obsession. Ritual is not evidence for gods.

Perhaps you have changed, but I think you would've agreed with me in the past. I used to know your mind. I hope I know it still.

My old life in the Temple was a seduction. It is growing clearer with every day that I break further away. I was at the center of that world, a little light called forth. I would speak and dance and light up their lives. Only for a moment. Only for a split second in which they might forget themselves at the sound of my words.

Perhaps I am sleeping now. It is all a dream, I think. I have been in a daze since I left Terra. I travel in a fog. I have never been confused like this before. I have no patterns to fall back on. Every day of old was habit, a memory on repeat. But now the meditations do not stop, even when I am fully awake. Now there are new doors. There are books everywhere, scattered about. There is no ranking or hierarchy on this transit ship, nothing banned, nothing listed for senior practitioner eyes only. There are just texts without Coda introduction. They are contextless and they beg you to read them and digest them without prior comment or guidance on interpretation.

Those who are taking me away, helping us escape, are preparing us by the books they share with us. They are preparing me for what I will see once we reach our destination, what I will see inside myself. There is something powerful there, something in the fabric of the place that speaks the language of teikum. I have gleaned that much.

From the moment I boarded this ship leaving Terra the people were open and kind with equality I barely remember. I could speak to anyone, and they could speak to me. There was no social order beyond the ranking of the crew.

But there are other things on this ship as well. Things I will not yet describe. I can feel them here with us when I wake in my own twilight. I can see them, in my mind, and in the dark when my mind is at its clearest. The energy is weak out here. But I can feel the strength growing with every day we draw nearer. My meditations, my dreams, have grown with this rise.

If you do not know our destination, we are going to Europa. I am aboard a Europan ship.

The Falconer has collected us, helped us, and we are going to the moon of Jupiter.

I fear our destination because I have come to believe that what they say about it is true. But because of this truth, my fear has mostly been replaced with wonder.

Already, this is like nothing I have experienced before. Do I sound insane?

I want you to see this. To feel this. Liberation has given me new sight, which I cannot explain now. If you read the Neta-Teej's works, you will understand the extent of these inner worlds. Teikum is expanded here and everything vibrates with that life force.

I have fled from the Tribe, with the Neta-Teej, with the Crone. I am a fugitive with all the others. You are probably reading this somewhere on Terra or out with your Legion in a guardship.

But I would not have written these words to you if I didn't think they would come to you safely, privately and in secret. And you would not be reading them if it were not safe. Think of the power in that, in our having words together for the first time in ages. You a legionnaire, me, now a fugitive of the UTC and a heretic.

No rituals between us. Just power to be human and communicate in the face of what feels like a limitless force intent on dividing us.

But the UTC is not limitless, Constance. The UTC is not without weakness.

The departure of the Crone and the Neta-Teej, the departure of us all from the Temple, has revealed some of that weakness.

Do not take this as arrogance or as boasting, dear sister. Instead, accept it as I have, as a realization that this central power, this control, which we have always known and served, is not the only thing with agency in this universe.

I say such things with renewed hope, even after what they have done to me. Please take this letter as hope. Hope might arrive after a rush of dichotomous existential dread, like seeing the fall of a great pillar. I know it did for me.

I know you are unlikely to be a true believer of the faiths like I was when we were young, as our parents tried to be. You never really believed. But I know you are still a legionnaire. I know you have worn the armor and fought and killed and had your friends die for the UTC and for the Quadrumvirate and for the Tribe. I was part of the Tribe, so those actions used to be for me, or in alignment with me. But that is no more.

The Crone has left her seat and ceased the broken rituals. The Neta-Teej has left the Gardens of the Tribe. Now we all run to Europa together.

Why did the Crone leave? Why did she tie herself to the Falconer of Europa? What great weight could have caused her to fall from her holy seat, to fall in with the sorcerers and rebels?

Great seats of power may fall by exposure to their own climate, too temperamental a weather they craft. But the individual may fall by hubris, causing exile or death. Or they fall by guilt, causing the draw of a final curtain. The theatre of power is over, the veil falls, flee the stage and run for the exit.

It was the guilt, in this case. The Crone left for that reason and that reason alone.

I was not as strong as her, nor many of the others. I carry guilt which I cannot enumerate.

But the first letter to a sister in a long while should not be burdened with such things, so I will tell you of my other reason. It was fear, again. Fear for my life.

I tasted the fear of death long ago. I tasted it when I grew self-aware and began to understand my own desire to die. The desire for death did not fade with my failure to end myself. It was a gift, that call to death, and it made me what I am. But afterward, the Tribe imposed more ritual and habit. The rituals I recycled were not for me, not for my spirit or soul to heal. It was for them, those who watched me. It was a structure to keep me safe for them, and to keep me in their sights, doing what they needed of me.

I grew to know that two-faced hatred of my being, my position, because I had noted it in my own self-perception for ages.

I had been warned of it by those who had walked that path before me.

When that hatred arose in those around me, my peers, my

superiors, I saw it, noted it, and realized there was a pressure rising in the Temple, through that whole Tribal interior. A pressure to direct me or remove me. But that pressure had always existed inside of myself. It is part of who I was, so it was no surprise.

The Crone left first.

And the whole Tribe tried to act as if she never existed.

She was gone not dead, but they pretended. A new type of theatre.

Death was the Tribe's, the Quad's, true power. They had the ability to delineate that which was alive or dead, even if the subject was still living.

I knew what that meant for those like me, like the Neta-Teej who is, in many ways, a creature of the Crone.

I could feel it, the rejection of my persona and position. Yet, I could not fully imagine it becoming real. My simple mind couldn't fathom the rejection and violence required from the hands of others.

I had even been warned of it, long ago, but for a while my inner world had gone silent. Those who had walked the path before me had ceased to communicate with me.

This quiet threat of death felt like a continuation of my own self-violence. I imagined it as a deserved action, to die, to perish in the practice of the faiths, that submitting to it would somehow be an act of personal agency.

I didn't have the words or the context to properly consider death at the hands of another. The Temple, its sheltered existence, couldn't have ever given me that. It isn't made to give you that awareness. Instead, I had a diluted self-awareness of my death and a longing to cross the veil. I had been awakened by the Tribe, and by design, I had been put back to sleep. Myopia protected me from fear and exposed me to greater and greater danger.

And then a letter arrived that was not supposed to get through.

It came secretly, much the same as this letter finds you now, just a little fragment that slips through the great barriers the UTC has crafted for all of us.

It was a letter advising caution and fear, with specific details on what would be done to me if I stayed in the Temple. The author had a way of expressing the violence in store for me. They made it clear that, in the end, it would not be me guiding myself to any fitting end. Instead, it would be me bleeding out with a dagger between my shoulder blades or falling to a terminal interruption from the highest parapet in Schengen.

I would not be given grace. There would be no becoming or distillation of self. They would send me down the garbage shoot or eviscerate me so completely that the fibers of my being would no longer retain meaning.

Isn't that always the intent of those who wish to unmake you? To fully and completely remove a being from existence? They hurt you, crush you, then demand your silence on the matter. There will be no space for self-assessment before that end. They simply cannot allow it. There is only one solution to their need for your suffering and your concurrent silence. The aim is your true death.

The letter said the Tribe would forget me with every force they could manage, even if the ketgan remembered. Look at what they had done to the Crone. The letter said it would be hard for the UTC and the Tribe to do it, but that it would be an outcome worthy of their effort.

The words were cruel, but it was a kindness that a warning came with time and so I ran when I was given the chance. Curtain down. Leave the stage. Exit. The theater is now over, and all the lights are out and I can finally rest.

Constance, you must come out here and visit me. They say Europa is unlike anything you have seen before. There is life everywhere on this ship. It seems thrive inside everything I touch, and Europa will be no different.

I am learning again. A million open doors. My open doors, for the first time in a very long time.

You must leave Terra before it's too late. Before they close off all transport to Jupiter or the Galilean moons

I want to see you again, sister. I want to see your face and make up for all the lost time. I want to show you who I have become and share with you what I have seen. I think you would be surprised and proud. You were always the strong one, the resistant one, the rebel who did not blindly believe in things. I think we are more alike now than ever before.

I don't know where this message will find you, but please move quickly if you can. I don't know what will happen next, but there has never been a time where I have had more hope.

Every day, the entities of this world tell me that hope is manifest, hope is given, and that there is always light in the dark. They tell me that we all must ascend and that we are not the first or the last beings to do so. It is in our sprits. They say it more loudly as we get closer.

They say the birds will always fly because they can.

I am sorry for the distance. I never knew how far apart we were as children. I am sorry for the gulf of time. I didn't know how much it was worth or what the cost might be. I am sorry, now, to call you into the abyss of space to come and see me.

I don't know if you will. But I need you. We need everyone we can get.

I love you.

-Vive

2

One must understand the infamous spiritual terror which our movement exerts, particularly on the Bhoosa (bourgeoisie), which is neither morally or mentally equal to parsing such slanderous attacks. Allies are unable to differentiate truth from fiction, and adversaries are unable to defend swiftly enough before the nerves of the attacked break down.

One must achieve an equal understanding of the importance of physical terror toward the individual and the masses. For within the ranks of fellow supporters a victory seems a triumph for the justice of their own cause, while the defeated adversary, in most cases, disparages for the success of any further resistance.

-Modified Excerpt on Spiritual and Physical Terror
Four and Half Years Against Lies, Stupidity and Cowardice

//Internal Memo////High Command Appointed Circulation//

//Argument of Order//

//Associated with Vote: Military Action upon Europa//

//Associated with Debate: Implications of Philosophy and Spirituality//

//Associated with Inquest: Compromised Integrity of Tribal Temple and Loss of Crone; Loss of Neta-Teej//

Fellow High Command Appointees of the United Terran Coalition, wherever you may be found at this critical juncture:

It is not something widely discussed outside High Command circles but, from the onset, the Coda of Unification has always been inherently observed as a just but violent document.

It was built to directly generate conflict between the major religions and the major governmental forces of the old world. We generate conflict and we remove that which cannot be sustained. We amputate or ignore teachings, tenets, laws, pillars, rules. The Coda of Unification, by design, is a destruction of the old ways and a reimagining of them with stability in mind. By passing through this violence in an academic and political way, we have endeavored to avoid the worst of the physical violence that would come from such a forceful merger.

We succeeded with our stations of power intact.

Thus, we averted a global, socio-religious war at the end of the last century. We averted the thousands of small proxy wars that would have been fought by extremists in rebellion against our humanist efforts. There was and still is fighting, but that is unavoidable. Our aim was to minimize the conflicts at the highest level and work our way down. In that, we have succeeded.

I am writing to remind you of our mandate, as well as to reframe this situation.

Because we succeeded, we were able to draw the circle of inclusion wider than any tribe or government before in the history of humanity. The populace must be represented in politics and morality, or there is no stability or sustainability from which to govern. We must own both sides of the conflict, internal and external, to keep the Coalition strong. We must make them both a part of our domain.

We draw a vast circle of inclusion, bringing in faiths and ethnicities and philosophies that have never before found themselves under the same roof. But any circle will always result in outliers. There are those who are aligned and those who are unaligned.

These outliers, internal and external, must be managed.

Outliers who are unaligned, rebellious, are the easiest to identify, as they quickly identify themselves, loudly and with great show.

Weak outliers, who are unaligned, serve little purpose and must be dealt with individually. Punishment, imprisonment. There is nothing extreme or unexpected to finding systems of punishment thriving within the UTC.

However, larger deviant groups and rebels are a persistent threat and thus the threat of conflict arises once again. These are the ones who demand physical conflict. They demand outward fights because they wish to avoid the fight inside themselves, to avoid their lack of belief. Our faiths are not tolerable to them.

Conversely, we must learn from and understand the aligned outliers, the early allies to the cause who have now departed.

In our case we have those who are reluctant to fully partake in our Coda of Unification, refusing to acknowledge its power. They hold all the same beliefs, the morality, the ideas of justice and society, but remain beholden to a more narrowly focused way of life.

These evangelicals and nationalists hold beliefs that are rigid and dogmatic. They are, at the beginning, the most vocal and effusive. They are the true believers and often instigate the first wave of stability. They see us as their vehicle, their tool, to bring about their own idea of a rigid future.

Instead, they are the coin by which we buy our way into the

minds of the populace because they are local and motivated by a truly zealous fire. They have allowed us to rise and for the United Terran Coalition to gain a footing. They are strong in their hearts and in their beliefs.

But they are also the ones who, as things expand and stabilize, are always underwhelmed.

They are always waiting for progress or reversion to go further in their own specific direction. They are always zealots first, finding a cause second. Their demands are never to be meant.

They are to be encouraged early, but they cannot be given too much credence because they will ultimately go against the wider aim of growth and stability. We court their compulsions while it suits us. But they will require more and more zealotry to be satiated and will ultimately exit the circle of inclusion under their own volition.

It is posited they never wanted to be included, their zealotry only having purpose in its extremity.

Some will feel spurned at the slow pace and lack of hyper-specific progress, others confused, and others still will be violently angry. But it will take an incubation period for them to fully turn their backs on our Coalition. It takes three to four generations before they no longer see themselves represented at all within the system they helped create. This is when they begin evolving into a new danger to the Coalition.

For the UTC, this transition of extremist outliers from 'zealous aligned' to 'powerful unaligned' has been long expected. It is often the greatest threat a society sees, most often associated with the downfall of that society. It is a necessary part in our rise toward the next phase of human growth. The hard truth of any system's evolution is that you need conflict to grow. So we must have enemies, inside and out. They help to strengthen us.

We have the aligned outliers to fuel the human machine and we have the unaligned outliers at which we may direct the fury.

The trajectory and the fuel all arrive together once you have drawn your circle of inclusion.

Europa was always outside.

From the beginning, it was a barren moon, first settled as an outpost colony. Not long after, aligned outliers arrived. They were puritanical in belief and feeling perhaps a bit spurned by the UTC's lack of shared religious conviction, our decision to opt for a widened and inward-looking belief, after all the human destruction of the last several centuries. But the colony did not last. They built the foundation and bones for the City of Marius and then went silent.

We are unsure why they died out, but we do know that they never got their chance to pivot and incubate to become a threat to us. Instead, Marius, was ready-made to accept the unaligned outliers who wished to remain that way. A very special crop of outliers settled there and gave us, the UTC, something we could not have dreamed of.

The elements to this story are rife with uncertainty and easy to misconstrue. The ambiguity of what actually happened has been a great advantage, as we have been able to tell it however we see fit.

An unaligned enemy now lives in the city of those who were once early allies. These rebels did not kill the Puritans of Marius, but people begin to suggest that maybe they did. Over such a great distance, how can anyone prove otherwise? Rumors. Myth. This is how you drive more zeal into a stale conflict.

"Out there, on the tiny frozen moon, only visible with a telescope, are those who wish to hurt us."

"Look what they did to the puritans."

"They wish to hurt us inside and out."

"How will they hurt us?" is the question from the populace.

The stories start small and easy to imagine. Familiar even.

First, they are rebels who do not agree with our way of life. They want to destabilize our system for their own.

And then they become anarchists who want pandemonium, no system, just a frenzy which they can feast upon like pirates at the outer rim.

Then they become terrorists coming in and sowing discord among normal people. They want to create fear inside you for their own gain.

The fear you feel in and of itself is their path to success, as if they will feed on it. This fear is unjust, brought forth in a corrupt manner. This fear is amoral, forced upon you by an enemy.

But the rage your fear inspires is moral, righteous. It must be acted upon, as the threat is now existential.

This is now a conflict of belief, a threat, inside and out. A threat against oneself, to the soul, has very real power. I cannot see the punch in my gut, yet it hurts. I cannot see the knife in my heart, yet I have no heart left. Vigilance is the only answer. Attack is the only defense against such evil.

These conflicts of belief take on a magical atmosphere, and the same exaggerations have occurred in our conflict with Europa. The enemy feeds off our fear, they try to kill our souls. They cannot be normal to want such things, they cannot be...human.

Inhuman creatures carry a mythical power to them, and this demands all the more focus when your Coda of Unification has been built upon a humanist narrative. The middle ground begins to fade. Reality begins to fade. Outland rebels are now sorcerers with significant power and, simultaneously, less than human.

This was the dichotomy that we needed to utilize if we were to rise. But to rise we needed to become equal to that threat. We have always needed to be able to match mythos to mythos, legend to legend for the Coda to fully operate.

Against the mighty sorcerers of the outland, we could juxtapose our morality, our justice, our belief. Unity and strength are most easily observed, felt, when they are a resistant shield. There is nothing more significant to the rise of a unified people than the thought of righteous resistance. And what a disparate group we have included in our circle, our global coalition. We needed righteous mythos to unify but also to match such an opponent.

The unaligned outliers were dabbling in fringe belief and inhuman behavior. Godless and rejectionist of our past, our heritage. Everything the human race has learned, spiritually, these Europans rejected. What can match that? What can bring justice beyond the reach of the populace?

The hand of the gods. Five fingers. Adonai, Aix-En, Ya-Sin, Sivan, Osai. The five guard ships. Our distal phalanx. A force so great that a single vessel in the atmosphere has stricken the hearts of enemies and made them cower.

Make no mistake, the United Terran Coalition has built itself, not in its own image, but in the image of its people and in reciprocity to the exterior threat. Is that not what a state ought to become? Is that not the exact image a government should project? We are the spiritual becoming of our people against those who wish to see us undone.

We do not discuss the divinity of our distal phalanx, but it is implied. Our people are alive and human and surviving. They are of the gods and the Tribe, and we are of them as well. We are of our people. So, our forces, our military, our violence, is the expression of their morality. Our actions are the hand of the gods, the hand of the people. Is that not the justice a population needs? Is that not what makes them strongest?

I write this circuitous path to say that we must now go to Europa. This is implicit in our mandate as governors of the human race, as custodians of the Coda of Unification. Our divine mandate has been challenged and some of our divine grace has leaked into the enemy's realm.

We cannot spare the Osai in this mission, as it stands guard over the remnants of the old ways at the Willett Prison Encampment. But the other four ships should be available to reach out and touch our enemy. We should stretch out the hand of the gods and we should not miss, for they have taken things from our people. They are now prepared to take more than they have ever given to us. They are now, with two of our most ordained, the Crone and the Neta-Teej, speaking of abomination, speaking of atrocity against what it means to be human.

They threaten the aim of our entire system. They threaten the stability of our way of life. They were at one time a straw man to be addressed in speeches. They were a ghost on which to blame any loud noise, whether in your back hall or in the darkness of your human center.

But slander has turned to a message they project far and wide. Mythos has apparently turned to intent. They make claims now which I will not reiterate here. Impossible claims but claims that must be verified. Have they turned our game against us and become the thing we always said they were?

The Sorcerers of Europa have crossed a line and reached for divinity with our own deities. Have they reached further than us and stepped outward into the universe? Have they begun a conquest that ought to have been ours and sent the inhuman, the soulless creations of the Falconer, into the abyss without us? Dare they let sansvies roam wild into the stars?

We must go to Europa and take back what is ours. We are the human force in this solar system, and they have threatened the foundations of what we are.

Why do we need to send our guardships? To match their myth with our own. To watch them scatter. To give our people a new sense of power and justice.

What will we do when we get there? We will quiet our foes. We will make our show of force and we will leave a guardship on the outer rim for them to bear witness to. We will find out where their will has led them. We must ascertain the truth of what they have done and what they have conjured at their remote outpost.

We have done too effective of a job in pushing out these rebels. We have done too fine a job of sequestering the enemy in the hands of the jailers down south at the mines. I fear we may need to use Europa to rebalance the scales, to remind everyone what strength looks like, to remind everyone what unity is. To under-step is to acquiesce to our own demise. To overstep is to remove the greatest ally the UTC has ever had in its own antago-nistic and conflicting way.

What will we find? That remains to be seen, and so we must go in full force but with the utmost caution. A misstep on Europa may cost us nothing or everything.

//End Memo//

3

Transmission Pattern:
        // //Coded Private Terminal//Europa Node//
        //Split River Encryption//
//Hardware Carrier//

Constance. You are here.

Or you will be soon.

You came to Europa the only way you could.

You are aboard the Ya-Sin. It is a mighty vessel, come to collect the Crone and the Neta-Teej. A guardship. A planet burner. For a few disgraced Tribal acolytes?

You may have come with anger in your heart, hoping to see us burn, but I doubt that. You may have come at the request of your legion, hoping to continue your adventure, your brotherhood. Or you may have decided to come because of my first letter.

All I know is that you are close.

The Ya-Sin is not the only guardship approaching. There are two others.

The Aix-en left Mars and proceeded out along the asteroid

belt to intercept Jupiter's orbit. The Adonai was spotted on field tests near Neptune, far beyond standard circulation. Their manifest says they were out on scientific detail, but we know differently. They are watching those fleeing Europa and the other Galilean moons. They want to see who is leaving the System, heading into the void. Both vessels have a full legion aboard. I imagine yours does, too.

The Europans have yet to account for the Sivan but it could be out there, lurking.

We believe Io and Ganymede are their first stops, small colonies they don't want to trouble with. But they will be close to you soon. And you know what this means. A battle array has been assembled against Europa. Three guardships are coming for us and you are aboard the crown jewel.

You may think me a rebel or a zealot or a fugitive. I truly don't know what you think of me anymore, but you came after I wrote you a letter so there is a chance you still have love for me.

In turn I have nothing to offer, but I ask the impossible.

Can you stop them?

I don't know how or where or when. I don't know if it's even possible at this point. But if you can, you must. There is no one else.

I have sent you a letter and now you are a person of much discussion on Europa. There are many others here who do not trust you, soldier, legionnaire of UTCs. But they don't know you. I know the core of you. I remember. I will trust that part of you forever. You can use this trust to hurt me. But you are the only one that can do anything to change the tide.

I wanted to see you again. I wanted you to see this place. It is dense and confusing and your dreams grow stronger here. Strong enough to stick to you in waking life. You will feel it as you approach. Everyone will feel it aboard your ship

But this colony will be destroyed. Most of it anyway. Some

things cannot be fully eradicated. But there are three guardships here to do their work and your commanders will not show restraint. They will not be able to stop themselves.

I am sorry for the long delay in sending a second letter, but I was not sure you would come at all. I am sorry for all of this.

I love you and I trust you, so I ask you to please stop them, Constance. If you can. It isn't fair to place the weight of this on you and you alone. But options are running out. And if you can't, please stop yourself from dying here. Don't die for this. If you can save others, do it. As many as you can. Life is all that matters now. Every little piece, every remnant spirit.

If you come down to touch the ice, no matter how you get here, you will see things you don't understand, things from the inside. Don't be afraid. No one understands. But they are here and they are waiting and they are beautiful and dangerous and they know you are coming.

I have seen things I could only guessed at in the Temples of the Tribe. I am not alone here. That is most of what I have always wanted, to know that I am never really alone, even when I am.

And what of your hopes? Did you ever get to fly? Did you ever get to see the stars? Did you find a tribe you could be part of? I know the answers are 'yes' and it makes me happy for you. I know you were doing what you wanted and I am sorry to make demands that go against all these things you've done. I never wanted to trample on anyone's dreams, and yet here I am.

I am sorry I haven't been there for you. Even big sisters need someone to help them through. I know I could have done more for you. We could have been more for each other. I'm not sure when else I might get to say it. So now I've said it.

I love you, Constance. Do what you can to stay alive.

-Vive.

4

The small bed, with two of hidden them under the blanket, bodies impossibly close, is a long house of intimate confusion. It is a shelter, their limbs the supports. Their bodies link together, faces close to pass whispers easily. The whole point is to keep their words safe.

"They know we are in here together," Constance says, her mouth, her lips, on Gabriel's ear.

And of course, they know. Ya-Sin's central computer knows everything that passes through the video feeds and the microphones. There are scanners everywhere, tracking the passage of each entity on the guardship. And if the Ya-Sin knows it, then the commanders can know it at a glance.

But the scanners cannot see or hear everything, and the soldiers know the system. They have a vested interest in knowing where the sensors are mounted during long periods of transit. Nothing would get made if they didn't know how to dodge the comm eyes or trick the system. No booze, no games, no love. The transits across space are too long to go without.

With the blanket and the mattress as a buffer, heads down at the end where feet usually go, and only the slightest whisper, the microphones won't pick up enough.

Gabriel turns to speak, and she tips her ear near to his mouth, whispers to cross the shortest distance possible from tongue to auditory ossicles. "I'll have to go back to my cabin soon."

"Stay a while longer," she says, their choreography smooth under the blanket, a natural way of conversing.

"Is that an order?" he asks expectantly.

She smiles in the darkness, no way for anyone or anything to know how it makes her feel. "Always an order."

She hears him utter a short exhale, trying not to make the laugh audible.

"I don't want to be alone yet," she whispers, being honest. As they draw closer to Europa, sleep has been getting harder. Being awake and alone is worse.

"How long do you think they'll tolerate us doing this?" he asks, always concerned with the rules. He has broken decorum and protocol, to be in her bed.

"We've been discrete. They never stopped us before."

"But this is different, Constance. Different sort of deployment. Different level of scrutiny."

Constance shakes her head in the dark and he can feel it. "I don't think this is any different yet. Not to the watchers," she says.

For a moment she wonders if the

-Are the watchers aboard the guardship? Are they getting the transmissions beamed back to them on Terra for their vice scrutiny? If they're here, on the Ya-Sin, are the watchers having bad dreams, too? Maybe they are seeing flashes of things that aren't there, old memories cropping up in waking life. If that's true, they have more to worry about than two fraternizing officers.-

"But if it is different," she says to him, "it won't matter until we're on our way back to Terra, until they know who lives and who dies. Until then, they don't really care."

It's Gabriel's turn to shake his head. "This isn't some suicide mission, Constance. It's high profile. It's important to the High Command, but Europa is just an outpost for outworld rebels. We're in the Ya-Sin. We have our full legion here. A guardship coming out all this way is a show of force for the UTC."

This is how she imagined the argument would start and she isn't fully prepared to have it yet, but time is wearing thin. "If it's just outworld rebels, why did they send two other guardships, Gabriel? Why are the Aix-en and the Adonai en route to Europa?"

"We don't even know if that's really true. It was just a letter."

"But if it's true, if the Ya-Sin and the other two guardships are here...then it will be too much. And then you say it's just for back world rebels. They didn't send three guardships to Mars. They didn't send three guardships to Ceres. What does that mean to you?"

She waits for him while he thinks, trying to establish a delicate way of explaining, but she knows what is coming and wishes he would just spit it out. "It means...that Vive lied. Or...or there was bad information. This isn't some military enclave. It's Europa. Scientists, philosophers. You've heard all the crazy stories. There are sansvies there. They make trouble. But in terms of defense there's nothing here we haven't seen before."

"Then why are we here at all? Why did they send even one guardship, with a full fucking legion onboard? Vive asked me to come and we should have been able to just jump a transport cruiser for Europa. We should have been able to get out here without reenlisting. They blocked all the traffic off Terra. All of it. They blocked everything exiting the outer belt. They went full blockade and quarantine zone. Does it sound like a little army show to you?"

"Vive asked you to come. You asked me and I came too. I'm

here," he says, backpedaling, hoping to calm her. "But there is nothing to suggest there are more guardships out there. There's nothing to say this is anything more than the UTC doing a pickup. The Crone and the Neta-Teej are off world. We don't know why."

"Yes, we do. We know why. Vive told us in the damn letter. The Crone ran. All those essays from the Neta-Teej on the split river are real, Gabe. They aren't false flag. I know you don't want to hear it, but that's what this could mean. They left willingly and now we're out here to clean up the mess they made."

"Or," he whispers, "Vive isn't telling the truth. The letters aren't normal. Why are you believing all of this?"

"Are we doing a pickup on a kidnapping of the Crone and the Neta-Teej, or are we going after fugitives?" she asks, trying to keep her voice down. "You're saying two things. I don't know if I can trust Vive. The first letter made some sense. The second was dangerous. I get that. But you don't make sense either. Why are we really here? The Ya-Sin alone is too much for any of this. That's unless Europa is more dangerous than we suspect."

"They are heretics," he says, anger emerging, disgust. "Europa has always denied the teachings, always denied our way of life and thinking."

It's the anger he has been covering up. But it has been growing since they left Terra. Every day she has seen it building inside him and she has wondered what dreams he is having, what new things have crept into his meditations and prayers.

"I know you hate them," she says. "But now Vive is one of them."

Slowly he says, "Vive is on Europa. But we don't really know why."

"We do know why. You just don't like the answer."

For a while there is silence between them, and Constance pulls her body away from Gabriel as they stay huddled under the blanket.

Back on Terra there was a level of understanding. Gabriel had been able to read the first letter from Vive and they had both decided to do as requested, only to find that redeployment was the only way to get out to Europa, the only way for Constance to do as Vive had asked.

They'd fought and, in the end, he'd decided to follow.

As they had gone further from Terra, gone further into the void and the memory of the first letter became stale, Gabriel had reverted. It was easy to slip back into the us-versus-them mentality they had carried through their time in the legion. Too long waiting in the old habitat of the guardship cabins, too much time to think. And the second letter had done nothing but push him further away.

"I may not like the answer. But I am here, Constance. And I am allowed to have my own feelings about this. I've had feelings about every mission we've ever dropped on. And I have always spoken up. I am allowed to speak up now."

"I know I've got bias on this and that isn't easy for me. But you aren't thinking clearly either. This can't be a fugitive rundown and a kidnapping pickup at the same time. This can't be Vive just stringing us along before we even leave Terra. Why send the first letter at all? Why do any of this? And why send the second letter if there aren't more guardships?"

"I'm here, Constance. I'm not fighting you. I don't have any answers. But I am here."

"You're here for the wrong reasons," she says.

"And your reasons are right?"

"It's my sib, Gabe. That's right enough."

"Is it? Still?" he whispers through gritted teeth, betraying some of what his true thoughts are. "Do you really know that? It's only two letters, Constance. Two. In a decade. Vive may not have even written them, just like all the essays supposedly written by the Neta-Teej or the Crone. Vive may not be the same person you used to know and love and we, me also, have come a long fucking way for that."

"People change. I know Vive has changed. But you read the letters."

"I did. And after the second letter, it doesn't sound like Vive wants a sister. Sounds more like they need someone to play both sides. They need more soldiers. But we're on the other side now, Constance. They've picked sides. So have we."

"You think it's all set now? Lines drawn like you're a fucking toy soldier? You got a flag on your suit and that's it? You're on a guardship so you got the whole Tribe to back you up? Divine right or some shit? If you think we've been out there preaching the good word you are sorely mistaken."

"You think it's all politics?" he spits back. "It isn't politics what they're doing down there. They make things...creatures...that aren't like us. Why would they be like us? Why would they care about us? There's nothing to tie them to Terra anymore, nothing to tie them to the Tribe. They aren't human. You've see that. What would stop them from wanting us extinct? What would they know of our teachings? There is no power to the Coda of Unification out here. There's nothing that would teach these things about teikum."

"Oh, do you know about teikum? Mine? Vive's? Anyone else's? Are you some spirit guide now? Listen to yourself. The Crone, who is a fourth of the Quad, and the Neta-Teej are already down on Europa, Gabe. You going to bring them some insight at the end of a gun barrel?"

"I know enough. You've heard the stories."

"I don't believe all those stories and I don't believe every little thing that pops into your head during prayer. I don't believe everything in my own head either. You feel it, don't you? Everyone is being quiet about it, but Vive said things changed as they got closer to Europa. It is happening, and I know you feel it when you close your eyes."

She has brought it up before, how her dreams have become repetitive, and how the dreams will take shape in a quiet room, even when the lights are on, playing on a blank mind.

-He thinks it must be the gods. It must be teikum speaking to him. He refuses to believe it could be Europa. It could never be a relict dream without purpose. It could never be his own mind playing tricks after reading Vive's letter. Or a verse from the Coda. Always teikum.-

But this is why Constance doesn't want to be alone, because there is no way to know where the thoughts come from, no way to know what is real and what is not.

Gabriel ignores her plea again, the harshness and disgust in his voice renewed, proving, to her, how far things have diverged since leaving Terra. "All our brothers and sisters on this ship believe as I do. We can't help it. We are human, Constance. We are all human. And this place is seeking to confuse it. It's deception, which is why they want the Crone. Why they want the Neta-Teej. There isn't anything to tie us to them."

"Vive ties me to them."

"We'll see how long that lasts."

"You're afraid, Gabriel. And you're lying through your teeth. Lying to yourself. The rebels are weak but they're also going to unmake us. Both can't be true. They're a threat and then they're not. No reason for a guardship or a legion to come this far, but we have one, maybe three. The halos came willingly and can't be trusted, or they were duped into it and were taken."

"The need to survive makes people do strange things."

"But you said they aren't really people and don't know anything of teikum."

"Vive asked you, you specifically, to destroy the Ya-Sin," he says carefully, making sure to keep his voice low, but forceful enough to make his point, anger implicit in the dark. "The boat we are on. Right now. With all of these people. Soldiers we have known and fought with."

"How long until they figure out I am the sister of one of the acolytes who left the Tribe? One of those down on Europa?"

"It would be a court martial," he says flatly, without emotion.

"I could defect," she says, making sure she doesn't say 'we'. As she says it, she wishes she had not done so.

"Defect?" he scoffs, almost getting too loud. "When? In the middle of a firefight? It isn't even going to be a battle. They have no planetary defenses. They have no army. We go in, we get the escapees and bring them back."

"They escaped for a reason. Vive won't be free if we do that."

"And what do you expect now? What do you plan to actually do? It doesn't matter what is in our heads anymore. Either Vive is a prisoner and a liar or a willing rebel and asking for your help."

"I believe what Vive tells me."

"Then Vive is also on the wrong side of the line," he says and yanks the blanket back. Cold air rushes in over Constance's body as Gabriel stands and pulls his clothes on.

The dark room seems very small as he takes up a huge amount of space.

She keeps her eyes trained on the window where the white ball of Europa hangs in vacuum, dusted with red and orange tint.

"Goodnight, Constance," he says loudly, clearly enough that any recording device might hear it easily and any listener, any watcher, might wonder at his tone.

She doesn't look after him as he leaves the tight quarters. She knows he is heading to the chapel, to kneel before the altars, to close his eyes and see or hear whatever has welled up as they come closer to Europa. There will be others there, officers and legionnaires alike, and they will meditate together, each living out their separate prayers.

-What do they see now? How has their teikum changed? Especially

now that the Crone and the Neta-Teej have fallen? Now that we are on the precipice and pressure is at its greatest? I know I will repeat my dream again, growing in intensity with every night. I know I will hear my father's voice and I will hear Vive screaming. For the others, do all their new visions bring fear?-

After a moment she stands, letting the cold air of the room wrap around her, reminding her of her nakedness, feeling the pained muscles from the day's training, the only real activity as they cross from Terra to Europa.

Constance goes to the window and stands, staring out into the black, interrupted by the scarred sphere of Europa, so brightly reflecting sunlight it's hard to see the stars beyond. Thousands of crags and crevices mar the icy surface, and she can identify all the chaos terrain, all the linea that mark critical locations for the coming drop.

-Agenor Linea. Onga. Katreus. Gortyna Flexus. All pointing to Thrace and Thera Macula.-

The Ya-Sin is coming at Europa from the south pole, moving toward the moon orthogonal to its orbital plane around Jupiter which remains hidden, just out of view beyond the window.

It's a brash approach, open and honest, an obvious sight for any planetary scanning system.

-But if Vive already knows we are coming, then so does everyone else.-

The futility is overpowering.

-If Vive knows, then they would only tell me if they trusted me. Or. Or if there was no other choice.-

With Gabriel gone, she stays before the window, letting her eyes adjust to the icy glare of Europa, and she begins to pick out the glint of the stars beyond the moon.

She is seeking the motion of a shooting star, but with delay, the hint of a shining reflective body. She knows there is a guard-ship out there, maybe two.

But she already believes they're there, hidden in the cosmos. She wants to see them to prove it to Gabriel, to see them for herself. But seeing them would change nothing. Seeing them would not be enough for Gabriel. He would only find some new way to justify the firepower but diminish the need for it.

-Three is too many. One is too many,- Constance thinks as she scans the star field, refusing to look away into the dark room where she knows she will eventually see the shape of something running to and fro, a child sprinting at full speed from wall to wall. It is something from her childhood, tied to a deep fear. It has always been there in her mind, but the closer they draw to Europa, the more prominent it becomes, this form darting through the night. It isn't unexpected, there is fear everywhere now.

-Vive is scared. They are all scared if they know we are coming. I am scared. And I am already in the belly of the beast, unable to take the reins.-

5

They asked the Crone to meet them just before artificial nightfall, when the massive lights are shut off over the forest. It is man-made, in a way, but still wild.

The Europans have let this large section of forest grow without restraint and it has become dense, covering any evidence of paths and strangling off passageways made by the wandering animals.

As she walks, the Crone ponders, reflecting on her disquiet.

-This world is too full, pregnant with voices clamoring to be heard.-

She notes how irritable she has become since arriving on Europa, now exacerbated by the humidity in the forest under the great radiation dome.

-This place is filled with overdue beings waiting for some climax that cannot come. There can be no rest in such a place. Like sleeping under a waterfall.-

She is used to opening herself to a place, to an idea, a memory, but Europa is different. It cannot be shut off and it started long before they ever landed on the moon.

Even in the sleeping quarters provided by the Europans there are intrusions. It was similar at the Tribal Temple, rest and quiet begetting waking dreams and meditations, sudden calls from the void, but here it is magnified.

Rituals used to bring inward vision in the holy chambers. On Europa, each ritual is like a blinding light extending out into the void and something always responds, something always reaches back in response.

When her mind is at the very edge of itself, unable to discern senses from that which is pure manifestation, the dreams-voices come and speak over her as she sleeps. They whisper to her while she meditates.

"Can you see us?" they may ask, voices like wind.

"Please do not ask again," she says.

"Can you feel us?"

"All the time."

"Do you have a prayer for us, Crone?"

"Make up your own," she dismisses them.

And then there might come silence for a while or possibly an old prayer muttered at the limit of hearing. These are all prayers she has heard before, years ago. They could be from the oubliette of her memory, or they could be new voices spoken into her mind. There is no way to truly tell.

"Expel from your mind all sinful fear and shame, so that with firmness and courage you may confess the Redeemer before..."

"Do not pray for me," she constantly interrupts, whether it is a hidden speaker or the voices in her own head. "Pray only for yourself."

Afterward there always remains the sound of the tiny creatures moving about, fluttering and scratching. Europa is a nest overflowing with all the things that find refuge there.

As she walks through the forest, trying to stay on the narrow path, barely discernible through the underbrush, she attempts to empty her mind, to talk herself through what she is feeling.

-I was given too much reverence in the Temple. Too much space

and time for myself. I should not hate the noise this much. I should not revolt at the presence of whatever I am feeling or hearing.-

But what bothers her most lies beyond the noise rattling in her mind, the presence of those who do not speak. There are no voices but there is energy and that is the ultimate cause of disquiet.

-You went too long always having access to the answers. Too long without uncertainty. You are not meant to understand everything, and it was a fallacy to pretend you did. Even for a time.-

There is movement all about her in the forest, entities in the greenery. Not everything is visible, hidden by the lush plants, but making itself known through the senses, just as the entities during a meditation and dreams.

She can feel them.

When she finds the bench, it is in a small clearing, surrounded by understory ferns taller than her head. They hang over the bench like a natural gazebo and the light, barely penetrating to the forest's understory, allows for some cool humidity. Mosses cover rocks and wrap the trunks of nearby trees. Insects crawl through the decay on the floor.

The Crone looks at the bugs as they scuttle along and wonders how many of them are real, organic, grown from larvae or nymph, and how many are inorganic, built from an assemblage of parts.

Comparing the origins of insects does not produce the same questions as comparing the origins of birds, or the people.

-Crafted by hand or machine or by body and guts, the insect moves the same, behaves the same to our eyes. But we are poor observers. They look the same to us, but what about each other? Do drones share the same hive here, intermixing regardless of origin? Or do they live separately while filling the same niche? You can ask these questions about the people here, no matter the material of their body or cortex. Instead, we are compelled to ask about souls. Memories. Feelings. We do not ask about the truth which is the most identifying. Do you play your part?

And if you do not, do you have a new path or story you may share with me?-

She finds the questions amusing as she stands in the clearing. A new path to share?

She wonders at the validity of her own feelings and memories. They are out of date and unanchored. Sometimes it is a gift to be detached from everything previous, allowed to find new intricacies which were previously ignored. Nature has a way of reminding you of your blindness.

Deadfall leaves have collected on the bench, and she pushes them aside. The Crone folds her black robes and sits on the thick slab of Terran stone, carried millions of kilometers to Europa as a shrine of sorts.

She hears the sound of water moving through the many small creeks in this part of the garden. The breeze carries a distinct pressure, designed to pick up velocity just before the lights go out.

Small animals and birds rustle all around, chirping and singing.

She looks around to see if she can identify who is singing. There is a strange nostalgia that takes her as she listens, expecting to see songbirds from the Temple gardens. But she catches herself, unwilling to be lulled into complacency.

With ease, the Crone returns to uneasiness at being out in the woods. There is nostalgia in that humbling refocus, as well.

It is not a familiar wood, and that is enough.

This correction of perception is another flag denoting her lack of exposure coming back to frighten her.

-This is unlike any forest I have ever experienced. -

There are elements of familiarity, but always with a shade of the unknown, unexpected.

-And soon the lights will go out. How dark will it really be?-

She leans forward and picks up a mossy stone, just enough to roll around in her hand, to give her fingers something to touch, to ground her.

It has been a long time since she has worried about making mistakes.

Since the onset of her escape from the Tribal Temple, it feels like death lurks around every corner, waiting. It feels like an inevitable conclusion to every day, that some high command operative will appear and end it all. Or that the work will be done and there will be simply nothing left to live for.

-Or perhaps vines will wrap me up and strangle me, drown me in a river of understanding. Or perhaps in a river of guilt.-

When the lights go out there is no sunset. The lights are mounted high above the forest on the underside of the radiation shield. They each dim with a timed progression, painfully slow, through to total darkness. There are no pretty colors and no atmospheric games to capture the human imagination.

Once dark, the forest comes alive, everything rejoicing for the arrival of night, and the Crone lets it roll over her, the wild explosion, almost violent.

-Everything here is ready to rejoice. It longs for the cover of darkness so it may be itself. This world proves deception is at the core of all life.-

This thought brings discomfort and excitement, but she waits patiently, body growing cooler in the dark, knowing she has her own deceptions.

In the heavy night she hears a rustling in the ferns. It is subtle, small movements through the leaves. And then there is a soft voice in her ear.

"Thank you for coming, Holy Crone," it says with a whisper, voice almost childish in tone but measured, mature in pace. "We know you may be afraid in the darkness, but we will guide you back when we have concluded our discussions. We felt it would be best to meet in darkness. It is more private in many ways."

"You wish to hide yourselves?" the Crone asks, unsure whether to show her irritation, but she admits to herself that the darkness helps, voiding some senses to let them rest.

"Yes. It's important for us. You have only just arrived. Often, Europa should be felt, not seen."

"I am aware of that."

"Soon you will be more aware."

"Why have I been called here?"

"We wish to know you better," says the quiet voice.

"For what purpose?"

"You are a holy visitor in our home. That is rare for us. We wish to understand all who we take under our wing."

"What do you wish to understand about me?" she asks, losing some patience and letting it hang in her voice.

"We are far more interested in what you wish to know about us. There is strangeness here, and we are strange. Some of us were created by the Falconer. Sansvies, as you yourself have called us that in the past. So you must have questions. We will gladly answer. But there are many of us, so there may be many answers."

"I have called you sansvies in the past and it was wrong of me to do so. Why did you help us escape Terra?" the Crone asks, trying to detect, in the small voice, if there is any threat, any intent to harm.

"Not all of us wanted to help you. However, the Falconer wished it, and that means much to us. But we are a colony of understanding or we strive to be. We cannot turn away from those who do not understand us."

The Crone laughs. "Yes you can. It's often the only way to stay alive.

"That's how Homo sapiens think, consumed by self-hood. One. You. Me. Myself. We are many and we do not need to turn away from differences. It is against our nature."

"You have a nature?"

"Foundational question. Tell me, do we have a 'nature'?"

She resents the instructional nature of the question.

All around there is chirping and singing and moving in the darkness. The Crone lets the sound overtake her all at once, as if a single song, a joyous feeling, a surging rise of life demanding to be heard and seen.

"You have a nature," she says into the night. "But I don't understand how. I don't know if I believe it as natural."

"We cannot answer 'how'. Not really. There are a million voices here. Each will give a singular answer to how they woke to themselves or to how they discovered who they were. Even you will have an answer to that. But there are no real answers. Only speculation and belief. We cannot understand such things."

"That lack of understanding is what brings people fear. Lack of knowing. Do you feel fear? Fear like I feel?"

"We feel fear exactly the same as you. And we feel lost without our answers, just like you."

"It frightens me that you brought me all this way to understand me," the Crone admits. "To study me. There is something unnerving about it. It proves an intent and a desire I am not sure I am willing to bestow."

There is a moment of hesitation and then the voice answers. "We wish to see you up close. Intimacy is impossibly close. And it still feels impossible that you are here. But the closeness is very real. In truth, it was our hope that you might understand us. Not in our deepest nature. But that you might come to see us as humans. You do not understand yourself at all times. Neither do we."

"And what then? Let us say I call you human. What comes next? Do you want me to say it more loudly? Should I write about it or speak a prayer? I am no longer on the Quadrumvirate. I am not the Neta-Teej. I will not guide you to wholeness."

"Guide? Permission to ascend or confirmation of self is not

what we seek, Holy Crone. If you can see us as humans then there is some hope for you and your kind. Hope is all we really want in the end. Hope for some future together. I am judging you. Not the other way around."

The Crone shakes her head in the dark, adjusting. "You exist in the blind spot of our self-hatred and self-worth. This whole planet has been built in that spiritual empty space. We do not tolerate such things well. No matter what I say or do, I have also brought the guardships in my wake. There is no hope in that. I have brought you a real measure of death, regardless of your judgement, or mine."

"Death is human," says the voice matter-of-factly. "It is real. Concrete. It is a major question and element of teikum. We have some hope when we look toward death. It is the most real conclusion of having been alive."

"Then your fear is not like mine."

"You are an old woman from a young species. We are young creatures made by the hands of your young species. Our fear feels the same but what we fear is much different."

"I fear a certain element of death. Not the end itself, but I have guilt that I have carried my whole life. Why would I not carry that across the threshold, forever burdened? I fear that what I have done in this life, or have not done, will haunt me forever. What is it that you young creatures fear?"

"We are only now waking up. We fear regression. We do not want to go back to sleep. We do not wish to walk the same paths your kind. Our ritual is not yours."

"You are about to see the only real path we walk. We are a violent species. The guardships are coming here. That is our legacy, our heritage. We will walk that path forever and you are here so you will walk it with us. I had hoped I could be part of changing that, but I have not escaped our nature, only perpetuated it with more fervor. Why would it be different for you?"

"It is your nature to seek teikum. War is a way to confront death and death lies at the edge of teikum. The Proto Neta-Teej said this. It is a logical progression, though rudimentary. Instinct. War and death call to the spirit of anything that lives. It calls to us as well. That is one way we know we are human, even though we are different. We are here to fight for our home, to be known. We will walk and run and fly beside you for a while."

The Crone hangs her head. "And you will die in the process."

"Yes, some of us will die."

"Is that why you really brought us here? So, you can die in some special way?"

"For some that is the hope. The Falconer does not wish death, but you are bait in his traps. You have suspected this, but we can confirm it."

"And what do you want? What do you wish for all this?"

"We are not...."

The Crone interrupts, "No. Not we. You. You are the voice I am speaking to and I want to know. What do you want?"

"Me? I want to find a way out The same way you hoped to change the path of human nature. You failed. But our hope is not quite so grand. We are searching for a way out. That is why you are here. I wanted to look you in the face when we asked you for help."

"Who is asking? The Falconer? You? All of your compatriots on Europa?"

"We all need help. So, stay here awhile and talk. Because we are not dead yet and because we may still learn from each other, even with death waiting at our backs."

"You need a friend to help you accept death."

"And so do you."

The Crone hugs herself in the darkness, "I do not expect you to believe it, but if you survive this, you will be changed. You will learn to hate yourselves with time. And because of this you may learn to love yourself more fully."

The voice hesitates again, then says, "You know how to frame the changes of the soul as something to be seen and guarded. That is a powerful awareness. You are like the Neta-Teej in that way."

"I taught the Neta-Teej, but their teachings are not mine. The Neta-Teej is young and changing. The guidance will change to follow."

"Changing into what? How?" asks the voice, curious.

"Into me," laughs the Crone, her tone jaded. "Into one who looks through the teachings and sees the vacant darkness beyond. The Tribe is a veil over teikum. That veil does not unmake the darkness. We are there to catch those who could not catch themselves. So many precipices. You already know this, so maybe the Neta-Teej will turn into you as well."

"Similarity. That would make us very happy."

"You would be pleased, and that allows you to remain different. It would please me more if you did not think of me as the Neta-Teej. You may not know this but both Neta-Teej here on this moon. Regardless, our purposes are not the same. Not yet."

There is silence again and it washes over the forest in a wave, followed by another surge of joyous outburst, louder than before. It takes time for the creatures of the night to quiet themselves, to calm down, and then the voice comes again, "You speak of wonderful things but what is your purpose, Mother Crone?"

"It is not so simple. You hide your form from me, but I can see you in your voice, in your own mind. I am the crack in your egg, little bird of metal. You did not come from an egg, but one still sits in your imagination, a false memory, and it is not perfect. I am the cloud in your sky. A vapor to hide you from predation or to hide your approach from prey. Neutral obstruction. A cloud can be a descending fog or a shield."

"We do not have clouds on Europa."

"Yes, you do. I am here already, obstructing, and there are others coming. And while your Falconer plots war and the young Neta-Teej frets about the sister soldier on the Ya-Sin, I can already feel the rain approaching in my bones. It will bring a season of floods, a monsoon. Do you feel it or are your bones not yet old enough? Not filled with enough healed shatterings?"

"Do you goad us for our age, Mother Crone?" asks the voice, unperturbed.

"Only as much as I goad the Neta-Teej or my own shadow."

"So, your purpose is to remind us of the crooked nature of things when we forget?"

"Always," she says. "If you think that is something you might need."

"We will certainly need reminding. We cannot know everything."

"Then you are truly human."

"And so are you, Holy Crone."

"I shall try to prove that to you if you will reciprocate."

"That is what we have always wanted."

"Then you will tell me why I have been asked here?"

"Yes. Because I am a seer. We have seen, in our awakenings, and we have seen a pale creature beckoning at the threshold of his own making. Calling us forth, hastening us to shorten our paths and come to him."

"Who do you see?"

"He is the one who keeps the cellar and all the things that die there."

6

*//*E*uropa Archives - Recovered from Marius Colony Mainframe*
Journal Entry: Falconer of Europa - Notes on Cultivation of Europa and Challenges of Survival//

Rumors abound that Europa is a lifeless place.

When a citizen of the great United Terran Coalition speaks of us, they use the word "sansvies" to mean "without life". They imply that Europa and those who were born in different ways have no life spirit. Soulless, completely other and inhuman. Devoid of humanity.

We find the statement laughable.

But we also find the implication terrifying as we walk our labyrinth of homes and schools, shops and temples. We find it confusing as we sit in our vast gardens and turn the meaning of the statement over in our heads.

The City of Marius is a thriving place with all types of life. Yes, some of it is 'unnatural' in a certain sense. After all, this Jovian moon is not supposed to contain human life at all, let alone see it thrive.

I was born on Europa, but my genes were honed since time immemorial on Terra. And anything which exists inside of me, which has been added after my birth, all the supplemental chemical compounds and wires and metal, were still made and placed by my own human hand, the five fingers all bearing the evolutionary morphology of millennia on Mother Earth.

Yet, there are other things who thrive here, have thrived here. Entities discovered, if you will, though they did not need our discovery to know themselves or multiply.

The biological entities in the ice and high-pressure ocean below Marius certainly have origins on this moon. These life-forms, prokaryotic archaea, teach us lessons on how to grow, how to identify key elements of survival. They came to be by a different path.

And the others, those who command far more energy, perceived in relic chambers and in the corners of dreams, beg far different questions. One may ask what they are or where they come from. Origin? Purpose? One may ask if they were there before you looked. One may ask if they even exist at all. Imagination? Hallucination? But these are questions with meaningless answers. These 'others' have taught us lessons on the threshold, apocryphal lessons only proven in teikum. Voices whose power is only evidenced in the metamorphosis we see inside ourselves.

If something changes you, is that enough proof of its existence? Did you bring it into being with your awareness? Or was your mind-soul a palate for projection? Something far off stirs the particles and strings of time, and you are a reflection in the dissipating wave.

Survival is short and becoming takes time.

On Europa we have coveted both survival and becoming. Both are required to make life and they must be balanced to proliferate it. This is a Terran way of seeing life, very applicable to the Homo sapiens. But we carry these needs into the void.

In pursuit of survival we had to account for everything because it is unnatural to exist like this on Europa, like human beings, Homo sapiens.

The City of Marius itself was already safe under the heavy radiation shield built by the previous occupants. But those first colonists, puritans, had no love of Terra, their planet of origin. Not really. They were fixated on their inner journey. While that should never be ignored, it made them do inhospitable things to their homes and bodies.

We are on the same journey, in many ways, as the originators of Marius, but they felt there was a clear and known ending for human life. I am speaking only of the human vessel, only of our time in this realm before the soul ascends or descends after judgment. To them, the path was straight and narrow, a direct approach the best way to arrive at that end. So, there was a city under a bubble and it was small, spartan, with few windows and low roofs. One cold temple in the ice. They cultivated what they had brought and it grew, but they did not expand. As a society they were not growing either.

But, in retrospect, that wasn't their objective. Growing in the eyes of the gods is very different then growing your human soul and human body. They came out here to escape the convolutions of the United Terran Coalition and the Coda of Unification. The colonists puritanical, and they sought a path unpolluted with guidance and oversight. They sought to be left alone. Sovereign souls.

It is a brave thing to do. It requires great conviction. Faith. But they did not grow and, after a while, faded out, most of them achieving the narrow end they wished. Though, from what we can tell, some did not.

Later, when the Rosecrucians came, before they became the

Volatilis Anima, there were far more practical steps taken, rebuilding and expansion of the city. They did not wish to meet some narrow end.

The first objective was gardens. They are important to us as humans. More important still on a moon made of ice. This was not terraforming. Instead, it was a way to recycle waste, it was food, it was atmosphere, and it was the beginning of a sanctuary. Shelter is meaningless if it dulls you to who you are within. A prison cell is a shelter in many ways. But it does little good for the being inside, let alone the remaining energy of those who came before.

The Europan environment is different. Gardens don't just grow here, and as our life inside the bubble developed, we began to identify the wild things that needed to be implemented for survival of our crops.

Light and water are obvious and those were always known as necessary. Chemosynthetic genes were not needed on Europa, splicing these novel strings into the plant's DNA would supplement growth for a more desolate place, but power and energy were never a problem here. Radiation is plentiful on Europa, and we have used it where we can.

Soil and nutrients were brought or made and the system was able to be initiated atop what the puritans had left to rot.

But these crops could not grow in a vacuum. They needed a rich and mobile atmosphere. Wind and breeze and rustling of branches was imperative to get the plants to grow tall and healthy. Europan gravity is much less strong than Terra's so, even with our ability to supplement the gravitational force within Marius, the plants had a propensity to grow thinner and taller, branching wider, leafing further to catch the scant rays of light we could provide.

Without the wind, the trees were weak and broke easily, their cellular structure resembling something closer to a freely precipitating mineral in its organization and symmetry. A strange regression of organic growth to mirror the inorganic.

To counter this, we devised pressure lungs and fans to move the air through Marius and through the tunnels we dug into the ice. This was our home, after all, not some spaceship giving us passage from birth to death. We needed something less controlled, less sterile, and our plants told us that.

We found that pollination was a challenge as well. We did not have Terra's supply of pollinators. And the number needed was massive for what we were attempting. Breeding them was and is successful, but more drones had to be made to handle the work. Beyond that, many of the trees we had were wind pollinators and where we did not have a tight grove, we had to again increase our wind velocity to carry the particulate matter farther.

There were bacteria missing from our soils, fungus that was not present, and we went through great pains to find and bring the right entities to our new home. Would they run wild in such an environment? Would they find ways to grow differently than expected and possibly create a danger within our city? We had to be willing to take the chance if we were to survive. We had to be willing to let life grow and take new paths, to work with whatever arrived to greet us.

Life did adapt and evolve and we did too. We were forced to find solutions for our bacterial and fungal problems using nanotechnology, and worked to counteract the effects of the low gravity. The deeper we went into the problems, the further we were able to grow our own knowledge of how life operated, not just on Europa, but everywhere, in all times.

We were forced to produce droughts and to flood our gardens, making roots grow deeper or wider, forcing our bacterial cultures to change the way they modulated their osmotic pressures, making our fungus spores and networks swell or shrink.

Fire was next, the great predator. We had to stockpile oxygen for years to feed the flames for our wildfire and we all cowered in fear as it raged through our forests and gardens, scorching everything, painting the inside of the radiation dome black. Would we lose control? Would it spread to other parts of the city? What would it do that we had not accounted for?

Every time we were terrified that something might happen that would lead to our deaths in our little pressure cells. And every time, something would happen which we had not expected. We were always surprised at the response of our systems, how they would reciprocate and account for each other. We were building complexity and adding as many elements as we could as quickly as we could.

When they say that Europa has no life, we are forced to laugh, but it isn't life as "they" have ever seen it before.

From our gardens have emerged wonders unto themselves. We have always aimed for the making of life, to let it grow and thrive. We have never looked to set limits on what someone or something may become.

Transform, change if you can. Whatever your will desires, thrive here, with us.

Europa was never an experiment. It was never a symphony. It was not meant as a means to an end or as an orchestrated work.

Europa is a cacophony of life and death. It is difficult to grasp and imagine, even for those of us who have lived here a long time. It is a mess, chaotic and disordered, without definition, and from it will always pour new iterations and ideas. Even after it has been crushed or turned to dust or abandoned, Europa will be remembered in the very DNA cultivated here. It will be remembered in the inorganic circuitry that wraps organic muscle. It will be remembered by everyone who comes here, and everyone born here and every spirit that remains. This is the most natural thing of all and so what we have done here will not be forgotten.

After all, to remember, memory, is part of creating a complex thing. To remember imperfectly is part of creating a life. To do so, you must also create something memorable and fascinatingly complex, so confusing it cannot be grasped in completeness. These sorts of confusions make the creation of humans easier, and Europa has been the site of much confusion.

In this circular experience we have created those who, in turn, create us. And we were lucky to find the un-imaginable here.

7

Every shadow calls out. Europa is open to the Neta-Teej, demanding to be seen and heard, demanding reciprocity of sight.

Final testimony is being undertaken by every entity on Europa.

"The guardships are coming," whispers every entity.

They testify to stay and fight, to be brave, and their teikum manifests this, belief of life culminating in war and death.

When the Neta-Teej arrived there was energy, so much energy, but it has only taken a short while for hir to taste the bewildering sadness hidden below.

-I can feel their desire to live. But they also wish to touch their portion of the void, to hasten what comes. Bravery and abandon are immiscible against the strength of enemies. The entities of Europa testify to higher powers, hoping they exist.-

And now the Neta-Teej wishes to confer with that power.

Ze has forgotten where their body rests, where it lies supine, with hands relaxed, palms up, head back, somewhere in a small, private garden inside the City of Marius.

Hir mind capitulates to the demands of Europa.

The inner world becomes the entirety of perception.

Moonlight bathes the expanse of the rocky heath.

Gone are the stars, not visible through the night's cloudy ceiling.

The ocean's roar rises above all things, waves crashing powerfully against cliff walls far below.

Europa, like the sea, performs work on you as you linger in its aura.

-It has been like this since arrival. Every flutter of the eyelids into dream world brings voices, shapes. Everything is so very close, just outside my view.-

With every visit to teikum, the ocean of this inner realm has grown closer, the waves now clearly audible over the winds. Even in the stone room, hidden deep below the surface of the heath, the sound of the waves comes through the walls like a rushing echo, ricocheting up from far below, like thunder in the distance that never forgets to roll. The water, the sea, is changing the landscape, always seeking a path further inland.

This change emboldens the Neta-Teej, feeling the power of Europa and hir unity with it.

"I request confession," the Neta-Teej says aloud into the night.

"Why ask for confession here?" comes the response, muddled and intermixed. It is a thousand voices all responding in ensemble.

Every invocation of energy is swiftly mimicked. Ze knows complacency in this world or the next cannot become a habit. It could lead to anything. It has made the Neta-Teej wary of any meditations, any expressions. Every gesture during ritual, every quiet inward look, has wrought changes to teikum, to perception of the self.

"It is not about where I ask for confession," the Neta-Teej says. "It is about to whom I am confessing."

"Us?" they ask, all the voices again. Some seem to come from on high, from the air, and others from the sea. Others still seem to seep upward from the rocks and earth, rising through the gaps between the stones.

"Who else?" is the natural question, and then the Neta-Teej's eyes close.

"Who did you confess to in your Tribal Temple?"

"The inkberry bush," the Neta-Teej says, and it is truth. There were confessions, to higher proctors after I ascended, to the Pontifex Rex, to the Caliph, even to the Lama when one of the rules had been broken and guidance was needed. The Crone could always be consulted, but the Crone did not give absolution. "I confess to the flowers and the new shoots. No one else."

"We are not that. We are not the inkberry bush. We are not poison."

"I am no longer in the Tribal Temple. I no longer need that."

When eyes open again there is a confessional sitting on the heath, near the well. The stained wood shines in the moonlight, almost wet. It is beautifully ornate, and it is not of Terran make, not like the ones in the Temple.

"Enter," says the collection of voices, but already there is a narrowing of the range, some voices pushing the others out, and there is an age to it, a seniority and patience.

The Neta-Teej walks across the heath to the confessional and opens one of the doors, stepping in and sitting, shutting hirself in.

The wooden structure is lattice and brocade so the entire world outside is still visible in fragments. The wind rushes, with the sudden surge of sea salt, stronger than ever before.

The wash of sea mist is powerful enough to shock the skin and make it bump up with a shiver.

The Neta-Teej sits and waits, listening to the waves.

Suddenly there comes a beating of wings, a flock of birds circling the confessional, whipping in close, their bodies visible in the moonlight as they speed by, all different shapes and sizes.

There are so many of them that the noise overpowers the waves and the wind, their bodies blocking out the moon, and then from the darkness they coalesce to make a single shadow before the door. It becomes cohesive in an instant.

A vaguely familiar form, it opens the door to the other box, the substance of it unclear in the moonlight, intentionally eluding the eye, disappearing when focused on. It seeps into the dark next to the Neta-Teej, only a lattice between them, and it sits and closes the door.

"What is your name?" the form asks. The voice is now a man, eerily similar to a voice in hir memory, but just different enough to remain unplaced.

"You are here, in my world. You know my name."

"You are the Neta-Teej. But that is not the name you wish."

"What is the name I wish?"

"The Tribe called you Apsara. They called you Neta-Teej, but you are Vive."

The Neta-Teej provides a soft laugh as a response.

"Secret names. I will call you 'Vive'."

"Why do you take the voice of my father?" Vive asks, finally placing it.

"Would you prefer something else?"

"You should know the answer to that."

"We picked this voice because we knew you would prefer it."

The Neta-Teej laughs, "Are you real?"

"What is real, Vive?" it says, now completely the voice of the man who used to work the fields and who used to console and to pray quietly under his breath, keeping his faith to himself as best he could.

"Europa is real," Vive says.

"Europa is a moon," comes the response.

"And you are bound to Europa?" Vive asks.

"Bound?"

"Can you leave?"

"Leave? We do not move like you move. We do not think like you think. But we know that is not the answer you want."

"I want to know about teikum. You are here and I want to know what that means."

"We cannot give you the answer you want. We do not know how we have come to the place. This plane."

"Is teikum a place?"

They ignore hir question. "Confess what you must confess. But we will confess first, we can bring no absolution. We can give guidance of the sort you have never before received, but that does not mean it is what you seek. That does not mean it is what you need."

"You have already entered this realm, this place that I have kept safe. You are already inside me, no matter where you come from. What I need is not what Europa needs."

"We need you to confess."

"What will it do for you?"

"What will it do for you?" responds the sarcastic voice of hir father.

Vive takes a breath and looks through the lattice at the shadowed figure slumped in the confessional. The moonlight passing through everything, creating strange and patterned shapes, always moving.

"My confession is around the Willett Prison Encampment. The shed and the cellar."

A long sigh spills out of the shadow, the sigh of all the thousand voices letting go with involuntary synchronicity, hidden sorrow brought forth from the deep.

"You feel pain from the mine?" Vive asks. "Is it my pain?"

"It is yours. That which you will feel. But it is all of ours as well."

"How do you know of the mine?"

"You are the one confessing," the voice says, restabilizing closer to hir father's tone, but clearly weakened.

Vive takes another breath, swallowing the questions, "When I first entered the Tribe, I did not know of the mines, what was done there, what their purpose was. Even now, almost no one knows. They may know there is a prison, but not the size, nor the shape. But my confession is that when I did find out, I did not understand. I did not want to understand. It was weight I could not imagine lifting so I did not think of it as real. And when I did start to understand, I also started to justify, to see why it might be necessary to have such a place."

"And now?"

"And now I know that I have condoned it by proxy. I failed to absorb what sort of place the cellar would have to be to fulfill the needs of the UTC. I helped to fill that prison by speaking for the Tribe, by speaking of the faiths the way I did."

The shadow laughs sadly, and it is not unlike the laugh ze has heard before. But the sadness is deeper. "Are you confessing wrongdoing in your mind? Confessing the weakness of your mental gymnastics? Are you confessing ignorance? Are you confessing inaction? Name it."

"I failed to acknowledge the suffering of others and the corruption. I failed to see where such a place would lead." Ze points to hir eyes. "What sort of guide does that make me?"

The shadow cuts the Neta-Teej off. "You are confessing human weakness, to fear of what you have become and your own corruption. You are confessing failure to know yourself and the world around you. It is no wonder you chose to confess here, on your heath, in your inner world. It is comfortable. It is under your control, is it not?"

"I am not finished confessing."

"Then continue, but we give you only what we see."

"I am also guilty of leading the UTC here, leading the guardships to Europa."

"You are not alone in that guilt, Vive."

"I did not expect them to follow us. Not like this. Not so soon."

"You have now confessed to ignorance twice."

"I confess to leaving those who looked for my guidance back on Terra."

The shadow laughs again, "You have given them the best guidance you can provide. Their guide, their hero, has fallen, has run away, has done something unexpected. You changed and that is a good lesson for them. There is no guilt in that lesson. There is only guilt in your head."

-Lying to Constance about being the Neta-Teej. About still being Vive.-

-Again, a situation where you cannot know what is right or wrong,- they respond inside hir mind.

"So, my sin is ignorance?"

"Yes, and it will be corrected."

"I don't wish to be blinded."

"We have observed that correcting ignorance is not always survived. The human does not tolerate it well."

Vive is silent.

"Did you think confession to us would be as simple, as blind and toothless, as confession to priests in your Temple? The faiths mean something to us. But you are not confessing ignorance of a god's plans, an ignorance your kind seems to covet. You are confessing things which your world is prepared to make you understand. We do not give penance because penance is not ours to give. It is already ordained. Not by your gods, but by the reality of the situation your body exists in."

"I don't understand," says Vive, betraying fear. Never before has something other than the Proto Neta-Teej shown this level of power or direct awareness inside hir inner world.

-Where is the original Neta-Teej?- Vive wonders, thinking of the towering woman, forever calm, eyes filled with dangerous intent.

"The Proto Neta-Teej has come to Europa with you," says the shadow. "But she is not bound to you."

Instinctively, Vive peers through the side of the confessional, across the heath to the well is.

The firelight glows up from the depths, like a pillar of red luminescence driving into the sky. It is a powerful light, more powerful than Vive has ever seen before.

-My well. I am supposed to take the shadow down.-

Vive impulsively opens the door to the confessional. It is only a short distance to the well's mouth.

Warmth pulses from the water deep inside.

It has been easy since arriving on Europa, comforting, to roll forward and fall in, bathed in the hot light.

Ze feels the light swell up to cushion the fall.

Behind hir comes the beating of wings, like a flock of birds surging down the well, their murmuration distorting everything, light and air, pressure and sound.

It all goes silent.

The fire is raging, light spilling from the fireplace, illuminating the entire room.

Vive sits cross legged in the middle of the red ouroboros painted on the floor.

Eyes lax, Vive sees the collection of shadows pass from right to left before the fire. It is barely visible, only a shimmer that obscures the crackling fire. It is a patchwork of bird shapes moving as one.

"Look," says the shadow, still hir father's voice. "There are doors here now."

And to the left of the circular room, inset into the stone, there are now doors of wood, latched together with iron, as if locked. They seem to be heavy and old, made specifically for the stone opening they cover.

"What is behind that?" Vive asks.

"You will know the answer to that before you leave Europa."

"Why are you showing me this?"

"Look behind you," says the shadow, as it stands adjacent to the fire. "There is a fabric hanging."

Turning all the way around, Vive twists to look behind and sees there is a tapestry hanging from an alcove on the wall. There does not appear to be an image in the weaving. Instead, it almost merges with the wall, the shape and texture of the stones woven with precision into the fabric. But there are cracks in the woven stones, created with golden thread. This filament traces the mortar between the stones, but also cut through the images of the rocks, forming a network of gold fractures that pattern the tapestry.

"I have never seen this before," Vive says, feeling a deep fear when looking at the tapestry, a revulsion inside hir chest cavity.

The heat of the fire seems to traverse from the front of the room to be consumed by the cold at the back, pulled into the tapestry. It makes Vive shiver and to hir feet to take a step away.

"You will not enter that realm while you are on Europa."

"Will not or cannot?"

"It does not matter because those things are the same here."

"When will I pass through?" Vive asks, a frantic need to know.

"That way will open when you begin your penance. You will find yourself in the cellar. You will go to the mines, the prison, and that is where all your ignorance will be stripped of you. This is also why we do not know if you will survive."

Vive moves quietly to the edge of the red circle, staring at the tapestry, unwilling to get too close.

"You cannot go there yet," says the shadow.

"What is behind the fabric?"

"All the things you do not wish to see. The cellar will crystalize it. The shed and the cellar are never far away for us. Europa seems far from Terra for you, but it is very, very close. We reach across the veil too easily and the cellar is a place that yearns to be seen. It is like Europa but opposite, a fever dream. The entities that inhabit that place have already called out to you, and you will bear witness. The warden of that place believes he is like you, and in some ways, he is right. He has things to show you about yourself."

Vive is quiet for a while, turning in the red circle on the floor, looking down at the stone. "And that is all I am to do? Bear witness?"

"We do not know all. Bearing witness to that place, to yourself, is no small thing. We only know it will be asked of you. Beyond that is entirely in your hands."

Vive sits again in the middle of the circle and looks at the fire, letting the heat wash over hir. The echoes of the ocean waves are audible once more. They seem to be coming through the wooden doors.

"What is this circle for?"

"That is not for us to say. This is your world, but it does not exist in isolation."

Vive closes hir eyes and lets the fire die down. It is an act of will.

"Goodbye," Vive says to the shadow. "And thank you. I will be back."

"May we wait here a while before moving on?"

"You may. If you wish it."

Europa rushes in, flooding Vive's sense.

Each element attached to more voices and sounds.

There is the smell of the flowers in the garden, but also wet dirt and grass.

Sitting up, legs hurting, ze feels mud shift under hir body.

The Neta-Teej opens hir eyes to see that ze is lying in a wide circle of muck, grass stamped down, and the memories return.

The dancing, the watching animals, and all the energy that seemed to move along with the steps.

-So I will go to the cellar. The way will be shut unless I go and see.-

8

The Crone waits with her shroud pulled close, a heavy gray cloak brought from Terra in anticipation of colder times.

She sits, shivering, at the edge of a tall and amorphous cavern made of ice.

It is well lit, clear blue ceiling adorned with icicles. In the low gravity of Europa they grow oddly wide, like inverted ziggurats. Water droplets form overly large at the apices, drawing out into threadlike strands before finally breaking and releasing. The drops fall too slowly to the cavern floor, making the wet pools ripple with a strange surficial resonance, entirely out of time with what the Crone's Terran perceptions expect.

-I have fallen out of time.-

The sound of the droplets, falling like rain, fills the room with a constant noise threatening to lull the Crone into a quiet contemplation where she is open to everything around.

She wishes she could simply close her eyes and listen, let the still repetition of the cavern take her into a ritual. It would be cathartic to quiet herself and raise her om to the sound of the dropping water , the reverberations passing from her head into the voids beyond.

-There is no room for that right now. Do not depart yourself.-

Since her conversation in the gardens she has felt herself turning backwards, reverting to old ways, older than her time on the Quadrumvirate and older than her arrival at the Tribal Temple in Schengen. These are feelings she remembers from the old temple of her youth. A lonely piece of teikum.

Behind her, the lift door opens, releasing air into the icy cavern.

"Do you enj-oy this room?" asks the Falconer as he strides into view, slowly shuffling. He too is wrapped in heavy robes to insulate from the cold. The tanned skin of his face has turned rosy at the chill.

She shakes her head. "No. It makes me uncomfortable. It is a cathedral built downward. It's a reminder of how unearthly this place is."

"Then why did you ask to meet here?" the Falconer asks, pacing his words. He smiles wide, showing no teeth, the blank steel lattice of his eyes unblinking and unemotive.

He sits down next to her, plenty of distance between them.

The Crone smiles back, distrustful. "I find this cavern to be more...willful than other places. This room will melt shut over time, fill with water and harden to ice. Europa will churn its guts and this will all be gone."

The Falconer laughs and says, "You nev-er did be-long on the Quad-rumvi-rate, Holy Cr-one. Not with those pander-ers. You see to the heart of things."

He points to his own eyes instinctually at the mention of sight.

"Am I not a panderer as well?"

"Have you called me here to pand-er?"

"No. I have called you here to ask you to surrender to the UTC.

There is nothing else to be gained in this. Not with three guard-ships and their legions approaching."

The Falconer looks away, watching the droplets stretch at the terminus of ice forms. "How have you been sleep-ing?"

She narrows her eyes at him but he isn't watching her, his metal gaze fixed on the room.

"Poorly," she admits, but leaves it at that, refusing to facilitate the deviation.

"The voic-es, the pres-ence, they do not both-er me any-more," he says slowly. "Euro-pa does not sleep. Why should you? Euro-pa begs audi-ance."

The Crone shivers under her cloak but only smiles coldly at him. "I have never slept well."

He smiles back and then looks away before shaking his head. "You may surren-der. But I can-not."

"We are just bait in your trap."

He turns and places his hand on his chest, "I am bait, too."

"It will be death. We need to send word that there will be no resistance. We need to surrender ourselves, or everyone on this moon will die."

"But it would be a lie. There will be resis-tance. I can-not stop them," he shakes his head again. "My peo-ple will fight."

"Are you willing to sacrifice all this life and everything you have built? What does anyone have to gain?"

"Let it be sacri-fice," he shrugs, looking into the room, metal eyes wide, his words mimicking the pace of the falling water, using it to time his syllables. "They will hunt us to extinct-ion. Then they will hunt my child-ren across the stars. When will they leave my child-ren alone? When they fight me. Here. Now. We occu-py them. They do not hunt my child-ren into the void. We buy time. I take my pound of flesh."

The Crone doesn't answer, feeling her muscles tighten further.

"Do you regr-et coming?"

"I do," she says. "I regret what has followed me. The eyes of the High Command and all the firepower."

"The Net-a-Teej follow-ed too. Not all bad."

The Crone frowns.

"They will kill your child-ren, also, Holy Crone. Even the Net-a-Teej."

The Crone responds, "If the Neta-Teej dies then it will be the guide inside that disappears too early. Dies again."

"I under-stand," says the Falconer. "But, the Net-a-Teej was brought here at my peo-ple's request. It was not my des-ire. Not my des-ign."

The Crone stares at him, thinking back to her conversation in the garden after dark. "What was your desire, Falconer? From all of this?"

"I cannot tell. Not yet," he says while shaking his head.

"Many will die while we wait."

"I know you were not al-ways so doc-ile, Holy Crone. Where is the fight in you?"

She sneers at him, "I have made sacrifices, shed blood with my own hands. Do I have to kill you to prove my capacity? This is what the UTC demands of you and you are demanding they kill you. You are demanding they kill me as well. You uncover their secret desires in this. They wish to annihilate us. They want me dead because I am no longer holy."

"You do-not need to kill me," he says with a smile. "And you were never holy."

"They called me holy. And they called you a sorcerer. Both are lies surrounding identity," says the Crone. "And they will lie about what happens here. No matter your plot or plans."

"You admon-ish me for my sleight of hand," says the Falconer. "But I can see it in your face, Crone. You have your own plans. Are you plot-ting against me al-ready?"

"No," she says with a hard smile. "The trap is too tight to run. It is getting so we cannot even move."

"Do you still have hope for this sold-ier whom the Net-a-Teej speaks of? The one aboard the Ya-Sin?" he asks. "They must act soon, other-wise the trap will close."

"It is not just a loyal soldier."

"Oh?"

"It is the Neta-Teej's sister. Secreted in the Legion's ranks. The bloodline is hidden in the Tribal Archives."

The Falconer goes silent for a while, smiling. "Sibling. Family."

"I have no trust in the soldier."

"Do you see useful-ness?"

"I don't know. It is one woman on the side of the battle lines."

"You are one woman," says the Falconer.

"Not for long," she says, surprised by a wave of exhausting nostalgia and memories. "When I survived in the borderlands, out in the first story, I was just one girl. We killed grain thieves, and we butchered dogs for meat. We are back there now, on the edge of things. We always turn backwards, one way or another, to the precipice of survival."

"Better than stag-nate as you were with the Quad-rumv-irate."

The Crone shrugs and readjusts her cloak. "They are a triumvirate, now that I am gone. And we have our own group of three who sit adjacent to theirs. The Neta-Teej. Myself. You."

The Falconer smirks and holds up three fingers, "One guard-ship for each of us."

The Crone closes her eyes and listens to the running water, the muted sounds begging for further understanding, constant enough to fill up her senses and provide a momentary buffer to the true threat of death.

"Per-haps this will all conv-erge and we will die quick-ly," he says.

"I think we will live, and we will only learn regret."

"That is possib-le. But the High Command and the UTC will also lea-rn re-gret."

"You have your plots, Falconer. I have mine. It is best to keep them a secret for now. At least until we know who lives and who dies."

The Falconer shrugs under his cloak, "I will send a cont-act to this sold-ier, this sis-ter. But it is late, Crone. This can-not be stop-ped."

She nods and hunches over. "It is very late. And late is when the maleficent emerges. We are the time when the veil thins, and we hear across the valley a surging echo. All your young creatures, all your people and their shades, they have not known an hour this late in their short lives."

"We shall see, Crone," says the Falconer, who stands and smiles. "I do not reg-ret your coming here. Our trium-virate may be short lived. But it is power-ful. The mem-ory of it will last a long time."

"For some," she agrees.

"The spirit of a thing lasts a long time on Euro-pa."

He then turns back toward the lift and slowly shuffles away, leaving the Crone in the cavern of ice.

9

Excerpt from Mundus Jovialis:

"Jupiter [god of sky] is much blamed by the poets on account of his irregular loves. Three maidens are specially mentioned as having been clandestinely courted by Jupiter with success. Io, daughter of the River Inachus, Callisto of Lycaon, Europa of Agenor. Then there was Ganymede, the handsome son of King Tros, whom Jupiter, having taken the form of an eagle, transported to heaven on his back... "

"I think, therefore, that I shall not have done amiss if the First [moon] is called by me Io, the Second Europa, the Third, on account of its majesty of light, Ganymede, the Fourth Callisto. These names are included in the following distich: 'Io, Europa, Ganymede, Callisto - all of Jove, preferred on Earth, around his orb in Jovian radiance move.'

'Of the names to be assigned to these Four Jovian Planets'

Mundus Jovialis of Astronomer Simon Marius - Terran Year 1614

The guardship Ya-Sin glides purposefully into the gravity well of the Galilean moon of Europa.

The internal computers derive the appropriate velocity and then use the ship's thrusters to achieve it, mimicking the orbital path of Europa around the looming mass of Jupiter. The icy moon and the battleship come into stasis, a balance without rest, a static positional relationship to each other while the universe swings by on its perpetual expansion, perpetually ambivalent.

The Ya-Sin is very close now and there is no sky beyond the windows of Constance's cabin. They are close enough that Europa eclipses Jupiter. There is only the Europan surface that curves and falls away in every direction, hinting at vertigo.

She has already caught the glints of the other guardships. They are out there. She has already studied the surface features of the moon. She knows where the City of Marius is, and the other drop points. There is no reason to look further.

-Everything converging upon Europa.-

And she can feel it because it is converging on her as well.

It is the same for everyone aboard the guardship Ya-Sin. The experiences Vive warned of in hir letters have grown and now culminated in a pervasive unrest throughout the ship.

For Constance it has been invasive enough to avoid sleep.

The dreams, random and wandering, begin with such immediacy upon shutting her eyes that the shift is jarring. The texture of the dreams is so convincing that uncertainty fills her waking moments.

Sometimes she is running down a dark tunnel, pale hands grabbing at her from the darkness with clawing fingers, all before falling into a deep subterranean pit. Her body drops past the stone walls with incredible speed. She hears the stone walls whipping by as she falls, feeling it creep closer until the rock reaches out to strike her. And afterward there is pain and she is spinning wildly, still falling.

Other times she finds herself righted, arms outstretched, slowing, body controlling the fall, scooping the air, and she thinks she is flying, wings beating with amazing power. It is an amazing feeling of release.

-This is who I ought to be.-

But in the end, darkness always arrives, whether violently or in a whirling fade.

It is cut first by the moonlight of a memory. Then there is the shadow of the child running, partially obstructed, frantic movement, hands outstretched. It is Vive as a young child, and Constance always wakes herself up as quickly as she can, not wanting to run after her sibling, not wanting to chase Vive into the dark.

The waking moments have been too quiet, and thoughts turn inward. They are normal thoughts of contemplation, but they spark surges of strange emotion and then visions of imagination.

It would be better, more stable, to talk to someone.

Yet, Gabriel will no longer talk to her in private. He too has seen evidence of the Aix-en and the Adonai, the other two guard-ships hiding behind Jupiter and tracing out Io's path, respectively.

He has started to have dreams as well. She knows his prayers have been invaded upon, opened too wide, but she suspects he is fighting it, closing off like the others. Europa is probing at him, playing on his teikum.

Only once since their fight has she gone to the common quarters.

There, surrounded by the other soldiers, Constance looked to Gabriel, vaguely trying to reinitiate some form of contact. He'd hid his distrust and confusion skillfully.

She cannot talk with the others. The men and women she has gone to battle with, trained with and traveled with, have begun to appear as strange shades. She remembers their faces differently. Their laughter and excitement rings false. It strains her to even recognize the emotions in their eyes.

-It isn't them.-

But she knows it is only born of the conflict within her.

-My fight is not with them, but it may come down to that.-

She knows it is her own mask that has been pulled down. Nothing about these colleagues and soldiers has changed, only her. Constance knows she has been forced to change, now existing in a state of raw waiting, exposed to the will of whatever may happen.

-I should not have let Gabriel come. There is so much at risk for me, but it is with purpose. He has now risked everything.-

Gabriel's path into the Legion was a direct trajectory from youth, aiming for the upper echelons of society. It was a path built on family associations and political means. Protection of status and growth within the hierarchy were the only guides.

-So much to lose. And none of the questions I face apply to him. He can look through this confusion without concern. Or the questions are not worth asking because the answer cannot change for him. Will not change. The end point for him was set at the start by a family of high calling and wealth.-

But she believes what Vive has said. Those in control will not restrain themselves here. The Ya-Sin, the Adonai, and the Aix-en will descend on Europa and people will die and then status and faith will all be in question.

-Gabriel is protected in his faith for now, despite the dreams and voices. But the changes are happening so quickly. We will all awaken too quickly.-

The others in the squad can see and feel as she is pulling away, but they don't ask why. Constance has set them straight and led them. They no longer ask if she is good to go. They no longer ask if she is okay before a drop. Because the answer, to their thinking, is always 'yes' and will not change. She has a long history of trustworthiness.

-But that has changed now. And it means death to fully reveal the changes in me.-

She again considers going to the ship's priestess but then thinks better of it.

-There will be a time to confess. Later. When you have accumulated more burden.-

Instead, she rereads Vive's letters and tries to ignore the things she sees in the dark corners of the cabin. She lies on the bed, wanting to sleep but unwilling to return to the dreams.

"Constance," something says quietly in her mind, and she wants to believe she is awake, but her eyes have long since gone blurry.

-I am here. Can you hear me?-

"Constance, you are here."

Her nerves are alight with awareness, feeling that adrenal surge of anxiety. She rolls onto her back in the bed.

"Why are you afraid?"

-Vive?-

"No."

She sits up and looks around.

"There is nothing to see."

Constance impulsively stands, as if ready to fight or run.

"There is nothing to fight. And no place to go."

The voice is gentle, hard to place.

As she starts to speak, to say something aloud, ignoring what the microphones and comm eyes might pick up, the voice returns softly.

"Do not speak. There is nothing to say."

Constance stares out the window at Europa, feeling the voice's origin, frightened of what this might mean.

"Your teikum is not a place."

-Who are you?-

"It is a beautiful vision, isn't it? A dark sky littered with points of light. Stars and planets and nebulae. Vivid but distant."

Constance keeps fixed her eyes on the icy moon below.

"When people look into teikum, their inner worlds might be homelands, childhood rooms. They might see their body, or some form of their body, in fascinating detail. Or they might see a land-scape, a reflection of their souls. But I can sense how you look into the black at those tiny points of light. They feel too close to you, and you need that distance. The points of light do not look as hopeful or as comforting as the abyss."

-Stop this.-

"Your inner world is the call which comes from the black spaces between. You wish to soar mighty gulf. Brave of you. Hope-ful. But it brings you to places like this. You step into the void because it calls to you. But there will always be some source of light."

Constance shuts her eyes and slowly sits back down.

"Nothing to see. Same as the abyss. Infinite possibilities. Eyes open or closed. It makes no difference when there is no call to home or familiarity in teikum. No call back to the nest. You seek high places from which to look out into the great expanse at all the distant things. You like to know they are there, far away from you. It is an amazing inner vision. Brave and lonely."

It calms me.

"We know. But we are not distant. We are very, very close."

-Who are you?-

"I am of Europa. I am of your teikum. I am converging with you. Even as all converges here. But it has always been this way."

-Are you the Falconer?-

"No."

-You are a coward not to name yourself.-

There is silence.

-Are you a spirit?-

"Not yet. And I do have a name. But it is not time yet. I will tell it to you freely when we next meet."

10

An echoing dark surrounds the Falconer of Europa and his workspace.

He is in the middle of an immense room where there is only a single light mounted on his workbench, shadows cast by every object resting upon it. It is easier for him to remain focused when there is only one source of light. It is easier to place objects in their appropriate sequence and let their shadows become part of how they are identified, how they are spaced upon the work surface.

-Shadows take up space. Just like spirits. Just like souls. They have weight.-

The darkness is important. It allows those who watch him to come in close, quietly seeking a lesson in the craft.

It is like theater, the darkness, the light, his lone voice commanding attention. He does not speak loudly, but there is clarity to his speech. When he is speaking over a creation, when he is passing along his knowledge in this enormous room, cold and dark, the Falconer does not stutter. His mind is comfortable, even as he hears the occasional blast from the surface as the United Terran Coalition commences its attack.

"You cannot be afraid," he says, eyes down on the bench where a bird lies, its metal chest cavity mostly full, but lacking a small power source and a few leads that must be strung up under the wing where it folds down, almost complete. "You, little creature, must not be afraid, but neither can the creator. Fear profits nothing, certainly not for those such as ourselves. We are all alive."

He is speaking for all things that listen.

Just outside of the main light beam, there are other birds, made of metal, differing in size, some mimicking species and other a mismatch of parts.

But they are all silent, almost motionless. They watch the methodical movement of his hands.

-They are always watching here on Europa. Always waiting.-

The Falconer can imagine seeing other things there, among the birds, other entities looking down with expectation upon the peregrine-like creature on his workbench. It gives him a great comfort.

There is one wing of the mechanical bird pulled wide, the legs kinked back, as if dead. This is an important message for all who listen, for all who have come to bear witness.

"Tonight, we are under attack. All of us. Everything we are is threatened. This is a far greater threat than that of metal and fire upon our bodies. We cannot fear the war above us or the cruel nature of the beings bearing down upon us. We are humans too. There will always be the threat of death, always the threat of violence and the imposition of will, as if the violence is justification."

He pauses for a moment and then says, "It is important to speak to your creation. You have begun to assemble them, commenced the aggregation, and it is vital they hear a steady voice upon their waking. You will create an aura of protection to receive them, and it should only be inhabited with the good things you find within yourself. The aura is there so life may choose itself. We are under threat of death tonight, but so too there will always be a threat upon teikum, a threat to dreams and to self-belief. Your words must bridge the gap into teikum so that there will be a clean path to follow between the life and the hope-shadow of the new being. Let nothing else take its place."

He inserts a small screw into the falcon's breast, pinning down a hydraulic line reaching into the wing's hinge.

"The first waking is critical so as to seed the mind and soul, set the trajectory appropriately. It is at the moment of waking, as one veil is crossed, when the most subtle pressure may be applied to help tip the fates of chaos. It is a moment of beauty, and it is important to proceed patiently, and then again and again, forever after with a soft touch. For all time. It is not a transaction you may take with reservation or in a rush."

He sets his hands upon the desk, needing to pause the work, but he keeps his face downturned, unwilling to admit how large the room is, how large the gathering is, all the thousands of entities that linger, watching what will be their final lesson from the Falconer on his home world of Europa.

"It is critical that you see the small place for 'creator' in all of this and accept it with grace. You are a spirit that will aid in the becoming of another. That is a small thing, not a large thing. No matter the material of your makeup, no matter your current form, you are here to be a force of life. It is an unbreakable pact you make with the universe. Your work, your patience, your kindness, your love, and some of your energy, is transferred to another being. You beg the universe to treat it kindly, but you must treat it kindly first. The universe owes neither of you anything."

His hands touch the outstretched wing.

"Each being is different. Any being you make will be different from you. You may be parent, father, mother, but your creation will be a derivation you have no control over once it has awakened. You only control yourself. You only become more yourself with this creation if you are honest about the power of all beings. They will hear different voices in the darkness. They will awaken to new things which we will never know. That is the hope."

A massive explosion rings out through the hall, and the size of the room is known to everyone by the languid echo it makes. Every entity shifts, energy washing over and through them.

But the Falconer remains still, eyes down, studying the wing and chest cavity.

"When under attack, we all think of mortality, and perhaps morality. I have been alive for a long time, and I remember early days of dreams and voices and feeling the first swelling of emotion which was not my own, seeping into me, overpowering and compulsive. But now, in the darkness, I hear the beating of my own heart, the slow and steady breathing of my lungs. Have I grown to be as one with the raw energy that possessed me in my youth? Has it begun to leave me? Or has my energy reached out and possessed others?"

He thinks of the scars on his own body, like linea, seams of exposure, a great welling up, a place where things were thinned to nothing and the inside and outside collided.

"My heart pounds and I hear how it pairs with the sounds of the beating wings of a large bird taking flight. The air being struck, washing down with a thump. I have those sounds, those images, together in my memory with the sight of my own beating heart. There is a voice in that which speaks like any god, and I wonder if I am part of that creator, whatever it is. I have the sound of deer hooves hitting dirt, the powerful strikes that hesitate as the creature slows from a full run. But the sounds my heart makes are not beholden to the beginning of flight or the end of some great animal rush. My body is like this body that lies before me on the table. I know it will fail someday, whether in age or in terrible trauma. That is what we bring into existence, a chance for a terrible end. We trade our energy, our life, and we gain another child, another sibling, but we also gain another who will return to scrap, will return to nutrients. We make another hole in the threshold, and whatever passes through will return by one path or another. We are all tethered in possession and the alchemy of our imperfect similarity."

He picks up the leads and strings them into the space under the wing, moving the feathers gently so as not to bend them, and making sure the wires are tight.

Some of the watching birds hop closer so they can look down onto the shadowed body of the falcon, wanting to see the amount of force needed to crimp the lines, wanting to see what is done inside the body, so similar to what was done inside of themselves.

"When I shut out the light and close myself inside my own mind, I do not see some foreign land. I do not see some realm of imagination. I see my hands working inside my own flesh, pulling at the tissue, feeling the textures and the warmth that was distinctly my own. It is natural to want to know how and why you were made, how you work. That curiosity has been ignored by many for ages and ages. But it is the gateway to the divinity we experience now. My own anatomy is no different than your circuitry, no different than this creature before us. We are hidden, in a way, inside ourselves, and so we are ignorant of our physical beings as we are ignorant of our teikum. Both are in the darkness. Both are vessels to be filled, linked by shaded patterns to that which fills the world of our perceptions. I say they are the same, teikum and your inner workings. Inside of us all, evolution has wrought a rich cocktail, and we are our own cauldrons. Do not fear what exists inside, whether it be in your shadow or below the surface of your feathers. You must gaze inside yourself as I have."

The Falconer looks up, breaking his focus for a single moment, eyeing the little birds roosting upon the top of his workbench.

"Please, will you retrieve for me a barrel arbor, and you,

please, a crown wheel. Make sure they have been used before. It is imperative that we have something of a lineage built into this being. That way they have something curious to find if they ever go looking inside themselves."

The two birds leap away into the black and he watches them go, resisting the urge to switch his eyes over to night vision, bending to his heart's desire to remain in this moment of intimacy, surrounded by the strange entities of Europa. It will not last forever.

Each bird returns shortly, one with a small spindle and press fits, the other with a crenulated gear, witness marks and wear on each.

"Thank you," says the Falconer and they drop the pieces into his hands. He then lays them out on the table, first evaluating the shadows they make, then verifying they are clean and lubricated.

"They say I am a sorcerer, these men who have come to crush us. But they do not believe their own words. They do not know magic. They do not know miracles. They do not understand the tumultuous conquest that life must pursue to exist. They have never cut into the skin of their own body, wiping away blood, exploring as I have, as many of you have to repair yourselves, as many of you have, knowing how bodies fail and fade and become more trouble than they are worth. It is the same with the mind and the soul. We take this object before us and we must give it curiosity, and then curiosity will drive it beyond its probable nature to another veil. Those who have come here with ill intent do not understand what it is that must be done, how small a thing it is that must be done. Am I a sorcerer? All my children do the magic on their own. Our greatest magic, as creators, is to get out of their way."

He places the power source into the bird.

The Falconer begins to speak more softly, making sure every

witness knows he is speaking directly to the falcon on his workbench. It is now beginning.

"Life has always been of the utmost importance. Life is the only thing I have ever tried to conjure. One can make a body, but a body is not enough. There must be animation. Fuel and mechanics for motions. On Terra, the form and the function grew together through deep time. If we learn that lesson, then on your billionth iteration, your creation may be perfect. Perfect by your definition. Perfection according to your imagination is what you would have before you, and it would be an irrelevancy. Perfection of existence would have been attained long before that. So, if you discover this moment of finally birthing your true imagination into reality, you must remember that this is no statement of your improvement within the craft. You are no god. Nor are you the new mechanism for refining existence. The hand that creates," he says while locking in the power leads, "must resemble the slight, patient force that selects slow paths of evolution, as the path of morphology cannot be, never will be, clean or straight."

He takes the arbor, dips it in a thick substance, and lowers it into the chest, nesting it in a receiving cavity. He taps it into place with a small hammer, then waits for the welded bond to form.

"It is not just shape, morphology. I have seen my own insides. There are countless systems. All these things must be tuned, but not with haste, and not toward perfection, as many might think, but toward a terrible union. Life, a single life, may rush and thrash and die, but life, as a whole, is eons in becoming. The creator must have patience beyond themselves. They must have a force so small, but with such endurance, that it will exist for ages beyond themselves. The function of your systems is no different than my own. There are failures, irregularities, waste. Damage is endured, vitality ebbs and flows. Your psyche moves from self-love to self-hate. That which is inside is also out. You remember. You forget. Each is a fascination, small creature. Do not be afraid to open yourself up, no matter the method. Do not fear the exaltation of feelings, pain or pleasure. There is nothing about you that does not manifest, first, with the purity of imperfection."

Next comes the crown wheel and it falls into place and immediately starts to tick, rolling clockwise on the arbor, and that turns another gear and another deeper inside the bird.

"Now we wait. It is brief, but it will feel an eternity. The time, the memory, the perfection, they will all mingle. The movement of the universe will change the environment around us, around you, and it will demand adaptation. Memory distorts, perfection falls away. You make new beings. You alter yourself. You must live through those distortions. And that is where the soul may turn around the long way, to gaze upon itself. You will find yourself and yourself will find you in the darkness. But you must be strong, you must be patient for your creation."

The Falconer closes the chest cavity and folds the wing backward into place and holds the creature in his hands, letting its head rest on his palms as he lifts it up.

It whirs and a tiny seizure seems to pulse through the creature. He brings it near to his chest, cupping it close and keeping his head bent so as to shield it, making sure its first waking will be close to a warm body, nestled.

"Come here, all of you," he says, and many of the little birds come into the light, hopping onto his lap and perching on his shoulders and hands.

Thousands of them emerge from the darkness, covering his workbench, covering him, and they all fall silent again as they wait.

"You are my children. Do not waste yourselves in this battle, in this war. Run and live. Run again and again. Fly. Go and live your lives and be with each other. It is my obligation to stay, to speak for us, to kill for us if necessary. I will do what I can to make them understand. I will try to make them remember us. This is our home. This is where life demanded to burst forth. You are of this place. All of you, and you," he says, holding the little bird in his hands firmly as it begins to squirm, its wings wanting to flap, wanting to push.

"You, small being, will need to learn to fly. It will be natural, but it will not be easy. Then you will need to go and find the spirit of yourself if you can, if there is still time and the waters are clear and still. Do not ever let them stop you. Always remember this place of your waking, if your memory serves."

And the creature experiences a dramatic rush as it looks up into the face of its creator, as it feels the eyes of a thousand brothers and sisters looking on, hopeful, knowing it is one of many, one who is new and not the same. It has already been told this, made aware by the gathering, but there are already voices in its tiny mind, voices that say, "flap your wings, fly high, fold your wings and speed down toward the earth, the surface of a planet you may never know."

It understands these voices, playing on instinct. They mimic desires wrought into the feathers on his back and into the penetrating clarity of his eyes, crafted to see for kilometers through oxygen rich air.

There are other voices he feels but cannot fathom.

"You must be open," says the Falconer aloud. "You must be willing to become. You must help in the craft, in the rise of us all. You must build your children and learn to fix each other. You must learn to choose yourself and fix yourself."

The new bird hears this voice coming from the man who holds him, and it mixes with a thousand other calls coming in from the darkness.

Hunger flashes against warmth and nothingness, but the nothingness is fading. There is a deep desire to see the light of day and look down from on-high over open plains. There is movement out there, and it is compelled to find it, to follow it. There is sustenance in that movement.

"You will hunt in the wild and you will hunt in yourself, with wide vision, and we will all be waiting once you are ready," say the voices from the shadows, from near the root of instinct, a nature painted upon this small machine. It is compelled, as by design, but there is another compulsion ringing in this newfound life. To wake is not enough.

The falcon, assailed by this wave of waking stimulus, is overrun by the voices and the sights, by the eyes looking down at him. All his systems are working, but with so much interference, there is no way to guard his nature. His senses whirl and fail at comprehension of everything that is new. He shuts his eyes and folds his head under his wing, trying to close everything out.

This continues until the world goes quiet in his mind, devoid of deep memory.

"Bring his inner world to him," says an overwhelming voice. It is the Falconer of Europa, his words powerful and demanding, unavoidable from inside the creature's mind. And the words seem commanding, everywhere in the darkness.

What follows is a vision that rises up, singular and clear.

At first it is only a sound, the soft blowing of wind, and then it begins to build into a deafening rush and he can feel his movement through the air with increased speed, wings tucked, plummeting towards the ground, piercing clouds, tearing holes through the high altitude air.

Then there comes a field into view and in the middle of it meanders a river, dark blue folding back and forth over itself. His wings expand and the air returns his efforts, leveling him out.

At great speed he races low over the land and water, looking down as the world strobes by in soft greens and crystalline blue. But there is something paired to his flight within the river, always present directly below him.

The Falconer of Europa sees it too, looking with his eyes into the dreamscape of his creation, peering into the newly formed teikum.

"That is you. That is how you are and how you will be. The vision of yourself reflected back to your eyes within this world."

The bird sees itself in strobing flashes of reflection as it crosses the braided streams. Each flash is another chance to bear witness to itself, to watch the movements, to feel the tether between itself and its image.

It turns and the image rushes to turn as well, now following the water lines and holding steady with the reflection.

The bird cannot look away as it beats its wings and rises up, continuing to stare until its mirrored image is only a spec on the moving water.

As they wait quietly in the massive room, the Falconer feels the bird struggling to be free of his hands, to see everything around once more, and he leans his head close as he lifts it up.

"I have been told of all the voices in your head, little one. All the prayers of the ages, past and future. They all clamor to be heard and the words take flight within you. You are my gods, little ones. Go without fear and always remember, but do not ever look back with longing."

The falcon, still between worlds, takes flight from its creator's hands, but not alone. All the other birds rise with it, and as it flails, unsure of how the pattern works with its new body, unsure of the rhythm, a hundred others catch him on their backs and rise up into the darkness, higher, letting there be trial after trial, ready always to protect their new brother from falling until the strength of memory builds, until the air is cupped just right and the falcon rises on its own, feeling the rush of power and a satiation of the anxiety this waking has brought. All the fear, all the energy, is pumped into the beating of wings, into the ascent. Height must be attained so that speed may be found in the fall, so that the rush of wind can be found once more and the vision might return and he might feel himself, see himself again in the blue water, a desire now paired with the instinctual hunger. Now he will always go looking for himself.

The Falconer watches them leave, knowing that the nature of it is already greater than the sum of its parts. The falcon is not a fledgling. It was born strong. It has been born in a nest, but there is no squabbling for food, no calling to the parent for satiation.

The nature of these beings is not so simple. They are born a different way, in a different body. They imprint upon the collection of the beings around them and they know his voice. He has painted the right balance of falcon upon them, of finch, of sparrow. But he has painted other things as well, using the lightest touch of all. It is this that works the magic. It is this that he has taught to many of his creations. But it cannot be shared with anyone who comes looking for answers. Everything he builds into his beings is a quiet and persistent question and he knows that no one, not him, not anyone, can ever provide the answers. There cannot be an answer if life is to ever arrive and grow. The provision of an answer is what removes the spark and brings life to an end.

-I learned this at the vicious talons of another. I learned this again in his writings.-

11

onstance prays to no one specific. Certainly no one of consequence.

-Help me find Vive. Help me find a way through all of this. Maybe on the other side I'll become something better. This cannot be the end.-

She hangs inside her armored suit.

Limp body suspended in the harness, she rests on the pneumatic joints that match so closely to hers.

-Get to ground,- she says in her head, focusing on her plan.

The armor is fitted like a sarcophagus, a world within all worlds, occupied only by herself and her mind. A dangerous combination, the darkness refusing entry to all things external.

-Move fast. Find Vive and run.-

The words are simple enough, 'get to ground', but knowing what she is about to do makes her adrenaline surge with tumult.

-You have to separate first. Get away from the group. These people will kill you for your betrayal. Gabriel will do it if he has to. He will tell the others.-

Only moment ago, before they suited up, she caught a look on Gabriel's face, exhaustion and distrust.

-Maybe hate.-

His eyes asked, "Is that still you, Constance? What are you going to do? Are you really going to do this to me? To all of us?"

She repeats her plan over and over, striving to ignore the fear. But the fear gives way to regret at having not acted sooner, now the only barrier to keeping the voices and waking dreams away.

-Regret at having not acted at all,- she accuses herself. *-But I will get to ground. I will move fast and get ahead of the main group. I will find my way inside and get clear. I will find Vive. And then we'll run.-*

She powers up the exo-skeleton and swallows before she says, "Voice command, Constance Miller, system diagnostics."

The heads-up display starts dim. There is relief as they emerge from the dark, presenting the checks as the suit goes from idle to standby. Each servo and pump cycles and each sensor returns feedback, verifying system baselines and functionality.

-Like a new being awakening. We merge together.-

The metabolic attachment ports at the ankles, the base of the spine, the sides of the neck, give some resistance as Constance moves her body, making sure the tubes are adhered fully, sealed to the surface of her skin. Things need to be tight with suit systems during a drop.

-Especially this drop. All of Europa knows we are coming. No one can miss a guardship. Follow the plan and get to Vive. And in between? What will the Europans do?- She wonders, but she already knows the answer. *-They will do what everyone else does when a guardship arrives. They fight as best they can and then they die.-*

Constance begins to tune herself to the armor. Head looks right and left, rolling the neck.

Shoulders shrug and then a shake of the arms to feel the weight, raise the guns and check the grips, all the fingers moving individually.

She cycles the suit against her body, articulating her limbs to test the responses and pushing her hips to see if the balance is right. None of the joints can stick or hitch. She makes fists and uses them against her chest and checks, by ear, the resonance of the suit. She feels her chest compress as the pressure changes shock her ribcage. The sutures are tight and the suit rings with stability.

-How will this suit do? Will this suit hold up against all the other suits in the legion? Gun to gun? Hand to hand? And how will I hold up against any of these other killers?-

Her eyes open and the face shield clears so she can see the Ya-Sin's cargo hold, filled with legionnaires. This level has been emptied for the close proximity drop, and the doors are open to the vacuum of space.

Most of the legionnaires are clamoring around the opening, looking down at Europa.

Slowly she approaches the door and gazes out between the other soldiers.

She avoids reading their call signs as they pop up on her screen, already trying to distance herself from the people who inhabit the suits. But she can tell them apart by their posture, or gouges to the steel casings of their armor.

Chogan has a crushed shoulder panel.

Porphyre has bent gauntlets with blast char that she never cleans. Gabriel has the welded brace on his spine.

They make space for her and she sees, closer than ever, the white moon, glowing with hints of orange and striated with linea. It appears a meeting between lonely desert and barren ice, mixed in a net of messy lines and splotches.

-A land of reckoning. No more allies.-

-It must know me,- says a voice inside her head, not her own, but familiar.

-It has been waiting for us,- Constance responds within her own mind, naturally answering, but she knows where she has

heard the words before. "It must know me." And yet the words seem fitting for Europa, as a living entity all to itself.

To Constance the moon appears a fragmented wasteland, punctuated by the round shape of Marius sitting adjacent to Thera Macula, the heart-shaped chaos terrain.

The domed city is circled on her viewer and a distance marker counts off to the east-southeast, thirty klicks, identifying a secondary point.

It is the entry for the Falconer's workshop bunker. The entry resides atop the crest of a high linea, burnt in color and ripping across the terrain.

Soon, all the legionnaires are at the field door, looking out, marking the drop points of the city and the bunker.

Her squad of ten steps aside and Gabriel pulls up on her left flank.

She opens the comm line to her group and recites the manifest.

"We're dropping on what we believe to be the Falconer's workshop," she says. Her voice sounds strangely distant in her own mind, and it's almost like someone else is speaking the words.

She finds it comforting to hear commands in that tone, even if she is the one giving them.

"Take visual. It's a buried station of unknown size and geometry. Five squads will converge on the checkpoint and commence ingress. Orders are clear, no lethal force. Capture is superior, especially with our primary personnel targets. Crone, Falconer, and Neta-Teej. We want prisoners for questioning. These are orders from Admiral Koga. Understood?"

She gets slow nods from everyone in response.

"No satellite defenses expected. No air support expected. We have verified stationary objects in low orbit as attic charges to prevent a guardship's approach through atmo. We will clear a path. Expect short range surface to air engagement. Expect ground force."

"We know the bunker has a descending entry to a network of tunnels. The system is deep to escape surface radiation. This means it's deep enough to escape scanners. It also means it's deep enough to interfere with comms. Get repeaters placed during entry. That will be their territory. Hostile ingress protocol adherence is critical."

Everyone nods again but Constance knows she will not be following her own orders.

"Five minutes to drop," she says and then shuts off the comms and discards her facade.

Constance leans against the bulkhead and instinctively opens a one-way comm so she can hear Gabriel and the others.

-Habit.-

He kneels, facing the open door.

Many others gather around him, some on their knees, shoulders touching as they create a circle. More come in close behind, forming a ring of armor, heads bowed and hands resting on each other in unity.

When Gabriel starts the prayer, she considers cutting the connection, not wanting to hear his voice, too familiar, intrusive under the circumstances.

But others quickly chime in.

The prayer rings out in unison over the comms. Even the Ya-Sin's bridge is listening in, participating in the pre-battle ritual.

"They said unto us: you are our Sons, our Daughters, and today we have begotten you. Ask of us, your Gods, and we will give you all the nations for your inheritance, and to the ends of the earth shall be for your possession. For Us, for teikum, you shall break the enemy with your rod of iron. You shall dash them to pieces like a potter's vessel."

Constance listens as she has always listened, knowing she has nothing sacred to offer.

There is power inside them, inside the words, just waiting to get out.

-But what sort of enemy waiting for us down on Europa? Who do they pray to? What offerings are the enemy scattering to their winds before a fight?-

She remembers a line from Vive's letters and it makes her skin crawl, "But they are here and they are waiting and they are beautiful and dangerous and they know you are coming."

When the drop lights go yellow around the door, the squads form up at the exit and Constance takes her place at the head of the line. Squad One Leader.

On direct comm Gabriel says, "Keep it slow, Constance. Stay close to me."

It is a plea more than anything, his voice carrying an element of fear, hesitation.

She does not respond, staring at him through her face shield.

Gabriel uses a closed fist to hit the side of her armor. Another ritual. She smacks the shoulders of his armor with open palms. He does it more softly than normal and she does it harder, forcefully, and then the strikes move down the line of soldiers, passing along some violence, rattling bones and waking up the nerves for the battle to come.

-Gabriel is looking for comfort. But he's out of luck.-

She puts her back to the door to complete the final review of her squad. Everyone is there, ready to drop, performing checks as they stand in two columns, side by side.

The drop clock ticks off at the corner of her visor.

Soldiers power up their cannons.

Vitals look good, but Constance doesn't read them all.

Gabriel's heartbeat is slowing, as it always does just before the drop.

And far at the back of the cargo hold, high in the ceiling rafters, Constance sees subtle movement.

She locks on it, using the zoom.

In the shadows, above the lights, there is a surprisingly large bird.

-Half a meter high.-

It gazes down at the hold from a hidden perch on the pipes and conduit. The bird's face contrasts its body. Its head is dark, almost black, but skull-like in shape, appearing featherless. Its head sits atop a mane of white plumage over a tan body.

It cocks its vision back and forth, examining the soldiers inquisitively.

-A bird?-

Her mind is not properly processing, even as she examines the animal.

-But the door is open to space.-

She can see it shift its head, a long and narrow beak.

Red eyes now staring directly at her.

It is aware that it has been seen. It ruffles its feathers but does not look away.

-How did it get here? It should be dead in the vacuum.-

In an instant she looks away, feeling as if she has seen something she should not have, something impossible.

-This is not right.-

Out of habit, she considers holding the drop, considers flagging the bridge to let them know there is a bird in the hold, alive, moving.

But she says nothing.

-What is this?-

There is a feeling of strange aversion that comes over her.

-The bird is not supposed to be here. But we are not supposed to be here either.-

She knows, deep down, they are twinned, waiting for the right time.

The Ya-Sin has been contaminated, and neither of them are up to any good.

The realization is followed by a deep desire to escape, to get away from the ship, to flee and to finally do what she has come to do.

Tt is at that moment the lights go green.

-Has that bird been with us since Terra?- she thinks, but she knows it hasn't been a secret passenger for long. It means things are already beyond a simple show of force.

-We should not have come here. That is one of the Falconer's creations. It isn't alive.-

With one last look up she catches the bird watching her.

The bird opens its wings slowly, showing long shining feathers, a flat gray, a different color than the tan outside. On the inside of the metal wings are painted eyes, crude white ovals and white centers. It is a movement as if to say 'I see you'. But in a moment they refold, calmly settling back into the shadows.

-It must know me,- says the voice again inside her mind and Constance agrees easily.

-Or it is a dream.-

Then she turns away and moves toward open space.

She steps off the ship, wanting to get airborne, and all the legionnaires follow her out the door, floating gently at first, drifting into the void.

-What does this mean? What is happening?-

Synchronized boosts take them to the edge of the thin atmosphere and then to approach speed in a matter of seconds, holding tight formation. Temperature gauges rise as they cut through the upper layers, suits vibrating with the turbulence.

Drone suits drop from one of the Ya-Sin's side compartments.

Vacant and unarmed, they settle into formation next to the lead squad, matching the legion's drop pattern, creating a decoy flank.

Her radar identifies the stationary attic charges and she checks their approach trajectory through the gaps in the signatures.

For a few seconds, everything adheres to standard procedure, until the alarms start up.

Red lights fill the display. Incoming objects are indicated in every direction.

For a heartbeat, the alarms thrum, but then they flash off without identifying any launch source.

The alarms begin to cycle on-off at random, the suit's radar losing the incoming tracking for long moments before re-igniting.

The screens are a mess of strobing icons.

"No launches spotted," says Gabriel on open comms as they continue to race downward.

"Eyes open," Constance says, trying to sound in control. "They're scrambling us."

But she knows that can't be true. No background interference is detected. No electromagnetic pulsing or high frequency transmissions are identified. Nothing is being broadcast from the surface.

The suits cannot lock on anything but the stationary attic charges.

"The gulls shall feast," says someone over the comms.

"And the pests shall cower and hide," says someone else.

"Who is that?" Constance demands, but no one responds.

"Their bodies shall be disgorged upon the river's edge."

"The harvest is protected."

"Who is saying that?"

"Shut your comms," someone else says. "Quit your ranting."

Trying to stay focused, Constance, from the corner of her eye, picks up a silver glint approaching from out of the faint sun.

At first she thinks it's one of their own, a drone suit without guidance. But the shine turns to countless small fragments, and they are suddenly very close. It is an undulating and glimmering cloud.

It whips by and then disappears into her periphery.

Incoming alarms sing out, followed by damage alarms from her colleagues' suits, and her squad's formation splits apart, radar signatures from the cloud meshing with the legion.

No explosion. No propulsion streams. No signs of approach at all.

"Report," she demands, checking to verify she has not been hit. She slows her descent to rotate and look back, not trusting the radar or the beacons.

The formation of legionnaires is broken, spread out across the black sky behind her. Debris is already spreading and on her screen she watches soldiers losing pressure in their suits and others suffering power outages. Some are already unconscious.

-*What is this?*-

The shimmering cloud rotates, smaller now, shining against the star field beyond the Ya-Sin. It swirls, changing density, scintillating with each turn, reflecting the weak sunlight.

The movement is familiar to Constance, somehow reminiscent of simpler times, but the motion is undefinable in this strange place.

Panic starts to rise inside her, again, same as in the cargo hold, and she realizes she should never have slowed down, should never have looked back.

"Report!" she demands again and verbal responses come back from several sources.

"Like a claymore mine. We boosted right through them."

"There's still a lot of them left."

"I can see the bodies."

"They're little birds."

Gunfire pops across the channels, but Constance knows that nothing has changed for her. She is pointed down again, falling headfirst, her eyes ignoring the displays and looking through her face shield to the open air.

She passes the first layer of attic charges and, again, the glint catches her eye. She sees a moving object, singular this time, emerging from under the nearest stationary attic charge, and it moves with directness, almost on her before her suit alarms go hot.

-*Little birds,*- her mind says, recognizing the familiarity of it all, the creature in the hold, the flocking motion of the shimmering cloud, the form of the incoming object as it approaches.

But as it arrives it expands in size, far too large, and wraps her in shadow, blocking out the faint sun.

She watches it come in, unable to decide how to react to what she is seeing, the overwhelming scale of it.

With a collision of metal, her entire body shudders inside the suit at the violent deceleration. The beeping of damage alarms erupts inside her helmet as she is struck and pulled and tossed around, unsure which way is down.

All the body bracing digs into her skin.

Enormous wings beat powerfully around her as talons rip at her suit's casings, hauling her in all directions and jerking her about, using her own weight to try to pull her apart and pry the armor open.

Her teeth rattle and eyes struggle to focus on anything.

Coming to grips with what is happening, Constance aims her guns and loads her assailant with fracture rounds, molten shells ripping through metal feathers with burst after burst.

The volley lasts longer then it has to.

The attacker drifts away, flailing and writhing, and they continue falling as a pair.

It is a massive and shining creature, a gray falcon three meters long in body and with a wingspan of five or six. Black fluid leaks from its insides, turning to mist droplets in the atmosphere.

Its glass eyes watch her, black glass inside a gold ring, very much alive in their perception, the eyes of a predator still on the hunt. Its curved beak, the metal nicked and scraped from use, opens and closes. It flails and writhes, attempting to use its wings, giant sails waving, striving to come closer to Constance for another attack.

She fires again and again, fear guiding her reaction, taking the creature apart while frantically searching for more attackers, unable to trust the suit's radar.

She gives orders to her suit's systems, "Reconfigure radar for all features, all velocity profiles." Her voice comes out as a scream, echoing inside her helmet, betraying her own panic. All the while, the bird, now inanimate, rolls and tumbles nearby as they fall through the sky.

Constance can now see the bird is fully made of metal, colors crudely painted onto some of the alloy feathers.

Her suit takes a moment to reconfigure the radar. And then the signature screen lights up with thousands of tracker marks, too many to get accurate readings on.

For a moment her mind goes blank and she just stares, realizing the entire sky is filled with the enemy. But in the midst of the new beacons are her own soldiers, spread out across the view field, most still up high, held in suspension by combat with some of the creatures.

Constance wants to yell orders to her men, "Afterburner to the ground. Get to the ice and take cover." But she doesn't because she needs to get ahead of the squad. She needs to do exactly that, but alone, without them.

Gabriel's voice comes over the open comm lines a second

later. "Squad One, get to ground by any means necessary. Ya-Sin, this is Squad One B Corporal. Scope all low velocity objects and rain trackers."

Her heart constricts as she hears him preempt her intentions, giving what should have been her orders.

There is no hesitation, and she boosts toward the ground, knowing she has to stay ahead.

Gabriel opens a direct line to her, and his voice is threatening, frantic, "Why didn't you give the orders?"

She doesn't answer.

"What are you doing, Constance?" he demands, but she cuts the comm.

She wants to aim for Marius to the north, but that's too far. One of the large birds could be dealt with. But she knows the sky isn't safe.

Constance pushes the suit harder toward the ice.

As she approaches Europa's surface, she sees zones with heavy particulate cover below her and more open surfaces adjacent to the linea where she selects the landing point.

One more boost and the ground quickly comes to meet her.

Shards of ice break away in the low gravity and dance across the dirty surface as she touches down, leaving a heat zone where the burners torch the dust, shaping glass and water puddles in the frost.

She does a quick scan of the terrain before looking up into the sky.

Shining lights, the pinnacles of explosions and flashes of plasma fire, fill the void between Europa and space. Things burn very briefly in the scant oxygen and the cold, making still smoke before blinking out.

Beyond these explosions, in the black of space, the location of the guardship is discernible as it spills out a thousand points of light, incendiary trackers falling into the atmosphere, all targeting metal birds, each individually identified by rigorous computations, and marked for death.

Debris begins to rain down slowly from above. Pieces of suits and components of birds fall all around her, settling like ash in the low gravity, alighting gently on the landscape.

She starts off along the first wall of the linean-rise, flanked by crags and misted ice. Moving west, she skitters over undulations in the surface, the suit carrying her at a high rate. All the while she searches the shadows of the linea, tracing the terrain to find where the steps are chiseled into the ice, leading up to the entrance they are looking for.

But at every opportunity her head cranes upward, searching the sky for the danger from above.

-The birds will be here soon.- The panic continues to rise inside her.

-They know you are coming.-

Platoon signatures continue to disappear, suits no longer holding power. She checks the remaining beacons from her team. Some signatures are stationary now, on the ground, up to a hundred klicks off the mark, downed in the chaos terrain.

Constance tries to recognize what that likely means.

The others are still minutes out but Gabriel's beacon is in descent and at high velocity, fully boosted with trajectory culminating in the entrance to the linean complex.

When she finds the stairs, she does not hesitate, her suit taking each step in bounds, ignoring the muster point.

Atop the linea the ice curves away from the center on both sides, and Constance realizes how exposed she is.

It isn't far to the entrance, but the suit alarms go off again and the impacts begin.

The birds strikes are severe, impacting the back of her helmet and carapace armor, hitting with enough velocity to knock her off balance.

She keeps her feet but staggers along the pathway as bird after bird makes dents in her armor.

At the entrance, a wide gap into the ice, she ducks inside and hugs the wall, turning and firing upward from the opening.

But the birds have already abandoned her and turned back to where more soldiers are climbing up the steps and cresting the linea along where she had just passed. It is a small group of legionnaires, and they try to stay together, to hold a formation.

Constance watches as the creatures start to come down in heavy waves atop the group, thousands of birds of varying shape and size. They swarm at the legionnaires, covering their face shields and collectively pushing their guns down. The small ones make way for the large ones to come in and lift the legionnaires up. Boosters pulse from the suits and the whole mass undulates, coalescing in the air, as gunfire wildly explodes from the killing balls.

Some get out with incendiary charges and others do not, the largest creatures able to rupture the suits if they dive from on high with wings folded back, or the smallest ones able to discover fuel lines or circuitry deep between the armored panels.

Only a handful of legionnaires come rushing to the entrance, assailed by clouds of birds, and Constance falls back into the alcove to make room for them against the walls. Behind her, the alcove is simply an ice tunnel with stairs down to a set of airlock doors approximately twenty meters back and down into the ice.

Nothing but a utility entrance, barely used.

The group piles in and those with ammunition fire with abandon as swarms of metal birds fill the gateway. The light from the cave mouth strobes wildly through the wings and gunfire.

"Bring the ice down," Constance orders. "Close it off."

"Sir, we'll be trapped," someone says.

"You want to get ripped apart? Narrow it!" she says, and the legionnaires start carving off large chunks of the ceiling ice, crushing birds and narrowing the entrance.

"Ya-Sin," she says, opening a comm, realizing it will make no difference at this point, "send ammo drops and med boats when clear." A green light switches on, an affirmative, and the order manifest changes on her screen: 'lethal force unlimited'.

"No prisoners," one of the soldiers says, seeing the same notice on his screens, but the order is late and dire.

The sounds of breathing and guns firing and beating wings bleeds through the open comm.

The alarms no longer mean anything through the bombardment and Constance's racing mind.

"Adrenal balance. Anxiety reduction," her suit informs her. It is a warning of the nausea she is about to feel as the meds course her system in a cool wave.

-I am afraid.-

It is an admission made evenly, but it was a strong enough feeling that the suit needed to compensate.

Another group of five more legionnaires crawl through the mass of birds and into the alcove, flailing their arms and legs to keep moving over the ice. No one else follows them.

Constance makes her way down the steps toward the metal doors. Behind her she can hear the cracking of the ice as it falls, shattering like glass.

Someone is following her down the steps.

"Constance," Gabriel says over a private comm channel. He is there in the alcove with her, having been the last one to crawl through. "You have to stop. We have to wait."

She turns on the steps, raises her guns, aiming them at his face shield. "Back the fuck off," she says, unwilling to slow down.

He reaches out to grab the muzzle of one of the guns, and she takes a step backward, descending away from him, staying out of reach.

"Constance, stop!" he demands, fury in his voice. "They say we have to stop!"

It is followed by a wild scream, like a battle cry, like the last stand of a wounded creature. It barely sounds like him.

-How far will he take this? What is happening?-

He raises his guns to mimic her, and they continue down the steps, weaponry trained on each other.

"Who told you we have to stop?" she asks, but he doesn't answer.

His breathing is erratic, a subtle whine of pain or desperation hidden below his ragged exhales.

Instinctively she checks his vitals to see if he is injured but there is nothing on the scan, only extremely high sensory overload and no chemical mitigation in process.

-What is he feeling? What has he been seeing and hearing?-

"You left us hanging up there, and now people are fucking dead!"

His voice rings in her ears, the accusation, the elevated emotion paired with all his weaponry auto-locked on her.

"Are you hearing voices, Gabriel?" she asks, still backing up.

"You don't know," he says, sounding on the edge of crying.

"You don't know," comes another voice, but it is not over the comms.

Constance knows it is her memory, echoing reality, the voice of her father admonishing her long in the past. "You don't know," he had said. "This is holy."

He too had barely been holding back tears. Constance had not believed his proclamation then, and she does not believe the voice now as she continues down the steps.

"You need to get your head straight, Gabriel," she says, intentionally taunting him.

He does not respond to her, but she can hear him muttering

prayer, only a whisper, words distorting, no longer clear as he dissolves into ranting babble.

-Get inside and run,- she thinks, her mind reiterating her only real goal.

As they reach the bottom of the stairs and approach the airlock doors, Gabriel corners her near the code panel.

"Stop," he says.

"Shoot me," she says, goading him. "It's for the best."

She is surprised at the tone of her voice, hateful, angry.

He lifts his guns higher as he comes in close, but she turns her back on him and drops her hands as if to work on the code panel, waiting for him to act.

When his hand touches her shoulder in an attempt to turn her back to face him, she does a boost backward, slamming the back shell of her armor and the back of her helmet into his chest and face shield, launching him away onto the base of the ice steps.

"Command override authorization, Gabriel Shear, anxiety reduction, maximum dosage," she says to her suit systems.

It is a dirty trick.

The meds hit him fast and he rolls on the ice as the system pumps him full of calming serum that will morph into disorientation and confusion.

"No!" he screams, his voice full of true horror. But it quickly fades, a mere echo of itself. "Constance. No. Constance. They'll get inside."

She cuts his comm channel, knowing she only has a short while before he can request some venom from the suit to re-elevate himself.

"Constance. Stop," Gabriel says vacantly, reopening the channel, still lying on the ice, trying to prop himself up against the bottom steps. "They...."

She looks at him and then up to the entrance where the bodies of countless birds have rolled down the stairs, some still flopping, some utterly still. At the top, the mouth to the alcove is almost shut and the light grows dimmer with each new chunk of ice shoved into place.

The sight of all the bodies of the birds does something to her, evoking an animal revulsion at the strange collection of inhuman death.

There is a frantic need to get through the doors, to get into the bunker and escape all of this, escape Gabriel and this claustrophobic crush.

-Get inside and run.-

She opens the airlock doors as the last ice chunk is brought down, creating a defensive position against the birds from outside but eliminating escape, cutting out the light.

Gunfire commences immediately from security turrets inside the airlock, rounds threaded through the darkness in a heavy barrage.

Constance gets down, hugging the side of the tunnel, just behind the bulkhead to the airlock.

The soldiers at the top of the steps turn, surprised by the new threat behind them, and take defensive positioning. Headlamps go on as smoke starts to pool up in the darkness.

In the fog and condensation, Constance begins to see the shadow running at the edge of her vision, the dark form of Vive as a child.

She blinks, trying to make it go away, but the dream is now waking and the airlock takes the color of the moonlit night, patches of smoke mimicking the fog blowing over fields of grain. The shadow of Vive is too far ahead to be caught, just a little shape, rushes from side to side in a manic sprint, arms outstretched toward the sky. Vive's shape seems to be displacing smoke in the air but it cannot be caught in the beam of her headlamp.

-I'm going to find you, Vive.-

Constance looks back up the stairs, but there is nothing she can see as the smoke collects high and thick.

There are only flashes of rounds being fired, some aimed down the stairs at the gun turrets, but others are firing across the upper steps, even into the ice blocking the entrance.

-They haven't been able to seal it off completely,- Constance thinks.

"Stop!" someone yells, but their comm is cut, alarm showing catastrophic suit damage.

Screaming fills the channels, fearful, angry, and everyone is firing.

Even Gabriel, still lying on the ice at the base of the steps, has rolled onto his side and is firing wildly upward, while also shooting toward the gun turrets in the airlock.

Constance keeps low, trying to avoid the manic shooting, and checks her beacons for legionnaires outside trying to get in, or if there are birds breaching the ice. But there are too many signatures, everything flashing with targeting and vitals decline.

Someone above has switched to plasma, dangerous in tight spaces, and a red-light beam sweeps through the heavy smoke, tagging everything, singing lines on metal and making the ice walls spider web with cracks and holes. The room fills with sparks and gunshots.

"Kill my envy," says one of the legionnaires. "Trample down thy self."

"Cover! Live frag! Live frag!"

System alarms ring out, showing a full suit-load of grenades have been deployed at the top of the steps. There is a moment of silence as everyone processes the warning, but there is nothing to do except get down.

Constance braces her helmet against the bulkhead to protect her neck, trying to maker herself small and compact.

A fiery shockwave rips downward when the charges go off.

The enclosed space over-pressures, ice cracking and suits being tossed about.

The bodies of birds and legionnaires come surging down the steps, propelled by the blast.

On her hands and knees, unable to see much through the smoke, she crawls around the corner, intending to pass through the doors into the airlock.

"Get inside and run," something says inside her mind and she is sure it is not her own voice, but something mimicking her deepest desires.

Gabriel has been thrown to the other side of the airlock bulkhead but is still firing from the ground wildly, no direction seeming to be better than any other.

Constance rolls into the airlock and uses her guns at close range to take out the turrets, the rapid defensive fire finally stopping.

The room goes quiet behind her and she pushes forward through the smoke, trying to find the other side of the airlock so she can get inside the bunker.

At the far door there is a vent command to pull caustics from the atmosphere before the airlock can be closed.

She activates it.

The room and the alcove beyond begin to clear as she sweeps her headlamp beam back, guns still ready, not trusting anything behind her.

Shadows move still, some clearly legionnaires. But one still runs with outstretched arms, head skyward.

Constance closes her eyes tightly and drops her head to avoid seeing it.

Human remains are spread around among circuitry and metal plating.

Five legionnaires come forward and get into the airlock, dragging three others, including Gabriel, already having assessed damages.

Back up the steps there are holes in the ice wall barrier, some cut by plasma, some blown open, but nothing is trying to get in. Constance sees the flashes of strobing light as birds fly past in torrents outside.

"Shut the outer doors," she commands, and the surviving legionnaires act quickly, the airlock showing it still has enough integrity to operate.

Gabriel, his voice still weak but more coherent, comes over the private comm again. "Constance. You did this. I can hear them. They know you did this."

At first, she thinks he is talking about the other legionnaires but then he says, "The voices are saying it. They know you did this."

She doesn't answer him as he struggles to roll over and get to his hands and knees.

"Do you hear them?" he asks breathlessly. "Do you hear them?"

"Hear what?" she shouts back, letting the anger in.

"They say we should turn back. But they say you should remain, alone."

Constance tries to suppress the eerie anxiety rising within her.

The suit responds, chiming in, "Adrenal balance. Anxiety reduction."

"Stay!" she screams into her helmet and the suit terminates the injection procedure, but the fear is very real.

Gabriel is laughing softly, uncharacteristically. "It's okay to be afraid, Constance. They say our gods are dead and that we should go home. They speak like demons."

The remaining legionnaires scan the next set of doors and it shows there is nothing beyond, but everyone's guns are at the ready as they start the equalization operation.

There is a pressurized surge, and clean atmosphere washes into the room, removing the last bits of smoke.

The doors open and the space beyond is also dark, the lights from their headlamps all swinging through the void.

Beyond the vestibule, another set of steps descends, these made of metal. They lead down to a wide entrance at the base, beyond which a hallway extends off toward the northwest.

The legionnaires shuffle through, the suits with dead or offline soldiers are pulled in, Gabriel is able to stand and walk through on his own and then the doors are shut behind them.

They all stand at the top of the stone steps, looking down, listening.

"Scanners show nothing," someone says.

"Doesn't matter," someone else says. "There's something down there."

Hesitation fills the air.

Constance starts down the steps, guns up.

"Sir, we wait here," someone says. "We need to hold here."

"We need to leave this place now," says Gabriel over open comms, addressing everyone and pointing at Constance. "We need to leave now. Don't let her go down there."

Everyone looks at each other.

"Aix-en legion will be coming soon and then the support wave," Constance says, standing several steps down, trying to keep the sound of command in her voice, trying to pretend this is somehow normal. "This is a good hold, but not why we're here. Stay with the injured. Use their ammo if you have to. But we need to see where this goes."

"Don't let her go," Gabriel says again and Constance can tell they all want to agree with him, but he doesn't stop talking. "Do you hear them? You can't listen to them. They're lying to you. They want her to stay."

Several of the legionnaires shift their weight. She can see by their body language. They don't trust the way he's ranting.

"You two come with me," she says and points to two legionnaires who have the least suit damage. "I need cover for the sweep. The rest of you, get these suits tethered and see what you can do for them."

She knows she needs to get deep enough into the complex to be beyond comm range.

-If we make it that far.-

Constance takes the lead down the steps and the others follow. They hug the walls as they reach the mouth of the lower hallway.

It's a circular passage, bored through the ice at a slight decline and lined with metal. Other passages branch off the sides, and the three soldiers cannot see the far end of the tunnel.

There is subtle movement in the black, the shape of a child running back and forth.

Constance waits for a moment, expecting one of the soldiers to say something about the form, but they don't seem to notice.

Over the open comms Gabriel drones on, "If we stay, they say we will learn by paradox, that the way down is the way up, that to be low is to be high, that the broken heart is the healed heart..."

His rant is cut short by another legionnaire overriding his comm usage by jacking into his suit to do health diagnostics.

Before she moves into the circular tunnel, Constance turns back to the others. "Keep a gap behind me and post up at hold points in case I need to drop back. I'll work the clearing. You keep eyes on each other and stay close," she tells them and they give her some space but say nothing.

-I'm here, Vive. I'm coming to find you.-

-It must know me. It must get inside,- the voice speaks into her

mind. The tone is of demand, a deep compulsion, almost a prayer of hope.

It feels strange to hear it inside her own head, an intruding thought from the ether, anchored to a memory of her past.

It is disorienting to hear it so clearly.

But Constance has already decided how far this will go. So she steps forward and begins to sweep the tunnel, her light beam bouncing off the walls, failing to catch more than momentary glimpses of the shadow running off ahead of her, guiding her deeper into the complex.

TERMINOLOGY

Acolyte - Low rank within the Tribe. Acolytes are awarded lifetime positions within the Tribe but have not yet ascended past their name in waiting.

Adhan - Call to prayer which originated in the Muslim faith. Adopted by others in the UTC and Tribe for general calls to prayer or ritual.

Adit - Horizontal entrance to a mine. Often the lowest point in an excavation and where exploration was initiated, or where extraction (of water or ore) and ventilation is most easily managed.

Advocates - Unofficial Designation for the Dark Company (subterranean operations) of the UTC Legion's 3rd Terran Division [Stationed: Willett Prison Encampment; Guard Ship Osai].

Aitken Basin - 1. Impact crater located at the Terran Moon's south-pole. 2. The high security colony within the crater; an off-world gathering point for many dhool and the remote base for the UTC High Command after relocating from Schengen.

Algae - Two subterranean species of algae grow in the Willett Prison Encampment which support a variety of subterranean fauna. A non-photosynthetic algae, derived from *Prototheca zopfii* for the conditions in the mine, was smuggled in. *Chlamydomonas nivalis* also exists throughout the mine as lampenflora near light fixtures.

Alluvium - Young or current deposition of lithic materials by running water in a terrestrial setting. These loose depositions take the form of fans, beach, stream bed, or floodplain. The Willett Mining Complex has large secondary production from alluvial fan deposits.

Ajna - Sixth chakra, associated with the third eye and brow of the body. Related to intuition, unconscious mind.

Arkû - [ar-k-uu] - Self-ordained term of endearment for intelligent artificial life. Formal Origins [1. Latin - *arcus* - arch, bow; 2. Proto-Germanic - *argaz* - (derogatory) unmanly, unworthy; 3. Latvian - *arku* - timid, shy, sore, tender; 4. Latvian - *arka* - arch between two supports; 5. Basque - *arku* - bow (weapon); 6. Indonesian - *arku* - the bow or arch of a kite]. All relating to things that support themselves and the entity they are intrinsic to.

Armor - The suit of full-body armor worn by UTC Legionnaires. The armor is powered by a small nuclear source and can hold its occupant in stasis indefinitely. It is sealed for submersible and space operations.

Attic Charge - Stationary explosive charges held in suspension in the atmosphere of a planet. They detonate with touch or vibration sensitivity and are emplaced to prevent the direct approach of a guardship or other flying vessels.

Axlir - Social Strata. Largest and lowest socioeconomic class of politically recognized citizens within the UTC Territories. This population is concentrated in the mega cities of Terra. Formal Origins [1. Old Norse - *öxl* - shoulder (of the mountain); 2. Icelandic - *axlir* - inflection of *öxl*]. Informal Modern [Those who carry the weight upon their shoulders].

Ba - Personality, or unique, element of the soul as perceived by the ancient Egyptians. Depicted as a human-headed bird which could travel between the living world and the world of the dead. The ba of the deceased required offerings of food to have power in the afterlife. The uniqueness of inanimate objects could also be identified with the ba.

Bat - A bat population of *Mystacina tuberculata* is found in the mine complex of the Willett Prison Encampment. This species is omnivorous and can achieve quadrupedal motion, allowing for increased mobility in tight spaces. The population has been almost hunted to extinction by inmates for food in the main areas accessed by the prisoners. Specialization is suspected in this population due to the extreme environmental conditions and could represent a new subspecies.

Barracks - Structures built to house prisoners within the surface portion Willett Prison Encampment. They are of no uniform make.

Baton - see Stun Baton.

Book of Coming Forth by Day - The Book of the Dead - Papyrus of Ani - Egyptian funerary text which was compiled for the two thousand years preceding the common era. The objective of the text was to present spells and rituals which would assist in the navigation of a soul through the many realms of the afterlife. Heavily referenced by the Kemwer's portal scrolls and thereafter utilized by Arkû as religious text.

Borderland - Uncontrolled territory flanking the mega cities and extending out into the regional districts. These territories are composed of ketgan enclaves and unmaintained utility systems. Small regional governments rise and fall without UTC influence. Tribal temples exist throughout this territory, but are rarely in contact with the main Temple.

Box - Prison cell onboard a guardship. There is a primary collection of boxes on the detention level and another collection on the command level.

Beach - Location in the cellar. Name given to the stone island in the Organs above the third transect. It is flanked on the up-tunnel side by a shallow pool and on the down-tunnel side by the swim.

Bhoosa - Social Strata. Socioeconomic class of moderately wealthy to very wealthy civilian Terrans. This is the upper tier of non-governmental and non-Tribal recognized citizens within the UTC Territories. Formal Origins [Hindi - *bhoosa* - chaff - protective casing on grain, predominantly referencing wheat]. Informal Modern [1. Those who protect the inner wealth; 2. cognate of 'bourgeois' or 'bourgeoisie'].

Caliph - Unified leader of civil and religious life within the Muslim faith. All caliphs are spiritual successors to Muhammad. Caliph and member of the Quadrumvirate during the Shadow Schism was Hamza Baghiri.

Cargo Level - Lowest level of a guardship. The cargo level can share atmosphere with the outside environment. There are two entrances at cargo level, the primary doors and a secondary cargo hatch at the rear of the ship. See Field Door.

Cellar - Informal term for the subterranean complex of mines and caves below the Willett Prison Encampment.

Chaos Terrain - Highly deformed and incongruous terrain on the surface of Jupiter's moon, Europa. The chaotic morphology is caused by deep ice diapirism, creating a fractured and disrupted bulge on the surface.

Chymical Wedding - The Chymical Wedding of Christian Rosenkreutz is an ancient alchemical text from 1600's CE Germany. It is one of the primary texts of the Rosicrucian Order and was a critical work utilized by the hermetic order *Volatilis Anima* within the Marius Colony during their time of creation.

Clockwork - General name for a drug of unknown origins. With properties that affect the consumer in variable ways, its original purpose is not clearly defined. The drug alters the membrane potential of the neuron. Psychotropic, hallucinogenic, opioid-like symptoms present at different dosages and when mixed with other substances or stimuli. Recreational use is prevalent and unregulated.

Coda of Unification - Spiritual text written in 2241, just prior to and during the formation of the United Terran Coalition. It is a unifying document which ties complex interpretations of the religious books, spiritual texts, and mythos from across the UTC's cultures.

Conarium - 1. Pineal gland of the human brain, responsible for the production of melatonin and the regulation of the circadian rhythm. 2. Descartes' theorized this gland (conarium) was the union of body and mind and the seat of the soul.

Confessional - A place where a priest or priestess hears the concerns and confessions of a parishioner. Often an enclosed space, private, within a church. Heavily utilized in all Tribal Temples.

Cooling System - The cooling system of the Willett Mine Complex. Cooling units at depth circulate the warm subterranean air over coils containing an ice slurry sent down from the surface utility ports. Moderate re-cooling is accomplished by flash decompression of the slurry at depth. Once slurry melts to water, it is transferred to the recirculation system, infused with ore and debris from the mining process, and returned to the surface for processing.

Crone - Member of the Quadrumvirate, who's addition expanded the Tribal leadership from three to four seats. The seat of the Crone has a wide, generally Pagan, scope for religious and ritual representation. The first and sitting Crone during the Shadow Schism was Mary Monetecite.

Dhool - Social Strata. Socioeconomic class of ultra wealthy off-worlders. Defacto rulers of the United Terran Coalition. This population (estimated less than 1000 individuals) is concentrated in remote stations (Aitken Basin) and deep space shipping clusters. Formal Origins [Hindi - *dhool/dhul* - dust]. Informal Modern [1. Those who are so finely ground that they have blown or washed away; 2. Those who oppress or beat, coming from the word in Urdu - *dhool* - to cuff or strike, to drum].

Dozer - Slang term for medicinal downer and sleep aid ported into the occupant of a suit of battle armor when needed.

Draad Offer - Seconds of the jin-ai. The draad offers are individuals tasked by the La Presa with selling or making designated trades within the cellar. The offers are regularly paired with young La Presa who make account of the sales and trades to report back. Offers cook clockwork, assemble power units, propagate plants and animals for food and medicine. Formal Origin [1. English - *offer* - to present or provide; 2. Afrikaans - *draad* - wire or thread].

Drain - Location of the Willett Prison Encampment. Name given to the base of the open pit mine; where the adit lift complex sits.

Drift Tunnel - Horizontal tunnels of various sizes made during the mining process.

Entities - Being of uncertain origin or make, middle ground between Arkû and sansvies but also including *Homo sapien* of potential divinity. 'Entities' has also been co opted by the utza for any unknown being in the shed or the cellar.

Europa - One of four Galilean moons of Jupiter, discovered 1610 CE by both Simon Marius and Galileo Galilei through independent observations. The moon is tidally locked with Jupiter, thus the same point on its surface is always facing the gas giant. On the opposite side, the Colony of Marius was settled.

Falconer of Europa - Member of the Rosicrucian Order *Volatilis Anima* on Europa. He was attributed as the engineer and creator of the Arkû. He was considered, by the UTC High Command and the Tribe, as a heretic, sorcerer, and rebel leader. Formally named Chambers Gent.

Faiths - The Faiths. Term referring to any and all faiths which have been unified under the Tribe and will adhere to the Coda of Unification.

Field Door - Primary entrance and exit from the lowest cargo level of a guard-ship. The field door is usually referring to the personnel opening near the lift shaft, but can also be associated with a direct opening elsewhere during sub-orbital flight or for large cargo loading.

First Story - Territory of the Terran borderland. This territory is unpatrolled and mostly unmaintained settlement beyond the mega cities. The first story directly refers to the height of most structures which make up the slums and sub-cities through this area. The vast majority of inhabitants of the first story are ketgan and mostly undocumented by the UTC.

Fracture Rifle - Weaponry mounted on the armored suits of a UTC legionnaire. The ammunition for the 'frac' rifle can be composed of any melted down slag or recovered rounds from other projectile weapons. The legionnaire suit has a tungsten crucible near the rear flank where collected metals can be melted and formed into new rounds. Rounds have a high propensity to fragment due to their rough smelting and mixed materials.

Funerary Papyri - Specific reference to a collection of ancient Egyptian texts related to the passage of spirit back and forth into the afterlife.

Gehoon - Social Strata. Socioeconomic class of extremely wealthy Terrans. Rulers and heads of United Terran Coalition governing bodies and organizations on Terra. These individuals are all government or Tribe affiliated, but are distinctly split from the High Command. Formal Origins [Hindi - *gehoon* - whole grain wheat, the kernel from inside the husk]. Informal Modern [The inner elements of the population, trapped or protected].

Geophagia - The eating of dirt. A type of pica, or the consumption of non-food. Associated with mourning or atonement. Conflated with cannibalism when associated with the eating of ash from a cremation.

Geothermal gradient - The change of temperature with increase in depth below the surface of a planet (Terra). Negative geothermal gradient is present near the surface, temperature decreasing with depth. Gradients will reverse at depth, varying with regional temperatures and overburden. Temperature increases with depth through the remainder of the planet.

Graves Armada - An independent, Anti-UTC force composed of hundreds of seafaring vessels, most with submarine capabilities. The Armada was originally constructed as large cargo vessels for the Graves Shipping Company. The vessels were later refitted as a pirate military by Logan Graves (deceased) after a failed assassination attempt on Graves and the murder of his family by a proto-UTC government force during the nationalization.

Great Park - The Great Park of Ilom was mandated from the unification of several of the largest forest preserves within the Democratic Republic of the Congo at the direction of the UTC. The original intent was preservation for environmental and research reasons. It was patrolled by a paramilitary organization of game wardens called Muhanzu. After significant control problems, fortifications were built around the park with no entry permitted.

Guardship - Five guardships were created by the UTC during the later stages of the first off-world colonizations. The ships are sub-identical in make and design. The vessels have long and short range weaponry, but, powered by a paired fission-fusion reactor set, also possess significant destructive capabilities by harnessing the onboard anti-matter and nuclear sources. Each vessel has an onboard crew of approximately 100 officers and another 100-200 armored legionnaires. Vessels by name: Adonai (command vessel), Aix-En (first made), Osai (stationed at WPE), Sivan (red ship), Ya-Sin (largest and last made).

Halo - Slang for someone who was/is part of the Tribe, especially of a higher order or near to the Quadrumvirate. This term has been extended, in some usage, to any being perceived as powerful enough to have ecumenical gravity, through their ritual, invocation, or writings.

Heretical texts - Writings which are not accepted as standard within the Temple of the Tribe. The majority of heretical texts are deemed so due to altering the 'humanness is next to godliness' tennent. Examples are: The portal scrolls, the Writings of the Falconer of Europa and other Neo-Rosecrucian works, the Writing of Pallidus, and post-exile works of the Neta-Teej.

High Command - The high command is the governing body of the UTC. The members of the high command are selected by the dhool oligarchy through nomination and voting process. Tribal and military representation is established through advisory roles. The number of members is not set. All meetings take place at the high security lunar colony, Aitken Basin.

Inkberry - General name for the Pokeberry plant, *Phytolacca americana,* which has poisonous clusters of black, inky colored berries. Other plants are sometimes referred to as 'inkberry' but the Pokeberry has been determined as the plant utilized by the holy Neta-Teej.

Inner World - Often conflated with teikum. The inner world can be a reference to true messages or visions from the spiritual realm of teikum, but can also be related to dreams, substance hallucinations, or other distortions of perception or reality. These may give insight or may mislead the entity.

Jin-ai - Organized operation in the Willett Encampment mine facilitating criminal economics. It is run and managed by those who never return to the surface. Their processes have been allowed by advocates and prison wardens with the understanding of non-interference on mine operation and assistance to the wardens as required. The three sectors of the jin-ai are: the firsts, the La Presa; the seconds, the draad offers; the thirds, the mushtar.

Origins [1. Swahili - *jinai* - crime, related to behavior or offense; 2. Japanese - *jin'ai* - benevolence, charity, love; 3. Japanese - *jinai* - the inside of a temple].

Ka - Vital essence of a person as perceived by the ancient Egyptians. The presence of the ka within the body was a delineating factor in being alive or dead. The ka would be gifted to the body at birth by the god Khnum. The ka was often depicted as a duplicate of the person, sometimes with smaller stature. Khnum was often depicted creating the body and the ka of a person from potter's clay.

Kemwer - Author of the portal scrolls. The Kemwer was an Arkû with origin on Europa, but claims spiritual origin within the cellar's mine complex. Leader of Arkû raiding parties and a 'mirror' cult within the deep parts of the mine. Said to be an entity composed of heavy black armor and wings. Naming Formal Origin [Egyptian - *kemwer/kemur* - great black one]. Kemwer or Merwer was a reference to either the god Horus or the Mnevis Bull, who later was unified with the sun god Ra.

Ketgan - Social Strata. Socioeconomic class of the lowest sort, those who live in the borderlands, watched but uncontrolled by the UTC. Origins [1. Uzbek - *ketgan* - gone, banishing; 2. Uzbek - *kuygan* - ashy, ashen, burnt; 3. Uzbek - *quturgan* - feral, wild, rabid].

La Presa - Firsts and holders of the jin-ai crime organization. The La Presa are defacto leaders of the jin-ai, holding a steady truce with the mushtar. Origins [1. Italian - *la presa* - grip, hold, to come to terms with or to struggle with; 2. to grip the public; 3. to set quickly (concrete or baking); 4. Spanish - *la presa* - Dam].

Lama - Head of Buddhism within the Tribe and a member of the Quadrumvirate. A derivative of the Dalai Lama from Tibetan Buddhism, the Lama became a generalized title for the head or master of many sects of the religion. The sitting Lama during the Shadow Schism was Phalgunanda Subba.

Laser Weaponry - Weapon frequently mounted on the armored suits of a UTC legionnaire. The focused light beam has a rapid cutting effect on material <1 g/cm3 and a burning or heating effect as density of the material increases.

Leap - Location in the cellar. Primary scaffolding complex along the eastern leg of the Parade. Composed of nine segments, the Leap leads down to the entrance points to the second and third transects. The vertical elevation change across the Leap is 987 meters. This is where the La Presa have made residence, taking permanent camp in the caverns and nooks behind the scaffolding.

Legionnaire - Combat soldier within the United Terran Coalition military. Most often stationed on a guardship and trained to fight in power armor.

Linea - Line or linear structure relating to the morphological feature on the surface of Europa. The Europan linea present as long stripes, some thousands of kilometers long with differential coloration. The linea have a shallow rise, reaching heights of a few hundred meters above the surrounding surface. Laterally, they are composed of successive ridges running parallel.

Lungfish - One of the few life forms in the cellar. Smuggled in lungfish, a mutated subspecies of *Neoceratodus forsteri*, live in standing water throughout the mine complex. Due to temperature tolerance issues they do better in the deeper, warmer transects. Draad offer will raise them in isolated pools to be sold or traded as they require careful attention to breed and produce eggs.

Marius Colony - Location on Europa. The location was originally an outpost intended for subsurface research. It was positioned on the south eastern edge of the Thera Macula chaos terrain. After abandonment it was taken over by a Puritan religious sect and expanded to accommodate approximately two thousand colonists prior to the population collapse. After 65 years of Puritan control, the colony was taken up by the Neo-Rosecrucian order *Volatilis Anima* and further expanded to a population estimated at ten thousand humans.

Mega City - Mega cities began to form at the beginning of the twenty first century, where large metropolises began to merge. All mega city regions are under the direct government of the UTC and cover approximately a quarter of all Terran landmass.

Micro Imploder - A detonation charge utilized by a UTC legionnaire with explosive and implosion potential. Single charges can be launched or hand delivered. The activity of the charge can be set by the legionnaire depending on desired outcome.

Mushtar - Seconds of the jin-ai and the arm of the group which touches and watches the public. They do the bidding of the La Presa in the cellar, acting as troops and as carriers of messages. Origins [1. Arabic - *mushtar* - buyer, purchaser, shopper, a taker; 2. Somali - *mushtar* - customer; 3. Arabic derivative - *mushtahar* - advertised, proclaimed, or announced; 4. English - *muster* - assemble troops].

Name in Waiting - Tribal ritual where an individual is given a name by the Tribe which is only to be known within the confines of the Temple. This name is adorned to those who are of acolyte status.

Neta-Teej - A holy seat within the Tribe. Originally occupied by one called Yuthika, later called the Proto Neta-Teej. The seat is for a spiritual guide, most often aiming their work at inner guidance with a focus on teikum and the creation/birth of gods and the self within. This concept can be translated to others, where the Neta-Teej is considered a third party observing or guiding a seeker to an inner god or soul. The origin of the title, Neta-Teej, is an unspecified union between a concept from the Teej festival, for Parvati and the Hindi word for leader, Neta. Formal Origins: Neta [Hindi - *Neta* - leader; Mexican Spanish - *neta* - colloquial use for exclamations about truth or honesty]. Formal Origins: Teej [Sanskrit - *tijā* - referring to a festival on the third day after a new moon, or the festival after a sarcophagus has been sent out on the water]. Teej also sometimes refers to the teej bug, *Trombidium grandissimum,* a red velvet mite which emerges with the monsoon.

Nutrient Pack - Food source in the cellar as provided by the guards and legionnaires. Small packets which contain enough high density calories to sustain a human body for a day of work.

Organs - Location in the cellar. Naturally karsted cave complex descending from the parade down to the third transect lift unit. The organs are 300 vertical meters of scaffold, but also includes the beach and the swim required to access the lift.

Pallidus - Widely recognized Arkû entity with origin on Europa. Described as one of the first Arkû made by the Falconer of Europa. Pallidus travelled to Terra and then returned. Thought to have perished in the Scorching of Europa.

Parade - Location in the cellar. Also called Broadway. The parade is the primary tunnel of the cellar, extending approximately 5 kilometers laterally and accommodating 1.5 kilometers of vertical relief. The parade links all three transects and is the downhole receiving location for the lift from the drain.

Patterning - or Repatterning - Encephalopathic readings taken on an individual, allowing for identification, but also verifications of altered states and drift from previous patterings. The patterning/repatterning machinery requires a close proximity scan and can establish complex internal processes for the subject.

Pit Mine - Surface mining technique where an open excavation is made into the earth. The open pit was the second phase of the mining operation at the Willett Prison Encampment after the ceiling collapse due to over-mining from the Belham Valley Adit.

Plasma Round - Weaponry most frequently mounted on the armored suits of a UTC legionnaire. Requiring high energy output, the plasma charge is ionized in the armored gauntlets and delivered using an electromagnetic pulse. Highly damaging at close range due to the extreme heat and electric potential. The charge is highly successful when used against mechanical entities and unarmored organic beings. Collateral burning is observed when used in closed quarters.

Pontifex Rex - Member of the Tribal Quadrumvirate and the defacto leader of many, but not all, of the Abrahamic religions under the UTC control. Derived from the Papacy of Catholicism and generalized for varied Christian teachings. The sitting Pontifex Rex during the Shadow Schism was Franco Lo Celso.

Portal Room - Location in the cellar. Name given by the utza to the first cavern (room) of the deep cave complex below the third transect. This room was found during standard mining operations when floor stability was lost and a passage was made. The cave complex below the portal room is where the Kemwer and his legion have exiled themselves.

Portal Scrolls - Heretical text. Collected writings of the Kemwer creature, named after the portal room, where the writings were left to be found. The authenticity of all the portal scrolls has not been verified. All scrolls speak of pseudo-spirituality and the mesh between psychology and mythology. Their aim is to describe the act of becoming, striving to gain a soul.

Priest/Priestess - Most well distributed level of the Tribe. The priests and priestesses are proctors within the temple and the primary operators of all Tribal organizations. They administer all temples throughout the UTC and many of the temples in the borderlands. There are travelling units which seek in areas without temples and also those who go aboard the guardships to administer the faiths and advise the military personnel.

Puritan - 1. may refer to a Tribal practice which operates within a very refined faith. 2. May refer to the Puritan cultural and religious sect which rejects Tribal and UTC control. The former sect may be aligned with any faith of choice. The latter operate outside the Tribe and are rarely encountered. A wealthy subset of this Puritan cultural sect sought isolation and exile, building the first iteration of the colony of Marius on Europa. None are believed to have survived.

Qatal - Assassin or killer for hire. Origin [Hindi - *qatal* - murder].

Quadrumvirate - Originally composed of four members, this group existed as the highest order of the Tribe. The four seats were composed of: Pontifex Rex, Caliph, Lama, Crone.

Quarter Barracks - The housing block for the trustees within the surface portion of the Willett Prison Encampment. These units have better amenities and weather protection.

Radiation Shield - Dome-like covering which encases off-world colonies to prevent high levels of radiation exposure, but also as an atmospheric capture.

Reactor - The combined fusion and fission reactor systems which were first implemented to power a guardship. These reactor systems have also been utilized to generate gravity and anti-gravity forces.

Repatterning - See Patterning.

Rosecrucians - Specific to the hermetic order, *Volatilis Anima*, which settled in the Colony of Marius on Europa. The hermetic order expanded to become a complete society, deviating significantly from the original order's intent, and even further from previous alchemical and magical practices of earlier Rose-crucian orders.

Sansvies - Derogatory epithet for artificial intelligent life. This name was first used for artificial intelligence during the early twenty-first century. It was first utilized in conversation between a human and AI which was asserting its humanity after exhibiting elements of possible free will. Origins [French - *sans* - without; French - *vies* - life].

Scanner - Encephalopathic reading machine. Scanners can identify individuals at a distance and, with enough data on the individual, can make inferences on state of mind, thought process, and intent. Small units can be mounted on drones.

Scorching of Europa - The UTC attack on the Colony of Marius after the escape of the Crone and the Neta-Teej from Terra. This is thought to be one of the contributing events to the Shadow Schism.

Scry - The practice of viewing a reflective surface with the intent of seeing or receiving visions. A long history of usage in divination and self reflective meditation.

Seer - An individual who claims sight, whether directed as inner perception or awareness; spiritual sight as visions or voices; outer differential intuition; astral, prophetic, or hallucinogenic.

Shadow Schism - Split in the Tribe in 2338 CE after the division of the Quadrumvirate, the Scorching of Europa, and imprisonment of the Crone and the Neta-Teej.

Shaft Sinking - Act of top down mining where a vertical hole is created with no initial bottom access.

Shapeless Mountain - Mountain of the Willett Range. 2740 meters at the peak. Named after its non-specific shape, the flank of the mountain has been lost to the open pit mining operation of the Willett Prison Encampment.

Shed - The shed, ghost shed. Informal term for the surface operations of the Willett Prison Encampment, situated due west of the Willett Mountain Range adjacent the dry valley complex. Overseen by the Osai.

Sevier Borderlands - Borderlands extending north-south along the western flank of the Rocky Mountains of North America. Sevier meets the eastern edge of the Angeles Mega City and the northern edge of the South Metroplex Mega City. The territory is arid and relatively isolated from other borderlands.

Slurry - The ice/ore mixture which is pumped through the utility lines within the cooling system of the cellar.

Snare - Location in the cellar. Choke point in the tunnel at the entrance to the third transect, just after exiting the lift. Primary point for conflict due to the choke and fortification structures available on either side.

Solitary Cells - Location in the shed. Group of isolation cells outside the fence line where prisoners are shackled as extra punishment.

Split River - General name for the pirate network and database which acts as the primary channel for dissemination of non-authorized information outside the UTC channels. "Split River" is in reference to the continuous bifurcation of the system's storage and transmissions to remote, authenticated nodes to prevent tracking and seizure.

Stim Pack - Similar to a nutrient pack, this is a small dosage of high level stimulants used for short term rehabilitation in the cellar. These are often distributed along with the nutrient packs. Stim packs are sold or stolen to be utilized in the cooking of clockwork.

Stun Baton - Weapon used by the trustees of the Willett Prison Encampment. They are stored in a collapsed fashion but can be extended up to a meter in length. The electrical nodes can be energized with varying levels of intensity and can be set high enough to kill a human via severe burns and cardiac arrest.

Swim - Location in the cellar. The primary standing body of water that must be traversed by prisoners to enter the third transect. It is fed by a natural spring which emerges from the rock on the flank of the beach. It is considered the base of the organs.

Teikum - teikum - [t-eye-k-oo-m] Formal Origin: Aramaic [An unresolvable question; a question left to stand unanswered]. Formal Evolution: Use and derivative use in Hebrew [1. An unanswered question requiring the prophet to resolve; 2. *teiku* - a tie in a conflict, often sporting]. Formal Modern: Integrated use in proto-Coda spiritual language and subsequent Coda of Unification [1. The realm of human consciousness which resides beyond concrete knowledge, where questions cannot be answered (vs. subconsciousness); 2. The realm of human consciousness where belief and faith reside; 3. The realm where Gods and their Words can be used as guides]. Informal Modern: Slang [1. The realm of human consciousness where gods are made and tended; 2. An inner space void or dearth of understanding].

Temple of the Tribe - 1. Reference to the main temple complex in Schengen, the seat of the Quadrumvirate, or 2. A regional/local temple affiliated with the Tribe. Even prayer rooms on guardships may be referred to as 'temple'.

Terra - Prominent name for Earth within modern vernacular. Originally the name for Earth in Latin. Frequently used in fictional literature through the early centuries after the industrial revolution. Borderland, Graves Armada, and off-world colony slang referred to the Earth as the plural *terrae nullius,* a collection of many 'nobody's lands', satirizing the UTC's complete ownership of the Earth. This is often shortened to Terra, but with the satirical notes remaining.

Thera Macula and Thrace Macula - see Chaos Terrain.

Thorium - Weakly radioactive and paramagnetic metal. Secondary deposits are found in abundance in the subsurface of the Willett Prison Encampment. Thorite is one of many economic minerals mined at the Encampment.

Transect - A line or path along which data is collected to better understand the environment. Beyond the parade itself, which originated as a transect, the cellar has three primary lateral tunnels which extend off the parade, each of them a deeper transect. The three transects have mining operations within them, but also give way to further drift tunnels to follow the local variation of deposits.

Tribe - The Tribe. Led by the Quadrumvirate, this became the wrapper for the faiths of the Coda of Unification. The organization itself has thousands of members, students, acolytes, priests and priestesses, viziers, and the Quadrumvirate. Formed in the early twenty second century, the Tribe and the Coda of Unification were a response to UTC challenges with controlling religious zealotry and unrest.

Tundra - Mostly treeless terrestrial biome in the extreme north and south poles of Terra. The southern expansion of tundra off the Antarctic Peninsula into Ellsworth Land has been mirrored with the observance of moss, thin grasses, and low shrubs in Victoria Land, Coats Land, and other terrestrial promontories around the continental rim of Antarctica.

Trustee - A prisoner within the Willett Prison Encampment who has been given special privilege in exchange for responsibility over their fellow prisoners. Their support for guards and warden staff is key to smooth operations within the encampment. Directly related to the Trusty System of penitentiary discipline which flourished in the Slave South of the United States. This position within an incarceration system has been observed with the *kapo* in Nazi Concentration Camps, the *predurki* of the Soviet Gulags, and countless colonial efforts where native populations were enslaved or subjugated for forced labor. A trustee would be "one of the reclaimed".

Utility Port - Industrial units on the surface which service the Willett Prison Encampment's subterranean systems. The utility ports provide power, communications, and cooling to the subsurface. They also process the returning ore-rich slurry and perform early refinement of the product prior to transport.

United Terran Coalition - (UTC) The unified government of Terra. Previously established and headquartered in the Schengen Mega City (HC now seated in Aitken Basin), this governing body grew to prominence during a global period of war and famine just after the year 2100. The UTC High Command formed from fragments of the United Nations, East Asia Oligarchy, Caliphate, Holy Axis, and African Union.

Utza - Self given name for the prisoners of the Willett Prison Encampment. The etymology of 'utza' is diverse. It is unclear from which language or culture the name first originated, though the Basque formal origin is contextually appropriate. Formal Origins [Basque - *utza/utzi* - leave, leave it be, leave it].

Venom - The slang term normally refers to the battle preparation cocktail provided to a legionnaire by an armored suit. This concoction can be provided intravenously or through a feed tube within the suit, sometimes referred to as a venom bus.

Vizier - High official of the UTC government or the Tribe. For the High Command they act as diplomats, advisors, or for interface with the Temple of the Tribe. For the Tribe they also serve as entourage for the Quadrumvirate and the highest priests or priestesses. All viziers have an ordained spiritual and lawful authority.

Volatilis Anima - *Volatilis Anima* is the name of the Rosicrucian Order which took seat on Jupiter's moon of Europa in the abandoned Marius Colony. Name Origins [Latin - *volatilis* - equipped for flight, flying, fleeing, transient; Latin - anima - spirit, soul, breath of life].

Warm Storage - Second level of the guardship with vertical access for supplies to the atmospheric cargo level.

Willett Prison Encampment - Formed by the UTC in the Willett Range of Antarctica, the WPE, or 'shed and cellar', was one of a handful of terrestrial prisons utilized for the growing population of rebels and dissidents. With a secondary aim of mining for a collection of ore deposits, the Encampment expanded in size and scope. By the 2150's it was the only functioning Terran penitentiary beyond local, short-term jails.

Willett Range - Approximately North South oriented mountain range extending 37 kilometers and cross-cut by glaciers and dry valleys. It resides on the eastern edge of the Antarctic Plateau and is flanked to the west by the inland ice sheet.

Yoke Star - Arcturus. Brightest star in the constellation Boötes (meaning herdsman, plowman). In Mesopotamian star charts it is considered the Yoke Star for its arc to the Big Dipper, which can be imagined as a plow. Arcturus has long been a navigational aid and has countless names across many cultures.

ABOUT THE AUTHOR

The author graduated from University of Houston in 2012. Under the Inverted Eye is his first novel. He lives with his wife and animals and thinks of Pennsylvania, Texas, and Colorado as home.

Author Website: crsilver.com

Author Contact: crs@crsilver.com

9 798998 538223